THE CANDLEMAKER OF MASS

THE CANDLEMAKER OF MASS

CALEB POSTEN

This is a work of fiction. Any resemblance to actual people, living or dead, events, or locations is entirely coincidental.

© 2025 by Caleb Posten

All rights reserved. No part of this book may be reproduced or reprinted without written permission of the author.

First Edition, 2025

Published by Posten Writes
www.postenwrites.com

Cover design by Amanda Posten

ISBN: 979-8-9995526-0-0

Printed in The United States of America

1

Philip leaned on the splintered edge of the watchtower's wooden parapet overlooking Bale's Victory, once known as Mirror Pool, a pristine and eternally calm water. The eyes of the ever-vigilant moon reflected off the pool's tranquil surface as it arced across the night sky, its splendor dousing the sparkling stars as it stood guard with Philip.

Scanning across the perpetual calm, Philip lifted his head toward the mountains of gray rock and white snow that shined like mounds of silver under the moon's brilliance. Great warriors had climbed those mountains, the Glass Mountains, the same that had conquered this land and banished the Great Evil to the bottom of Bale's Victory, to never awaken from its eternal sleep. Not as long as the Sentinels kept guard; great men and women, like Philip, who had stood on the very ledge he stood and watched over the waters stretched before him. He was in the ranks with those great warriors. The thought brought him pride as he breathed in the cool night air.

He looked at his belly and noticed he was farther from the edge than normal. He smiled thinking about his sweet Elizabeth's potpies and how they were making him round in the middle and happy of the heart.

Philip looked at the other watchtowers, set at the cardinal points on each side of the lake. All was quiet, as it always was and would continue to be as long as the Sentinels, stalwart as the Glass Mountains, remained stout at their posts. But now it was time for lunch, or whatever you call a meal taken halfway through the night.

The warped parapet creaked as Philip relieved it of his weight. He rubbed his paunch and took a seat on a bench below the ledge.

Pulling his pail toward him, he rummaged through it. Ah! a piece of mincemeat pie wrapped in cloth and a half-pound of pound cake for dessert. A pleasant meal!

Swiping the first bite of cold mincemeat, Philip leaned back against the parapet and looked down at the tops of the buildings and homes of Sentinel's Village. Not a light shined, but the moon glowed across the rooftops, as it did every night in the Kingdom of Mass. His Elizabeth slept down there, content and dreaming of the return of her valiant husband, Philip hoped. He grinned at the thought and finished his midnight lunch.

The pound cake settled like a pile of sand, and Philip's breath slowed as he eased further in his seat. He thought of Henry the Steadfast, who had cleared the land around the lake and defended it with his band of Sentinels—the first Sentinels! And of Sharon, the brave queen who sacrificed her life to save young Prince Bale, who would grow to become the most heroic king of all time, the king that drowned the Great Evil: Magic—the vilest scourge that ever landed on the Kingdom of Mass.

Philip thought fondly of King Bale, as did all of Mass. He wished to one day see the city of Umbrate—the King's city!—and the towering statue of the great King standing on the neck of the terrible wizard Xenerac. He dreamed of seeing it proud and tall with crowds of other pilgrims gathered at its base.

There would be a festival in Sentinel's Village in the coming months to mark one-hundred years since the exile of Magic to the depths of Bale's Victory. Rumor circulated that King Bale would be coming to celebrate with them. The great King would be one-hundred-and-ten! A smile of admiration crept across Philip's face.

"One-hundred-and-ten," he whispered to himself.

He thought of King Bale and Henry the Steadfast a moment longer, and if there would ever be great tales of his own exploits, before his mind drifted to the cakes and muffins and stewed meats and smoked chickens that would be at the festival. His eyes closed but a sheepish smile remained across his face. With his back against the parapet, Philip slept, as did the sentinels in the other watchtowers.

A bubble rose from the depths of Bale's Victory and burst at the surface, sending a ripple all the way to the shore. The first wave, however small, that Bale's Victory had seen in nearly a hundred years, and only the second in its history, and none were awake to witness it—none except the ever-watching eyes of the moon.

2

A small boy, no more than three, sat in the grass and ran his fingers through the dry sprouts that had bloomed with hope and died in dejection under the shade of the spindly oak that reached for nutrients from the leaden sky above. His mother smiled from a bench at the fresh bloom of her lost love.

People moseyed in and around the out-of-the-way square with carts and feet wobbling over the cracked and lumpy cobblestones. An old woman sat nearby, gazing at the boy with the same kind eyes as the mother. They were the only ones watching, the rest simply wandered through with little care to look at anything but the stones below their feet.

It was often quiet and cold in the city of Umbrate with the sun so distant, so frail, and the faces of its citizens reflected it, with the exception of the mother and the woman watching the child.

Night closed in, and the square cleared of carts and people, leaving the three in their peace. The old woman stood and approached the child. The kindness in her face told the mother to fear no harm as she squatted and ran a wrinkled finger across his delicate cheek. He beamed at her and the whole square seemed to blaze with light before he returned to running his fingers through the failed sprouts of grass.

The old woman looked around the empty square and back to the boy. Much to the wonder of the mother, she swirled her hands until a glowing orb formed from their motion. The boy stared with awe as the light expanded between her shriveled fingers and the particles of the air assembled into a healthy stem and bud. She spread her hands apart and the light emanating from the top hand unfurled the bud into a white Iris hemstitched with purple.

The boy and mother watched, mystified by the birth of Magic within the worn hands. The light faded and the woman presented the brilliant flower to the child, whose smile competed only with the brightness of the flower in the dreary city. Putting an overworked and tender hand to her chest, the mother felt a flutter of fascination she once thought dead. She began to laugh before she could stop it.

"What's this?" asked a gruff voice.

All three turned sharply. The man wore the insignia of Bale's City Guard, a bronze shield split into four quadrants, on his left breast. It was the only bit that shined on his drab gray attire, though he carried a sword at his hip—and they bet it was shiny—and a pair of well-used handcuffs on his other hip. He approached the old woman and lifted her from the ground.

Snatching the Iris from the boy's hand, he shoved it into the woman's face. "Looks like a bit of Magic to me."

The boy began to cry and beat his fists against the man's leg.

"Give it, it's mine," he yelled, tears rolling off his untarnished cheeks.

"Get off!" the guard grumbled, kicking the boy to the side. He pulled the faded silver fetters from his belt and secured them around the old woman's wrists behind her back. "I'll be seeing a nice bonus for capturing an old hag performing Magic—in public of all places," he mocked.

The mother lifted the boy off the ground and began to back away when the man grabbed her wrist.

"Where do you think you're going, pretty? You're complicit."

She fought to free her hand as the boy clung to her side.

"Let them go," the old woman slurred. Her weight seemed to grow too heavy for her body. She began to sway. "They had nothing to do with this. It was all me. They're so young they've probably never seen Magic."

"I can't take that risk. You're all going in," he growled.

"You coward!" the old woman spit; her voice weak. She lurched and wobbled.

The guard turned and watched her dizzying sway. A vicious smile crept across his face.

"Enjoying those shackles, witch? I bet you're feeling sick about now." He sneered in her face as her eyes rolled in her head. "Made by our Magical Advisor Kylan, they are. Very sinister. Very powerful against your kind."

The mother jerked to free herself, pulling the guard's attention from the old woman.

"That's enough! You're coming in whether you like it or not."

She resisted and he grabbed her with both hands, letting the old woman drop to the ground in a fit. They struggled back and forth with the child screaming and swaying as he held his mother.

"Let us go!" she yelled, tugging in vain to free herself from his relentless grasp.

He pulled out a second set of fetters and grappled to put them on the woman's wrist.

"No!" she yelled, breaking free for a moment before the man grabbed her again.

"Give me that hand, witch!"

"I'm not a witch!"

"That's for the clergy to decide. Now, on the ground!"

The guard grabbed her other hand and forced her to her knees. She lurched upward and smashed her head against his nose. He released his grip and grabbed his face as the woman pulled her child away. Blood trickled in a thin rivulet from his right nostril.

"You wench!" he hissed. "Come here!"

The boy clung to his mother, forcing his face into her dress skirt as the man grabbed her elbow. She pulled back as the guard pulled forward, and the boy tumbled to the ground in the quarrel.

"Mommy!" he screamed, tears dripping from his eyes. "Leave her alone!"

"Run, child! Run!" she yelled, but he sat on his rear and cried and screamed as the guard wrestled her closer, tightening his grip on her elbow as the blood trembled over his grimace to his chin.

"Stop fighting! There's big penalty for those that resist!"

The boy howled and blubbered, his voice screeching higher with each pleading word.

The man squeezed her elbow, his knuckles whitening. She squealed in pain and grabbed him with her free hand. White light flared between her clutched fingers, and the guard hollered in agony before he fell limp and crumpled to the dry earth at the base of the tree.

The mother flopped to the ground with wide eyes staring and agape mouth gasping for air. The boy ceased crying and looked at her in blank awe. She wavered in shock and brought the child to his feet.

"Are you all right?" she asked, searching his eyes and smoothing his hair. He gave her a slow, vacant nod.

Turning to the unmoving guard and the limp woman, she ripped the shackle keys from the man's belt and freed the old woman's hands. Her sagacious eyes popped open and she sat upright, scanning the scene before her. As much of a smile as she could muster started on her face.

"I knew there was something special here," she said. "I thank you."

The mother pulled her child in close and nodded, stuck in shock.

A man walked around the corner of stone and stopped, taking in the curious state of the square. The whites of his eyes grew in the fading light and all went quiet. He turned and bolted, yelling: "Help! A witch has attacked a guard!"

The old woman grabbed the mother's arm. "Go! Find somewhere safe. I'll hold them off."

She stared back, dumbfounded, her child whimpering in her lap. The old woman struggled to her feet and urged: "Go! Now!"

The young woman came to and lifted herself off the ground with her son in her arms.

Two guards came around the corner and called: "Stop!" but the woman already turned the corner with her child.

A flash of white burst behind them and the world fell silent. The mother pressed her child's face into her shoulder, his tears wetting her tattered garment, and she fled through the streets and alleys of Umbrate to the only person she could think to ask for help.

◐

The streets throbbed with commotion when the mother and her child stepped out of a tenebrous alley and knocked on a door with a dingy and faded sign above it that read 'Chandler.'

A straggler running to meet the mob of guards ran past. She tucked the child's face into her chest, feeling the boy's warmth at her breast one last time.

She knocked on the door again, harder. It opened a crack and a pair of tired eyes peered through.

"Shop's closed," he said. "You'll have to come back in the—"

"Please, sir, it's an emergency," she interjected with quick words. Her son sniffled at her chest.

"Then find a clergy leech," he replied. The door started to close and she forced her foot into the crack.

"Paulette Grindholm was my grandmother!" The pressure on her foot decreased but didn't let up. "She said if I ever found myself in trouble—any trouble—that I should seek you."

"Get her!" and "String her up!" came the shouts of a man and a woman as they sprinted by. The pair passed and the door opened, permitting entry to the mother and child.

The Chandler's shop was clean and tidy, with here and there bits of clutter expected of all back-alley shops. Flickering flames filled the room from each corner with more light than the typical candle afforded. The walls and shelves were covered with candles of all sizes, colors, and designs. Some were covered in a fine layer of pewter dust and some were freshly made. The room smelled of wax and oils that coated their nostrils. But the new party seemed not to notice any of this.

The woman put her child down and knelt to look into his gloomy eyes. She smoothed his hair and smiled weakly.

"Are you all right, darling?" she asked. The Candlemaker watched from the side as the boy nodded in response. Her smile grew a little more. "Of course you are. You're very brave the way you stood up for mommy."

"He was hurting you," the boy said. Heroic tears trembled down his face.

"Not anymore," she said.

"What happened to him? What was that light?" the boy asked.

The woman looked over her shoulder at the Candlemaker, whose stern face loomed over his tattered robe. He was stroking the long and wild hairs on his chin.

"It's difficult to explain, darling, but," she paused to stay her tears, "but I'm going to have to leave you here."

"What?!" said the boy and Candlemaker in unison.

"You can't leave him here! I couldn't possibly take care of a child," he said.

The woman stood and met him face to face. "You knew my grandmother—very well by the sounds of it. You knew she was … unique," the woman leaned in closer, her countenance sullied with pain, "and she was killed for it. Something happened in the small east square today. We helped an old woman, who was also unique, and a guard was hurt … maybe even killed."

The Candlemaker breathed in and stroked harder at his chin hairs, on the verge of pulling them out.

The woman leaned in even closer, nearly touching noses with the Candlemaker, and whispered: "I must give myself up, or they'll come for my son as well."

The Candlemaker dropped his eyes and stepped back. "I can't. It's not possible."

"My grandmother said you would help. She said you were a good man with a kind heart." She turned to her son. "They will take him and turn him into one of them. That's no life for a boy, for anyone."

"Don't let them take me, Mommy!" the boy said, rushing to her side and grabbing hold of her draping skirt.

The Candlemaker watched with terror in his eyes. He took another step back as if to see the situation clearer.

"Take him in. Make him your apprentice. He's very intelligent."

"No! Don't leave me!" The boy cried and beat his fists against his mother's legs.

"Please, take him," she pleaded. "You've heard what they do to children in the Reformatory."

The boy shoved his face into his mother's skirt, muffling his cries. The shouts from the expanding mob grew louder outside. Guards scoured the streets for her.

The Candlemaker looked at the door. He swallowed hard and nodded.

The woman gasped and pulled him in for a hug and kiss; the Candlemaker accepted both stiffly.

"Thank you! How correct my grandmother was," she panted, relieved. She kneeled and took her son by the shoulders. "Mommy has to leave you now."

"No! Please, don't leave me!" he begged, wrapping her in a tight hug. She embraced the fire of his youth.

"You're going to grow to be a strong man, darling," she said, smiling. The Candlemaker watched through glimmering and distorting pools. She peeled her son away and kissed the dejected boy on the forehead. "Whatever happens, remember that mommy loves you. Understand?"

The boy, with slumped shoulders and broken heart, nodded. Tears spilled down all their faces. She stroked his hair one last time before she stood, took a deep breath, and headed for the door. "Thank you," she said to the Candlemaker as she opened it and stepped through. The shouts in the distance moved ever closer.

"Wait!" the Candlemaker said. The woman stopped, turned. "What's his name?"

The woman smiled lovingly at her son one last time and said: "William," before she closed the door on the sound of wailing.

3

The Candlemaker and Will bounced atop their cart as the donkey pulled them over the cobblestone streets of Umbrate. People passed them on their own business as the kingdom's comers and goers funneled through the gate. A guard wearing a leather vest over a hauberk stepped in front of their cart and halted them. His other hand rested on the hilt of his sword, and the tarnished silver handcuffs clicked at his hip.

"Morning, Will," the guard said to the boy, who nodded. "Where're we headed today, Del?" the guard asked the Candlemaker.

"Off to the apiarist for wax, and to see a woman about some white earth and soot, Phin," Del replied.

"Soot? If you'd have just asked, I would have lent you one of my nephews, they're always covered in it," Phin said, laughing. Del joined him, more out of obligation than humor. "Will that be all then?"

Del nodded. The guard looked over his shoulder at the other, more stern looking guards and leaned closer to Del. Looking up shyly, he asked: "I was wondering if you might have something for my sister's new babe? She's had a terrible cough for the past week. Nothing she does seems to help the poor child." Phin's face carried the concern in his voice.

Del looked across at the other guards frisking and searching people as they went in and out the gate. He reached into the breast pocket of his long coat and pulled out a small purple candle about three inches long. He passed it to Phin, who shoved it into his leather vest after another peek over his shoulder.

"Tell your sister to burn the whole candle through the night while the child sleeps," Del explained. "And keep her clean of soot. That's where her problem lies."

"Thank you, Del," Phin said sincerely. Del smiled and nodded to him.

"Phin!" yelled a hoarse guard. "Back to it!"

"Yes, sir!" Phin yelled back. "On with you," Phin said to Del. "I'll pass your kindness onto my sister."

"No need," Del said. "Just do as I instructed."

Del slapped the reins across the donkey's back and they went through the main gate, off the cobblestone streets of Umbrate, and onto the smooth dirt road, the King's Carve, that snaked across the gray plains of Mass from Umbrate, through the Grim Forest, and all the way north to Sentinel's Village.

People scurried to their left and their right until the travelers thinned. The donkey clipped and clopped his way up the road at a pace he thought fit, and Del and Will rode along with no authority to make him go faster. The King did not allow them to have horses (they were too fast, meaning someone might use one to escape Umbrate), so a donkey they had, and at a donkey's pace they plodded.

Will looked over the landscape scattered with struggling grass and scrubby trees. He enjoyed it when they left the cold stone of Umbrate and went on a journey across the plains for candle making supplies. It wasn't much, but Will liked spending a day away from the stuffy chandler's shop and out of the room filled with boys and girls his age learning the history of Mass.

He turned to Del, slouched on the bench, and asked: "What was in that candle you gave Phin?"

Del looked out of the corner of his eyes as if disturbed that Will had cut his train of thought.

"Lavender."

Will looked at him curiously. "Does that grow around here?"

Del scoffed. "Nothing grows around here, boy."

Will went back to looking at the sparse countryside.

"Instructor Luceen says that this land was once filled with all sorts of plants, but the scourge of Magic destroyed them all. It's been nearly a hundred years since Bale's Victory and the land is still recovering."

"Hmm," Del said rather distantly.

Will looked around, searching for more things to ask about. These monthly trips outside of the kingdom were the best time for him to ask questions. The rest of their time was spent working in the shop, where Del was preoccupied with his own tedious tasks, and if Will wasn't working or in school three days a week, he was wandering the streets of Umbrate, often alone. Will brightened with a question he hoped would interest Del.

"What other plants help with coughs?"

"Many others," Del said.

"Like what?" Will persisted.

Del turned to him, not cruelly but not kindly, and said: "When you get a handle on dipping the candles, I'll teach you more."

Will slumped into the box seat, turned to the blank landscape, and traipsed back into his mind.

Charlie, the apiarist, and his apprentice Kip, both dressed in heavy canvas suits with diaphanous nets on their heads, were tending the hives by King Bale's grain fields when Del pulled the donkey to a halt some distance off.

"Hello, Del and Will," Charlie called, coming to their cart. Kip, a lanky and nervous boy of fifteen, continued to work at Charlie's bidding.

"Hello, Charlie," Del and Will said.

Will very much liked Charlie. He was kind and loquacious, and possessed the caring, pacifying attitude necessary for beekeeping.

Charlie removed the net from his head and presented them with a smile.

"How are we today, gentlemen?"

"Fine, Charlie," Del said. "Here for our monthly pickup."

Charlie's smile faltered; he looked at Will and it regained some of its brilliance.

"Will, you look older than the last time I saw you."

"I do?" Will said, perking upright.

"You must have had a birthday," Charlie said cheerfully.

Will slumped back. "I don't think so." He shrugged modestly. "Well, I don't know when my birthday is, is what I mean."

Charlie looked from Will to Del, who wore a countenance of parental guilt that fit him rather well.

"Not a problem," Charlie said, mustering his cheer. "We'll pretend it's today. You go and have a bit of honeycomb while Del and I have a talk."

Will looked to Del, who nodded his permission. Will smiled and jumped from the cart, patting the donkey as he passed.

"Kip," Charlie called. The twiggy boy looked up like some sort of blind one-eyed insect with four sharp-jointed legs. "Give Will a bit of honeycomb, and have a bit yourself." Kip cheered as Will approached a safe distance from the hives. He entered the honey shack and the golden treats were on glorious display before him.

"Charlie never lets me have any honeycomb. What's the special occasion?" Kip asked, freeing his head from the net.

Will looked over the dripping blocks of honey, sure that gold rectangles reflected off his face as his mouth watered in anticipation for the sweet and sticky treat. Bees buzzed about the room, looking to reclaim their hard work, but neither boy paid them any mind. Will least of all. "Will?" Kip brought his attention back.

"What? Oh, Charlie says it's my birthday."

Kip furrowed his brow. "Well, is it?"

Will shrugged. "I don't know?"

"You don't know?"

"I'm an orphan. I don't have a birthday … Del and I never celebrate it, at least."

"Oh," Kip said, trying to fit all the pieces right in his head. His face said he was thinking much too hard for his brain's capacity, so he stopped. "Happy birthday, then. How old are you?"

"Eleven … or maybe twelve," Will said. He could smell the inviting honey, desperate to get it on his hands and face.

Kip brought out an old, bent knife and split a five-inch block of comb in half. They each pinched a half between their fingers and Kip tapped his against Will's in cheers.

"Here's to turning eleven, or maybe twelve." He smiled and they each took a greedy bite. "This is fresh stuff, we cut it out today." They turned and walked toward the door of the honey shack into the dim light of day. "It's awfully difficult staying out of the honey when you work with it all day. It's near torture. But Charlie never lets me dip even a finger in the pot," Kip said, pleased to have a contemporary to talk to. "He says the bees aren't doing well."

Will chewed laboriously on the honeycomb, enjoying the work of extracting the saccharine sweetness. "Tastes like they're doing fine," he said with a full mouth.

"They aren't producing like they used to. Even I've noticed."

The boys fell silent, listening to the gentle buzz of the bees in the hives nearby.

Realization struck Kip. "Hey, if you're twelve, you'll be up for Selection soon, right?"

Selection was an event looked forward to by most boys and girls of Umbrate. It was the time in their lives where they left school instruction and entered into the King's workforce. The 'Selection' Kip referred to denoted the selection of children for training in Bale's City Guard. All children, boys and girls, coveted the opportunity to rip Magic from all corners of the kingdom. Their training was the best, their food was the best, their clothes were the best, and it was the greatest honor for a child to join their exclusive ranks.

"Do you think you'll be selected into the guard?" Kip asked

"I don't know," Will said. To say he hoped not would have been blasphemy, but it was what his heart told him. "I probably won't because I'm already an apprentice with Del." He tried his hardest to look sad.

"I wish I had been selected," Kip said, looking into the distance. He took a bite of honeycomb and the nectar brought him back. "But being a beekeeper isn't so bad."

"Being a candlemaker isn't so bad either," Will said. They fell silent and watched Del and Charlie speaking in hushed tones as the bees spoke in their own hushed tones.

"What do you think they're talking about?" Kip asked.

Will, with honey dripping down his chin and wrist, wondered the same thing.

◊

"I'm shorter than usual on wax, Del," Charlie said, crestfallen. Del looked at him with subdued concern. Charlie explained further, nearly pleading: "The crops produce less and less each year, and the bees aren't as healthy because of it. Things aren't growing like they used to. The sun is too weak below this pall."

Del stroked the hairs of his chin. "I understand, Charlie. You're a good beekeeper, and you care for them the best you can. I'll take what you have to give and no more."

"If anyone was going to understand, I knew it would be you, Del," Charlie said. "The King's bakers aren't so understanding."

"They have much to be concerned about," Del said.

Charlie looked over his shoulder and saw Will and Kip chewing on honeycomb by the shed door. He dropped his voice: "And there's been people around, Del."

"People?"

Charlie nodded. "I can't be sure, but I think they're men of the Guard in disguise." Del squinted to bring Charlie into tighter focus. "They've been coming with the field crews. Two of them seem less interested in field work and more so in what Kip and I are doing. I discovered one digging through the shed the other day. He made some excuse about confusing it for the field worker's shed. It's troubling, Del. I'll be nothing if they take my bees from me." Tears formed in Charlie's eyes.

"Troubling indeed." Del's concern was less subdued now; his hand more aggressive across his chin. He looked over Charlie's head at Will watching from the shed door. "Keep me informed."

Charlie nodded and called Kip to help load the beeswax. And after the cart was filled with heavy blocks of wax, Del and Will continued on their way, each with much to think about.

On the jostling ride to meet the woman about the white earth and soot, Will began to ponder as he extracted the last bit of sugar from the honeycomb. It had not occurred to him that he might get selected for the City Guard. It was an honor given only to those who seemed to always have their noses in the business of others, or those in high-esteem with their instructors, or orphaned children that floated from home to home. Will was none of these. He was content with candle making, and he was content with the space Del gave him.

Life with Del was not all bad, but an inward boy like Will had a tendency to wonder what life might have been like if he hadn't been abandoned with Del. He tried to think of his mother and could hardly remember her face. The tender start of his life was fuzzy and stinging, like opening his eyes in cloudy, soapy water. He thought little about it now, but sometimes his mind wandered back to see what it could find. Often, very little.

He chewed the wax until the effort of biting into the thick wad made him sick to his stomach and he pulled it out and put what remained in his pocket. They entered a country with more hills and scant trees, nearing the home of the woman, Grace Sandler, who provided them with white earth and soot. The soot, Del had explained, was added to the liquified wax to trap impurities, then the white earth was added to clump the impurities together and pull them to the bottom so the wax would come out clean and pure. These jobs were dirty and, needless to say, Will's responsibility.

As they neared, Del pulled up the reins on the indifferent donkey. Another cart was already there, a cart much larger than Del's that was being filled to capacity with white earth by two men of the Guard.

Del gritted his teeth and slapped the reins across the back of the donkey. Grace saw him first and ran from her porch to greet him. Disappointment clouded her naturally jovial face.

"They've taken nearly all of it, Del. I couldn't stop them. They said the King needs it for his textiles," she explained.

"Are they paying you for it?" Del asked.

"The bare minimum."

Del shook his head and said: "I'll take what you have left, and pay you a bit more."

"They'll take what I give you if they see it. But I've some stored away," she whispered. "We'll load the soot first." Del nodded to her and pulled his cart next to the guards'.

"There won't be any left for you, old man," the first guard said as the second smaller and younger guard struggled to load a sack.

"I'm not here for white earth, just soot," Del explained with contained anger seeping from his words.

"Soot! What, you struggle to find that in the city?" the guard scoffed.

"The fires in Umbrate are fueled with twigs and dung," Del said, angrily. "That doesn't make good candles."

"Soot for candles? What good does that do?" the guard asked. The second guard stopped to take a breather. Will looked at him and recognized him as one of the older boys he used to attend school with but, hard as he tried, he couldn't recall his name. The young guard turned away, grabbed another sack.

"I don't have the patience to explain it to an oaf!" Del said just above a whisper.

The guard sneered. "Be careful who you call an oaf, old man. I'd be pleased to bury you out here."

"You'd bury the man that makes the King's votive candles?" Del said.

The guard raised to answer but stayed his tongue. He pointed a finger at Del. "You've been warned, fool," he said, turning in defeat to help the other guard with the last sack. He got in the cart and pulled away with a glare.

Del watched him go, and Will watched his old schoolmate bounce next to the man in tired despondency. Their eyes met for just a moment, and Will saw the desperate dejection he wished to avoid.

When the guards were out of hearing range, Del came down from the cart and approached the woman. "I'm sorry for my anger, Grace. I hope I haven't harmed you in any way."

"No more than they have," she replied. "C'mon, I've some bags stashed in the cellar. You'll need a strong back to get them out though." Will knew what that meant.

Grace opened the cellar door on the side of her small home and Will dropped into it.

"They're in the corner to the left, Will," she said.

Will crawled on hands and knees to the three bags stacked in a pile.

"Newt can barely keep up with their orders," Grace said with hands on hips. "He's been working more hours than are good for him. They just show up unannounced and expect us to have what they need. I don't know how their fullers can keep up with it."

"What are they weaving?" Del asked. Will came into view dragging the first bag in jerking strokes.

"Banners and fine clothing for the centennial festival of Bale's Victory," Grace said. "Can you imagine? Them making clothing to dress up for a party while the rest of the kingdom starves in rags."

Del shook his head. Sadly, he could imagine it.

Will came up and they tugged the first bag from the cellar. He went back for the other two.

"If you ask me, it's time for a reckoning," Grace said. Will dragged the second bag over and they hauled it out. "And Newt and I will be the ones to give it to them if they try to take our home or our mine."

"There's no sense in that, Grace," Del said.

"Of course there is! This is our livelihood. They have no right to take it from us. And for banners, of all things!"

"Things will go back to normal when the centennial festival is over and done."

"And what's normal to you, Del?" Grace posited.

Del retreated to silence until the cart was loaded and the pay was settled.

"We'll be back in a month," he said.

"And we may have nothing for you," Grace said with frost on her tongue. "I'll say it again: it's time for a reckoning." She put her palm to Will's filthy cheek and smiled. "If not for us, then for the children."

Del remained silent on the matter and climbed onto the cart. Will smiled at Grace's warm touch and left her in front of her home with nothing left to give.

Del turned the cart onto the road, back toward the King's city.

Halfway back to Umbrate, and after much silence beyond the clipping of the donkey's hooves, Will turned to Del and asked: "What do the fullers do with the white earth?"

"They clean the wool with it."

"Like we purify the wax?"

Del nodded, keeping his eyes ahead.

Will thought a moment, then ventured to keep the conversation going: "What do you think is wrong with the bees?"

Del shifted in his seat. "What do you mean?"

"Kip says they aren't doing well. He says he's even noticed it himself."

This surprised Del; Kip never struck him as the type to notice much at all. The Candlemaker often withheld the truth by saying nothing at all, but Del saw no point now.

"Charlie says the crops are poor this year. The bees need a good crop to stay healthy, they need plants to pollinate and what not. They die off without them."

"Will that affect how we make candles?" Will asked.

"Yes, though the thought of less food concerns me more. Many of the common people are already stretched thin, while the king eats as he wishes and makes banners and fine clothing," Del added with venom.

"You think we'll go hungry?"

Del looked at him from the corner of his eye. "We won't go hungry." The truth was vacant from Del's words; Will had been around him long enough to know.

"Are we going to have enough white earth and soot for our candles?"

"We'll make it work," Del said. "The dip and votive candles are the most important. We have to fill the king's order before we can worry about the others."

Those were the most boring candles to make, and were often Will's task to make them. He had made thousands of them, and yet Del never seemed impressed with his work.

"Are there other ways to make candles?" Will asked.

"Of course. Tallow is the next best, but it's as hard to come by as beeswax these days. And it's not as nice to burn."

"Why?"

"The beeswax is just better."

"No, I meant why is tallow hard to come by?"

Del turned and looked at him seriously. "It's hard to grow animals when you can't grow any plants." Something in the way he ended the sentence told Will the conversation was over.

They continued down the dusty King's Carve, the donkey struggling mildly with the added weight. And when they arrived at the front gate, it relieved Del to be greeted by Phin once again.

"Back so soon," Phin said. He went to the back of the cart and lifted the tarp that covered the load. "Load looks a bit lighter than usual," he said.

Another guard approached behind Phin, who looked over his shoulder and tensed.

"White earth, I see," he said. "We just had a load come through for the King's loom. The guards said they took all of it." He sneered with a contorted smile. "Apparently not."

"He's fine, Fred," Phin said. "He gets his supplies once a month."

"Once a month?" Fred said. "And what do you do with these supplies?"

"He makes—" Phin began.

"I didn't ask you!" Fred screeched, turned to Del. "I asked him."

Del remained calm, kept his eyes ahead. "I make candles for the king."

"Candles for the king?" Fred said. "And why should I believe that?"

"Because it's true," Will said. They all turned to him. "Who do you think makes the votive and dip candles for monthly mass?"

"Not an insolent little boy, that's for certain," Fred replied angrily.

"Come, Fred," Phin said, pulling him aside. "You don't want the king to hear about this."

"He'll hear about it all right. He'll hear that someone has been taking his white earth from under his nose!" Phin pulled Fred aside and gave Del the nod to go through.

Del slapped the reins across the donkey's back and burned Will with a furious glance. Will crossed his arms over his chest and looked ahead.

They unloaded the supplies and returned the donkey and the cart to the stable before Del slammed the shop door and turned to Will.

"Never speak like that to a guard again!" he shouted. Will, anticipating the reproach, didn't flinch.

"He was wrong to stop us," Will said. "He was just being mean."

"That's his job! And if we comply, they leave us alone," Del said. "Now, get to work on those dip candles. And make sure the water is cool enough. The last batch was too soft!" Del stormed out of the main shop area and slammed the door to his own workspace.

Will clenched his fists in anger. He wished to throw something but knew it would only make matters worse. Instead, he doused his anger with work.

The large workspace was filled with square vats, deep pots, and warped wooden tables. Frames holding dip candles hung from the ceiling and votive candle molds were stacked high like muffin tins in a baker's shop.

Will started a fire under a deep, square vat of wax for dipping candles, and while the fire liquified the wax he laced spun wicks through a frame until twenty-five of them hung down like the tentacles of a jellyfish. He set the frame aside and lifted the lid off a copper vat of similar size by the wax vat. He dipped his finger in the water and decided it was, after Del's kind observance, too warm for dipping the candles.

Leaving the vats, Will went to an edge of the room the clutter seemed to avoid and lifted an opening that led into a crawl space. He jumped in and rubbed his arms against the cold. Packed tight into the corners, the previous winter's snow had solidified to ice. Will chipped at the nearest block and went out quickly. He replaced the door and dropped the ice into the copper vat to cool the water. Will dipped a pewter spoon in the water, and then into the wax. It hardened to a pale white: ready for dipping.

He dragged a long platform closer to the vats and stood on it. Grabbing the frame and its swaying tentacles, Will lowered it slowly and evenly into the hot wax. After holding steady a moment, and at the correct height, he pulled it from the wax and dipped the frame into the cool water.

"One," he said to himself, and dipped them into the wax again, then back into the water. "Two."

Thirty dips, if conditions were perfect, and Will would have flawless candles, though Del would find a flaw in them—he always did, but he still accepted and delivered the candles anyway, so Will didn't take it too hard.

Life would have been difficult for Will if he took the Candlemaker's contemptuous looks or backhanded comments each as a pin in his side. The man was his guardian, but he treated Will as his full-time apprentice. Will didn't mind it, but in truth, he knew no other way.

"Eight," Will said, dipping the thickening wicks in the water. He attached the candle frame to a holding platform and checked the water again. Too warm. He gathered more ice, checked the temperature, then went back to dipping.

A gentle knock hit the shop door when Will hit twenty-one. Del opened the door by the third hit as if expecting the visitor. In came

Mrs. Grissom. She was elderly and kind, short of stature but full of cheerful smiles. She held her burlap bag close to her midsection as she entered.

"Hello, Del," she greeted. "I came for my order."

"Yes, Mrs. Grissom. Right this way," Del guided her to his workspace.

Mrs. Grissom stopped on the other side of the vats and looked at Will.

"How are you, Will? It's been some time since you've been by for a cake," she said. They weren't really cakes. Mostly they were whatever Mrs. Grissom could mix together to resemble a cake of some fashion. Often, they were the spent grains from the brewery, stripped of their sugars, but still sweet enough for Will to enjoy. Sometimes they were made from the material that was sifted off the grist, a hard to digest chaff that stuck in his teeth. Will preferred the spent grains, but he appreciated the variety.

"I'm sorry, Mrs. Grissom. I haven't made a personal delivery in some time," Will said. "How is Mr. Grissom?" Mr. Grissom was the reason Will made special deliveries to the Grissom household. He was frail and ill beyond his years, and Del sent Will with specialty candles meant to help Mr. Grissom feel better so that he could work. Mrs. Grissom paid with what she could, usually her cakes, which Del detested but accepted because the kindness and honor of the woman's heart wouldn't let him do otherwise.

"Mr. Grissom is much better when he has visitors," she said, winking. "So you come by soon. A young heart gives him hope."

Will smiled at her as she went into Del's workspace. Del came up next to the vats and dipped his finger in the water. He pondered over the temperature before he looked at Will.

"Good," he nodded once, "add ice after two more dips." Del left him and closed the door between Will and his workspace. It always ended that way when Del had special orders.

Will knew to add ice after two more dips because that was always Del's instruction when he inspected his work. He dipped the candles back in the wax and listened closely to see if he might catch a hint of what they were saying behind the door. In all the years he'd lived with Del, Will had only been in his workspace a handful of times. He could see it now when he closed his eyes. It was little more than a closet. There was a table over a small stove with an array of deep vats filled with waxes of all colors, and the shelves were filled with blocks of colored wax, vials of strange oils, and knives and other tools for shaping designs in the candles.

Will saw the spectacular candles Del made in there, candles with wings and curves and flowers carved and folded into them, and sometimes the aromas of the oils leaked under the door and hypnotized him. That was the type of candle making Will wished to do. It was elaborate and fantastic and, unless for special occasions, the candles were made to help people like Mrs. Grissom. Will desired nothing more than to have the opportunity to help people with his work, like Del did.

"Thirty," Will whispered to himself. He hung the frame from the ceiling, next to the others, and the candles dangled like elongated and uniform fruit.

Del and Mrs. Grissom emerged from the closet, Mrs. Grissom beaming as she gazed at the intricate candle in her hands. It was deep blue on the outside with waves of green and light red running through the curls and swirls Del had cut into it. Two birds of the same design graced the top. Will looked at it with the same awe as Mrs. Grissom, and Del looked at it with tired admiration.

"Make sure you put that in your bag before you leave, Mrs. Grissom," Del instructed kindly. "And that should give your husband more energy and vigor if you burn it like I've instructed."

Mrs. Grissom hugged the candle into her chest and got onto her tippy-toes to kiss Del's cheek. "Thank you, Mr. Chandler." She looked away with remorse that carved lines into her kind face. "I've nothing to pay you with today."

"No worries," Del said, waving her off. "Mr. Grissom will be back to work soon and you can pay me then."

"Thank you," she said again. She placed the fine candle in her bag with a hint of reluctance and turned to Will. "Please come visit, dear. Mister and I would really appreciate it." Will smiled and said he would as Mrs. Grissom left with a radiant smile erasing the remorseful wrinkles.

Del came to Will's side and inspected his work hanging from the ceiling.

"Adequate," he said. "Now, onto the votive candles. The delivery for monthly mass is due next week."

Del turned with a slight smile on his face, and Will turned with mechanical repetition to prepare the molds for the votive candles.

4

Three days a week Will and all the other children of Umbrate, ages three to twelve, were required to attend school. They gathered in their age groups and were admitted into their classrooms by rather stern teachers dressed in spotless gray robes. They were clerics of King Bale and, judging by the looks on their faces at each morning gathering, many of them were perturbed by the prospect of teaching unintelligent children. Instructor Luceen taught Will's group, and she was the sternest of them all. Will was sure she hated him because she never paid him any notice, but if that was the only consequence of being disliked, he didn't mind.

He stood in his group of twenty or so boys and girls and waited for Luceen to open the door. Will looked to his left and saw the younger class gathering next to him, not much different than his own group. He looked to his right and saw an empty hallway: the end of his instruction. He sighed deeply. The other children talked about Selection and which part of the kingdom they hoped to police someday, and about all the magical deviants they would bring to justice if the honor of being a guard was bestowed upon them. It was rare, nearly a hundred years after Bale declared Magic outlawed, for the Guard to find anything magical or any magical beings. It had been eradicated long ago. Now, Will believed, the men and women of the Guard just bullied others because they had nothing better to do. Will didn't hate them, it wasn't kind to hate your fellow Umbratian, but he disliked them very much, and he knew Del felt the same way, though he was less inclined to speak about it openly.

Instructor Luceen opened the door and a dusty light spilled into the hall. The children hushed their fantasies and career endeavors and looked straight ahead. She counted them quickly and stepped aside to permit them entry to the classroom.

The room contained three rows of long wooden tables with long wooden benches worn smooth by elbows and rears after years and years of instruction. The children sat in their spots assigned to them by Luceen as she watched in front of a slate wall with chalk writing across it that read 'Review.'

The children made as little sound as possible as they sat. They had learned by their second year that talking was not permitted unless you were called on by the instructor, and any superfluous noises received threatening, reproachful glances. Classes were conducted by the instructor, not taught. No debates over the information took place, and creativity bowed to indoctrination. The children wrote on bits of parchment provided to them by King Bale, and they all echoed in answer when the instructor asked a question.

"Today, we will be reviewing for your final examination," Luceen said. "I do not need to tell you how important these exams are for your Selection."

A trill of hushed excitement vibrated through the class. The results of the final examination were a great indicator of where a child would be placed at the time of Selection. With Will's future already in place as the Candlemaker's apprentice, he didn't share in the excitement of his classmates. Orphans like him were often selected into the Guard because they had no other place to go, but he had a place, and an apprenticeship, and that put him ahead of his classmates in many ways. He looked around the room at their smiles and enthusiasm. They had always seemed so childish to him, and it was probably why he had only one friend. No one was ever mean to him—meanness toward another was not tolerated—but they had never been friendly either, and Will had never been friendly with them.

Luceen picked up the tome of *Mass and Umbrate History* and began to hurl questions at the students.

"How many years ago was Magic outlawed by King Bale?"

"Ninety-nine years ago," replied the children in rote obedience.

"What caused the banning of Magic?"

"The murder of the Brave Queen Sharon committed by the evil wizard Xenerac," said the children.

Will always thought the questions were so obvious and broad that any child could answer them if they had paid any attention over the last nine years.

"How old is our mighty King?"

"Soon to be one-hundred-and-ten. Glory to our King!" the children said.

At the beginning of every year, their new instructors took the students to see the great statue of King Bale standing on the neck of Xenerac. Will thought it was a grand statue the first time he saw it, until it occurred to him one day that King Bale was only ten-years-old when he defeated Xenerac and outlawed Magic. The statue embodied a grown man, a great warrior crushing Xenerac, not a ten-year-old boy. He guessed many children saw themselves that way: bigger than they were, older than their minds, something they were not, and Will supposed he had been guilty of the same imaginations.

When Will was about ten, he pondered what it would have been like to have made the decision of banning Magic. It seemed a great deal of responsibility for a ten-year-old boy, but the kingdom appeared all the better for it, or at least pretended so.

"William?" Luceen said coldly. It was not a good thing to have your named called in class. Will scrambled to tether his trailing mind.

"Yes?"

"Who is King Bale's magical advisor?"

"Kylan Godea," Will said. The other children stared at his insolent inattentiveness with open mouths.

Luceen nodded to him. "Correct. Now pay attention." Will maintained eye contact and nodded meekly. "And what are Kylan's duties?" continued Luceen.

"To advise King Bale in the areas of Magic and Magic eradication," the children answered.

Kylan Godea had always been of great interest to Will. He himself was a magical being, a great wizard from before the time of outlawed Magic. He had renounced his magical ways to advise the king in magical matters. It was also rumored, in hushed tones in back alleys, that he was the one that determined the punishments and vetting methods for people caught in magical acts or with magical items. Will had seen the effects of the handcuffs Kylan had created, rumored to be made of silver cursed with the blood of dead magicians. And he could only imagine what sort of torturous things went on within the walls of the Reformatory of Magic: the place where magical beings were interrogated and imprisoned. No sound ever escaped, and its solid wall let in no light from the outside. Will had asked Del about Kylan and the Reformatory, but his eyes clouded at the mention of either and he would refuse to talk about it.

Instructor Luceen asked questions for the next three hours, and the children answered promptly and correctly, Will along with them. Luceen slammed the tome shut and dismissed the class in a tight line.

Lyle, Will's only near-age companion, came up behind him once they reached a safe distance from Luceen's piercing eyes.

"That's no way to get selected," Lyle said.

"Then I'll be sure to keep it up," Will replied, smiling.

"You're hopeless, Will," Lyle said. "Why would you not want to be a member of the Guard? They get the best food, the best clothing, and they're always in the King's favor."

"And always in his vision," Will said. "Besides, the son of a miller shouldn't have any worries about food."

"Just because my father mills it doesn't mean we get to eat it," Lyle clarified, nudging Will amicably. They walked out of the stone school building into the stone square, surrounded by children of all ages, each dressed similarly and according to the status of their parents. Some in clothes with only fine threadbare and others in complete rags.

"Are you concerned about the final examination?" Lyle asked.

"No. I'm sure my selection has already been made," Will said. "You?"

Lyle shrugged. "Yes and no. The worst that can happen is that I go to work with my father and continue to live my same life—the best is that I'm selected into the Guard."

Will knew of Lyle's eagerness to be a member of the Guard. A desire Will could understand but not himself want. The Guard members, it was rumored, did get all the best food and clothing, and the King often visited them, but they lived together in large barracks and were not as free to roam as other workers in the kingdom, and they worked long shifts with no breaks. It was not what Will wanted, but he was not hungry, and Del, despite his shortcomings, did provide for him the things he needed. Besides, Will wanted to be a candlemaker as much as the other boys and girls wanted to be members of the Guard.

They walked down the winding cobbled roads toward the Chandler's shop and the homes of the millers.

"Do you want to play this afternoon?" Lyle asked.

"I can't," Will said reluctantly. "I have to help Del finish the votive candles for mass."

"Fine," Lyle said. "See you at school. Don't forget to study." Lyle started into a run and disappeared around a curve.

Will watched him go before he turned and tried the door. It was locked. Del must be out, Will thought, so he grabbed the key from atop the door frame and let himself in. He stopped abruptly once inside. Del was there, speaking with a man wearing the King's colors, not the bland gray of the City Guard and the Clergy, but a robe striped with flaming orange, deep red, and soothing brown, like a sewn-on field of autumn. He wasn't a typical guard—no, this man was much higher than a member of the City Guard, he was a member of the Royal Guard that tended to Umbratian royalty. The man was as stout with youth as the colors of his robe were strong. His broad shoulders, thick beard, and dark hair made Del look like a sickly old man next to him. The men looked to have been in a tense conversation, but the appearance of Will seemed to smooth it out.

"Ah, I see your apprentice is back," the man said. "I'll take my leave, then. Good day."

He smiled and stared at Will, almost studying the boy's face, and left through the door. Del looked distressed, but pleased to see Will.

"Who was that?" Will asked.

"One of the King's men," Del replied. It was unusual for a man or woman of such prowess to enter their shop, or even to be seen outside the castle. The only time it ever happened was if a lowly cleric came by with a revised order of candles for the castle or mass.

"What did he want?" Will prodded.

Del faltered. "Special candles for the centennial festival."

"Oh," Will said, surprised. "Big candles?"

"Yes," Del said. "Elaborate, too."

"Can I help you with them?"

Del looked at him and gave a small smile. "Perhaps. Now, please finish the candles for mass. We have to deliver them tomorrow." He turned to enter his workspace.

Will stopped him. "I have my final examination next class."

"So soon?"

Will nodded. "And Selection is right afterward."

"Ah, and do you hope to be a member of the Guard?" Del asked, his voice timorous.

"Well, no … I was hoping to continue working with you," Will replied.

Del smiled. "Good." Silence filled the space, as it often did, and, without a word, Del closed the door between them.

Will dropped his parchment on the counter and took his place by the vat of hot wax. He inspected his previous day's work, and once he deemed it fit, proceeded with the next batch, thinking about Del's finely dressed visitor.

5

Del woke Will early on the days their deliveries were due at Bale's Cathedral. It was their largest order of each month, and Del, like everything in his life, kept it prompt and consistent. Though Del never told him this, Will knew that the fulfillment of this order kept the shop open and enough food on the table, even though the King's pay was meager. And special consideration was always given to businesses and people who provided important products or services to their king, and Will guessed that was also why the shop remained open, and why they weren't cast into another trade under closer scrutiny of the king and Kylan.

He looked into the thin porridge before him. It was mostly chaff that stuck to his teeth, but he ate it without complaint and wondered about the man wearing the king's colors that was in the shop the previous day. Their faces had been too stern for them to have been talking about special candles for the centennial festival. Will tended to notice things like that.

He gathered the last watery bite on his wooden spoon as Del conducted the final count of the candles. The count always made Will anxious. It was the final verdict on whether he had completed the task appropriately or not. Del and Will lived in a small home on the backside of the candle shop, and Will could see from his seat at the small table Del counting and inspecting each candle in turn, which was no small task considering there were one hundred votive candles and one hundred dip candles per order.

Will cleaned his bowl and joined Del in the workshop. He watched from behind as Del inspected and marked on his order sheet, inspected and marked.

Del turned and said, "Good," to Will's surprise. Del always had something to say, even if he accepted all the candles. "Let's load the cart."

The wooden crates of candles were too heavy for Will to carry by himself, so he and Del each silently grabbed a side and loaded the four crates into the back of the old wooden cart, as was ritual.

The donkey waited patiently for them, eager to be out of the harness and away from the cart, but he knew the schedule as well as Del or Will, and in the dark of the morning, he started pulling up the cobblestone road as Del and Will settled in their seats.

Will enjoyed making deliveries in the dark, damp morning. He could see the candles, ones he'd likely made, and oil lamps forming halos in the apartments and homes they passed, but most windows were dark, and the few people they saw in the streets were nothing more than shadows that slipped by like a wisp. It wasn't a long trip to Bale's Cathedral, but it was pleasant to be in the streets with no one about. The streets within the walls of Umbrate always felt empty, even when there were people in them, but it calmed Will to know he was one of the few people meandering through, and he wasn't a blank, wandering soul, just a soul on a mission, and the rest, he hoped, were having pleasant dreams in their beds or sitting under the light of his candle.

They stopped at the side door of the Cathedral. Friar Emesh looked up from his lamplit work through the window by the door. He smiled at them. Will couldn't help but smile when the kind friar did. His face was worn and friendly, doleful and sensitive, and he was much more approachable than most of the clergymen and women in the kingdom. Will always wondered what it would be like to have Emesh teach one of his courses, but the man was too kind, and kindness from an instructor was frowned upon. Instead, he was in charge of handling all the goods coming into the Cathedral and royal castle.

"Morning, Gentlemen," the friar whispered, as if he might disturb the sleeping.

Del smiled—a rare thing to see; the friar had that effect on him as well. "What, are you afraid you'll wake the king?" Del said at full volume. His voice echoed off the high stone walls of the Cathedral.

Bale's Cathedral was the largest and grandest building in Umbrate that the common people were allowed to enter. Mass was held once a month in honor of their king and his banishment of Magic, and all in the city were required to attend. Will thought it a boring experience, similar to the repetitiveness of going to school and answering the instructor's endless questions. All citizens chanted back, as Head Priest Renalt asked question after question. The truth was that it was not much different than school, just for everyone, no matter their age. They asked the same questions and the citizens returned the rote answers. Then they all bowed as King Bale entered, old and frail, with the Magical Advisor Kylan Godea leading him down the long aisle of the nave. It was not unlawful to look at the king and Kylan, but most kept their heads bowed out of fear. Princess Briella (or so Del said she was), the King's cousin, always followed behind, veiled, and surrounded by royal guards. Of course, everyone *did* look at the King and Kylan, but it didn't mean it was polite to talk about it, only mention how old and frail the king looked later in a dark alley with his friend Lyle. And after the King lit a votive candle for his mother, the Brave Queen Sharon, Kylan led him back down the aisle and out of the Cathedral with Briella and the guards following. The rest of the people waited with their heads bowed as the lower priests lit the rest of the votive and dip candles in their candelabras to represent the light that their king gave them. When the last one was lit, the patrons were allowed to leave, and the Cathedral was lit for as long as the candles burned to represent the king's enduring throne and the sacrifice of the citizens of Umbrate to the crown. Or so they chanted back to the Head Priest Renalt.

"How's the order this month?" Emesh asked.

"Fine, as usual," Del replied.

"I don't doubt that," Emesh said smiling.

Will and Del each grabbed a side of a crate and hauled it in through Emesh's office and into the main Cathedral area where they stacked them by the Altar. The dark of the Cathedral made Will's skin lift and go cold. Despite being a place of mass gathering and reverent worship, it was also a place of tenebrous mystery. Rumors circulated about the priests and the quiet things they did. Lyle's father was a great source of these rumors. And it wasn't just what the priests did, but who they might be doing it to. Directly behind the Cathedral was the Magical Reformatory, and beyond that the royal castle stood tall and proud, with Kylan's tower standing the tallest, casting its long shadow over the Cathedral by light of the faint sun. And all in Umbrate knew that nothing good grew in the shadows. Will had seen many grown men and women shudder after walking out of the Cathedral, and he often shared their sentiment. Will's combative advantage was that he knew the kind and courteous Emesh—a kind light in that damning place.

"Wonderful quality," Emesh said inspecting the candles on top.

"You can thank Will for that," Del said, offering more unexpected kindness. "The boy is coming along nicely."

"Fine work, Will," Emesh said, grinning and shaking his hand.

"Selection is coming soon, and he's hoping to join me full-time in the candle shop," Del said, feeling quite talkative this morning.

"I don't know, a strong, smart boy like him might get selected for the Guard," Emesh said. He subscribed to the public opinion that all boys and girls wanted to join the Guard.

Del and Will dropped their smiles. Emesh saw and changed the conversation. "Well, here is your compensation." He dropped a bag of coins in Del's hand. Del counted it with his fingers. His face clouded over.

"Will, do you mind giving us a moment?"

Will nodded, thankful to be leaving the dark Cathedral for the struggling light of morning. The rumors were ancient and tangible under the eldritch roof. He joined the donkey outside and ran the back of his hand down his cheek. The old boy grunted at him.

Will watched Del and Emesh talk from the corner of his eye. There had been too many secret conversations for Will's liking as of recent. Both men turned downcast.

Del whispered now, "I hate to question your count, Emesh, but this is not the normal amount."

"I'm aware, but the king is cutting things tighter now. He wants …" Emesh's inexhaustible cordiality turned his eyes toward the ground.

"He wants what?" Del said.

"He wants to save the resources for the festival," Emesh admitted. "That means many are getting cuts in pay … including me, Del."

Del put his hands on his hips and shook his head in frustration. He looked out the open door and saw Will look away.

"And you won't take a stand against this?"

"Will you?" Emesh asked, almost hopefully.

Del deflated. He knew he would not, could not.

"The king is absorbing the entire kingdom, Emesh. His men took all the white earth from my supplier and now I have none for my candles. And do you know what for?"

Emesh dropped his head to the solace of the ground again. "For banners, for the festival."

"And fine clothing, my supplier said. She's hardly getting paid for it. They're the only mine around here. If the king had enough skilled men to work it he'd simply take it from them, same as my shop."

Emesh looked into the dark Cathedral and his face changed.

Del continued in frustration, "People are starving out there. Their children are running around in rags and he's making fancy clothes, let alone banners."

He turned his face back to Del in disbelief. "Our king is kind; our king is benevolent. He would not let his people starve."

"I see it every day, and now it's affecting my work." Del didn't notice the change in Emesh; his back tightened and worry wrinkled his face. Del struggled to find the words that Emesh was trying to prevent him from saying. "I might … well, I might not have enough supplies to make a full batch of Altar candles next month."

"And why is that?" said a raspy voice from beyond the door leading into the Cathedral. The figure stepped through. It was the old and red-nosed Priest Renalt, the leader of Bale's order and the conductor of monthly mass.

"Father Renalt, you're here early," Emesh said, a titter of nervous laughter escaping him. Renalt looked to him with bloodshot disdain in his eyes. He turned his painful and rheumy stare back to Del.

"Why will you not be able to supply a full order of Altar candles?"

Del's eyes seemed to have grown heavy because he couldn't lift his head up from the ground.

"There aren't … well, I'm low on …" he gathered himself enough to lift his gaze. "I'll make it work, Father Renalt."

"Yes, you will," Renalt said. "Now, away with you."

Del turned and left before he had to stare another second into that malevolent face.

Renalt ran his fingers down his rigid jawline. He turned to Emesh and said: "Tell me what you know of this man."

Del walked past Will and jumped into the seat of the cart. "Let's go, boy. We have other work to complete today."

Will stopped petting the donkey and ran around to sit next to Del, giving a passing glance through the Cathedral's side door as he did so. His eyes met those of Renalt, and Will could feel the cold, stinging poison of them. Many of the disreputable rumors stemmed from Renalt, and the meeting of their eyes explained them all.

Del clicked to the donkey and the cart wheeled around, back down to the Chandler's shop. The morning light matured and the streets filled with the hardworking citizens of Umbrate. Will could sense Del's discomfort.

"Was that Father Renalt?" he asked.

"Yes," Del said.

"What did he say to you?"

Will knew from Del's glance he wasn't going to get the answer.

The pair returned the cart and donkey to the stable and walked through the waking commotion back to the shop. Wax preparation always followed delivery to the Cathedral. Del and Will would gather the blocks of raw beeswax and throw them into the largest vat they had. Will would maintain the fire and stir the wax as Del completed his calculations of soot and white earth additions. Will was never sure what he calculated, but he would observe Del as he stirred the melting wax with the cumbersome wooden paddle that strained his developing arms. Then he would check the fire, add wood if necessary, and continue stirring.

As he stirred that day, he realized the wax in the vat was much shallower than usual. He looked at Del making his calculations and realized why he and Emesh had appeared so distraught after they dismissed him: the wax in the vat was not enough to complete the Cathedral's orders. Will reached into his pocket and pulled out the bit of honeycomb Charlie had given him. It was mangled with bite marks, but Will had kept it to chew on in case there might be some sweetness hidden in a crevice or crack, or at the very least to imagine there was. He turned it over in his hands and tossed it into the vat. Will turned and saw Del looking at him. A feeble smile crept across his face.

"You're a good boy, Will," Del said, standing. "As you can see, we're short on wax." Will nodded. "We'll gather what we can and make due."

Del took his calculations and went to the bags of soot and white earth. He mounted one side of his large scale with the weight he desired and piled the soot first. His hands were black with the stuff by the time he had it weighed and dumped into the liquid wax. Then came the white earth to contrast the dark and sticky soot he wore. The air filled with the throat-sticking dusts as he dumped and Will stirred.

"What will happen if we don't have enough?" Will asked.

"We'll have enough … this time," Del answered. "Even if it takes a bit of," he paused and looked at the boy, "ingenuity."

"What does that mean?"

"It means we have to be clever." Del winked at Will, much to his surprise. "Now, keep stirring and try not to get any on the ground."

Del left Will to stir the viscous liquid. He pondered what sort of cleverness Del was considering. The boy had never seen wax pulled from thin air, but Del was intelligent, and crafty, two skills he showed in his ornate candles like the one he made for Mrs. Grissom, and as long as Will had been with him, he had never missed an order of Altar candles. This time would be no different, but Will wondered about next time. He watched the paddle glide through the wax with effort, until he became entranced by waves as the soot and white earth sank the heavy, dirty bits to the bottom of the vat, increasing the clarity of the hot liquid. His mind wandered to school and the final examination he would have the next day. It excited him to know he would be working in the shop more. Maybe Del had been waiting for him to finish school before teaching him more about the trade. Will hoped so.

The clear wax swirled before him, and as Will looked into it, he could see his future. And it excited him. Working in the shop each day would be fun, and it was a good career with the potential to help people like the Grissoms or Phin's niece. He hopped off his step and fed the fire, then returned to stirring the wax, his zeal for his work increasing.

6

Will met Lyle outside the school the morning of the final examination. His haggard eyes stared at Will as his teeth worked on the last bit of thumbnail they could find. The children were quieter than usual, especially the twelve-year-old children who were soon to meet their futures with rapid speed.

"My father wants me to get selected into the Guard," Lyle said with fear written in bold across his face.

"I thought that was what you wanted," Will said.

"It is," Lyle said, looking at him severely. "He said if I get selected it will improve life for my entire family. He was so serious this morning." He stopped and shook his head. "I'm scared, Will."

"You'll be fine, Lyle. It's not as if you really have a say whether you get selected or not. Your father knows that. He just wants you to have something different than what he has," Will said.

"Easy for you to say. You've already got your apprenticeship in place. Instructor Luceen hates me. She'd never select me in a thousand years," Lyle said.

Will smiled and put his hand on Lyle's shoulder. "Luceen hates everybody, Lyle."

Lyle lifted his downcast face, where a smile started.

"I suppose you're right," he said.

"Let's go," Will said. "Luceen certainly won't select anyone who's tardy."

The boys entered the school, then their classroom, soon to shake hands with destiny.

◊

The process of Selection was not known to be a grand event. It took place immediately after the completion of the final examination. The children were forced to wait in silence as the tests were graded and the selections revealed.

Will completed his test first and had the boring task of waiting for the other boys and girls to finish. Some of them worked feverishly, writing down every last piece of information they had memorized over their nine-year tenure. Others seemed at a loss for words, as their lead hardly scratched the parchment. Lyle was a member of the latter. Will cheered for him in his head, but he doubted Lyle could hear by the way he worked so slowly.

Two other clergy members joined Luceen that day to help with the grading of the examinations. They scanned the room with glassy, pensive eyes, often landing on Will, who felt forced to look away. They graded each examination as it was turned in, and then the triumvirate whispered together before they wrote on the examination and stamped it with Bale's wax seal of approval. They spent little time deliberating over Will's; his fate was sealed before he had arrived that day.

What did happen to be a grand event was the presentation of the new Guard at the monthly mass after Selection. It was a sight to witness: all those children, some scared, some proud, all uneasy about being presented at the Altar to accept the King's personal approval as the common people recognized the new crop that would be trained to protect and intimidate the kingdom. It made Will laugh to think about it now that the King's sure stamp had solidified on his quick lot. He rested his head on the desk and waited for Selection, the last thing he would do in that classroom.

"Rise, children," Luceen said, rousing Will from his daydream. "We will now begin the Selection. Those selected for the Guard, turn to the left when you leave the classroom. Those selected for other trades, you are free to go home. The master of your trade will contact you within the next month."

She stood at the front of the class with the two clergy members standing stiff behind her. Their gray cloaks blended in with the slate, making their heads look suspended in the faint afternoon light streaming through the tall, skinny windows. The day was moving toward a close. Will had been waiting a long time. Some of his fellow students danced as if they had to go to the bathroom, and some probably did, while the others stood starch still in anticipation of their verdict.

Will looked at Lyle and gave him a tired smile; Lyle returned it. They turned to the front.

"Eric Andrews—Guard," Luceen said. A quiet relief escaped the boy in a whimper. He came forward, took his stamped exam from Instructor Luceen, and was given a bronze Guard badge by one of the clergy members.

"Lauren Heathertow—Seamstress … Johnathon Herndon—Mason … Bethany Minx—Textiles …"

Nobody cheered or clapped as Instructor Luceen insipidly doled out destinies to children but remained silent as had been beaten into them over the years. Some who had wished to be members of the Guard shed silent tears going to get their papers that designated them as blacksmiths or hospitality workers for the Cathedral or King's residence. Will found it to be much more depressing than he thought it would be, seeing his classmates, of which only one he mildly cared about, get their dreams and hopes of their tender youths crushed so violently by heavy, monotone syllables, and with no one to cheer for them or comfort them.

"William Chandler—" Will perked at the sound of his name, "Guard."

His mouth dropped open before he could stop it. He remained in place long enough that Instructor Luceen lifted her head from the papers in her hand to gaze at him. The remaining students turned to stare.

"William," Luceen repeated dully. Will turned to Lyle, his countenance a curtain of shock and pain that kept any light or happiness from shining through.

"It's not correct," Will whispered, looking at Lyle.

"Excuse me," Luceen said. The uncommon emotion in her voice brought the children's faces back forward. "Are you questioning the King's ruling?"

Will turned to her and put his head down. "Apologies, Instructor Luceen. I am surprised by my selection."

"Selection is final," Luceen said. "Come forward and leave to the left so that we may continue."

Will did so without further hesitation and received his papers and Guard badge from the clammy hands of the clergyman. He turned at the door for just a moment to see Lyle's bewildered face. His friend wouldn't look at him.

"Peter Bernard—Guard …" Luceen continued.

Will turned left outside the door, feeling out of breath. The harvest of future guards stood in a tight line down the hall. A stern man stood in front of them. Will moved so slow that Peter Bernard caught up with him.

"Hop to, Will," he said with a smile as he passed. Delight was written on the boy's face; delight Will could not find.

"Come down, boy," the stern guard said, his face shadowed by the fading light in the hall. Will approached the group. "Stand directly behind this young woman. Line your shoulders up with hers and keep one arm's distance away." He explained before he went silent again.

Will reached his arm out and distanced himself from her—Patricia … something—his brain was so lost he couldn't remember her name. He avoided the gaze of the guard and stared over his shoulder at the classroom door. Lyle came out and stopped. He turned his head to the left with tears of betrayal shining a trail down his face. Will's heart stopped. Lyle looked at him a moment before he turned right and exited the building. Pain struck Will's gut like a glowing spear. He watched Lyle leave.

"Eyes forward!" the guard said.

Will turned to look up at him. The shadows on his face made him look rigid as stone. He leaned forward into the light of the embrasure window. Will's eyes widened further. He recognized the guard.

"I would suggest you get used to doing what you're told," he said, sneering.

"Yes, sir," Will said. He stroked his hair down and turned his eyes to the back of the girl in front of him. Another child approached from the classroom; Will didn't turn to see who it was.

The Guard told him or her how to stand, and Will could feel the quivering fingertips touch his back for distance.

The hall was silent except for the excited and scared breathing of the children. Will looked up into the face of the guard, sure that he knew him.

"That is all," Instructor Luceen's voice called behind them, cleaving Will's years of schooling with her pithy statement.

The guard gave a smug smile and looked at his new recruits.

"Let's begin."

◊

Will walked in the dark with a listless keel that pushed him from stone wall to stone wall. The only place he had to go was back to the Chandler's shop, the very place he wanted to avoid. He let his feet take him where they pleased, wandering around corners with his hands scraping over the stones to support himself. The night air was cold and dark, but it felt much colder and darker to Will.

He thought of the guard's stern stare and familiar face; he thought of Lyle and the pain he must be feeling; he thought of Del and how he would handle the news; and finally, he thought of himself and the life he would spend in service of King Bale … and whatever leader came after him.

Will stopped. He knew where his feet were taking him, and he aided them by bursting into a run. There were still people going about their business in the streets; it was not too late to visit friends, especially those that had invited him.

He took the curves and turns with a child's agility and found himself at Mr. and Mrs. Grissom's house. The lights were off. Will tapped on the door, but no response came. He knocked harder.

"Mrs. Grissom, it's me, Will," he said to the door. He heard no sound on the inside. He looked up to the sky. It got dark early in Umbrate, so far from the sun, but he knew it wasn't very late. He tried one more time before he peeked through their small window, through a crack in the drawn blinds. All was quiet and cold and alone. It appeared to be abandoned.

Will went back to the door and tried the handle—it was unlocked. He poked his head through the crack and called in. The hollowness of his own voice was the only response. Entering, Will closed the door on the peering eyes of the outside world. It was dark and dank, and a cold humidity wrapped him. He put his hand over the stove and felt no warmth, touched its side and felt only cold iron. Their house was small, as all were in Umbrate, and Will could see most of it from where he stood. He looked to the large chair Mr. Grissom often sat in and repeated the same stories as Will munched cakes and sipped the thin tea Mrs. Grissom always had in a pot on the stove.

Will turned his head from the chair and looked about the rest of the dusty and disheveled room. Mrs. Grissom had worked on the King's hospitality crew until she couldn't walk up the stairs anymore and was released of her duty; her house was never dusty or disheveled, and certainly not both together.

Will's heart beat faster. He looked about the main room and kitchen before he turned his attention to their bedroom door.

"Mr. and Mrs. Grissom," he said with shaky voice as he approached the door. Silence.

He lifted his trembling hand to push it open. It gave way with a creak. He could see their lumpy bed and what small belongings they owned, but the Grissoms were not there. He looked through their room, inspecting every corner, and did the same in the main area, but he couldn't find what he was looking for, an item that would have stood out like a red rose in a field of wheat.

The candle Del made them was missing.

Will opened the door to the Chandler's shop and quietly stepped in. Closing the door, he turned to see Del sitting in the light of a small candle.

"Where have you been? Did Selection take that long?" Del asked, his voice quaking.

"No, I ... I went to see Mr. and Mrs. Grissom," Will replied.

"You did?" Something in Del's voice told Will the old chandler knew they weren't there.

"Yes, but they weren't home. They haven't been for some time by the look of the place."

Del pulled at his chin hairs with patient but nervous fingers. "Yes, I'd heard they … moved on. I was waiting for the right time to tell you."

"Oh." Will had no energy to fight or ask further, and he carried his own news he wished not to share.

Only the flicker of the candle offered any conversation for a moment. Del looked as if he was trying to find his words when Will stopped him.

"I've been selected into the Guard," he said.

Del sat upright, silent. "I see," he said after a few moments. It was difficult to distinguish in the small light, but Will thought he saw sadness deepen the aged man's eyes. "When will you be moving to the barracks?" Del's face told Will he wanted to say more but lacked the words, or courage.

"The man said we would be moving there in thirty days. He said it was enough time to gather our things and prepare ourselves."

"What man?" Del asked.

"Head Official Yan Coaler." Will said. His eyes went blank. "The man who attacked my mother."

The grave words from such a small boy rattled Del. "Are you sure it was him?" Del asked. He stood and began to pace; the firelight wiggled as he did so, creating a greasy orange wave in the halo on the back wall. Will stared with acute eyes that glowed in the wavering light.

"But I thought he was … no, of course not. You would be sure. You're an intelligent boy. And one does not easily forget something like that, no matter how young." Del turned to him. "Do you think he recognized you?"

Will shook his head. "No."

"Good," Del said, stroking his chin as he paced. "What shall we do about this?" he asked himself.

"What can we do?" Will answered, his voice quavered with emotion. "The King's seal is already stamped on it." Will presented Del the papers and started toward bed.

7

The common people funneled into Bale's Cathedral, quietly and efficiently, with mothers holding the hands of fearful children, and fathers observing all with glancing eyes. Silence was part of the ritual on the mornings of mass. Even the small children who had no cognizant idea of what they were doing huddled close to their mothers or fathers in daunted silence.

Four clergymen, dressed in robes, stood by the door and took count as the citizens of Umbrate filed through. All citizens were required to attend unless they were unable to walk or illness left them in bed, and only if the clergy permitted their absence.

Del and Will walked by the counting clergymen. Usually, they were gray faces in a gray fold, but today Will wore the bright bronze badge representing his fresh admission into the City Guard. Children gawked as he passed and men and women stared at him, some with honor, some with pity. Will only felt the pity. They followed the line of people down the aisle, into a pew, and to their seats. Del sighed as he sat, and Will sighed with him.

Will looked across the aisle and saw Lyle sitting with his mother and father. Lyle caught his gaze and looked ahead with steadfast anger and malleable shame. Will felt the badge burning on his chest. It seemed to collect what little light came in the windows to shine brighter than anything else in the Cathedral. The man sitting next to him turned and saw his badge. He leaned over and, rather out of mass tradition, spoke to him.

"What an honor it is to be selected into the Guard. Congratulations, young man."

Will gave him what smile he could muster, nodded, and looked toward the Altar.

Once all the citizens were seated, Father Renalt took to the pulpit and began the process of rote preaching before they all kneeled for the entrance of King Bale and Kylan Godea to light the candle for Queen Sharon to commence the lighting of the dark nave as the king and Kylan left in shadow. Princess Briella followed, veiled so that her face could not be seen, and beside her walked the man in the autumn-colored robe who had been at the candle shop the other day. Will could not mistake him. Why had such a high official been in their shop, he wondered? Not simply for decorative candles.

Will would be blessed by the king that day. As the others remained with their heads down, the new recruits were brought to the front and presented to the king, the king's Magical Advisor, and Father Renalt. The thought of standing before King Bale and Kylan Godea spurred Will's heart into a drum beat that pounded in his ears, rushing with the fear of staring into the eyes his own were never meant to meet.

"Now, if the selections for the Guard would please come forward to receive their blessings," Renalt said.

Del looked out the corner of his eye and put his hand on Will's shoulder. He squeezed, keeping Will seated. The boy looked at the man who had been his guardian for so long as if it were their last moment together. Before today, Will had wondered if Del felt relieved to be rid of him, but the glimmer in the chandler's eyes told him otherwise.

Will stood, feeling the tears rise, and scooted his way down the pew to the main aisle. The other selected boys and girls sprouted up from the bowed heads and joined him from all corners of the Cathedral. Will counted nine in all. A boy and a girl were ahead of him, approaching the Altar slowly for fear of being the first. This was one of the few times that the King allowed any of the common people to get so close to him, but Will forgot he was not one of the common people anymore, but one of the few chosen to lead his community. The guards stood above the common people, viewed as elite because the king and his society believed it, and they were treated as such.

Will could see the hateful gazes he would meet in his future, and all the fearful tears that would spill on his account. He thought of Mr. and Mrs. Grissom getting their house sacked and their lives taken because of a candle they had. They were likely beyond the wall that held up the Altar, in the Reformatory, being questioned about the magical qualities of a stupid candle. They would never tell where they got the candle from, and that truth mixed with the fact that the chandler did the King's work kept Del protected. Will hated Del for just a moment, but it dissipated before he reached the Altar, for displaced hate alters the veracity of the true enemy, just as they wish it to.

The boy and girl ahead of him kneeled and bowed on the steps before the King, Kylan, and Renalt. Princess Briella and the royal guard stood behind them. Will joined the kneeling, with one last look at the votive candle—the candle Will had made—King Bale lit for his mother, the Brave Queen Sharon. Will had made all the candles on the Altar that were now being lit by the men and women of the clergy. He wished to knock them all down, to cause an uprising that lifted the people's bowed heads. Deep inside, he believed it was himself that had borne the evil that tore at his heart because he had made those candles; the ones being lit in strange honor of the process he did not want himself or others to be forced through. And more than all that, he didn't want to be above his fellow man in any way. He wanted to make candles—candles that helped people, like the ones Del made. Simple candles that lit rooms and provided warmth. As a member of the Guard, Will would not be able to help people, and he believed that; he could only wield fear with that badge on his chest, not aid.

"William Chandler." The voice of Father Renalt ripped Will from his introspection. Renalt's cold fingers lifted Will's gaze to stare into the stern face of the priest, the frail face of King Bale, and the indifferent face of Kylan. "Do you vow to do the King's bidding as the King sees fit?"

Will fought the urge to look down. He looked into the veiled face of Princess Briella, getting a glimpse of its blurred outline through the intricate lacing. The royal guard looked down from beside the princess.

"Yes," he said, for no other answer was optional.

"And do you vow to make it your life's purpose to destroy all magical beings and all magical entities within the walls of Umbrate and throughout the Kingdom of Mass?"

"Yes."

King Bale presented his bony hand, the sinew and tissue worn away from years of disuse. The fingers were pale and thin, and Will could see all the way through the skin to the snake-like veins and tendons writhing below. Will looked away from the decrepit hand toward Kylan. The old wizard's eyes were haggard but sharp. It took effort to gaze into them for more than a moment. The man looked through him, reading the shame he bore on his heart for the act he completed. Will looked to the only solace he could find: the faded face of his princess, and the strong face of the young guard.

"Kiss the hand of the King to seal your allegiance," Renalt said.

Will did so, and the triumvirate moved onto the next child. He looked at Kylan one last time and thought of his mother, and if she had ever met the demented wizard. Kylan gazed at him, and Will bowed his head to hide the tears he couldn't hold anymore.

"Peter Bernard. Do you vow …" Renalt continued.

It was done.

More candles of Will's making were lit, pouring light across the Altar. The nimbus of that light touched Will, at the edge where he was severed from the people he lived among, the people he wished to serve. And just like the candles Will and Del made for the King, Will was now the King's property. But then again, he always had been.

8

Work continued as usual during Will's last month with Del, being the only way they knew how to conduct themselves. They didn't talk about the Selection, or the moment at the Altar, and both seemed fine with that. Will was back to being an apprentice, but only for the time apportioned to him.

People looked at him differently now that he was a fledgling of the Guard. They moved aside as he walked past, and some sneered at him with scornful eyes. It stabbed him to see it. He even tried to visit Lyle after mass, but his old friend wouldn't see him. The sun was darker than usual, and the work he busied himself with and the food he ate was insipid and dry. It was the natural course of things and Del appeared unaffected by it, and that hurt Will the most.

On the morning of their last supply run together, Del and Will conducted themselves as usual. Will went with him to the stable and harnessed the donkey to the cart. It occurred to the boy that the poor beast had no name. Soon Will would have no name—people would simply call him Guard. He ran his hand down the cheek of the donkey and stared into his dull eyes. His ears swiveled and turned as Del attached the harness. The donkey had worked hard in service to them, and Will believed he needed a name. He looked deeper into the animal's eyes in search of one.

"Clyde," Will said to himself.

"What was that?" Del asked.

Will hesitated, feeling a bit foolish, before he found his confidence and stared at Del sternly. "The donkey's name is Clyde. I would like for you to call him that after I'm gone."

Del made no attempt to dispute. "As you wish."

Clyde snorted in approval. Will smiled at him and ran his hand down his neck and across his back before he got on the cart to make his last journey to pick up beeswax, soot, and white earth.

◊

Phin greeted them at the city gate with a grand smile that morning. He raised his hand to shake with his new comrade.

"Will, I'm pleased to call you a member of the Guard," he said. Will shook his hand, gave a small smile, and said nothing. "What will you do now that you won't have a strong boy around to do all the heavy lifting?" Phin asked Del in jest.

Del turned to him seriously and said: "I don't know." And it sounded like he meant it.

"Well," Phin said with an oblivious smile, "I suppose you'll figure that out in time. Maybe the king will provide you with a new apprentice." Phin stepped back from the cart and let them through. "I can't wait to share a spot with you at the gate, Will. It'll be an honor."

Will and Del stared ahead as they passed the ever-cheerful and removed Phin. The other guards saw the badge on Will's chest and nodded to him as they rode through the gate amid the flurry of people entering and exiting Umbrate.

The possibility of a new apprentice needled into Del and Will with each jostle and bump. They shifted with uneasiness as it worked into the quick with painful dedication. A thought entered Will's mind as he bounced and rocked on the slow-moving cart, but he kept it there. It was dangerous for members of the Guard to think such things, no matter how intriguing they might be. And he knew if he proposed the idea and somebody found out, Del would find himself in trouble as well, and Will did not want that. He pushed the thought aside and tried to conjure something to say, but Del beat him to it.

"I really *don't* know what I'm going to do without you, Will," he admitted. "I don't wish to have another apprentice."

Now Will's thought didn't seem so outlandish. It dashed forth from its cage.

"What if we left?" his voice sounded weak, childish.

Del jerked his head to the right; Clyde's ears swiveled to listen. "Left?" Del questioned.

"Yes, left Umbrate. Maybe the entire kingdom," Will paused and scrunched his face in curiosity. "Are there other kingdoms?"

Del looked at him with the same curiosity, still stuck on the prospect of fleeing. "Across the sea, maybe. But we would be caught before we made it to Miner's Cove or Bale's Bay. We'd be criminals—outcasts and defectors. That'd mean serious trouble for us, even death."

"But couldn't we go … somewhere else?" Will grew excited; he could see Del had considered this before.

Del shook his head to sift down his tempting thoughts. "All places are the same. They're all poor; they all hate Magic; they all do the king's bidding." Del slapped the reins across Clyde's back, much to the donkey's disapproval.

"We could go live in the Grim Forest."

Del turned to him, perturbed. "What do you know of the Grim Forest but its name, let alone surviving there?"

Will shrugged. "We could figure it out. We could grow our own food, and hunt wild things, and … and—"

"Enough of this madness!" He looked around to make sure they were alone, and lowered his voice. "I won't have you suggesting such ideas any longer. Mass is where we live, and Umbrate is where we reside. It's a great honor for you to be a part of the Guard. You will be well-fed and taken care of."

"But I don't want to do it!" Will screamed. The tears spilled from his eyes as he put his blubbering face into his hands.

Del looked around again to make sure they were alone. Clyde stopped the cart as if he could read the old man's mind. Del leaned over and hovered his hand above Will's back before resting it down awkwardly.

"I know you don't want to be a member of the Guard, Will, but you were selected, and now it's your duty to serve your king as he sees fit, same as the miller, or the blacksmith, or me, the chandler. We all have jobs that need completing."

"For the king's cruel bidding," Will said. He lifted his stormy face to Del. "I know you believe it too, Del. You believe it the same as all the others do." Del searched for words but could find none. "They already treat me differently. They see me in the streets and they move aside. Some look at me unkindly because they know now is their chance to do so, before I'm above them. Even Lyle won't talk to me anymore. I hate it! I won't be a good guard."

"Of course you will," Del said.

Will turned to him angrily. "You think so, do you? And what happens when they order me to take you in?" Del sat up stiffly. "I know Mr. and Mrs. Grissom were taken to the Reformatory because of the candle you gave them."

"That's preposterous." His susurration lacked conviction.

"Then why else were they taken in? I went through their house, Del, I couldn't find the candle."

"Are you accusing me of performing Magic?"

"No." Will calmed himself. "I know it's not Magic you put into the candles, just oils and such that make people feel better. But the members of the Guard won't believe anything like that."

Silence filled the void between them. A bird chirruped alone in the distance. Clyde snorted and stamped his feet. Will stared at Del, who held the reins up and looked ahead.

"Did you know?" Will asked.

"Did I know what?"

"Did you know that it was the candle that got the Grissoms sacked?"

Del looked down between his hands. "Yes," he admitted.

"Is that why the man in the King's colors was at the shop the other day? The Royal Guardsman?"

"Yes," Del said, breathing deep and looking up again. "He's an old friend. His mother was deathly ill once and I helped him, before he joined the Royal Guard. He knew I made the candle." Del faltered. "He told me the Grissoms wouldn't say my name, no matter how much they … they tested them."

"Hurt them, *tortured* them, you mean?"

A single tear dribbled down Del's wrinkled face. "Yes." He turned to Will. "I won't make any more candles like that. The Guard will have no reason to come find me."

"What about the man who informed you?"

"He's indebted to me," Del said. "He risked his position to tell me." Del's eyes remained focused on Will. "This is the world we live in, boy. You'll have better luck in it as a member of the Guard."

Del slapped the reins on Clyde's back and the tired donkey proceeded down the road.

◊

Del stopped the cart a safe distance from the hives as he always did. Kip rushed from the shed to the hives, his canvas suit and mesh hat falling off like loose skin. He worked with nervous, hasty hands, nothing like Charlie's caring easiness, and the bees swarmed him with fury. Del and Will watched with strange fascination.

"Kip!" Del yelled.

The skinny boy lifted his head and adjusted the mesh head cover to see. His bewildered eyes pierced through, wide and shining, and his skin glistened with sweat.

"Are you all right?" Del asked.

Kip realized who they were and moved toward them, away from the cloud of enraged bees.

"Del, Will, I-I-I'm sorry, but I don't have your order ready," Kip said, taking his mesh cover off as he approached. "I've been trying to fill the King's kitchen with honey."

"Where's Charlie?" Del asked.

Kip looked shocked. "Have you not heard? He's been taken by the Guard."

"By the Guard?!" Del said, flabbergasted. "For what reason?"

"What reason?" Kip responded, baffled that Del should ask such a thing. "For performing Magic, of course. What other reason would they have to take him?" Kip looked to the ground and shook his head. Del turned pale and sickly.

"Charlie? A magical being?" Will asked, as baffled as any of them.

Kip nodded, sad and angry. "And here I was working with him all this time, and without a clue about it," he said, as if trying to convince Will and Del of his ignorance in case he should be suspected next. "What a fool I was letting the old coot lead me along."

"When did they take him?" Del asked, looking rather washed out.

"Not too long after your last visit, only a few days. They just came out of the grain field one day and arrested him."

"Why didn't they arrest you?" Del asked.

Kip looked at him crossly. "I'm not a magical being. I'd never touch the stuff, not even for a joke!"

"Did they give a reason why?" Del asked, tripping over eager syllables.

Kip shook his head. "Not to me they didn't. I'm sure they gave him a reason though, right before Kylan Godea gave him what he deserved, the old liar."

"Enough of that!" Del blurted. Kip jumped. Del's countenance turned apologetic. "I'm sorry, Kip, I'm just a bit worked up. Charlie's been a friend for a long while. It's disturbing to learn he'd been engaged in illegal practices all this time."

"No one understands your frustration better than I do, Del," Kip said with downcast eyes. "I'm sorry I don't have your order ready. If you come back in a week, I'll have it for you."

"That'll be fine, Kip," Del said.

"I don't want to disappoint the King. I'm sure his eyes won't be far away since I'd been working with Charlie. I can't believe the old fool would choose to put me at risk like that. He should have turned himself in years ago. Now they'll probably be watching my family as well. How I hate him," Kip hissed, though his voice lacked the vile he intended. He looked to Will. "You remember that I'm not magical when you get into the Guard, Will. Don't let them tear me away from my family."

"I'll remember," Will answered, still reeling from the shock.

"I have to get back to work," Kip said, replacing his mesh cover. "I can't keep up. If they don't send me some help the King will be without honey." Kip turned back to his work, leaving Del and Will staring at each other.

"Do you think it's true?" Will whispered.

Del looked over his shoulder to make sure Kip was far enough away.

"No, Charlie was not a magical being, just a good apiarist," Del said.

"Then why did they take him?" Will asked, distraught. He had always loved Charlie, and in a moment of selfishness he saw himself having to strap on the horrible silver handcuffs cursed with the blood of dead magicians harvested by Kylan himself.

"I don't know," Del said. "Maybe they were bored." Del slapped the reins on Clyde's back and turned the cart back to Umbrate.

"What about the white earth?" Will asked, looking over his shoulder.

"What's the point if we have no wax to add it to?"

Del slapped the reins again, meanly, and Clyde's hooves clipped into a trot. He never trotted. Will slumped. It was not the ending he wanted for his last supply run.

9

It took Will everything he had to not barrage Del with questions in his last few days living in the back of the Chandler's shop. Questions about if he would have enough wax for the Altar candles; questions about Charlie's arrest; questions about their future together.

Will had thought long and hard about what happened to Charlie. He couldn't remember the last time a true magical being was captured, or even the last time they discovered a magical device of some sort. Word always got around if someone was taken in for questioning, but Will and Del had heard nothing until Kip told them. It could have been that their own situation occupied his mind, but Will doubted they would have heard *nothing* about the arrest of their friend for magical malfeasance. Something sinister lurked here below the surface.

It was not uncommon for people to get lifted by the Guard, but few among the common people believed that the ones they took into custody were actually magical. There were, it was known, great incentives granted to guards that caught magical beings. And every time the Guard took a captive, folks were quick to chalk it up to the bonus a guard received, but it never slowed the rumors of possible Magic.

Del had been acting strange since the news of Charlie. He had gone out without Will a number of times, and the boy had not seen Del but for meals the last few days—the last few days they had together. Tomorrow was the day Will moved into the barracks to begin training for the Guard. His stomach turned thinking about it.

Will fiddled about the shop as his mind wandered hand in hand with the possibilities. There was still no wax, and that meant no work for the boy to occupy his hands, so he paced, logging the shop's humble details into memory. He wondered if he would ever be back. He guessed not, and part of him, as a member of the door-busting guard, certainly hoped not.

A heavy knock hit the door. Del emerged from his workspace to answer it. The fierce pounding continued until he opened the door. He cracked it part way and the knocker forced it open the rest of the way. It was three members of the City Guard. Del jumped back; Will jumped up. Head Official Yan Coaler came in first.

"Is this the residence of William Chandler?" he asked Del.

Del nodded, pale and sweaty. "Yes, he's just there in the shop area."

Yan and his two men were well dressed, even for men of the Guard, and they stood with great prowess in the entryway, making the space look too small for them.

"William Chandler," Yan said, stepping into the shop area. His men followed. Del bent over and grabbed his chest as if an iron vice squeezed it.

Will stepped forward stiffly. He looked around the thick, well-fed frame of Yan. "Are you all right, Del?" Will asked.

Yan looked over his shoulder with little care. Del stood upright to catch his breath.

"Yes, boy, they just gave me a start is all."

Yan looked back at Will, indifferent toward the old man's hardship. He gestured over his shoulder. "Looks a little old to be your father."

"He's not my father," Will said, staring him in the face. He refused to be afraid of Yan.

"What about your mother?" Yan asked.

Will gritted his teeth. "Don't have one. I'm an orphan."

"Ah, that explains why the name is Chandler," Yan said. It was often the way of things in Umbrate for orphans to take on the name of their guardians or their assigned trade. Chandler was not only Del's last name, but his trade as well. Will often wondered if he had been an orphan, but Del employed creative ways to avoid discussing his childhood or past. "What happened to your parents?"

Will's courage faltered. "I-I don't know. They died when I was very young."

Yan nodded like he cared—he didn't. His goons stood behind him at attention. Yan looked about the place.

"Nice shop you have here," he mocked. "Can't say I've ever been in it. How's business?"

Del came to Will's side and put his arm over the boy's shoulder. "Fine enough."

Yan looked to say something smart, as he did when he entered other homes on Guard business, but held his tongue and remembered why he was there.

"I came to see how my new recruit is faring," Yan said, scrutinizing Will. "Prepared for tomorrow, I hope?"

Will nodded to him. "Yes, sir."

Yan stepped forward, removed Del's arm from the boy's shoulders, and placed his own large hands there. He inspected the bony boy with rough, prodding fingers. He examined his shoulders and neck, his eyes and ears, his legs and crotch, making Will more uncomfortable with each invasive touch.

"A little scrawny, but you seem in good health, William," Yan said, stepping away. "It is a great honor to be selected into the Guard. We are pleased to have you. You and the other eight recruits will meet me at the front of the Cathedral at dawn to begin the process. Do not be late, or you will be presumed a runaway from your duty, and you will be hunted down." His mechanical voice carried a weight of seriousness.

Will, desiring to look away, kept his eyes on Yan as he spoke. "I'll be there, sir."

"Where?" Yan quizzed.

It took all the strength in Will's neck to keep his eyes up. "The front of the Cathedral, at dawn."

Yan flashed a wanton smile that made him all the more difficult to look at; Will had seen that malicious grin before. "Good! I'll see you then."

A knock hit the door. All five of them turned to look at it; none of them moved. The knock came again. Yan turned to Del.

"It would appear you have a customer, Chandler."

Del remained planted, stiffly staring at the door. Yan signaled for one of his men to open it.

The guard did so without delay, but he appeared as startled as Del when he opened the door. He turned to Yan.

"Sir, it's Alphonse, of the Royal Guard … here to see you," the guard said as if it were a question.

Alphonse stepped in. Will recognized him as the man in the King's colors he had intruded on the other day talking to Del, the same that had walked with Princess Briella at Will's induction into the Guard.

"Is there business dealing with the Princess, Alphonse?" Yan, breaking his sure demeanor, appeared as surprised to see him as anyone else.

Alphonse smiled. "No, Head Official Coaler, I'm not here to see you. I'm here to see the candlemaker."

They all turned and gawked at Del. Alphonse remained the only one that wasn't nonplussed.

"My business can wait until you are finished," Alphonse said, breaking the silence. The colors of his robe were brilliant and clean, and he made even the finely-dressed guards look drab and lifeless, even more so Del and Will. Members of the City Guard Will had been selected into were not the same as members of the Royal Guard. Those individuals were selected on an as needed basis only once every few years to protect King Bale and Princess Briella. Will had thought a lot about the princess over the past few weeks. It was said she was as beautiful as the sunrise on the Glass Mountains around Bale's Victory, but Will had never met anyone who had seen her face, just her veiled figure at monthly mass, and rumors circulated whether that was even her or not. The king and the princess were the only surviving members of Bale's royal family, and the guards that protected them were almost as rare as the royals themselves. Will could not even recall one being selected at his age of twelve.

Yan gathered himself. "We're done here, sir. I was just checking on my new recruit before we begin the first wave of training tomorrow."

"Ah, good," Alphonse said. "William is a good lad. Del speaks highly of him." The words baffled Will. He had only met this man once, and they had only exchanged glances.

Yan looked even more surprised. "You do a lot of business here, Alphonse?"

Alphonse remained cool, untouched. "Of course, Del is the man that makes the Altar candles for the King. And the King has commissioned specialty candles for the upcoming centennial festival at Bale's Victory."

Yan turned to Del with fresh admiration. "Well, the king thanks you for your services," he said.

Del accepted the feigned kindness with a single nod and a straight face. Silence gathered between them as Yan and Alphonse locked their unbreakable eyes. Yan broke first, turning his gaze back to Will.

"William, I'll see you at the Cathedral at dawn," he reiterated. He turned to his fellow guards. "On to the next house, men. Alphonse," he acknowledged as they moved out the door with three pairs of eyes on their backs.

Alphonse closed the heavy wooden door behind them. His face turned grave as he turned to Del. "We have business to discuss."

Del nodded, turned to Will. "We'll be just a minute, Will." He forced a smile. "Then we'll have supper." They entered Del's workspace and closed the door on Will with a thud.

Alphonse turned to Del, breaking his relaxed demeanor. "The apiarist spoke your name."

"Me? Why?!" Del said, bludgeoned by the report.

"They tortured him," Alphonse said. "They were his last words before they ended it. His confession and the candle they found in Mrs. Grissom's possession is enough for them to take you to the Reformatory. You are no longer safe here."

"But why would Charlie say *my* name? Our conversations dealt with wax and bees; he knew nothing about me."

"It doesn't matter," Alphonse reasoned. He rubbed his thick beard, attempting to calm himself. He let out a heavy sigh. "Goodness, I thought they had already gotten to you." He paused and regained himself. "You're very fortunate your orphan was selected for the Guard, or Yan would have been here on other business today."

"Why would they wait?" Del asked.

"They don't want an incoming guard with angry blood against the king. Their numbers are not as large as they make them appear. They would take more children, but other industries are already overworked. The king and his people enjoy their goods and services."

"Why are you telling me this? Why are you risking your position?" Del knew how hazardous it was for a man as high up as Alphonse to appear in public, and to get caught purchasing for the King would raise the curiosity of men like Yan—men who did rash and dangerous things when their curiosity was stoked.

"The princess knows of your work. You've helped those she keeps close to her. She knows you do well for the poor and the sick of Umbrate. She wishes to do the same. She believes the king cruel, heartless. And …" Alphonse stopped, turned sentimental. "And you know you have helped me as well." Del did know. "You must leave—tonight," Alphonse continued. "I've created a window for you to slip through."

"Leave?! I can't leave!"

"You have no choice!" Alphonse hissed. Del could smell his hot breath and see the beading sweat on his brow. "You will die if you don't, the same way the apiarist and Mr. and Mrs. Grissom died. And what happens if you give an innocent name just so they'll ease your passing like Charlie did?"

Del sat back on a stool, feeling dizzy. There was truth in his words.

"Where will I go?"

"I can get you out, but it's best if I don't know where you're going."

Del rubbed the pulsing ache in his forehead. "What about Will, what's going to happen with him?"

"You'll leave a note that says you've gone for supplies, he'll join the Guard, and you'll never have to worry about him again. Once he's on the inside, they'll have no reason to suspect him," Alphonse said.

"Can't the princess do more than this? Can't she protect me?"

"She already has," Alphonse said. He breathed deep, almost reluctant to speak. "Things are in play, and she believes people like you will be of great importance soon. You must take this opportunity." Alphonse put his hand on Del's shoulder. "It's the only one you will receive."

Del looked at him with pale face and downtrodden eyes. "Tell me what I must do."

Will pretended to busy himself when the door opened to Del's workspace. Alphonse walked by and nodded to him.

"Best of luck with the Guard, Will. It is a great honor. Maybe one day we'll serve together in the Royal Guard," he said.

Will thanked him and watched him go. Del stood in the doorway, looking quite ill.

"Are you all right?"

"Yes." Del gave a weak smile. "You're a kind boy for asking." He came toward Will and looked him in the eyes. He tried to stretch his smile further but failed. "Let's have supper—a big one! It'll be our last together."

Will stared at the ceiling of his room that night with a full stomach and an empty heart. They had eaten nearly everything in the small pantry, despite Will cautioning on doing so, and Del's face remained cheerless through all of it: something more than him leaving distressed the chandler. He thought about Alphonse of the Royal Guard and the talk he had with Del in secret. It worried Will, and mixed with his concern about joining the Guard the following day, he pushed sleep aside to remain awake and alert.

All had been silent for some hours as he stared up from his bed that was beginning to be too small for him. Much too silent for Will. Normal nights were filled with Del pacing the floor of the shop or snoring in his bed. If he wasn't pacing, he was snoring, and vice versa. Now the harsh stillness of all awake and listening filled the void of silence.

Will heard a creak and sucked in the breath held tight behind his lips. He listened for the usual patterns of Del's pacing, closed his eyes to concentrate harder. Del sounded rushed, strained in each step. No flickering light waved under the door as it often did when Del rose in the night. Will sat upright; the bed groaned beneath him. Del's footsteps halted—he was listening as well.

Will stood with bare feet light on the floor and stuck his ear to the door.

In the main shop area Del gathered the things he had packed in secret hours before. His heart trembled and his hands shared its sentiment. He fumbled here and there, pondering over what he had missed and if he was taking too much. He only owned two books (most were banned for magical implications) and neither were worth their weight to carry, but it still pained him to leave them. He had helped Will learn to read with them: *Heroes of Mass* and *The Lineage of King Bale*. Both dreck as far as Del was concerned, full of lies and redactions, but it was what they had. He would leave them in case Will wanted them.

He looked at the molds that formed the votive candles and wondered who would make them now before he realized he didn't care. They would probably announce to all of Umbrate at monthly mass that they had been lied to and cheated by a magical person attempting to poison them with magical candles. The crowd would gasp, for that would be the correct response, but not even half of them would believe it, and the other half would pray that enough poison had made it into their systems that soon they would perish. Then the powerful Father Renalt would announce that they would be using oil lamps from then on out. Del scoffed; it was the way they were heading anyway. They wouldn't miss his candles.

He turned at the slight groan of wood from Will's bedroom, holding his breath. It was a groan he'd heard many times before. He must have rolled over, Del thought, continuing to gather his things.

He turned to the front door and could see the boy's poor mother dropping Will in his lap. He had been so resentful, so hateful of a little boy for so long, and now he was leaving him behind. It wounded Del to think of it, worse than he thought possible. Will would have a good life with the Guard. He would be well-fed and well-clothed, and he would not be beyond reach of the king's favor. The boy was good of heart, and he would rise in the ranks, maybe even work with Alphonse in the Royal Guard. Though good of heart was not an applauded attribute of a guard, Del thought, stroking his chin and shaking his head. What a kingdom they lived in.

He considered what Alphonse said about Princess Briella. Was it possible that she was considering an uprising, a coup to tear down the King's throne? Del didn't think so. It had been attempted before, and because of that attempt, Briella was the only surviving member of the family, and likely because she had been only a baby at the time. Kylan Godea had renounced his magical power, but only for doing good, and he was not the only one with magical ability in the King's household. He shuddered at the evil the man had done.

Del pulled his mind back to his task before it wandered to the evil Kylan might do to him if he missed his window of opportunity. He pulled on his heavy cloak and placed his makeshift pack on his back. He turned toward Will's door.

'Please, take him. You know what they do to children in the Reformatory.'

The words of Will's mother struck his chest like a specter swinging an oak club.

"No," he whispered to himself. "He'll be fine—he'll have a good life."

Del turned toward the door.

'Please, take him. You know what they do ...'

Del closed his eyes to silence the distress in her voice. It was as if she were there, tugging at his garment with tears streaming down her face as she had that night. No, she had been stronger than that ... because she knew she was doing the right thing. Del shook the thought away.

He put his hand on the knob of the door.

'No! Please, don't leave me!'

Will's childlike voice raked across his brain.

The boy wants to leave. He asked to leave! Del's conscience hollered in the distance.

He took his hand away from the knob and turned. Will stood behind him, barefoot and quivering in the dark of night.

"Get your shoes and cloak," Del said. "We're leaving."

10

Del raced ahead of Will, exceeding the swiftness of his years and selecting their course with prudent deliberation. They blended with the walls and shadows, cautious of running into guards around every corner. Alphonse had promised Del safe passage and they were receiving it.

Will did not know where they were going, but he knew it was not to the front gate. Del stopped at a corner and peered around.

"Where are we going?" Will asked, coming up behind him with bated breath.

"Shh!" Del hissed. He searched all angles, then dashed toward a small side door in the city wall. A man stood beside it. Will, close behind, matched his footsteps.

"You fool! You can't bring the boy!" It was Alphonse; his voice quiet but harsh.

"I couldn't leave him," Del said with a touch of shame. "His mother would not have wanted me to."

"His mother is not here!" Alphonse said. He looked at Will. "I'll take him home. You continue on."

"No!" Will shouted. Alphonse glared at him.

Del put his hands on the boy's shoulder.

"You risk not only your life, but mine and the boy's," Alphonse said. He towered over Del. The colors of his clothing shimmered in the silver light of the distant moon.

"I can't leave him. They'll change him, Alphonse. I made a promise to his mother. Not spoken, but agreed upon."

"You've also made a promise to me," Alphonse rationalized. "This boy is expected to be in Guard formation at dawn. They'll go searching for him if he's not. And when they find that he *and* you are gone, they'll go hunting."

"They won't find us," Del said.

"Of course they will!"

"They won't," Del said with calm sureness. "You said yourself they don't have enough guards. They won't spare even a few to hunt down an old man and a child."

"An old man they believe is magical!" Alphonse said.

Will sucked in his breath. Del and Alphonse both looked at him, then back to each other.

"I have friends, Alphonse, people willing to help us," Del said.

"Like the apiarist," Alphonse countered.

Del shook the comment away before it lingered long enough to cause a ruckus in his brain.

"No, stronger people. Runaways."

Alphonse stroked his beard in frustrated suspense. A pair of voices caught their ears.

"The window is closing," Alphonse said. "Out, both of you." He opened the door and shoved Will through. He stopped Del. "If they catch you, don't mention my name, or the Princess's work will be finished."

Del faltered, but nodded. The voices came closer.

"Go," Alphonse whispered, pushing Del out. "And do not forget Princess Briella's kindness."

The door closed, leaving Will and Del walled off and terribly alone. They looked at each other for a moment, terror palpable on their faces.

With one last look at the door, at Umbrate, the two set off, searching for a place to hide across the vast, dry plain.

11

"Peter Bernard," a guard called from the Altar of the Cathedral. "Present," Peter replied.

"Eric Andrews," droned the man. "Present," Eric responded.

It was an early dawn for the eight children that stood at the foot of the Altar where they had kneeled and pledged their allegiance what seemed only a few days before. And it had felt especially early because none of them had slept a wink, whether from fear or excitement, hope or anticipation, as they stared at the ceilings of the rooms they would never sleep in again. Some saw joining the Guard as a promising endeavor, while others wished to be nothing more than what their fathers were, and their fathers before them.

But a different fear seized them now that they were there. Only eight of the nine selections were present, and those that dared to meet the eyes of Yan Coaler saw his anger grow as his fellow guard called the names and the children answered one by one— until one did not.

"Harriet Miller," the guard called. "Present," came the girl's feeble voice. All that were present had been called on. Harriet fought the urge to look to her left with the hope of seeing a small boy just beyond her peripherals.

"William Chandler," the guard called. His voice quavered when he called again.

Yan's rage permeated from his eyes to the tense lines of his jaw.

The guard calling roll turned to Yan. "It appears one is missing, sir."

Yan burst with anger. "You think I can't see that?!"

The children trembled, looked down. The guard held his ground, acclimated to the fury.

"What do you wish to do, sir?"

Yan ran his fingers through his hair and collected his thoughts a moment.

"Gather a troop. Have them check the boy's residence at the Chandler's shop. If they don't find him, or the Chandler, have them prepare for a hunt."

One of the children, perhaps Harriet, gasped. They all knew what that meant for quiet Will. Yan looked at his new recruits.

"Let it be a lesson to you all. Deserters and betrayers, no matter how young or experienced, are found and ripped to shreds!" Spittle flew from his lips.

"Yes, sir," the children answered weakly.

"Find them!" he yelled to the guard, who sprinted out of the Cathedral to gather a force.

12

The yellow halo of dawn cracked over the horizon. For once, Will and Del were happy to see the weak light rising. They had made it far with the few hours they had but were still exposed on the open, shrubby plain, and they knew there would be a hunting party not far behind with the discovery of Will's absence. The landscape began to roll with small hills waving up from the stillness of the flat plain. It was where Del wanted to be, but he'd hoped to have been there much earlier.

Grace and Newt Sandler's cabin was ahead. Del breathed a sigh of relief. His old frame hunched as his legs weakened with the forward progress. Will's youth kept him upright, but even on such a cool morning sweat rolled down his face as he quickly sucked in and released air from his lungs.

Grace stepped onto her porch and waved to them. Newt, a stout man built hard with labor, came up behind her and put his hand on her shoulder.

"I didn't realize we were expecting you so early, Del," Grace said. "You didn't show up for your usual pick up the other day."

Del stopped at the foot of their porch and leaned against the post. Grace and Newt stared down at them with furrowed brows.

"What's the matter? Haven't you brought a cart?" Newt asked. "We have five bags stored away for you."

Del fought for breath to speak but couldn't grasp it.

"We need shelter," Will, youth bringing his breath back first, finally said. "They'll be chasing us by now."

Grace and Newt turned grave, but wasted not a moment.

"Stay where you are," Grace said. Newt rushed inside the house and emerged with a bag of white earth.

◊

Del and Will sat in the cellar behind bags of white earth, covered in the stuff from head to toe. They appeared as nothing more than blinking bags of white powder.

The day advanced, and Del and Will had been there for what seemed like hours, fighting the urge to sneeze with every inhale.

Grace and Newt had had them walk up the road some distance before they dusted them with white earth and brought them back to hide in the cellar. They said it would hide their scent from the dogs. Del and Will, in the dark with treacherous thoughts of being ripped to ribbons, were not so sure, but it was the best option they had. They shivered at each hint of sound as they huddled close in the cool cellar. Grace paced the floor above them, each creak vibrating overhead. Newt had gone to work, acting as if the day was as normal as any other.

Del and Will tried to avoid thinking about the atrocities that waited for them upon being caught, but the time and the silence imprisoned their minds in the dark cages of those cruel, prodding thoughts. Del, having seen people brought back torn to shreds by dogs and sent to the Reformatory, knew what waited ahead; Will had only rumors and stories to guide him in this darkness, which opened even more terrible alleys for a boy that had experienced so much loss in his youth. He envisioned the terrible acts happening to himself, and then he thought of them happening to his mother years ago. His eyes burned with tears.

Three quick stomps rang through the boards of the floor: the signal Grace said she would give if somebody from the Guard arrived. Del and Will sucked in their final breaths before the long hold.

They heard the barking of the dogs first. Will whimpered and Del placed his arm over him—his body quivering with fear. He pulled the sack material over their heads to blend them into the pile. In complete darkness, they heard the gruff voices of the guards in the hunting party.

Grace's feet shuffled through the house and out onto the porch.

"I didn't realize the king was in need of more white earth," she said. "I wasn't expecting you to be back for another week."

"We're not here for white earth, you old loon," a winded and rough voice came back. "Can't you see we're on the hunt?"

"Hunt? For what?" Grace asked convincingly.

"That's none of your business," the guard replied.

"I just aim to help is all," Grace said. Her feet turned toward the door. "I'll leave you to it."

"Wait!" called the guard. "Have you seen any travelers this morning?"

Grace turned. There was a long pause. Del closed his eyes and pictured her with a persuasive thought on her face. His mind warped the picture to her whispering to the guard where they were hiding. Opening his eyes to fight the thought, he found himself in deeper darkness. He pulled Will closer.

"Can't say that I have," Grace replied. "Seems your dogs have though."

The dogs snarled and barked, on the scent Del hoped they would soon lose.

"The king offers great incentive if you have any information on their whereabouts," the guard said invitingly.

It was true that the king offered more food or money or prestige to those that helped him find and oust magical beings or those accused of conducting magical acts. It was the source of many souls rotting in the Reformatory, and the cause of death for many innocents.

"I said I haven't seen any, and I mean it," Grace said. "I wouldn't lie even to get a sack of grain for it. I'm not a liar, and I'm not a thief."

The dogs barked, covering the guard's response.

"No, I live here with my husband," Grace said, her voice losing some of its confidence.

"And where is he?"

"He's in the mine," she said, "digging out the King's white earth."

"And there's no one else here with you?"

"No, of course not," Grace said. Del could see the guard moving closer, intimidating her.

"No morning visitors?"

"None that I've seen," Grace said. "Though you refused to describe them to me, so how would I know?"

"Are you getting smart?"

"No, sir, just being realistic. I've seen none, and greeted none except you and your party."

There was silence.

"Search the house!" the man said brusquely.

The dogs barked louder and shouts of men were heard. Intimidation was a chief tactic used by the Guard to get people to open their mouths, but Del, shaking, couldn't help but wonder if they were aware of the visitors in Grace's cellar. Had Grace given them up to save herself as the poor apiarist had? Some good it had done Charlie, the kind fool.

Light feet and claws pitter-pattered across the floor above them as heavy boots of soldiers thumped about the place. The hovel was small, but it sounded as if the whole Guard tramped around inside. Dust sifted through the boards in the floor and rested lightly on their sacked heads. The footsteps ceased.

"All clear, sir," a guard reported.

"Take 'em around the house," came the next order.

Will shook like dry grass in a circling wind.

"Stay still," Del whispered. The boy's shaking slowed. He breathed deep and it stopped.

"There's a cellar door, sir," a guard called. His voice loud, close.

The light steps of the dogs were audible, but the barking had stopped.

"The dogs aren't smelling anything," the guard yelled.

"Send the young'un down," the head guard said.

Del squeezed Will in close. A flash of light burst into the cellar. They heard a thump ahead of them; breaths locked in their chests. All went completely still. They expected the soft steps of a dog, followed by snarling and growling and tearing at flesh. There was movement toward the cellar door, but it was crawling.

"What kind of a person has a cellar?" the guard asked, his voice heavy with accusation. "Have you something to hide?"

The shuffling continued, closer, but it wasn't the sniffing, searching of a dog.

"Of course I've nothing to hide," Grace said curtly. "I'm married to a miner, and miners dig."

The shuffling, crawling sound moved away. "I don't see anything but some sacks," the voice echoed from within the cellar. It was the voice of a young man—maybe the voice of the young man Will had seen there the other day, the one he knew from school.

A thick, thinking pause followed. The head guard said, "Get him out and let's get on before the dogs lose the scent."

Darkness filled the cellar again. The dogs began to bark as they found the trail once again. Their sound faded, stopped for a moment, likely where Del and Will had been dusted and turned back to Grace and Newt's home (Had Grace swept the white earth away from where they had been dusted?), and then continued on until there was no sound but Grace's gentle steps on the floor above. After some minutes, she stomped twice: all clear.

Will and Del breathed deep. Del removed the sacks from their heads and pushed the full sacks away from them. He pulled Will in tight. The boy looked at him, and in the dark he could see the streaks of tears trembling trails down the white earth on his face.

Some hours passed before Newt opened the door and called into the cellar.

"You're safe to come out now, gents."

Will and Del crawled and scooted stiffly toward the door. Del needed assistance to stand, and even Will's youth acquiesced to the strain in his knees. They looked up to find Newt covered from head to toe in white earth, just as they were. Newt helped Will pull Del out. Grace stood behind them with a blanket wrapped over her shoulders.

Del turned to her suspiciously. "How did you know the dogs wouldn't smell us?"

Grace smiled. "Look at my man. He works and sweats all day in the mine and comes home smelling fresher than I do." She patted his shoulder and dust flew up.

In light of the troubling day, they couldn't help but smile.

◊

Gathered around Grace and Newt's table, only a small, weak candle lit their faces to prevent any unwanted eyes from seeing in. They had eaten a little porridge, better stuff than they usually ate, and all sat in silence, pondering the day survived.

"You can stay here as long as you'd like, but it will be long days in the cellar for you," Newt said, staring, unblinking, into the light of the candle. Grace nodded her agreement.

"No," Del said. "We can't put any more risk on you. You've already too many guards here as it is."

"Where will you go?" Grace asked.

Will looked at Del, and Del at Will.

"They'll be coming back down that road sooner rather than later once they realize the dogs don't have anything," Newt said.

Del ruminated over the warning. They couldn't follow in the wake of the soldiers that had passed them up. And they would surely be caught if they stayed on the road. Del searched Will and thought about what the boy had offered earlier.

"Do you know of safe passage to the Grim Forest?" Del asked. Will perked with excitement.

Newt and Grace glanced at each other and smiled.

"We can help you with that," Grace said.

13

"In there?" Del said, standing in front of a hole in the ground that was no more than four feet tall and wide. Will looked into it, intrigued.

"Yep," Newt said with pride. "This is the mine."

They had allowed themselves a few hours of sleep, but it was still some time in the night, with Mass's ever-shining moon in the distance, when they stood before the hole, a low-lit lantern between them.

"And it goes to the Grim Forest?" Will asked, putting a hand on the top edge of the hole and looking into it.

"Well, this will take you most of the way," Newt said. "To get to the forest, you'll have to take a smaller shaft."

"Smaller?" Del squeaked, feeling woozy.

Newt could see the man's face turn pale even in the dark of night.

"It's your best option, Del." He paused and reconsidered. "Or, the best option I can provide you."

"How far is it?" Will asked.

"Yes, how far?" Del asked eagerly.

Newt bought some time while pretending to think. He knew the distance exactly. "Half a league."

"Half a league!"

"Then another half in the smaller shaft," he admitted further

"A full league underground!"

"Wow," Will said with awe.

"It's the best way, Del," Newt said. "They know nothing about it."

Del swallowed hard. "What side of the forest will we end up on?" The Grim Forest was split down the middle by a swath of the

King's Carve that was nearly half a league wide itself. King Bale had the center of the forest burned down to provide safe passage between Sentinel's Village and Umbrate. It was rumored that magical things still resided in the forest, and entrance was forbidden by all who weren't a part of the King's Guard, though none dared enter more than a few feet, and only to prove a bet.

"The west side," Newt answered.

"Good," Del replied. "That's the side I wish to be on."

"You've a plan, then?" Newt asked. Will looked back at Del, more intrigued with the idea of a plan than the mine shaft.

Del looked from Will to Newt. "Let's see if we make it through this first," he said, gesturing toward the opening.

"Good." Newt smiled kindly. "I'll lead the way."

Newt, carrying the lantern, ducked into the hole. Will jumped in behind him. Del took one final breath, as he did earlier in the cellar, and followed close to not lose the light.

Newt stopped ahead of them and turned to shine the halo of light on the smaller hole.

"Here it is," he said, sweat dripping down his face after the endless stooping walk in the warm, damp mine. The hole wasn't quite half the size of the one they were in, but it was close.

"You can't be serious," Del said. His back ached and his clothing stuck to his clammy skin.

Will peered into it. "It doesn't look that small," he said.

"Of course it doesn't look that small to *you!*" Del countered. Will shrugged. Del looked down the shaft they were in. "What's that way?"

"A dead end," Newt said. "This is the only way through, or it's back to the cabin and into the cellar."

Del huffed and puffed, his anxiety growing too large for the small space.

"Calm yourself, Del," Newt said, tilting his head to Will. The boy's face paled with apprehension, reminding Del he was not alone in this.

"Yes, you're right, Newt," Del said. He would have stood taller if he could have. "We'll be fine, Will. Just a bit further." Will nodded back to him. Del turned to Newt. "Lead the way."

Newt looked at the small hole and sighed. "You men will be making this one on your own," Newt said. "I don't have it in me to make it all the way there and back again, and some parts are a bit tight for me," he admitted, looking at each broad shoulder with betrayal. He reached into his pocket and pulled out some lengths of burned candles. "Take these for light."

Del felt sick. He looked down at the candles. He wanted to lift them from his hand and launch them into the man's face, but he knew the amount of help Newt and Grace had given them would tip the scales of all other help he had received in his life.

"Keep your candles," Del said. He kneeled down. "I packed a few special ones for such an occasion. Get them for me, can you, Will? The light blue ones."

Will searched through the pack and pulled out two six-inch candles.

"Good boy," Del said, stretching a feeble smile across his face. He turned to Newt. "Give us a light, friend."

Newt put his lamp down and removed the glass chimney. Taking a candle in each hand with care, Del dipped the virgin wicks into the flame. Both flared, illuminating the small space with the light of day. The three shielded their eyes from the radiance.

"Well, would you look at that," Newt said, smiling as bright as the candles. "You really are quite the chandler, aren't you?"

Del smiled and handed a candle to Will. "They're very hard to put out, and they'll burn all day. Old secret," Del said with a clandestine wink. "We have little time to waste, Will." Del pointed toward the hole.

Will held the candle upright and turned to Newt. "Thank you, Newt, and please send my thanks to Grace. I will not forget it." Newt wiped a tear from his eye as Will stooped and went into the hole.

Del squatted deeper into his aching legs and looked into the shaft. Will's light progressed away. He turned to Newt.

"If some of the spots are too tight for you, are you sure it leads to the forest?" Del asked.

"Quite sure," Newt said, though later Del would ponder the confidence in his voice.

Del looked into the hole again. Will was already some distance ahead, crawling on hand and knees with the light forming a caged halo before him.

"And will I be able to fit?" Del whispered.

Newt put his hands on Del's shoulders to comfort him, though Del felt a bit like he was being measured. He pulled Del in close. "You can make it. I'm sure of it," Newt said, his voice still suspicious.

Del took a deep breath, shaking the powerful light of the candle between them. He watched the shadows dance over Newt's face. He grew diffident, feeling out of place in such a situation, but the words needed to be said.

"Will and I are grateful of your courage, you and Grace both. We thank you, and like Will, I will never forget it."

The tears waved in Newt's eyes. "You're welcome, Del," he said. He pulled the old Candlemaker in close and whispered: "When the time comes, don't forget about us." Del looked at him curiously, trying to decipher the miner's intent. "Now, on with you before the boy gets away." Newt gripped Del's shoulders tighter and handily pushed him into the hole.

The white light filled the void. Del covered his candle and could just see Will scooting and crawling ahead of him. His knees already hurt, and the closeness of the space gave him a headache, but it was time to move, even if it meant enduring a little pain.

Del tried to distract himself from the pain in his hands and knees by counting the seconds and minutes and hours, but he lost count somewhere around two hours, and that had been at least two hours ago.

He caught up to Will, sitting with his back to the wall, shaking the light of the candle with his heavy breathing. The boy was not catching his breath but hyperventilating. Del sat next to him in the largest bit of space they had seen since they left the main shaft. He grabbed ahold of Will's arm. It was cold and clammy. The boy didn't notice his touch. He was in a panic. Del touched his forehead, and Will turned his pallid face and wide eyes toward him.

"There's no end, Del. We're not going to make it." His voice was weak, hopeless.

"Of course we are. Grace and Newt wouldn't have led us this way if there was no end. Just a bit further."

"There's no end," Will repeated, weaker, quieter. The boy's bloody hands shook the candle. Del pulled him closer, pushing aside his own dismay.

"Close your eyes," Del said.

Will did after two lethargic blinks. The darkness behind his eyelids gave him no comfort. He tried to open his eyes, but Del put his fingers over the lids. The old man breathed deep, saying a few quiet words to himself. Will, even through closed eyes, could see and feel the illumination of the candle in his hand dampen. He felt the comforting rush of cold water over a parched throat, and he lolled back in sleep.

Will opened his eyes sometime later. Del lay beside him, sleeping. Both candles were propped between the cracks of rocks, and both were a bit shorter. He checked the old man to see if he was still breathing, and once he confirmed he was, nudged him.

"Wake up, Del," Will said, his voice renewed.

Del blinked himself awake. His haggard face beamed with the hope of waking on a new day before the cold realization of the cave crushed it. He looked at the candles, and then to Will.

"How are you, my boy?" Del asked.

Will felt around his own body in search of evidence for the answer.

"Much better," he said. He looked strangely at the old man. "What did you do to me?"

Del leaned his head back, closed his eyes, and smiled. "I did what I had to. You were in quite a panic."

"I was?" Will tried to remember but couldn't. Del didn't answer. "Thank you," Will said. Del nodded and opened his eyes. He looked at the candles.

"We've been here for some hours." Del moved to his hands and knees, adjusted his pack, and grabbed a candle wedged in the rocks. "Time to move. Just a bit further."

Will turned onto his knees, much easier than Del, grabbed a candle, and proceeded down the dark tunnel.

"There's light ahead!" Will called back, his voice lifted in triumph. "Just there, I can see it."

"Keep quiet!" Del's sibilation slithered over the stones of the cave. "We don't know who might be about."

Will lowered his voice. "We're almost there. We've made it to the Grim Forest!" A comment few in the Kingdom of Mass uttered with jubilation.

Will scooted on. The cave tightened as they neared its aperture. He turned to offer Del a hand. The two scooted and pulled, scooted and pulled until they could feel the cool breeze sifting through the opening. They stopped and basked in it, each closing their eyes to its cleansing mercy. Will squinted and went for the light with avarice. Close behind, Del followed, eager to be away from the damp, apathetic tunnel.

Will pulled himself through and out, birthed into the light of day. He turned and pulled Del's hand to liberate the man of the tight entrance. Once free, Del stood upright and wrenched in pain. He sat, and Will looked around.

They weren't in the Grim Forest. They were standing on the side of a steep, rocky hill, overlooking a flat gap between them and the green wall of trees.

"We still have some distance to go," Will said. "Half a mile or so."

Del looked across the expanse with exhaustion. "I need a moment to rest, then we'll continue."

Will sat beside him. Both were filthy, with torn knees, hands, and cloaks. He looked at the sky, shielding his eyes from the sun. It was warm and bright, but he guessed all parts of day felt that way after being in the cave for so long.

"In my pack," Del said, fatigued. "There's a skin of water and a bite of food. Be a good boy and get both."

Will scooted to Del on his rear. Rocks broke away at his feet and tumbled down the hill.

"Did you hear that?" A voice said over the hill above them.

Del and Will tucked back against the rocks, holding tight to their breaths.

"I didn't hear anything," came the uninterested response. "There's nothing out here."

Boots came closer to the edge. Del and Will flattened themselves against rock. Loose pebbles tumbled from above and accumulated on Will's shoulder. He tilted his head back and could see the toe of the man's boot.

"Come on, let's get back before they have all the food ate," the indifferent man said.

"No, I'm sure I've heard something. Voices!" the first man responded.

"You've heard nothing but the wind," came the reply.

The toe stepped away from the edge. "I've had enough of your insolence. I'm your superior!"

The other's voice went quiet. "Yes, sir. It's just, we've been at this for two days now, and not a whiff of them since the beginning."

"That's no excuse to shrug your duty … or honor," the man barked. "Now, back to the hunting party and get me two of the swiftest dogs. I'll stay here and have a look around."

"We were told not to separate, sir."

"Do as I say, or you'll be tried for treason against the king!"

"Yes, sir," the voice said, and his boots crunched away.

The other man milled around the edge, kicking pebbles and dirt onto Will and Del. Will looked at Del with renewed fear. The old man looked up, then to the boy, the life restored in his face. He knew that if they could just get to the bottom, they could outrun the man to the forest, but they could not outrun the dogs. Now was their chance.

He pointed down the steep hill. Will nodded and began to skitter over the loose rocks like a spider. Del followed beside him.

Halfway down, Will began to slide, creating an avalanche of dry dirt and rocks that sprayed up a cloud as he rode atop it. Del got caught in the swell and the cloud expanded overhead until they skidded to a stop on the hard, level bottom. They stood quickly, wasting no time to dust off.

"Stop!" the man yelled from the top of the cliff. They turned to look at him. He was nothing more than a lone tree atop a bare hill.

"Run!" Del said. "Into the forest!"

The guard ran across the top, looking for a safe place to bail over the dangerous ledge. Standing at the bottom, Will and Del could see that the hillside they emerged from was as wide as it was tall, and a precarious ledge reached over it like the white cap of a wave. They watched as the dutiful man jumped the ledge and tumbled down the hill.

Del grabbed Will's cloak and pulled him along. Will turned to see the guard caught up on something, dangling as he reached to free his foot. He turned to Del pulling away from him and sped to catch up, not looking back again until they reached the forest edge some minutes later.

Will stopped at the tree line and saw the guard wedged in the same spot. "He's hurt!" Will announced.

"And so will we be if we don't keep running," Del said, grabbing hold of Will's loose cloak.

They entered the Grim Forest, where the dense canopy erased the light of day.

14

Gnarled oak, beech, and ash grew together in a prudent attempt to keep Del and Will from getting very far in. They struggled through the dark forest as they had in the mine shaft, but here the air felt much closer, much denser.

Will had heard rumors of the forest, and its namesake was the foundation of them. He was taught that all of the oldest and evilest Magic was born there, and that some of it still resided within, too afraid of King Bale to ever emerge. It was in the Grim Forest that King Bale had ripped the greatest Evil that ever lived like a rotten tooth from its root and banished it to the still waters of Bale's Victory for all eternity.

The forest felt old, as if it held secrets that would break Will if uttered nearby, but it did not feel evil, just uncomfortable and suffocating.

Del stopped and searched the forest feverishly as if looking for something.

"Yes, yes," he said, stepping over a fallen tree. He put his hand to his chin, became confused, and stopped. "No, that's not correct."

"Where are we going?" Will asked desperately.

Del turned his head, sniffed the air.

"What are you—"

"Shh!" Del hissed. The sound of dogs rumbled in the distance. Fear shook them. "Stay close," Del said before dashing into the trees.

Will covered his face to fight off the assaulting branches that slapped back from Del rushing ahead. They emerged into an open clearing. Del stopped, spun in a circle. The barking closed in, and the voices of men could be heard. Del turned his frantic eyes to the ground and saw a smooth white rock protruding from the earth.

"We're getting closer," Del whispered. He darted away from the clearing back into the thick trees. Will followed, reaching his arm ahead to feel Del's cloak. Del stopped, and Will ran into his back. The barks were close enough that Will was sure he could smell the bloody breath of the dogs, and the men were shouting louder and louder, goading the beasts ahead.

"Here!" Del exclaimed, pointing up. Will came around him and looked up at two oak trees growing close to each other. Will followed Del's finger to two branches, or rather one that was a part of both trees. He tilted his head at the illusion.

Del grabbed him, sprinted in a wide figure eight away from the shared limb, and dashed under the arched branch into a wide circle of cleared land. He stopped and bent over, breathing deep.

The barking and haranguing moved nearer. He turned back toward the way they came and could see the branches rustling and breaking with the pursuit of men and ravenous dogs.

Will turned to Del, who was now sitting on a fallen tree, unconcerned—relieved, even. Will rushed and grabbed his arm.

"Get up! Get up! We can still outrun them."

He wrestled the man's arm, but couldn't budge him. Del smiled kindly, infuriating Will further.

"The chase is done, Will. We've no further to go," Del said.

Will punched his arm as the angry tears ran down his face. "Why did you bring me if you were just going to give up. I can't believe how selfish you are. You *want* to die. I hate you!" Will slammed his fists into the old man's arm until Del caught his barrage and forced him to sit next to him.

"Watch," Del said, pointing toward the pursuing dogs.

The first mutt popped through the trees, pulling his guard behind him. He stopped moving, stopped barking, and perked his ears as drool dropped from his toothy mouth. Will looked into his eyes, and he was sure the dog stared right back at him.

"C'mon, you stupid hound," the guard said, kicking the dog.

The kick reminded the pup of his duty. He sniffed the ground in the exact figure eight Del had stamped out, away from the two oak trees, and back to where they emerged from. Another dog and guard hurtled through the trees and the same thing happened. The dogs walked in circles until the whole hunting party was bumping shoulders and grumbling at the revolving dogs.

Del leaned back and sent forth a deep belly laugh. Will watched him with a dirty face, bewildered by his raucous laughter as the group of men and dogs bumped and grumbled like blind and deaf beasts.

"What are they doing?" Will whispered, flabbergasted. "What are *you* doing?"

"I'm enjoying the show," Del said at full volume. He looked at Will with tears of joy in his eyes. "No need to whisper, boy, they can't hear us. And, clearly, they can't see us either." He snickered at the foolish animals, man and beast alike.

Del leaned back further and found a comfortable spot on the log.

"Worthless dogs lost the scent," a guard said.

"Let's backtrack," offered another.

"They were here, I'm sure of it. Even I can still smell them," one guard with a good nose yelled.

"If *you* can smell them, then why can't the dogs?" said a guard in offense.

The man with the good nose decked the offender. A scuffle broke out and the other men fought to tear them apart in the closeness of the trees. The dogs watched with puppy-like curiosity, with tongues and heads lolled to the side, as confused as the men.

"Enough! Enough!" yelled the man who appeared to be in charge. "Half of us will backtrack, and the other half will head in that direction." The guard pointed to his left, away from Del and Will. "It seems the clearest path."

The men did as ordered, with more bumping and grumbling as they sorted themselves and cleared away.

Will turned to Del. "What on Mass was that?"

A victorious smile appeared on Del's face as he pointed to the shared branch. Will looked at it again and saw a stout stone trilithon, acting as some sort of doorway.

He turned back to Del, even more confused. "Why couldn't they see it?" He paused. "Wait, why couldn't I see it?"

"Because you weren't looking for it, and neither were they," Del explained.

"But I could see the shared branch. Why couldn't they?"

"You could see it because I showed you."

"But—but—none of this makes any sense. They were right there. I bet that man really could smell us," Will said, attempting to reason with his pursuer.

Del put his hands behind his head and laid back on the log. He closed his eyes and smiled, smooth with relief like Will had never seen him before.

"Welcome to the world of Magic, Will."

15

Will sat on the log and looked down at his dangling feet. His mind seemed to consider all things and nothing in the same thought. The mocking world had been flipped on its head and now it was waving and smiling at him. Del slept next to him, a small smile on his face. To add to the conflicting thoughts and feelings, Will hated and loved the old man as he watched that gentle grin resting on his face like a butterfly on a flower, as if it was supposed to be there, though Will had never seen it before.

Will knew Magic was real—he had learned that in school—but Magic was the Great Evil of their world; Magic had killed the Brave Queen Sharon; Magic was filled with shame and hatred for all things that weren't magical. But, Will thought as he looked through the trilithon doorway, Magic now protected him. Magic hadn't chased him down with dogs that would have ripped him and Del to flaps of skin and meat as the guards laughed and pointed because he ran to avoid being forced into the Guard that took his mother from him. The thoughts made his head spin as they passed like swooping swallows. He was getting nowhere.

Now, for the first time, Will considered why Del was fleeing Umbrate in the night. That had been nearly two days ago and Will hadn't stopped to think about it once. The old chandler was leaving when Will came out of his room, and Alphonse, their liberator, had certainly not expected Will to be with him—even to the point of taking him back to join the Guard. And what was all that business of Alphonse saying Del was suspected of being Magical? Del had known about the shared-branch archway, and that it would protect them once through. Will thought about the candle Del gave to Phin for his ill niece, and the even more elaborate candle he gave to Mrs. Grissom and the way she smiled when she held it, even the way she died instead of saying Del's name. And what about the candles in the cave that seemed to burn eternally bright? And what had Del done to Will to calm him into sleep?

Will looked at Del resting with that silly, content smile on his face. His thoughts ceased to swoop by and paused to smile at him and nod. The realization grew on his face, along with disgust and intrigue. Combat waged in his head between the things he had been taught and the things he had witnessed all those years as the Chandler's apprentice. It had all happened right under his nose, hidden like a terrible secret. Was Del a …? Anger raged in him, but he knew not what to do with it. He stood to shake Del awake in his fury when he caught the glint of two watching eyes. But it was more than a pair of eyes, it was a whole human—a whole woman to be exact. She made no effort to hide, just stood some distance away and watched Will fight with his thoughts and his desire to throttle Del. She was old and thin, and her hair and clothing were disheveled (though it looked intentional to Will), but her sagacious eyes peered right into his being.

Will turned his anger to concern and nudged Del.

"Del, wake up," Will whispered, never taking his eyes off the woman. Del didn't move. Will nudged harder, rocking the old man on the log. "Del!"

"Stop it, boy. Get some rest," Del mumbled. "We're safe here."

"There's a woman watching us."

Del sat upright, almost pushing Will to the ground in the process. He looked at the woman, jumped to his feet, and slowly backed away. Will came to his side, grabbing at the old man's cloak to stay close in case he darted.

The woman raised one bony finger, her eyes aflame with rage. Del turned his head, cowered behind his hands. Will imitated his defense. The fury of Magic was true and before him, just as all those instructors had taught him. The woman opened her mouth to speak, to cast a spell …

"I thought it was you, Delier Chandler," she said with a voice that sounded like the opening of a creaky coffin. "Always smelling of wax and oils, you are. I hate it!" She lowered her ominous finger and spat on the ground.

Del clenched his fists and found his courage. "A woman shouldn't spit. It's not honorable."

"Ha! He leaves without notice to make candles for a rotten king, and now he's lecturing me about honor." She spit again.

Will stepped back from Del, unsure of the quarrel he was witnessing.

"I did what I had to do and I'm not ashamed of it," Del said petulantly.

"Not ashamed!" She turned to Will. "Do you think he's back on my doorstep because he's *not* ashamed?" Will looked from Del to the woman, from the woman to Del, and slowly raised his shoulders and hands in confusion.

"Don't bring the boy into this," Del said, rubbing his forehead in frustration.

"Looks like you brought him into it," the woman said, crossing her arms over her bosom. "I can't believe you found a woman that would let you father a child—and at your age." She looked nearly impressed, in a cynical way.

"I'm not his father," Del said. He looked at Will guiltily and explained further. "I mean, he's not *my* son. He's an orphan, and my apprentice, and I take care of him."

Her face turned to surprised disgust. "Who would let you take care of an orphan?"

"The granddaughter of Paulette Grindholm," Del replied. He crossed his arms over his chest and turned to the side with hauteur.

The surprised disgust dropped from the woman's face. She came closer to Will with affectionate interest. Will backed away as she neared.

"I won't hurt you," she said, fascination across her face.

"Don't believe her, Will," Del said, still turned, still petulant.

The woman cocked her head sharply. "Don't trust an old fool still milking blood from old wounds," she said. Del waved her off and turned further away.

She looked at Will and the cracks on her face smoothed with joy, like she was greeting an old friend. The woman rested her cupped hands on Will's dirty cheeks, and he allowed her. They were warm and worn, and they gave Will a comfort he had forgotten. She looked at his every feature like a painter about to embark.

"Yes, yes. I can see it now," she smiled genially. "What was your mother's name, Will?"

"Isabella," Will said. Del turned to look at him. The poor child had never uttered his mother's name until now. Del had wondered if he even knew it.

The woman looked at him more lovingly. "Is that right?" she said, smiling deeper and brighter. "That's my name as well, but everyone calls me Isa …. I'm your great-aunt."

Will stepped away from her hands. He turned to Del for the truth. It appeared Del didn't want to give it, but he nodded.

"It's true, Will, she's the sister of your great-grandmother Paulette."

Will turned back to her. He fought the urge to hug her, feeling it an awkward gesture for someone he just met.

"Nice to meet you," he said timorously, raising a hand to shake.

The woman shot an annoyed glance at Del. "I can see you've raised him with a lot of love." Del rolled his eyes. She turned back to Will. "I'm your great-grandaunt, dearie, and aunties get hugs." She embraced him, and Will, fighting it at first, embraced her back, feeling tears burn his eyes. They hugged for a long while, each reluctant to let go. Del watched from the side, his heart aching.

Isa let Will go and smeared the pools away from her eyes.

"What a joyous day," she elated, standing. "Come with me, Will. You look hungry and in need of a wash."

Isa began to walk away, but Will stayed in place. He turned to Del, who stayed put with his arms crossed.

"Um," Will said. Isa turned. "Can Del come with us?"

Isa put a hand on her hip and waved a malicious finger at the Candlemaker.

"Only because the boy asked," she said, turning again and walking away.

Reluctantly, Del grabbed his pack and came to Will's side. He held his arm up. "You lead the way." But only to keep a buffer between him and the new entry, it seemed.

Will followed Isa with slow feet as she walked ahead of them on a skinny path worn deep from years of foot traffic. He turned to Del and asked: "Is she really my aunt?"

Del nodded. "She is."

Will looked at her back, confused. "And, how, well … why, um …"

"How do I know her?"

Will nodded.

"And why does she hate me?"

Will nodded again, stepping gently into the strange territory.

"She's my wife," Del said.

"*EX*-wife!" Isa called back.

Del shrugged. "That's more accurate, actually."

Will tried to pull the loose strings from the convoluted knot in his head. A few minutes ago he had no family, now he had an aunt, and …

"So … you're my uncle?"

Del looked up as if realizing the fact for the first time. "I guess I am," he said, grinning.

"*EX*-uncle," Isa scoffed. Del scowled at her back.

Will looked to the ground and was reminded of his initial question. He wasn't sure if he wanted the answer to it, but now seemed the best time considering he'd never seen Del so talkative and honest.

"And you're a … a, uh," Will began, but stopped. Del looked down at him.

"Go on …"

"And you're a wizard?"

Del smiled at the boy and nodded.

"*EX*-wizard!" Isa clarified. "And not a good one at that!"

"How dare you say such a thing!" Del yelled back.

Isa turned and they began to quarrel, but Will heard none of it. All the exhaustion of running and the flood of honesty caught up to him. His head began to swim. He wavered and fell backwards, and the world went black before he hit the ground.

16

Yan Coaler ascended the steep steps to Kylan Godea's quarters. It was not often that the King's Magical Advisor called upon him, even as a Head Official of the City Guard, and if the past proved anything, the visit would not be a pleasant one. The steps twirled in a spiral that seemed to reach all the way to the sky, and Yan almost wished that it did to give him more time to think.

He knew the steps well enough to know that he approached the door at the end of them. Stopping, he leaned against the stone wall. It was still cool, though the temperature rose the higher he climbed. Yan had heard these high and steep quarters, with only a narrow stair up and down, were selected for Kylan after he denounced his magical powers—a prison cell with no bars, guarded day and night in case the old wizard decided to change his mind. It was Kylan's punishment for ever believing in the evil of Magic. Yan didn't believe any of it for the width of a fly's hair. He believed that Kylan wanted to live there to force his lower subjects to make the painful climb and to give them time to consider, and *over*-consider, the destination ahead. Yan believed this because it was working on him at that moment. He gathered himself and began to climb again.

Two men of the Royal Guard stood at the door of Kylan's quarters, their outside shoulders touching the stone wall, their inside shoulders touching each other. They were the wall before the door, a wall with the stern faces of duty.

"Rufus. Gregory," Yan greeted, slightly winded. Neither reacted except to step aside to admit Yan into Kylan's tower. Yan breathed deep and opened the door.

Kylan stood looking out the window through a brass contraption with a long tube and all sorts of glass lenses protruding from it like the legs of a bug. He paused and wrote his notes on a nearby podium. Yan looked to a chair and decided against sitting to prevent prolonging the meeting. He stood at attention, waiting for Kylan to finish. The old wizard dipped his Raven quill and continued to write. Yan would have to wait longer. He turned his head to look about the small room.

It was an office and a living space. The sheets were pulled tight across the small bed, as if it were a guard's bed in the barracks, and Kylan's desk was relatively free of clutter. In the corner, Kylan looked through his contraption. Yan had seen it many times but had no clue about its function, or why the wizard always seemed to be looking out of it. Beside the contraption, there were three large bookshelves that extended from floor to ceiling. The shelves were bare but for four books. One was the tome of *Mass and Umbrate History*, another was *The Great Evil*, written by King Bale himself. Yan could see that the third book was titled *Sky Over Mass* by Kylan Godea. He tried to decipher the last one before Kylan replaced his quill in its holder and took his seat behind the desk.

"You've something to report, Head Official Coaler?" Kylan said. His voice was old and wise but with a defeated and indifferent vibration to it. Yan hated looking at the man whose bony face seemed eternally sunken in thought, but his honor required him to.

"Yes, sir. We have raided the chandler's shop to find Delier Chandler and William Chandler gone," Yan reported. "We have found nothing out of the ordinary, sir."

Kylan looked up, his eyes tired and dull, but their mien deceived Yan not.

"Nothing out of the ordinary except two missing citizens. One ordered to be present at Guard call, and the other soon to be a resident of our Reformatory. Is that not out of the ordinary for the basic Guard, Official Coaler?"

Yan hated how the word *basic* rolled so easily off Kylan's tongue; he desired to free it from the wizard's mouth. He remained calm, professional, proud, as he replied: "Excuse me, sir. It *is* out of the ordinary. I just meant—"

"I'm aware of what you meant!" Kylan yelled back. His eyes exposed their true fire, if only for a moment. He dipped his desk quill and began to write, cooling the embers. Yan waited in agony for him to finish, both in fear and anger. Kylan returned the black feather to its holder.

"Any news from the hunting party?" Kylan asked.

"Very little, sir," Yan replied.

"And have they found any sign of them?" Something in his voice told Yan he already knew the answer.

"Yes, sir, and they are following that sign with many men and dogs," he said officially.

"And have they found nothing but sign?" Kylan prodded. A man of lower rank would have looked away or shuffled his feet, but Yan did neither, though the urge was stronger than he wished.

"Last word was that they were in pursuit of the criminals, sir, but—"

"But?!" the syllable shook Yan, thinking he might feel the evil of Magic. He closed his eyes and gathered himself for the final admission.

"The men lost the trail in the west forest, sir."

Yan waited for castigation, but it never came. Kylan grabbed his quill, dipped it in the ink, and began to write again—Yan's death warrant, he guessed.

Sweat beaded on Yan's head as the heat of the high tower suffused through him. Kylan replaced the pen.

"Since your men have failed, we have no choice but to put our best dogs on the trail."

"Sir, I assure you that if my men can't find them, no—"

"Silence," Kylan said. Yan had no choice; the threat of Magic affected even him. "They will find them, and they will finish them."

"And if they can't?" Yan asked.

Kylan looked up with his indifferent and hateful eyes. "Then we'll burn the forest down."

◊

Rufus and Gregory were relieved of their duty, and they said not a word as they descended the stairs, feeling the pain in all four knees with every step down. Neither complained, and neither ever would.

At the bottom of the steps, Gregory turned right, Rufus left.

"Aren't you returning to the barracks?" Gregory asked.

"Captain Alphonse requested to see me after my duty." Rufus replied. Gregory nodded and went his own way.

Rufus marched to Captain Alphonse's quarters. He knocked on the door and admitted himself once granted permission.

"Rufus, what can I do for you?" Alphonse asked, sitting behind his small work table.

Rufus looked through the cramped space to make sure they were alone. "They have escaped in the west side of the Grim Forest, their trail lost," he whispered.

Alphonse leaned forward, intrigued. "Anything else?"

"Kylan plans on sending monks," Rufus said, mechanically.

Alphonse's countenance clouded over as he leaned forward. "Are you certain?"

"Yes, sir," Rufus said. Alphonse breathed deep, thought a moment.

"Thank you for the report, Rufus. You may go now."

Rufus gave a curt nod and turned for the door. He turned back.

"He also said he would burn the forest down if the monks couldn't complete the job," Rufus added, leaving without waiting for a response.

Alphonse stared at the door, stroking his beard with concern. Monks? For a candlemaker and a kid? He shook his head in dismay. Things were more troubling than they appeared.

17

Will rushed out of his dream, sat upright, and looked around. It was a place he didn't know, and it smelled like he didn't know it. He looked down at the sheets that covered him and at the bed he rested in. The sheets were clean, the bed was larger than his, and the frame was made of real wood logs, smoothed from sanding, unlike the prickly planks that made up his twisted and creaky bedframe in the house behind the chandler's shop. It was comfortable, like resting on an evening sky after the rain. He fought the urge to lay back down by putting his feet on the bare dirt floor. He looked around the small room and landed on the wooden door. Hushed voices bickered on the other side. He got to his feet and the voices hushed further; he moved toward the door and they went silent. Whoever talked on the other side sensed his listening ear. He reached for the handle, ready to reveal himself, when he stopped and dropped his hand. The world beyond that door was changed.

Will stepped back and took a seat on the bed, giving himself a moment to think. The voices seemed to know his ears weren't close enough to hear what they were saying and began to bicker in hushed tones again. The boy slumped back and looked around the room. The bare walls gave way to a dirt floor. There were a few items beside the bed and all looked to be handmade or hand mended. Atop a small table to his left stood a figurine carved out of wood or bone, Will didn't know which. Picking it up, he rolled it over in his hands. It had the grains of wood and the stark whiteness of bone, but it was made of wax. It possessed the form of a man, about four inches tall, with broad shoulders and determined hands at his sides. He stood tall and proud for such a short thing, Will thought. He put it down out of fear that he might drop and break it.

The voices lifted beyond the door—voices of those familiar with the art of bickering. Will had never heard Del talk so much in his life—the world really had changed.

"I've had enough of this!" Del's voice rang out. Will heard the stamping of feet and the slamming of a solid door against a solid frame, followed by a voice mumbling words that probably weren't very kind.

Will turned to look at the bed. It called him to lie back down, like a whispering warmth on a comforting breeze. He was tired, and lying back down would give him more time to think. He yawned and rubbed his eyes. The figurine stood out like a pocket of snow on a gray mountainside, stalwart and stable. Will had had enough sleep. He stood and opened the door.

Isa sat at a small table by a large fireplace in the kitchen. Her face turned from revulsion toward Del to joy at seeing Will.

"Ah, come here, Will, have a seat and have something to eat and drink," she offered, with refreshed kindness in her voice.

Will did, and a plate of food and a cup of some sort of tea were before him in a moment's notice. Hardboiled eggs rocked back and forth, staring up at Will from beside a biscuit.

"Eat up, dearie," Isa said. "I doubt you've had anything good to eat in a long while." She slid two crocks across the table. "Butter and honey for your biscuit."

It was more food than Will had seen in a long time, and not fake like the stuff he got back in Umbrate. They were fresh eggs, and the biscuit looked like it was made with milled flour, not chaff that pretended to be flour. The butter, an unheard-of treat in Umbrate, glistened, and the honey was smooth and gilded. He didn't feel hungry, but he didn't think it right to let such good food go to waste.

Isa watched him, smiling, as he bit into the first egg. Her stare made him uncomfortable; he was used to being ignored.

"How long was I asleep?"

Isa shrugged. "All of yesterday and through the night. You've had quite a journey."

Will took another bite to avoid the discomfort of silence. He scraped the butter thinly over his biscuit with a wooden knife and pulled the honey dipper from the other crock. He watched the thick golden treat flow with wonder. Its pureness surprised and entranced him, and before he knew it the nectar flowed over the side of his biscuit. He put the dipper back, embarrassed that he had taken so much.

"Sorry," he said. "I'll be sure to eat it all."

Isa laughed at his embarrassment. "There's plenty where that came from, Will. You take as much as you want. I've boiled a whole pot of eggs and made a whole tray of biscuits just this morning."

Will looked by the fireplace and saw the proof of her words. There were small crocks and large crocks spread across the kitchen counters, and vegetables and herbs hung from the ceiling. His eyes wandered through the rest of the house. It was much larger than the one he and Del lived in, or rather, used to live in. Its quaintness matched its comfort, and it smelled of biscuits and honey and herbs and life. He turned back to the delicious fare on his plate.

"Where did you get all this food?" Will asked, hoping his question wasn't too impolite.

Isa laughed, and answered, "I grew it."

Will took quick inventory of everything again. "All of it?"

Isa looked at her small kitchen with pride. "Well, I can't take much credit for the eggs or honey, but most everything else, yes. And what I didn't grow I found in the forest."

"Wow." The word leaked out of Will.

Isa smiled at his small wonder. She pointed to his plate. "Don't be bashful. There's enough, and much more."

Will finished the food on his plate, stopping only a few times to answer or ask innocuous questions. And when his plate was cleared, he looked with a guilty stare at the tray of golden biscuits going cold on the counter. He averted his licentious eyes. Isa saw his gaze and stood to grab a biscuit. She shared half with him to allay his self-inflicted shame. He couldn't help it, the world that brought him up had made him that way.

Once filled, Will turned to Isa, who smiled and stared at him like he was a shining jewel. She fingered something hanging from a chain on her neck, hiding beneath her tattered shirt. Will turned away, looked about the house.

"Where's Del?" he asked.

The smile was stripped from her face.

"Outside, pitying himself … the old softy," Isa said.

Will turned and looked to the door he guessed led outside.

"You can go talk to him if you'd like," Isa said, growing kinder.

Will stood and went to the door. He stopped and turned to Isa. "I know you don't get along, but he's been good to me," Will said, "for his own part at least. Without him, I'd be dead … like my mother." Isa's shoulders slumped at the hard truth. "Please be kinder to him." Pools formed in Isa's eyes as she wrapped her fingers around a clay cup with one hand and grabbed whatever pendant hid below her blouse with the other. She nodded.

Will went out the door and found Del looking at a row of bloomed and brilliant flowers as he slouched on a log. They were white with purple edges and their flowy symmetry entranced the Candlemaker. Will sat beside him. Though he had Isa now, beside Del was still his place of comfort.

"Glad to see you're awake," Del said. "I'm sure you've had quite a shock."

Will nodded and looked around the homestead. They sat in a circular opening, sun-drenched and full of daylight, but when Will looked up, he could see a hint of trees as if he stared up at them through water. He rubbed his eyes and looked again. It appeared as though there were treetops above him but no trunks to support them, and below was brilliant sunlight.

"It's a cover," Del said. "She put it up so that her home would be well hidden." He said *she* with much disdain.

"You mean, it looks like there are trees over us?"

"Yes," Del said, giving most of his attention to the flowers.

"Wow!" Will said in awe, just above a whisper. It was a word he guessed he would be using a lot now.

Will looked at the flowers. He had never seen anything like them in Umbrate, but somehow they were familiar to him.

"What are those?" Will asked.

"Bearded Iris," Del answered. He looked up at the sunbeams piercing through. "They love the sun, and once upon a time they grew wild all over Mass … before all went so dark."

Will looked deeper at them. "I think I've seen one before."

Del looked from the blooms to Will. "Not likely, my boy. These are the first I've seen in many, many years."

Will slumped at the rebuttal. He stared at the dazzling flowers with melancholy their beauty could never induce. Del sighed at the sight.

"The world has changed very quickly for you, my boy," Del said, "and I'm sorry for that."

Will turned to him. "Why did you never tell me?"

"Tell you what? That I'm a magician?" Del paused, expecting Isa to yell '*Ex*-magician!' She didn't. "That I'm your uncle? That you have a witch auntie that lives in the woods I've never mentioned?"

"Well … yes," Will replied.

Del tried to smile but strained under the guilt on his face.

"Because I'm a coward, Will," he said, looking the boy in his fresh eyes. "But I have a feeling you already knew that about me."

Will made no reply, and none was necessary.

"How did you prevent yourself from being captured all these years?" Will asked. The flurry of questions began to swirl through his mind again, but this one seemed a safe enough place to start.

"I turned into a gray man," Del said. "I fell into a crease in the fold and did as they instructed me. I thought once that I might be able to provide help to people, to those that were really oppressed."

"With your candles? Were they magical?"

"Some were, some not, but they helped those with sick children or burdened hearts."

"Like the candle you gave to Phin at the gate, and to Mrs. Grissom?"

"Yes," Del said, his voice sticky with remorse. "It's always been risky, but the risk was always worth it to help, that is, until the King ordered me to make the Altar candles for mass. After that, it became rarer and rarer that I could help someone in need. Phin's candle had very little magic in it. It never would have been detected, and Phin's a good man who cares about his family. The candle I gave to Mrs. Grissom, though …" his voice trailed away.

They both looked at the ghostly trees overhead.

"So, Magic is not … evil?" Will asked after some time.

"All power is evil in the wrong hands," Del replied. "King Bale is only cruel because he's a king that's surrounded by cruel people. It's easy for him to order others around because he has power, and always has. He was just a boy, younger than you, when he outlawed Magic. He might have known better but for the whispering voice in his ear. The death of his mother upset him, and he made a foolish decision because of it."

"Was Queen Sharon really killed by the wizard Xenerac?"

"She was, but not for any of the reasons they've taught you in school." Del turned to him. "Her grief led her to evil, same as Bale."

Will looked toward the ground. "And were you around for all of this?"

"Yes," Del said.

"And you knew my grandmother Paulette?"

"Yes."

"And was she a witch?"

Del seemed to grow weary. Will wondered if he'd slept since they arrived.

"Let's take this conversation inside. Isa can provide more help than I can," Del said. He stood and made a slow, reluctant step toward the door. Will matched his gait. "Did you get the figurine?" Del asked.

"Yes," Will said, curious how Del knew about it.

"Good. I made it for you after we went to Charlie's place and he gave you the honeycomb for your birthday. I meant to paint it but I ran out of time."

"You made it … for me?" Will asked, still confused.

Del nodded. "I haven't always been good to you, Will. And I'm sorry for that. I—" he stopped and rubbed his head, "I hope you like it."

"I do. Thank you," Will said. Del glanced at him and smiled. They neared the door to Isa's home. "Who is it? The figurine, I mean." Will asked.

Del stopped and looked at the false trees overhead. "There are no men left with any honor. It has been stripped from them or melted away over the course of their long, laborious lives. So, I made a man of the future, a man to look up to." Del looked down at the boy. "I carved the man I believe you are going to someday be."

Without waiting for a response, Del turned and went into the house. Will stood outside with his mouth agape. And it was the mere morning of his day of discovery and understanding.

18

Isa sat at the table with a cup in her hands, patiently awaiting the return of Will and, if she had to, Del. Del walked in first and they exchanged quick scowls—like lovers do—but they were fleeting, for Will's sake. Will came in behind, his mouth still agape and his mind trying to find something stable to grab onto.

They sat at the table with Isa. All was quiet, and Will knew they were waiting for him to begin. His mind reached for questions like grasping at windblown snowflakes, until one landed on his tongue.

"How did you get the trees to do that?" he asked. He hated that it was the first thing out of his mouth, and Isa was clearly not expecting it.

"Oh, well, it's quite simple, really. Just a small charm, and poof! it hangs up there like a sheet in the breeze and lets the sunlight in while keeping me protected," she replied.

Will nodded and stuck out his tongue for a more substantial flake.

"Was my grandmother a … a witch?" The word rolled off his tongue as if it were deplorable—after all, he'd been taught his whole life that it was.

Isa smiled. This question was closer to the one she was expecting. "Yes, we were twins."

"Spitting images of each other," Del said as if reminded of a gentle memory. Isa fought to not glare at him for interrupting.

"Yes, we were identical," Isa said, smiling at Will like she could see Del's gentle memory herself.

Will thought of the history he had learned in school. They never withheld the gritty parts from the children, and it made him wonder about his own lineage.

"Does that mean I'm a … wizard?"

"Not likely," Isa said. "It's not hereditary—passed from parent to child, I mean—and if it is it hardly crosses genders. It's more likely your mother was a witch than you are a wizard."

A flash of light blinded Will's mind. He remembered very little of his last day with his mother, but he remembered that blinding light when Yan grabbed her. It had seared the man's face into his memory.

"Magical beings are rare, Will," Del said. "Even at our pinnacle, there were only a few dozen of us across all of Mass, maybe a hundred. And your grandfather—I can't seem to remember his name—was not a magical being."

"Virgil," Isa said. "He wasn't Magical, but he was a good man."

"Yes, I see much of him in you," Del agreed, trying to find his way onto Isa's kinder side.

Will slumped at the idea of not being magical, but his history lessons came back to him.

"If it's not hereditary, then why did they eliminate so many babies and families of magical beings when King Bale first outlawed Magic. Thousands according to Instructor Luceen." It disgusted Will to say it. *Eliminate*—the word used by his instructors to soften their horrendous acts.

Isa shot fireballs in Del's direction—not real ones, but Will thought she might by the way she stared at him.

"You forced him into those indoctrination classes?" she screeched.

Del crossed his arms in defense. "No, King Bale forced him."

"Oh, that's just like you to blame a senile old man."

"I couldn't have done anything about it," Del replied, his arms tightening across his chest.

"That's a cowardly lie," Isa said. "You could have—"

"He's telling the truth," Will shouted. Isa and Del turned to him. "They check all the homes for children. I was discovered by the Guard and forced to attend. It's just like monthly mass at the Cathedral. All citizens are required to go." Isa relaxed back. "Now, why did they eliminate so many people?" Will asked.

Isa breathed deep. "They didn't eliminate anyone. They *murdered* all of them. Most of them innocent people with no more power in them but to start a fire with sparks and kindling."

"Then why did they do it?"

"No reason other than mass hysteria and malicious intent. People were taught to hate Magic. It had killed their queen, though she was no blueberry, and they believed it would come after them."

"So, Magic *is* evil?"

Isa turned her blazing eyes to Del again; she couldn't blame the boy for his upbringing. He shifted uncomfortably. She turned to Will in earnest.

"Get comfortable, Will. We've a long story ahead."

19

This story begins long before Bale seized his reign, when he was but a boy and nothing more than a prince. The King of Mass always had a Magical Advisor to aid in the fairness and well-being of all people, magical or not. The Magical Advisor in those days was Xenerac Torvio, and he advised King Abiri Hornblower, husband of Sharon and father of Bale.

King Abiri and Xenerac were revered across Mass, and they shared a great reverence for each other, some even say a friendship. Magical people and common people got along in those days. The magical people provided wellness to people and animals, growth and health to the crops, and protection for all across Mass. The common people prospered and had healthy children with the aid of the magical people, and all was well in Mass, and particularly well in Umbrate. The streets teemed with people and commerce, and citizens were only poor if they wanted to be, and very few did. Times were pleasant and all loved King Abiri because he loved them. He would often walk the streets with Sharon, Bale, and Xenerac, and he would greet the people and show his thanks. He was a good king, and good kings make happy kingdoms. All seemed in everlasting prosperity, until the day that King Abiri suddenly died.

The entire kingdom mourned with Queen Sharon; her wails floated through the streets of Umbrate, quieting all. She walked the streets no more, and her presence was only heard in the howling from the king's tower. A shroud covered Umbrate, and darkness replaced cheer. Work continued, as it always does, but there was less joy in it without knowing who the work was for.

One day Queen Sharon, in the depths of grief, called on Xenerac. She was the rightful ruler of Mass, and he was her

Magical Advisor. She asked if he knew anything about bringing a loved one back from the other side. Xenerac refused to entertain her ideas, explaining to her that only Dark Magic could bring a soul back from the other side, and with consequences too great to consider. He said he would not do it.

Queen Sharon took his advice, but not in the way Xenerac intended, and went in search of Dark Magic. Every strong statue has a shadow, and Magic is no different. Sharon found the witch Mallory, known far and wide for the evil she willed forth.

Sharon gathered Bale and took him to meet with Mallory at Abiri's catacomb in the dead of night, for that is the only time such Dark Magic can be conducted. And with her she brought a girl that worked in the castle's kitchen. They were clothed in a mist of secrecy, waiting for the old hag to complete her incantations. She kneeled the obedient and unknowing girl in front of her and slit her throat, for Dark Magic requires sacrifice of the witch or wizard or a poor soul to be complete. As her blood spilled, a hazy purple light began to shine in the king's catacomb, and Sharon's face began to cheer for the first time since her husband's death.

Young Bale hugged her tightly and begged for it to stop, but she promised her child that soon his father would be home to comfort him. The old witch chanted louder and louder and the purple light intensified as the blood drained from the lifeless body. A tear was ripping through to the other side, where silent screams penetrated the gash, piercing deaf ears.

Xenerac stepped into the royal graveyard and yelled: "Stop this madness!" His second in command, Kylan Godea, behind him.

The old witch turned to him, and he flashed a killing curse at her before she could attack, but Queen Sharon jumped in front of it. The old witch Mallory and Sharon both dropped dead in the graveyard.

Bale watched his mother fall, the purple light still on his face. Kylan pulled the boy aside as Xenerac stepped forward to seal the rip between the worlds. The harder he focused the more the screams of the undead sharpened, until the purple light, intensified by the second and third sacrifices of Mallory and the Queen, flashed and blew him back. The doorway was closed, cutting off the light, but the curse had been complete with the sacrifices, and a black smoke rolled over him like an avalanche, the shrill screams following it.

Xenerac sat upright once the stampeding smoke vanished. He looked at the three dead women, and then at Kylan restraining the crying boy.

Young Bale attacked him and beat on him with his fists. "You've killed my mother!" the boy cried.

Xenerac looked to Kylan. "Care for the boy. I must gather all the magical beings. A Great Evil has been unleashed on this night."

Kylan took the boy back to the castle, as the people of Umbrate were being jerked awake by screams deep within their heads. Xenerac roused all the magical beings in Umbrate and sent word to the rest in Mass of his desperate need for them, of the desperate need of all.

The Great Evil plagued the farms and killed the animals. The sun darkened under its course, disease set on the forest, and the earth was scorched where the great horde of fiery, dead, insatiable locusts traversed, never ceasing to erode the border between the world of the living and the world of the dead on the course to make them one realm.

Lives and homes were lost, and it took all the magical power in Mass to contain the horde and banish them forever in Mirror Pool, now called Bale's Victory, where the light of the sun and moon shine eternally bright upon the calm waters. Good Magic needs light, and the light keeps the dark imprisoned at the bottom of the pool forever. Mirror Pool was a symbol of Mass. A place where all could look at its placid surface and see the reflections of the past, the reflections of evil. It was a place to observe and remember. Sentinels were trained by magical beings to watch over the pool, and the wizards turned back toward Umbrate, back toward the destruction birthed by the selfish queen, to heal the land and people.

But in their long absence, Kylan had chewed his way into young King Bale's mind. He had convinced the boy that Xenerac had killed his mother in cold blood because he wished for Abiri to remain dead so that he could take the throne for himself, and that Xenerac would have done the same to Bale if Kylan had not been there to protect him. Being only a credulous child, Bale put all his faith in Kylan, his Magical Advisor, and when Xenerac returned, King Bale presented his ultimatum: Denounce all Magic and serve the throne, as Kylan and the other magicians had vowed to do, or commit his life to imprisonment and death. Xenerac answered by fleeing the king's hall only to be captured by Kylan's magical underlings, who later became known as monks in the clergy of Kylan's dark religion.

Wizards and witches, including Paulette, Isa, and Del, returned to Umbrate to find themselves in another battle. Magical numbers were depleted and dispersed after the war with the Scourge, and magical beings were forced to fight alone or scatter into hiding. They couldn't gather great enough numbers to fight Kylan's relentless forces, armed with cruel devices designed by Kylan to harm magical beings; devices formed in silver and cursed with the blood of dead Magic—a great sacrifice allowing Dark Magic to rule.

Kylan filled the Magical Reformatory with wizards and witches who spent the rest of their lives in eternal darkness, where Light Magic can neither live nor breathe. And as Magic disappeared from the land, the sunlight over Umbrate seemed to go with it, leaving behind the death and decay carved out by the Great Evil from the other side, and with no Light Magic to heal, the Kingdom of Mass was left never to recover …

20

Will rubbed his temples like an ache punished him somewhere behind his eyes.

"But if that's all true, why didn't the common people stop it? Why did they just let it go on? Why didn't King Bale stop it if he's so great?"

"They were scared," Isa explained. "The good magical people were all off fighting the Great Scourge or dead, and they felt they had no one to stand up for them against Kylan and his monks, or the king that backed them."

"The Guard was originally made of normal citizens acting as bounty hunters that would arrest any suspicious people for a bonus of food or money from the king," Del added. "People became hungry after the Great Evil wiped the land of crops and animals, and terrified that if they revolted they or their children would die."

"And Bale was a mere boy when all of this began," Isa said. "Just thinking about Xenerac killing his mother, whether an accident or not, fueled his hate. He and his army had dug in too deep before they realized what they had done, if they ever realized. And many magical beings were more than eager to pledge their powers to Bale to keep themselves alive and fed, and so were the common people. It became a silent battle among the citizens for food and safety."

"So Kylan pledged his powers to the king?" Will asked.

"And many others," Del said. "Though many wonder of Kylan's motivation in convincing Bale to outlaw Magic."

Will pondered that a moment. "Do you know why he did it?"

Del and Isa looked at each other. "Some believe he did it to be the most powerful wizard of all time," Isa said. "Others think he did it to take the throne after Bale dies. Still more think he did it because he despised the way King Abiri loved Xenerac."

"Do you really think he could take over the throne?"

"It would be an easy transition for him," Del said. "He's been a symbol for the people as long as Bale has been. It would be nothing for him to convince a broken and defeated kingdom to let him rule. Their grandparents were the last to remember how life used to be, and they're all dead now. Kylan could just wait for Bale to die, then kill Briella with a whisper. She's been silent so long no one would ever know. Nothing would be in his way then."

"Then what is he waiting for?" Will asked. "Why doesn't he just get it over with?"

"Wizards and witches live a very long time, Will," Isa said. "He is waiting, planning, and when the time comes, Kylan will be prepared."

"Yes, he's very smart," Del said. "He won't move too soon. I'm sure he's been keeping Bale alive with Magic for so long. The frail old man should have been dead long ago. For what reason, I don't know. Kylan must have a plan for him."

"And what about Xenerac? What happened to him? We were taught in instruction that Bale killed him, but you said Kylan imprisoned him."

Del and Isa again shared a glance.

"Nobody knows what happened to him," Del said. "There was word at the time that he was killed. But some believe he's still alive in the Reformatory."

"And what do you think?"

"I think he's dead," Del admitted.

Will looked at Isa. "And I think he's alive. He'd be a good man to have on hand if things ever turned."

"You think Kylan is stupid enough to keep the most powerful wizard that ever lived alive all these years?" Del inquired, mocking her. Anger rose between them.

"I don't see why not," Isa said, crossing her arms over her chest. "What harm would it do Kylan to keep him tied in a cage? He's probably been warping his mind all these years so that he can join his wicked cause."

"I don't believe that for a minute," Del said combatively. "I think—"

"Do you think my mother could still be alive?" Will asked. Del and Isa, pausing their fight, turned to look at him, then to each other. "They say only magical people are reformed there, and you said it wasn't likely my mother was magical." Will sat patiently, waiting for one or the other to speak. Del took the leap.

"It's not likely, Will. She attacked a guard, and people, magical or not, who attack guards are put to death. The king is too proud to reverse course on anything. Once arrested and sent to the Reformatory, nobody leaves."

"And those that aren't put to death wish they were dead," Isa said. She shuddered before adding: "Wizards left in the dark for too long begin to decay, slowly. That's where Kylan is said to harvest the blood for the chains and bars and manacles he uses to incapacitate and imprison witches and wizards."

A memory flashed through Will's mind. The old woman in the square, sick on the ground after Yan put the dull silver cuffs on her.

"What's so bad about magical blood?" Will asked. "If Magic is so good, then why is the blood bad?"

"Dark Magic requires sacrifice, Will, and to bleed a magical being out is the ultimate sacrifice," Del said. "Death is the remembrance of Life—a reminder that we once lived but now have ceased. Dead Magic is worse than no Magic at all."

The painful words set in. Will thought of his mother; Isa thought of all the dead witches and wizards and innocents that didn't deserve such endings.

"What did you do after you helped banish the Great Evil into Bale's Victory—I mean, Mirror Pool?" Will asked after suffering the time alone in his mind.

"We came here," Isa said, smiling. "Del, Paulette, Virgil, and myself. Paulette gave birth to your grandmother, little Annette, in this house. It wasn't long after that her and Virgil left with their daughter. I tried to convince them to stay but ..." Isa went silent. Such regrets aren't worth reviving.

"What happened to them?" Will asked, eager to find out if he had grandparents as well.

Isa's eyes filled with tears. "I don't know. But I do know that my sister is dead."

"How do you know that?"

Isa tried to smile at Will but what stretched across her lips was redolent with pain. "Twins know these things, Will. I could feel it when she passed." Isa wiped the tears away. "Del left not long afterward."

Del tried to hide his face, but the sharp truth chimed there like a noon carillon.

Will, desiring to keep away from that subject, asked: "What do we do now?"

21

Del and Isa looked at each other, and something in their look told Will they had already discussed what to do next, and they had disagreed. The fading light outside darkened the inside of the small home.

Isa sat upright, shifted in her seat, and said: "It's time for a revolution, Will."

Del slumped and put his hand to his forehead. A groan escaped his lips.

"As you can see, we're not in agreeance," Isa said, scowling.

"And why would we be? An old witch and wizard—who can't remember a bit of real Magic—against the entire Magic-hating world," Del said.

"More will come!" Isa shouted. "And not all hate Magic. They just pretend to, to keep their lives intact."

"More?" Will asked.

Isa leaned in, smiling with excitement. "I've sent word to all corners of Mass, to all magical people."

"When?"

"Yesterday after you arrived," Isa explained. Her cheer at the proposition of an uprising replaced her anger for Del.

"How?"

"Birds and butterflies mostly, but whatever moves swiftly."

"And they do what you tell them to?" Will asked with a skeptical upturn.

"I can speak with beasts and birds, flowers and trees, and so could your grandmother," Isa said, nonchalantly. "They're my familiars." Will nodded as if he understood what she was talking about.

"And you think your message will reach them?"

"Of course it will," Isa said, taken aback. "People will come—I assure you."

"And then what?" Will asked, intrigued.

"Yes, and then what?" Del echoed reproachfully.

"You know it's time, Del," Isa hissed. "We've stood to the side for too long, watching our friends and family die. If we don't stand up now, our opportunity will waste away, and all the good Magic with it."

"There's no good Magic left," Del said. "There's no good left at all." He sat back, pitying himself.

"And what about the man of the Royal Guard that helped you escape? What about the things he said about Princess Briella, huh? How about the people that risked their lives to hide you and help you to the forest? Were they not good?" Del looked away from her. "You're free to go back to living in fear and hatred, making stupid candles for a stupid king, but I won't do it anymore."

"We can't go back," Del barked.

"Then stand and fight!" Isa pleaded. "You were a great wizard, Del. One of the best. And you will be again, but not without standing here—now!"

"I'll stand," Will said. He got to his feet. Isa smiled at his bravery.

"No, you won't," Del said, wiping the smile from Isa's face. Will looked at his feet, embarrassed, and sat back down.

"And why should he not be able to fight?" Isa asked.

"Because he's just a boy," Del said. "I'm his guardian, and I won't allow it." Del crossed his arms with steadfast arrogance.

Isa stood from her seat and towered over Del, who struggled to maintain his hauteur in her shadow.

Isa came closer; Del melted into his seat. "You, his guardian? Ha! I bet that's the first time you've accepted that role. You're lucky this boy isn't just like them. He would have turned you in long ago, and you'd be the one in the Reformatory in need of rescuing."

Del sat upright, attempting to regain his dignity. "How dare you—"

Isa's voice forced him back down. "How dare *I?!* How dare his own flesh and blood aunt?! You've nearly ruined this boy by keeping him from the truth. He has good in him, and if you believe yourself his guardian, you'll fight for him, and let him fight for what he believes!"

"So that he can die like his mother did?!" Del blurted.

The room fell silent. Isa and Del glanced at Will. The tears brimmed in his eyes, but he remained strong, willing. "She died protecting me from evil," he said, his voice quavering like a dry leaf in a breeze. "And I'll fight to protect others from it as well—even if it means my life—because she did it for me." He stood and went out the door. Del stood to stop him.

"Leave him be," Isa said.

"But it's dark out," Del replied.

"He's safe here." Isa ceased towering over Del and sat back down. "He's lost just as much as we have in all this madness," Isa said, not angrily but factually.

The fighting stopped, and both fell silent in gloomy, unforgiving thought.

Will stepped out under the dull moonlight streaming through the false canopy. His heart and head hurt equally bad. He turned his eyes to the moon. It peered back at him as it made its constant loop over Mirror Pool many miles and histories away. He thought of the Sentinels that watched over it, their families, and the people that did the same before them. Did they know the truth? Did they know why they watched over Mirror Pool, or why Magic was outlawed in Mass? He guessed they did not, as he once did not.

He moseyed away from the house and took the path they had walked down the morning he lurched into the world of Magic. It glowed at his feet, and he wondered if he walked on Magic or if it always looked that way under the opaque canopy. Will followed it for some time, caring neither where he was going nor when he would return.

Stopping near the edge of a clearing, he looked across it and squinted in the failing light. There was a pool in the distance and, unless his eyes deceived him, the figure of a woman sat beside it. He looked down the trail, toward Isa's home, then back toward the figure.

Try as he might, he struggled to remember seeing the pool when they passed by before. He wondered if he had already fainted before they reached it. Squinting for better sight, Will tried to discern the shape of the body. It was a woman, that much he was sure of, but that was all he could make out. He duck-walked back down the trail and into the trees to get a closer look.

Will shimmied his way through the small openings between the dense trees, stopping occasionally to get a better look at the woman. She was dressed in a light gown that seemed to glow with the faintest light, like fine dust shining in a sunlit window, as the trail did in the silver light of Mass night. Her feet were dipped in the pool, and she scooped her hand in the calm water and dripped it over her arms and legs. Her alluring fingers rubbed the drops of water into her skin.

Will couldn't look away, fearing she would vanish if he blinked. A cool breeze rose out of nowhere and wrapped Will's face. The scent of the woman floated to him, cool and relaxing, halcyon and familiar. She lifted her head and smiled. Her eyes glowed like her gown. Her gaze met his, and there was no denying that she was looking at him, into him. Will tried to avert his eyes, but they were locked like magnets.

"You can come out now," she announced, her lithe hands never stopping as she rubbed the droplets into her skin.

Will emerged from the trees without thinking and without guilt for watching. He approached the pool, but maintained his distance.

"It's not very nice to watch a woman in secret," she said. "Didn't your mother ever teach you that?"

"My mother is dead," Will replied.

"I'm sorry to hear that. Every boy needs a mother." She dipped her hand and dribbled more water onto her skin. Will watched, waiting for her to tell him what to do.

"What is your name, child?" she asked.

"Will," he responded without hesitation.

"Well, Will, I'm sure if you had a mother, she would have taught you that it is impolite to continue to stare after you've been instructed not to." Her words were light and without vitriol, and her smile developed her message further.

Will looked away for a moment, but his urge to stare quickly pulled him back. "I'm sorry."

The coquettish smile remained as she continued to rub her skin. She stared at him deeply. Her eyes glowed, Will was certain now.

"Come, sit next to me, Will. Dip your feet in the water. It's quite cool," she said, running the palm of her hand over the surface. The ripples flowed away from her, and the glow on her gown and in her eyes rippled as well.

Will approached her, slowly, as a hunter approaches a deer.

She laughed in gentle vibrations, like the slight undulation across the pool. "Don't be afraid, Will. I've no reason to harm you."

Will, trusting her words, jogged the rest of the distance between them and sat close, but not too close, with his knees hugged to his chest. Her beauty had increased in the short distance, and her scent floated to him, unabated. He gazed at her with awe, and she smiled down at him.

"Go ahead, put your feet in," she offered.

Will shook his head.

"And why not?"

"Because it's your pool." He looked away for the first time, embarrassed. "I don't want to dirty it."

Her laughter floated from her throat like clouds across the sky. "I wouldn't have invited you if I thought you might dirty it, Will."

The fire rose in Will's cheeks and he looked down, hiding his happy shame. He glanced at her feet, the right one sliding over the left, the left over the right, as her smooth legs did the same. She offered him her hand.

"Come closer, Will," she said. "No need to be afraid. It's just water."

He hesitated, before he released his arms from around his knees and rolled to his hip to reach for her hand. He could feel the heat from her palm as he hovered his hand over hers, a comforting heat Will did not want to abandon. He stared into her placid face and placed his palm in hers.

The glow in the woman's eyes flared from night-blue to vicious violet. Will jerked away from her fury. Her palm squeezed his painfully as her other hand grabbed his elbow. He looked down at her once lithe hands, the tight grip burning and sending shivers of pain up his arm.

Looking back into her face, he stared into the dark, hollow hood of a cloak. He pulled to free himself, and nearly succeeded when another pair of arms gripped him across his chest from behind. He was lifted from the ground, writhing and screaming in the powerful grasp.

"No! Let me go!" he yelled. The arms across his chest squeezed the last word flat. Will's head swam with a rush of hot liquid, and the vice tightened with every excited exhale until there was no space left for his lungs to fill.

Will struggled to stay conscious as the attackers pulled him into the forest. He looked out with his last moment of lucidity and saw a large figure burst through the trees. The cloaked man in front of Will turned and was met with a burst of light. He crumbled to the earth. The man holding Will dropped him to fight the new emergent and met the same light as it flashed like a shooting star over Will's head. The second man went limp and dropped on top of the boy.

Will grunted and remained still, too scared to do anything but lay there, struggling to regain his lost breath under the weight of the body. Looking overhead from his position he saw the large figure leaning over the first cloaked figure he struck, inspecting him. He came to Will, without haste, and lifted the body off.

"You alive, boy?" he said; his voice deep and thick.

"Yes," Will wheezed, feeling the pain in his side for the first time.

The man ran his hands over Will's midsection, and stopped on his left side. "You've got a broken rib," he said. "Stay still. This will hurt a bit." Will, stuck in paralytic fear, did as he was told.

Light formed under the man's hands as they moved back and forth over the painful spot. Then, suddenly, he brought his hands together and hit Will's ribcage, sending a loud snapping sound through the hushed night. Will groaned. He looked at the man with betrayal in his eyes until the agony dispersed the way a drop of blood suffuses through a bowl of water, until it was completely gone.

"Better?" the man asked.

"Yes, thank you," Will said.

He pulled Will to his feet with ease. Will looked at him for the first time. He appeared to be twice as tall as Will, and he wore a cloak over his features that made him almost indistinguishable from the ones that grabbed him. Will looked at the two, crumpled and crooked on the ground.

"Are they dead?" he asked timidly.

"Yes," the man said with remorse. "I had no choice. They would have killed you. Because you and an old wizard fled Umbrate."

"How did you know that?" Will asked.

"A bird told me," he said. He removed his hood and peered down at Will with dark eyes. His bald head reflected what moon dared to shine upon it, and his dense beard made his eyes look even darker than they were. "My name is Elias Alder. I'm an old friend of Isabella and Delier."

Will relaxed. He looked at the dead again and averted his eyes.

"What were they doing? I mean, the one looked like a woman, and then they attacked me."

"They were luring you in," Elias said. "They knew your weakness and exploited it."

"What were they?"

"Monks. Dark wizards from Umbrate," Elias said. "I've been following them for half-a-day. They moved fast, with a mark in mind. They lit the path at your feet and put the glow in the woman."

"So, she wasn't real?"

"No, just an illusion."

"But I could smell her. She smelled like …" Will's voice trailed away.

"Your mother … your weakness," Elias finished.

Will hadn't recognized it, but it was true. He felt embarrassed and angry. "If you were following them, why didn't you stop them before they attacked me, or before they got so close to Isa's house?"

"I needed to know where they were going," Elias said. "They're very powerful wizards, and with few scruples while under the guise of Kylan's work. They would have killed all three of you if they had the chance, but I had no desire to kill them until I was sure of their mission: you, apparently."

Will dared a glance at the bodies again. They were empty, hollow, like a box with bygone use.

"Run along and tell Isabella and Delier that I've arrived," Elias said. He looked down at the bodies. "I'll take care of them."

Will looked across the clearing toward the trail. He hesitated to move.

"You'll be safe, Will. I assure you," Elias said.

"How do you know my name?"

Elias smiled and the moon's reflection moved from his head to his teeth.

"It was a very talkative bird," he said.

Will smiled back, and returned to the trail, dark now, then to Isa's home.

22

Will entered the home listlessly after his life revealed itself as nothing more than a bit of thread on his walk back. Del and Isa watched curiously as he entered. He could tell by the ting in the air that not a word had passed between them since he left. He looked up and met Isa's gaze. Her face turned down at the sight of his.

"Are you all right, Will?" she asked coming to his side. "You look like you've fallen ill."

"I was attacked," Will said lethargically.

"Attacked!" Del exclaimed, getting to his feet.

"There's a man out there," Will said.

"A man!" Del looked toward the door. He stood as if preparing to pounce and paused.

Large footsteps crunched on the dirt outside. Del faltered. Isa stood.

"Get behind me," she said.

"No, he's good," Will said. "He saved me." They didn't hear him.

Isa and Del, ready to fight, watched the door open slowly. The large figure ducked his cloaked head in. Del poised his fists; Isa pushed Will behind her. Elias pulled back his hood and smiled through his thick beard.

"That's no way to greet an old friend, Delier," Elias said.

Del dropped his hands and turned as pale as Will. Without a word, he leaped forward and embraced Elias.

"That's more like it," Elias said, laughing.

Isa came forward. "Elias, you got the message." She had to pull Del away to give him a hug herself. "I'm guessing it was you that scared the boy."

"I told you he was good," Will said. "He saved me from the attackers."

"Attack*ers*," Del said. The aged couple turned to Elias—his face now clouded with seriousness.

"Yes," Elias said soberly. "Two monks." They gasped. "I ran across their path around midday. They formed an illusion to attract Will. If I hadn't been there, they would have taken him."

"But I didn't feel them cross the barrier like I did when Will and Del came through," Isa said.

"You forget how powerful they are. They knew it was there. They stopped at it for a long while and tried spell after spell to break it. They cut a hole right through. I sealed it behind them," Elias said.

"Yes, we forget that Magic hasn't been outlawed for them," Del said, gritting his teeth with contempt. "They have remained strong while we have turned feeble."

"Not all of us," Elias said.

Del turned and took his seat at the table. He leaned back in deep thought.

"Have a seat, Elias. I'll get you some food," Isa said, scurrying into the kitchen.

Elias removed his pack and cloak and left them by the door. His shoulders were broad and he had to duck under the beam that held the house up. He appeared even larger to Will in the small space than he had outside. Isa placed a plate of bread and a bowl of cold vegetable stew in front of him. They watched him eat, waiting patiently for the conversation to continue. Elias pushed the plate and bowl forward once finished. He thanked Isa, who cleared the table, and then they fell into silence, each hoping for another to speak.

"What animal caught up with you?" Isa asked with some cheer after the long, ear-ringing silence.

"A swallow by the name of Terron," Elias said.

"Oh, he's a good bird. A fast flyer. And very—"

"Talkative," Elias said, smiling kindly.

"Yes," Isa said, returning his kind smile. "Talkative."

Silence consumed them again. The metallic ting returned to the tense air. Will scanned from one to the other. The only one that looked at all powerful was Elias. He appeared at least a decade or two younger than the others. Will wondered how long magical people lived. They were well over a hundred years old if they had been around when King Bale took the crown. Isa and Del appeared geriatric, but life and mettle remained in Isa where it was lost in Del. Will gazed at him with pity.

"How did you get out of Umbrate and all the way here without being caught?" Elias asked Del, cutting the silence.

His voice roused Del. "Oh, uh, friends," Del replied, dipping back into his thoughts.

"They must be good friends," Elias said. "It can't be easy getting out of Umbrate as a future guard and an accused wizard."

"Yes," Del smiled, "they are very good friends. Will and I owe them much." Del seemed to not care how Elias knew so much about their journey; he seemed not to care about anything at all, in fact. They sat around the table like old friends that had nothing in common any more, which surprised Will after their genial greeting. Isa spoke again to try and spark the tinder of conversation.

"Where were you when Terron found you?" she asked. "You've arrived very quickly."

"I was lurking along the east side of the forest, trying to avoid the King's Carve," Elias replied. "I noticed a large number of Guards around. They appeared to be hunting something. Your bird told me what. I crossed the road to the west side of the forest and ran into the Monks. I knew their path would lead me to you."

"And thank goodness you saw them. I hate to think what they might have done to Will." She looked at the boy and saw something the others could not. She shook the dark thought away.

"Mmm," Elias grunted. He looked at Del intently. Thought filled the space again with impatient silence. Will, seeing all the awkward glances, wanted them to talk, to say anything that might help, or anything that might lift them out of the dreaded stillness, but all seemed reluctant to start the revolution Isa had been so fervent to suggest.

"How many do you think will turn up?" Isa asked Elias. He looked down at his sinewy fingers interlaced on the table. The chair creaked beneath his heavy, uncomfortable movement. Isa's face grew concerned. "Elias?"

The man shrugged his large shoulders. "It's difficult to tell. Many will need more time to arrive."

"Have you seen any recently? On your travels?" Isa asked. Del continued to stare into the distance.

Elias shifted again. "No," he answered.

"Nobody?" Isa said.

Elias shook his head, "Rolph and Gertrude were the last I've seen besides you … that's been a decade, probably more."

"A couple of old kooks," Del interjected. Isa shot him a glance but didn't deign to bickering.

"Then they are in hiding?" Isa asked, turning to Elias.

Elias shrugged his broad shoulders in answer.

"And you've neither seen nor heard from anyone else?" Isa pressed.

Elias breathed deep. "Those that haven't been hunted down have gone into hiding." He looked at Isa with deep regard. "The common people are hungry, and any reported hint of Magic puts more food on their tables."

Isa shivered, troubled by the thought. She covered her eyes and left the table. Elias looked at Del, emotionless and staring.

"How have you managed to survive so many years in Umbrate?" Elias asked.

Del breathed deep. "I played the part, held the guise. It helps that I was commissioned by the king to make his Altar candles for monthly mass. A job like that adds a bit of protection."

"So you've participated in their lying games," Elias said, and not kindly.

Del turned to him, fear and anger fighting for position on his face. "I did what I had to do … and I provided a home for Will while I did it." Del and Elias shared a long, thoughtful survey of each other. Will wondered if Del feared the large wizard. Del looked at Will. "Speaking of which: it's time for bed." Will knew Del used him as an excuse to look away. The boy didn't hesitate, and nobody stopped him. He got up from his seat and came to Elias's side.

"Thank you," he said, offering him a quick hug; he was getting used to it.

Elias gave him a dutiful nod. Isa came from the kitchen and hugged Will.

"What would you like for breakfast, Will?" she asked.

All he knew for breakfast was mealy porridge, so he said: "Anything you make will be fine." And he turned and went to bed.

In the dark of his room, Will sat on his bed and held the wax figurine. He listened by the door to see if the conversation continued without him, but it either didn't or they kept their discussion in their minds with some Magic he couldn't understand. The figurine glowed in the weak light—More Magic? Will traced his fingers over all its features, memorizing each curve, resisting sleep. He didn't know if it would come for him that night, but he didn't want to lie down to figure it out.

Was a revolution even possible? Maybe. But Will, like Del, the man that raised him, couldn't help but question its potential for success.

Will rubbed over the strong arms of the figurine. *"I made the man I believe you are going to someday be."* Del's words surprised Will, even more now than they had when he first heard them. Will placed the wax carving on the bedside table and rested his head. He let the day catch up with him, and he slept with the promising words of Del running over his mind like a fall of crisp, sparkling water.

23

Two days passed … then three. And no sign or sound was seen or heard from any others. For the first day, Isa tried her hardest to entertain her nephew until she realized he needed no entertaining at all. She then turned her efforts to other tasks, as did the others. She cooked and cleaned and waited outside for reports from her returning birds and animals and would arrive home sadder than when she left. Elias patrolled along the magical border during the day, and he let Will follow, but he only talked when prompted, as Will discovered to be his way. And Del sat around the house, deep in thought or indifference, no one could tell.

The only time they gathered was around the table for meals. And their hushed nature proved unbearable, even for Will, who was raised in it. Isa tried to talk of old times, but the men would not engage for lack of interest or fear of bringing up old hurts, and the only discourse was silence. Will wished for some discussion to open for him to ask questions, but the minds of the others traveled elsewhere, and he wished not to bother them, as he had been brought up not to.

But at dinner on the fourth night, Del finally spoke.

"Well, we've tried," he said. "Now it's time to call it an end."

Isa and Elias put down their wooden utensils and looked at him as Will's arm froze in midair with vegetable stew steaming on his spoon.

"It takes more than four days to get from other parts of the kingdom," Isa said, incensed.

"It takes four days from some parts, but not all, and not where we're located," Del replied, snidely.

"Some travel with more caution," Isa said.

"And if so, how many would that be?" Del turned in his seat, facing them for the first time in four days. "A hundred? Fifty, even? Not likely by the looks on your faces."

"You can't lose hope, Del," Isa pleaded. "Aren't you sick of hiding? Aren't you sick of seeing people you can help starve and die?"

Del rolled his eyes. "It's a new world. We might as well get on with it."

"You mean lay down and die?" Isa asked. "You've always been skilled at that."

"Better than dying for a foolish cause we couldn't possibly win," Del retorted.

Elias, pensive always, watched, and with not a little anger for Del. Will realized his spoon was hovering and dropped it into the bowl. Isa looked across the table at him with worry worn deep in her wrinkles.

"And what about Will? Do you want him to grow up in a world that erodes more every day? Even an old ass like you will live beyond that, and so will I. I don't wish to see this world burn while I can do something for the weak in it," Isa said.

"And why is it that you've just now discovered yourself to be so brave? Is it because a few wizards showed up at your house? We're more likely to have a successful card party than a revolution," Del said. Four days of brooding fountained from his words. "Three is not enough to tear down a kingdom."

"Four," Elias said, nodding at Will. The boy grinned and blushed.

"Four is better than none," Isa said. "Now is the time." Victory emerged in her voice.

"And what can three aging wizards do against a great regime? An anti-magical *magical* regime, by the way. I've forgotten all I know. I can hardly light a candle without a fire nearby."

"I've not forgotten," Isa said.

"Nor have I," Elias echoed.

"Oh, I don't believe that for a moment. It's been a hundred years! A hundred years with no books, no open Magic. We've all forgotten things. The monks will defeat us as soon as shoo a fly."

"Not the monks that attacked me," Will said. They all stared at his fresh voice. "Elias handled them without trouble."

"It's true," Isa said.

"Yes," Elias said. "And we can get books."

"They've destroyed all the Magic books," Del said.

"Not all of them," Elias said. He exchanged a knowing glance with Isa.

"What do you mean, of course they have," Del fought.

"Elias is right," Isa said. "Some still remain."

"And where might those be? In Kylan's chamber?" Del mocked.

"No, in the Mausoleum of Magic," Elias said.

The fight leached out of Del, along with his blood.

Isa sat upright with encouragement. "Yes, the Mausoleum of Magic."

"And how do you expect us to get in there?" Del asked.

Will chimed in before anyone could answer. "What's the Mausoleum of Magic?"

"It is a stone hall where they've stored all the last copies of magical books and leftover magical items," Elias said. "It's located deep in the east side of the Forest."

"Why would they keep that stuff?" Will asked.

"Like Del explained: they're an anti-magical *magical* regime," Isa said. "People like Kylan still have use for the books."

"As do the dozens of Monks that guard the Mausoleum," Del interrupted. "So, I ask again: How do you expect us to get in there?"

"There aren't dozens, not anymore," Elias said. "I've been over that way recently. There were only two guards at the door, and only one appeared to be a monk."

"Then the others were inside having lunch," Del exclaimed.

"No, I believe they are less concerned about it with fewer and fewer magical beings around. That, or they don't have enough guards or monks to spare. It's been said Kylan doesn't let his monks far from his sight these days."

Del quieted a moment. He remembered the words of Alphonse during their last meeting: *Their numbers are not as large as they make them appear.'* Alphonse had no reason to lie to Del. Elias's words were believable, but not wholly convincing.

"If that's the case, then what would be your plan for getting in?" Del asked, calmer but still somewhat scaly.

Elias looked at Will. "We create an illusion of our own."

24

Kylan drummed his fingers on his desk as he waited for a report. It had been five days since he sent the two monks, and word had not returned. Kylan was a patient man, but his patience was wearing to nothing more than a diaphanous sheet. No magical beings had ever escaped him, and certainly not ones that lived right under his nose.

"Call the leaders of the two Guards," Kylan called in the empty room. "Yes, sir," came the reply through the door.

Yan and Alphonse showed sometime later winded from their rapid climb up the steps. Kylan wasted no time addressing them.

"I sent two monks in pursuit of our escapees," he said. "It's been five days and no word."

"Patience is necessary, sir," Alphonse said. "Even more so if you believe the old chandler is magical."

"Patience!" Kylan hissed at the acrid taste of the word. "I've given enough patience as it is. They must be caught, destroyed!" The room fell silent as the last syllable echoed.

Yan spoke: "What do you propose we do, sir?"

"I propose we stick to my original plan. We burn down the forest."

"That can't be our only option," Alphonse blurted. "The king surely doesn't approve of this."

Kylan turned his slate gaze to Alphonse. "I am the king's advisor, and this is what I would advise him to do," he said. "A magical being on the run is a dangerous thing for the sovereignty of our kingdom. What if he were to release the Great Evil on these lands again?"

"But what about wood? We need wood for the king's fires. We need wood for the centennial festival. And we need game to feed the king. It would be unwise to burn our supplies for an old man and a boy. They've likely already died on their journey."

Yan gave a nervous glance from the corner of his eye. "I agree with Alphonse. There's no reason for us to believe they are alive at all. We should wait longer before we take such drastic measures."

A grim smile formed across Kylan's mouth. "Your advices have been heard. Now, send thirty men from each of your Guards."

Yan looked at Kylan in disbelief. "Sir, I don't have thirty men to give."

"Nor do I," Alphonse said.

"You will give thirty men apiece on the king's order. Pull them from where you will."

Alphonse stepped forward. "I advise you against—"

"And I advise you to follow your orders!" Kylan stood and yelled. "They are the king's orders, and this is the king's business! Magic *cannot* run free across these lands!"

"Yes, sir," Yan and Alphonse said.

Kylan sat back in his seat, collected himself. He pulled his dark quill and began to write. Yan and Alphonse shared a worrisome side glance. Kylan finished writing and replaced the Raven feather.

"Now, you are correct: it would not be wise to burn the whole forest down," Kylan began. "But it only takes a small fire to smoke the rats out of the haystack. So, your guards will go to the site where they lost the wrongdoers and they will start a fire to flush them out. Is the king's order understood?"

"Yes, sir," they replied.

Kylan lifted his quill and wrote again. Alphonse could hear Yan's excited breath over the scratching on parchment. Kylan replaced the quill and looked up at them with a smile.

"You may go now," he said. Both bowed low and returned to the door. They knocked and the outside guards freed them from the suffocating room.

Halfway down the stairs, Yan said: "He's mad! Only a fool would do such a thing for an old man and a boy. I can't give up that many guards. I'm already stretched thin."

Alphonse avoided saying what he wished to say, and instead replied: "We'll do as we are told." After a few more hurried steps, he added, whispering: "Then maybe they will learn their lesson."

25

Will, Del, Elias, and Isa stood outside of her home, each weighed down with a makeshift pack. Isa looked at her empty house, and the empty pens where her freed animals had once given her so much company, and despair wrinkled the corners of her eyes. Del exploited her questioning glance.

"We don't have to do this, Isa. It's a fool's proposition." His words echoed the feelings he had been making clear since the formulation of the plan.

Isa knew he was wrong. Kylan would soon discover that his monks would not return, and he would send more, possibly many more. Now was the time for action, movement.

"You're still free to leave, Del," Isa replied. "I'm sure they'll welcome you in Umbrate with open arms."

Del scoffed and turned away.

Elias, always watching, always anticipating, spoke: "We must be moving. Daylight is waning and we need to be at the King's Carve by dark if we wish to cross in shadow."

Del looked at Will. The boy was quiet, serious. He kneeled beside him. "Are you sure you want to go through with this?"

Will nodded without hesitation. "I have to. I can't go back to the city."

Del knew what he said was true. He stood and turned, and the conversation was over. Elias started down the trail, and Del followed close behind.

Isa looked at her home and sighed as she turned away, knowing in her heart it would be the last time. Will watched and waited to walk until she came to his side.

"It's all right, Isa. We'll be back soon enough," Will said.

"I don't think so, Will." Isa put her arm around him and smiled. "But sometimes it's best to sacrifice a few small things for something greater."

They walked some distance down the trail, with Elias and Del pulling away.

"Do you think we can do it?" Will asked.

Isa pulled him closer. "I wouldn't be leaving my home if I thought we couldn't," she said. "C'mon, let's catch up before Elias leaves us and Del runs off." They shared a grin and picked up the pace to catch the men.

After they crossed the magical barrier, all turned silent and vigilant until they reached the edge of the forest at dusk. The other side of the forest was little more than a green wall in the failing light as they looked across the expansive King's Carve, half a league wide, dividing the west side of the forest from the east. The road appeared empty now, but the eyes of Bale always watched. They rested in the trees some distance from the road and waited for the cover of darkness.

Will observed Elias's watchful, forbearing eyes as he nibbled on a biscuit. Del slept, and Isa appeared lost in troubling contemplation. The traveling had been rough and far, through dense trees and thick undergrowth, and the exhaustion crept into Will's bones. His eyelids felt as if they had weights on them. He tried to think about tomorrow to stay awake. They would be breaking into the Mausoleum of Magic, a place he didn't know existed until last night, and he was key to their success. He stared across at Elias, who gave Will a nod, and the boy fell asleep.

Will awoke, staring up into the mottled canopy and trying to blink through the faint, gray light. He thought he had been asleep only a few moments when he realized it was the purple light of morning fighting through the treetops, not the silver light of night. The setting moon peered at him over the top of the trees. He sat up and looked around.

Del and Isa slept with their backs leaned against the same oak tree, a safe distance apart. Elias sat at the base of another tree; his eyes unblinking as he remained on incessant guard. He looked at Will and nodded him over. Will left his pack and moved to Elias's side quietly to not disturb Isa and Del. He peered through the miles of trunks and tangled limbs and wondered what Elias watched for.

"Are we on the other side of the forest?" Will whispered.

"Yes," Elias said.

"How did you get me across?" Will asked.

"Del and I carried you."

"Del?" Will asked, louder than he intended. Isa and Del stirred but did not wake.

"Yes, he's quite strong … for an old man." Elias smiled. Will snickered and looked across at Del, then back to Elias.

"Why didn't you wake me?"

"You needed your rest. We have a grand task ahead of us."

"Do you need your rest?" Will asked. "I can keep lookout if you'd like."

Elias shook his head. "Del, Isa, and I took turns in the night," Elias said, though Will wondered if he was lying. "Besides, a traveling wizard gets little rest in these strange days."

"You don't have a home?" Will asked.

"I move from place to place trying to help people as I can," Elias replied. "Though few understand the healing power of Magic nowadays."

"And you've never been caught?"

"I'm a very good hider … with some very good hiding places." Elias winked.

Will grinned. He looked at Del. Elias followed his eyes.

"I'm not as good a hider as Del, though. How he's hidden in plain sight so long, I'll never know."

"He's been cowering," Will said, feeling the guilt of the craven word.

"There's little difference between hiding and cowering, especially now. From magical people to common people, we all do it, and we all have a reason for doing it," Elias said. Will's face evened out. "Del did what he had to do, and he protected you in the process."

"He never wanted me," Will said.

"No? Then why did he save you from servitude in the Guard? Why did he risk his life to escape with you? And why is he here now?"

Will mulled over the questions, feeling the guilt rise again.

"Are you nervous for today?" Elias asked after some time.

"A little," Will admitted.

"As am I," Elias said. Somehow the admission made Will feel better. "We will protect you, Will." Elias leaned in closer. "You may not know this, but Del is a great wizard."

"He is?"

Elias nodded. "One of the greatest I've ever known. Second only to Xenerac himself if you were to ask me, only a little less obvious than the great wizard. Del's always been quiet, distant."

"But Isa said—" Elias stopped him.

"Del and Isa have issues of their own. She would have admitted the same once."

Will looked at the geriatric man scrunched against the oak tree.

"If Isa or I can't protect you, Del will," Elias assured him. He leaned back and closed his eyes. "I think I will take that rest now— if you don't mind keeping watch, that is?"

Will had no time to answer before Elias's breath slowed and deepened. He stared at Del again. As many secrets as there were between them, he wondered if he knew anything about the man that had taken him in and raised him since his first solid memory.

Overhead, the sun snuck up behind the moon to relieve it of its duty. The forest came to life, and Will watched over his magical counterparts and considered the task ahead.

26

Breathless and steady, Will peered through an opening between intertwined branches. A day and a half of traveling on sore feet, and in the clearing before him, like a monolith risen from the dirt, was the Mausoleum of Magic. The crypt was larger than the ones in the graveyard of Umbrate, and Will could make out the intricacies carved into its sides like the mausoleums that housed the bones of Umbrate's former royalty.

Two guards stood in front of its great door, so still that Will wondered if they were real or not. They adorned the same cloaks, gray with red trim, that Will had seen on the monks the night they snatched him out of the alluring illusion.

He closed his eyes and shuddered. A strong hand grabbed his shoulder and pulled him back. Containing his gasp, the heavy grip turned him until he faced Elias, Isa, and Del. The palpable fear on their faces pulled Will further into the reality of their situation.

"I searched the whole area," Elias said. His lips moved but barely a sound came out. "I can only see evidence of the two guards. Both appear to be monks."

Del swallowed hard, louder than Elias spoke. They all looked at him and he turned away, embarrassed. The light of the sky ventured toward dusk. Time wore thin.

"Ready?" Elias asked. They nodded, one by one, Del last of all. "Into position."

Del and Will shared a glance before the three magical beings moved in separate directions away from Will. His body shook as the distance increased between them. He had to trust them. He had to trust himself.

After giving them time to get into position, Will began.

"Help!" he yelled at the top of his lungs. The monks jumped at the sound. "Help!" he yelled louder. The guards broke free of attention and took a step away from the Mausoleum.

Will yelled once more and began to crash through the trees. "Anyone! Please, help me!" The sound echoed in the clearing as he burst through the trees making as much noise as possible. He could see flashes of the Monks moving in his direction.

"Help me, please. Help! They're chasing me!" Will emerged into the opening; the sky darkened overhead.

The monks jumped at his appearance, taken aback at the sight of a small boy so deep in the Grim Forest. Elias stepped out of the trees to the side of the monks. Will dropped to his knees and covered his head. A flash of light filled the darkened clearing and one of the monks screamed. His body thumped on the ground.

Another flash filled the space and Elias howled in pain. Peeking from beneath his cover, Will saw the remaining monk running toward him, just a few strides away.

Del stepped out of the trees and hesitated. Will looked at him. The monk followed Will's eyes and sent a beam of purple light in Del's direction. The old wizard jumped back into the woods as the light flashed and cracked into a tree behind him. The monk grabbed Will and pulled the struggling boy into the cover of the forest.

"Let me guess," he said, containing the boy's arms to his sides: "William Chandler?"

"Let me go!" Will gritted his teeth and tried to free himself, but the more he squirmed the tighter the grip squeezed.

"No reason to fight anymore, boy," the monk said. "The first man is dead and the second is a coward."

"No! Let me go!" Will shouted.

"And why would I do that?" the monk asked. "There's a large reward for your head."

Will heard quick footsteps and felt a dull crack rumble through the monk before he fell limp.

Will rolled out of his grasp and saw Isa holding a heavy oak log, one half dangling where it had cracked over the monk's head.

The hood pulled away from the monk's face as he lolled back; blood trickled from his hairline.

"I would have used a spell, but I was afraid of hitting you," Isa said. "Go and find Del and get him to Elias. I'll take care of this scum." She said the words, but Will could see it pained her to do so.

The monk lifted his head and tried to blink his eyes open.

"Go!" Isa said.

Will stood and made his way toward the clearing. A flash of light followed him out; he flinched at its intensity.

Del walked out from behind the tree battered by the monk's spell. He appeared lost, dizzy. He wobbled up to Will.

Will stared at him with fury emanating from his small stature. "He said you would protect me!" Del looked away, avoiding his glance. "He said you would protect me, and now he's dead!"

"Not yet, boy," Elias said. He stumbled from the trees holding his bleeding arm.

Will ran and hugged him; Del followed behind.

"I'm sorry, Elias. I-I," Del paused and gathered himself. "It's been so long since I've used any real Magic."

Elias grimaced in pain and sat down. His gaze told Del he didn't want to hear anymore.

"Help me now, then, Del," Elias said.

Del hesitated at the sight of Elias's mangled arm. Isa rushed from the trees and came to Elias's side, inspected his wound.

"Come, Del, give us a hand," Isa said, composed.

Del put his hand to his pale forehead. "I-I can't."

"You what?" Isa said, turning to him in anger. "I just destroyed a man of misguided Magic, a man of *our* murdered race, and you can't help a friend?"

Del opened his mouth to speak but no words came out. Isa spurned him and turned back to Elias. She peeled away his tattered garment to get a look at the wound on his upper arm. She grimaced. It looked as if a great cat had gashed him with jagged claws from the top of his shoulder to his elbow. His striated muscle quivered as if the blood that ran over it burned. Will inspected the wound. It hurt him to see his friend like this, a man who had saved him, and even more so to be so helpless.

"Can I help?" Will asked.

Isa looked at him for a moment and nodded. "There's some water in my pack. Run and get it, please."

Will got to his feet and dashed into the trees before anything else was said. He walked by the dead monk, the blood drying on his forehead, his graying eyes staring up into the trees. Wounded by the sight of it, Will looked away from the cooling, bloodless face.

He grabbed Isa's pack and carried it back. Del, his eyes dazed and hollow, sat some distance away with his knees brought up to his chest. Isa and Elias talked in hushed tones as Will came to their side.

"Good boy," Isa said. Will looked at the exposed wound. Blood trickled from it but was slowing. "Take the water, give Elias a drink, and run the rest over the wound."

Will passed the waterskin to Elias. He drank the cool draft with sweat beading on his brow. Elias gave him the skin back, and Will ran the cool water over the wound. Elias winced, and Will stopped.

"It's all right," he said. "Keep going."

Will dumped the rest, and the blood drained away in pink rivulets. Elias's ripped muscles pulsed, and Will looked from the jagged wound to Isa. She seemed somewhat hesitant herself. Catching his gaze, she focused back on the wound. She raised her hand, closed her eyes, and breathed deep.

A radiance materialized in the space between her fingers and Elias's arm. It pulled in the light of the failing dusk, illuminating the wound. Will watched the bleeding stop … then the smaller wounds began to close. He turned his fascinated eyes to Elias, who squinted in pain; he looked at Isa, her eyes still closed. By the time he looked back to the wound it was almost healed. And as he watched the last gash close shut, the light faded between Isa's hand and Elias's arm. Both sat back, exhausted.

Will stared at the wound. Without realizing it, he lifted his hand and touched it. Elias hissed and grimaced. Will jerked his hand back.

"It's not healed all the way," Isa said. "It takes very strong Magic to heal deep wounds, and I don't have it in me right now."

"You've done fine, Isa," Elias said. Beads of sweat dripped down his forehead. Del came up behind them and dropped the last of the packs.

"It would be prudent for us to get away from here as soon as possible," he said. Too exhausted, no one turned to him in anger. In fact, no one turned to him at all.

"He's right," Elias said. "We know nothing about their comings and goings here. Help me to my feet, Will."

Will and Isa each provided Elias a hand and, with some struggle, pulled the large man to his feet. He wavered with the swimming in his head and put his large hand on Will's shoulder.

"You did excellent today, Will. I just wasn't quick enough."

Still no glance or word went in Del's direction, but Will could only guess how he felt: helpless, just as he had staring at Elias's wound.

They dragged the packs down to the Mausoleum and rested them beside the door. Dusk faded to night, and the white stone building absorbed what light remained. Del pulled two candles from his pack and looked over the door. He ran his fingers over the seamless stone frame from the top edge, down the side, until he hit a diamond-shaped keyhole. He pulled a key from his cloak and inserted it.

"Where did you get that?" Isa asked.

"I took it from one of the monks when I retrieved the packs," Del said.

"There's no way that will work," Isa said. "Kylan wouldn't let the door to the Mausoleum of Magic be opened by a simple key."

Del turned the key until it clanged and the door swung inward on smooth, noiseless hinges.

He glanced at Isa. "It appears Kylan placed too much confidence in his monks."

Del lifted one of the candles and lit it with a touch of his finger; he lit the second one with the first. They were the same brilliant candles Del had furnished in the arduous tunnel. Their bright light illuminated the frustration on Isa's face. Del couldn't ignore it.

"Lighting a candle is not the same as healing a wound," Del answered her contemptuous gaze. "Even the boy could tell you that."

Del thrust a candle to her and forced the door open. It swung in easily, without a moan, and he peered into impenetrable darkness. Again, Del hesitated.

"Well, if you won't, I will," Isa said, entering first.

Elias looked at Del, and into the gloom. The light shined on Isa's figure and nothing else. The impregnable dark consumed and prevented even the halo of Del's brilliant candle from touching anything but its holder. Elias entered.

Will looked up at Del. "Come on," Will said, following Elias.

Del stared through the opening. He could just see the top half of his traveling companions in the luminous ring. Then the realization hit him.

"Wait!" Del yelled. The three heads floating in the nimbus of light turned as the heavy door slammed shut between them.

Kylan had made it easy to get in, but it would be much more difficult to get out.

27

Rufus rushed to Alphonse's quarters. He knocked twice, and Alphonse permitted his entry.

"You wished to see me, sir?"

"Yes, Rufus. It has been brought to my attention that two monks have gone missing in pursuit of our recent escapees. Kylan has informed me that he wishes to send thirty members each from the City Guard and Royal Guard."

"Thirty members!" Rufus exclaimed, "But, sir, we don't—"

Alphonse put up a hand to stop him. "Kylan's orders are the king's orders." Rufus acquiesced with a nod. "I have selected you to lead the force for the Royal Guard."

Rufus shuffled his feet but maintained his professionalism. "Yes, sir. It will be an honor to carry out the King's orders."

"Good," Alphonse said.

"May I ask our mission, sir?"

"You are to flush them out by burning part of the forest down."

"That's absurd!" Rufus retorted, his professionalism hanging on the point of a hook. "I refuse to—"

Alphonse's powerful hand stopped him again.

"You will do as you are ordered," he said, remaining calm. He stood and came around the table between them. He whispered to Rufus: "If you see them, offer them protection any way you can. Princess Briella wishes them alive. They have avoided and possibly killed two monks; she believes the escapees are very powerful."

Rufus looked at him out of the corner of his eye.

"Silence any opposition if necessary."

Rufus breathed deep. "Yes, sir."

The pair went silent for a moment, each testing the trust in the other.

"Good," Alphonse said. "Now select your men and meet with Yan in the city's square. You leave immediately."

"Yes, sir." Rufus exited the room.

Alphonse had little hope in the mission. But some light was better than none.

28

The wind from the slammed door snuffed out the flame of the candle. Will grabbed for Isa and hugged her midsection, the silhouette of Del outside still flashing in his mind. It was all he could see, whether his eyes were open or not, and it made no difference if they were, because the room was a box of inky darkness, void of light and the use of sight.

No one spoke, but heavy, hyperventilating breaths filled the space. They were stuck, abandoned from the outside world by a slab of stone.

"Will, are you there?" Isa said.

"He's here," Elias replied.

Will realized he was holding Elias's waist. He should have known when he couldn't get his hands all the way around, but his frazzled mind found no room to think about such things. Elias's panicked breath heaved up and down. A floating hand hit Will's head.

"Oh, thank goodness!" Isa said. She kneeled and put her arms around Will.

"Are you all right?" she asked, squeezing him with a terrified hug.

"Yes," Will answered, "but Elias needs help. I think he's in pain."

Isa felt for Elias with blind, shaking hands. "Elias, are you hurt?"

"No," he said. "But the darkness …" He breathed deep to get control, and both felt his body shaking.

"Light the candle," Will suggested.

Isa fumbled in the dark. She slowed her breath and sparks snapped between her fingers and the candle, lighting the terror in their faces with mind-imprinting flashes. Isa tried over and over, but the only light produced were the fiery specks that lit and remained in Will's eyes long after they were gone.

"It's no use," Elias said. "There's not enough light in here. Kylan is too clever for that. Cruel but clever." He breathed in as if pulling his last breath before a long plunge. Will stopped hugging him but he could feel his body quivering in the dark.

Isa scooted past them until Will could hear her put her hands on the stone door. She patted across it, searching for anything that might open it.

"It's solid," she reported. "I can't even feel a crack in the stone." She banged a fist on the door. A flat sound came back. She hit it again and again, but she might as well have been hitting the outer wall of Umbrate. She wondered if Del could hear her.

"Del!" she yelled, the echoes rattling Will and Elias. "Del, can you hear me?! We're stuck!"

No response came through the stone. She turned and crawled her way back to the others.

"It's going to be a long night."

"With no promise of dawn," Elias added.

Del gawked at the solid slab before him, his jaw hanging on loose hinges. Instinct told him to wait, stand there and see if they could open it from the inside. He waited a full minute, then two … then five, and nothing, not even the sound of shouting, rang out from behind the stone door.

He looked down and remembered the key dangling from the diamond keyhole. Gently, he grabbed the bow and closed his eyes before he turned it, waiting for the deep clang of the lock he had heard before. The key turned, and continued to turn, until Del opened his eyes and realized it had made a complete circle. With the flick of his wrist the whole key spun like a well-balanced top on a smooth table before it worked its way backwards and fell to the ground.

Del fell with it, raving. On his knees, he pounded on the door and called out: "Can you open it? Is there a knob on the inside? Can you hear me?"

His voice sounded as puny as his pounding on the solid door.

"Nonononono," he repeated to himself. He searched the door and wall in front of him with numb fingers. Nothing gave way, nothing moved, nothing spoke to him. He turned and looked at the sky. Night reached over the top of the trees and a few stars speckled overhead.

Del stepped away from the door and walked around the building with his fingers and eyes inspecting every inch and finding each one more impenetrable than the last. By the time he circled back to the front, panic and sweat oppressed him like a humid cage.

He put his ear to the door to listen. No voices, no heartbeat, nothing. The sky darkened overhead, but the space around the Mausoleum appeared even darker. Del got on his hands and knees and scoured over the ground to find the candle he had dropped when the door slammed shut. His fingers rolled over it and he picked it up—its flame snuffed. The realization struck him that if his flame was out, then the one on the inside was likely out as well. Any hope he had that Isa or Elias would get them out was doused with oily dread. The hope remained with him, but he found none to call upon.

"Think, think, think," he said to himself. He rubbed his forehead and his hand slicked over the beading sweat. He closed his eyes and breathed deep. There is hope in light, he thought. So he started by lighting his candle.

Though impossible to tell in complete darkness, Will was sure a whole day had gone by. He fell asleep at one point, only to awake again in the absence of light with the promise of a new day snuffed. They spoke little, but Elias's heavy breathing continued endlessly. Isa and Will tried to calm him any way they could, but the wizard would only reply that he was fine as his whole body shook in a fit. Will thought it might have been his wounds that were hurting him, but soon discovered it was the fathomless gloom.

Good Magic needed light, Will had remembered Isa saying that to him. And the traveling wizard had probably never seen such darkness before—none of them had. It took a truly evil sorcerer to create such a place of never-ending night, to let invaders die of insanity in the absence of light. Will had always wondered what it was like inside the Reformatory of Magic; now he believed he knew, and he could feel the deeper depravity of it hearing a great and powerful wizard like Elias shake and hyperventilate like a child jolted by a fear of the dark.

"Does anyone have water?" Elias asked. His voice rose out of the gloom like a specter, so close that it stunned Will.

They didn't have any water, or food, or light, and that had been settled some hours ago, but Elias continued to ask in his delirium. They all sat within an arm's length of each other, and Isa never took her hand off Will, and Will guessed she never took her hand off Elias either.

The first few hours they had tried to find something, anything to help, but now they didn't venture from their little circle by the door for fear of finding more Dark Magic, but as far as Will could tell, the Mausoleum appeared empty. He had envisioned a huge hall full of books and staffs and cauldrons and all sorts of things he had learned were the instruments of the Great Evil of Mass, but even when he reached around him, he felt mostly open space besides some small bookshelves.

"Do you remember much of the old days, Elias?" Isa's sweet voice echoed in the hall. Elias's laborious breath continued. "I know it's been a long time, but I often sit and think of them."

No reply came back, just quick, strained breaths.

"It was green and bright then, Will," Isa continued. "There was food enough for all, and people were free to roam as they pleased, and work as they pleased, and live as they pleased. Del and I lived in the forest. It was called the Verdant Forest back then, none of this Grim Forest nonsense," Isa soliloquized. "Children used to play in the streets of Umbrate, unabated and unafraid. Bale's father, Abiri, was king, and all life basked in the satisfaction of existence."

Elias's breath began to slow.

"All were healthy and clothed, and the people gifted with Magic cohabitated with the common people like butter and honey. There was little hate in that time, for there was enough for all that wished to work for it. We needed the common people as much as they needed us. Elias traveled all over Mass, and the people in small, thriving communities would greet him with such cheer."

Elias's breath slowed even further.

"Del was a master healer, and he would travel far and wide to heal anyone—from a child with a splinter, or to ease the passing of an old woman. And folks would bring their sick animals to me, or have me give life to their wilted crops. How pleasant it is watching a living thing thrive the way it is intended to, with enough food and light. You may have never seen it, Will, but it's like nothing you could ever imagine."

Elias's breath eased to that of a sleeping man. Isa stopped and let it continue. The sound comforted them after the long hours of panicked respiration.

"How are you, Will?" Isa whispered.

At first he didn't answer, then he said: "I've lived my whole life in darkness."

"Then you must be handling this quite well." He couldn't see her, but he knew she smiled at him as she fumbled to caress his cheek and smooth his hair. "One day the light will shine again. I can assure you of that. And Mass will be glorious once more."

"Del really was a great wizard, then?" Will asked after a while.

"Very much so," Isa replied.

They stopped talking for some time. Elias's breathing remained calm, and things didn't feel so bad in that moment.

"Do you think Del can get us out?" Will asked.

"Magic is as much in the heart as it is in the head once you awaken, or, in Del's case, reawaken what's inside of you," Isa said. "Del's Magic has been asleep a long time."

Will found little comfort in her words, but he knew the truth of them.

"If he can, he will get us out … especially you." Isa scooted to Will's side and hugged him close. "He may not be able to show it very well, but he loves you, Will."

Will laid his head against Isa's chest and listened to Elias's tranquil breath.

◊

Night came and went, and now day returned to night. Del had taken the packs into the trees to hide while he thought. He anticipated someone, anyone, to come along, if only to relieve the guards, but he remained alone with his thoughts and the accompanying guilt.

He had spent much of the night inspecting the Mausoleum only to find his own insanity. The building was seamless, without fault; not a crack to let in light, or stitch to pry open. The sun began its downward turn, and Del began to look more at the pile of packs than at the crypt his friends were dying in.

It would be easy to leave. No one would even suspect that he had been there. And, eventually, someone would arrive and find three bodies inside. Del shuddered at how effortlessly the thought came.

No need to shudder, they're already dead, his mind rationalized. The thought comforted Del, and he hated himself further for it. But if a powerful wizard like Elias can't get them out, how can I? he asked.

They have no light, a voice answered. He peered into the small clearing below and took a sip of water he'd taken from Isa's pack; he despised himself for quenching his thirst while his friends remained parched, while Will remained parched. He pulled the waterskin from his lips and looked down at it with distaste.

Curiously, he looked in the trees around him. The light in the trees, even under the dense canopy appeared brighter than the light in the clearing. He stood and moved closer to the edge of the opening to see it was true, as if a magical dome like Isa had around her home to let the light in prevented the light from reaching the Mausoleum. It was Dark Magic.

Del stroked his chin as he paced a path between the trees. Dark Magic always intended to inflict pain, and it required a conviction to break the natural order, and the sacrifice of one's own being or the soul of another. It was power beyond all belief if one committed themselves to it. It hated light, for light showed all the gruesome cracks in its faith. The Great Evil was released by Dark Magic, and it was forced to the bottom of Mirror Pool to ever be under the barrier of Light Magic as the sun and moon wrapped their endless courses over it.

Light! Del thought. The true weakness of Dark Magic. He rushed down to the Mausoleum. The large door remained sealed, stalwart, and scornful. He channeled what Magic he could muster. It was there, as it once had been. He closed his eyes and lifted his hands. Breath after breath rolled through him and, when he was ready, he thrust his hands forward. A small burst of light hit the door. Del watched, but nothing happened.

He closed his eyes and tried again. A larger, brighter burst hit the door and thrust him back. But the Mausoleum remained sealed. Another burst and the building appeared to become stronger. Del's head grew light and he backed away from the door and fell onto his rear.

Light wasn't the answer. Del gathered himself and checked the door and found it locked with arrogant pride.

What weakens Magic? he thought. He looked around him and remembered the dead monks.

"The blood of dead magic," he said out loud.

He turned and ran up the hill toward the dead monks. He approached the first one, slowly, his hair rising as he did so. The body laid face down. Del kneeled beside it and rolled it over. Dead eyes stared back at him and his stomach rolled looking into their emptiness. Avoiding the inanimate stare, Del pulled up the sleeve of the monk's cloak and exposed a cold, pale arm.

He looked around and picked up a rock with a sharp edge. Sucking in one last breath, he sliced through the rubbery skin with the edge of the rock and squeezed above the wound. A blood-like liquid plopped out of the veins. Without thinking, Del put his hand under the coagulated ooze that leaked out. It filled the palm of his hand, and he turned and made his way to the Mausoleum door. When he reached it, he rubbed the blood around the keyhole. He waited a moment and leaned against the door. It didn't budge. He pushed harder. Nothing.

Del looked down at the blood on his hand. Why wasn't it affecting him? He had seen many magical people brought to their knees by the horrible cuffs made from silver and cursed with the blood of dead magic, but why wasn't he feeling the effects of it?

He still gripped the rock he used to cut the dead monk. His eyes shifted from the rock to the bloody palm, and back again.

"Dark Magic requires sacrifice, and as much to undo it," he said to himself.

Without hesitation, Del put the sharp rock to his wrist and sliced through the skin. The blood fell in dizzying drops, but he stood, with his life flowing out, and smeared his blood all over the door, from top to bottom. Once finished, he gripped his wrist to slow the bleeding. If he was wrong, he was dead.

Staring hard at the door, he put his shoulder to it and fell into the Mausoleum of Magic.

29

Will and Isa scrambled toward the light as Elias woke and sucked in the fresh air with desperate relief. Del lay prone on the floor, unmoving. Will rolled him onto his side with the help of Isa and they stared with terror at the fresh blood smeared over his front. Even the dull light of dusk blinded them after being in the dark so long, but they squinted over Del's body to find the source.

"He sacrificed part of himself," Isa said with awe. She put her hand to the wound and held it tight. She turned to Will and said: "Let's get him into the light," her voice urgent but calm. Will grabbed Del's leg and began to pull with Isa. They struggled with the weight until Elias came and moved him by himself. The great wizard looked exhausted, as if he'd ran from Sentinel's Village to Umbrate in one day, and he rested beside Del, soaking up what light and air he could. He put his hand on Del's chest.

"His heart beats, but weakly."

Judging by the spilled blood, Isa understood the need for urgency, but her hands were trembling and her mind frail. She hovered her fingers over Del's wound. Light sparked from her fingertips but didn't strike. She breathed deep and tried again. A weak beam formed, and held, but it wavered. Will watched with dancing anticipation, eager to help but with no idea what to do.

"Come on, Del," Will whispered. Tears fell from his eyes and landed on Del's chest.

Blood still trickled from the wound and it closed much slower than Elias's had. Isa's hand shook and the light began to spark. Elias breathed deep, reached over, and wrapped his large hand over Isa's. The light enhanced and the wound stopped bleeding.

"It's working!" Will elated, his tears streaming onto Del's chest.

Their locked hands shook and sweat formed on their pale brows, but the light remained steady. With a last moment of effort, Isa and Elias's shaking hands sealed the wound. Both fell away in exhaustion.

"You did it!" Will yelled. "You've saved him."

Del didn't move. Isa rolled over and put her hand on his chest. "He's alive, but he's not saved yet." Will looked at Del intently. Isa laid back by Elias.

"You saved us, Del," Will whispered. "It was so dark in there, and you saved us."

Del's eyes flickered for a moment and he put his hand on Will's leg. Will looked into his subdued face with relief. He leaned over and hugged him.

"Del! Are you all right? Can I help you?" The eagerness in his voice raced ahead.

"Water," Del whispered.

Will looked around. "Where are the packs?" he asked. Del pointed up the hill. Without hesitation, Will jumped to his feet and raced away with sore and cramped knees from sitting so long. He stumbled upon the packs and dragged them back down faster than he went up. Rummaging through them, he found a waterskin and some bits of dried biscuit and bread. The water and food tempted his dry throat and empty stomach, but he resisted the urge to drink before the others.

He lifted Del's head with his small, tired arm and tilted the water to his lips. The first sips cooled his aching throat, and life reappeared in his cheeks.

Del dropped his head. "For the others," he said, nodding to Isa and Elias.

Will took the water to Isa and put it to her lips. Life revived in her and she sat upright.

"You first," Elias said.

Will could see he wouldn't drink until he did, so he tipped the waterskin back and let the cool rush smooth his parched throat. He wanted more but only drank enough to satisfy Elias. Will passed the waterskin and the large wizard took his portion. Will took the rest and tipped it to Del's lips. Isa and Elias sat upright and rested their backs against the cold stone of the Mausoleum.

Del's eyes flickered with life. "Help me sit up." The boy wrestled him to the wall and Del smiled at him. "You're a good boy, Will." Will smiled back.

"The light is stronger in the trees," Del said. "There's Dark Magic over this crypt."

Isa got to her feet with the help of Will. "It's almost dark," she said. "We should get away from this evil place."

They all agreed. Elias struggled to his feet and came to Del's side.

"Can you rise?" he asked.

Del looked up at him. "I need more time."

Elias nodded and turned to Will. "See if you can find water." Isa and Elias leaned on each other as they made the arduous journey up to the trees, away from the dreadful Mausoleum.

Will gathered the waterskins and started off in search of water when Del stopped him.

"I'm sorry it took me so long," he said, just above a whisper.

Will kneeled beside him. "You got us out, Del. That's all that matters." Will turned to leave and Del grabbed his arm.

"I-I," he put his head down in shame. "I wanted to leave you," he confessed. "I wanted to leave you in the tomb … and I wanted to leave you in Umbrate. I was scared, Will … nothing but a small coward."

The words did not shock Will. He put his hand on Del's and looked into the eyes of the man who had taken care of him for so long. "But you didn't leave me, and you didn't leave us," Will said. "And you've been the one that has sacrificed the most." Will touched Del's wrist, where the old wizard had spilled his life-giving blood to save them.

Del looked at the young boy, no more than a child, with sad admiration. They shared a teary-eyed moment before Will left in search of water.

Del cried alone with what energy he had left, satisfied with what Will had become.

◊

Will discovered a spring down the hill from the Mausoleum. After his scare with the malicious illusion of the woman, he waited, watching the tempting water flow from the ground. Once he deemed it safe, he approached and dipped his hands and mouth and face in its freshness. He filled the waterskins and returned to find Elias and Isa carrying Del up the hill.

They put him down in the last light of the sun and shared the water in silence. Night lay ahead, but at least the dull light of the moon would be accompanying it. Will hated to blink for it reminded him of the cruel darkness of the crypt. It stared up at them, its door open and taunting.

They ate what crumbs of food they had left and laid back to rest. The defeated four stared down at the Mausoleum. It mocked them, and its derisive words reminded them of the evil powers in the world.

"Let us sleep," Del said, tearing the mocking words in half. "If it's still open in the morning, we'll take what's ours and leave."

None of them spoke of the horror of the dark, and none of them needed to; it was wrapped tight to their hearts like a black growth that hindered the beating.

Will relaxed onto the grassy turf below the sparkling sky, and he counted what stars he could before his heavy lids closed and he fell asleep.

◊

The sun pushed the moon away for the sake of dawn and woke Will; it was his to bask under again. His rested bones ached with their first movements. He looked down at the Mausoleum, its door still wide open, but the promise of morning light quieted its jeering. A noise startled Will to his left. Isa was gathering all the waterskins they had drained the night before. Del and Elias both slept with slow breaths lifting and dropping their chests. Isa gestured for Will to join her, and he got up and led her down the hill to where he found water.

They drank to their heart's desire and filled the vessels one by one from the vitalizing liquid that flowed out of the earth. Once finished, they rested back and watched the sun rise over the trees. Isa closed her eyes and soaked up its power like a cat on a porch ledge. Will could see her color return, and she appeared to grow younger the longer she turned her face to its invigorating rays. After some time, she opened her eyes and turned to the boy watching her.

"It's a powerful thing, the sun, the light," she said. Her face turned down. "I thought we were never going to get out of there, Will." He said nothing. She gazed at him and smiled affectionately. "You're a very brave young man. I'm proud to call you my nephew." Will smiled back at her. "Something tells me this journey is just beginning," she said, facing the sun again, "and we'll need much more of your bravery."

"And yours, and Elias's, and Del's," Will reminded her.

"That's very kind of you, Will. But if we had more bravery when it counted we wouldn't be stealing our books and lives back from the same evil we handed it to." Will thought over her words as the sun glinted off the trickling water. "Cowards took our lives, but what were we to let them," Isa said. She turned to him; her age returned to the wrinkles and cracks of her face. "It will hurt to enter the Mausoleum today, but it's what we are forced to do to denounce our recreance. Things will only get more difficult from here, I'm afraid. But when we were in that darkness, I could see the light again, I could remember for the first time in a long time what life used to be like. And I want it back, Will. Not for myself—I've had my chance—but for those to come." She took a moment to remember something Will couldn't perceive. "Hiding in fear is no way to live, and I've consented to living that way for near on a hundred years. I didn't believe Del, a mere candlemaker, would get us out yesterday, but he found something deep within himself, something that a scratch on the surface could never reveal, and it gave me the courage to do the same."

She basked a moment longer, reluctant to leave.

"Yes, that's what I want: a life of freedom, a life with more heart, more light to illuminate evil."

Isa picked herself up and looked at Will intently.

"What do you say we go fight for it?"

Will nodded, gathered the water containers, and followed her back to Del and Elias.

Both men were awake when they arrived, and both appeared in higher spirits, though Del's age and Elias's fragility showed under the morning's revealing brilliance.

They thanked Will and Isa and drank their fill of the cool spring water. All stared down at the Mausoleum, the symbol of their individual pains. Not one of them desired to enter it, and if one had suggested leaving without doing so, the rest would have followed without a word. But none suggested it, and as soon as the sun reached a safe height, they gathered their things and went into the shadowed clearing to claim what they came for, what was theirs.

The bloody door swung inward toward the unassailable darkness. Its greed for light swallowed all that tried to penetrate before it reached beyond the door's arc.

Del pulled his blue candle from his pack and lit it. Isa pulled the one the door had snuffed from her pocket and Del lit it for her. He stepped forward.

"Wait," Will said. Del stopped. "Won't it close again?"

Del considered the door a moment. "I don't think so, or it would have closed overnight." The ones that had been trapped inside peered into the darkness; trepidation trudged over their faces. "I'll go first," Del suggested. "If it closes on me, you know what to do."

No comfort was found in his reasoning, but Del strode forward, holding the candle as steady as his hand allowed. He leaned against the door to allow more sunlight in and peered into the gloom. He could see shapes that looked like bookcases and shelves with various items on them, but his eyes could not distinguish anything. He turned to see silhouettes of his three traveling companions staring back at him.

"It appears safe," Del said. None stepped forward.

"I'll stay out," Elias offered; panic dense on his face.

Isa put her hand on his shoulder. "Come, Elias. Together."

Elias looked at her, then around the Mausoleum. He walked some distance into the trees and picked up a rock the size of a large dog curled in sleep. He placed it between the door and the jamb.

"Now I'll go in," he said. And he did.

Will grabbed Isa's hand and they entered together. Watching, Del waited just a moment for the door to slam shut and break the rock into sand, but the door remained open, and the frail light trickled in and faded against the darkness, like a mist against a flame.

Del turned to the books. There were three large shelves, though not very large indeed considering they held the last of all things believed to be magical in the Kingdom of Mass. Del held his light over the spines. Most were worthless books with little or no Magic in them, just words that were suspicious to senseless fools. *Plant Apothecary, A Guide to Crop Rotation, Rudolph's Apiarian Insight.* Del scoffed at some of the titles that were burned to ash and the final copies placed in a deathtrap. He landed on one that interested him: *The Essential Chandler's Handbook.* He flipped through the ancient pages with a small smile on his face. He would keep this one.

By the time he had scanned all of the first shelf, and found mostly duds, Isa exclaimed: "Oh, I've missed this book." Del turned to see her flipping through a copy of *Flora and Fauna: A Husbandry Guide.* He grinned at her elation. She hugged it snug to her chest and continued to search.

Though the collection was small in context to its ancient content, it was the most books Will had ever seen. In fact, the only books he had ever read were the tome of *Mass and Umbrate History* (which mostly his instructors read *to* him), *The Heroes of Mass,* and *The Lineage of King Bale.* It was a glory of knowledge for Will to witness, and his small eyes took it in with curious glances. He had no clue there were this many books in Mass at all, total, and certainly not this many condensed into one place.

Some of the shelves were bare of books but lined instead with items that appeared to be nothing more than trinkets to Will. Elias picked up what looked like an iron ball, small enough that his fingers could completely wrap around it. He rolled it through his hand and smiled.

"What is it?" Will asked.

"It's an illumine." Elias marveled at it. "It can create days of light, or a great burst all at once." He tossed it into the air and caught it. "If only we had known this was here, then things wouldn't have been so dark." He passed it to Will, who weighed it in his hands.

"Wouldn't it need light to create light?" he asked. "Since it's magical, I mean."

"No," Elias said. "It was created by Magic but it's not magical. Even you could use it if you wanted to."

"How?"

"Ask Del, he invented it," Elias said. Will peered at the clandestine chandler, who scoured the shelves with fervor.

Del fingered through the volumes, his hope of finding what they needed waning. His light passed over three volumes with nothing written on their tattered spines. They didn't look like the rest of the books in the place: nice and neat, and without dust from being locked in the airtight tomb so long. No, their spines were worn, and the oil of hands from use attracted dust and dirt to them. He slid the first one out: *Dark Magic* by Xenerac Torvio.

"Yes," Del said to himself. He pulled out the second one: *Magic of Light* updated by Xenerac Torvio. He balanced the books and snagged the third one: *Writings* of Xenerac Torvio.

"Will, be a good boy and get our packs for us. We have a lot of books to carry."

Will nodded and turned to get the packs. He kneeled beside them and looked down at the illumine in his hand. Iridescence danced over it in the sunlight. The ball was smooth, but Will could see markings under the sheen. Its beauty gathered all his attention and Will became lost in it.

"Will, are you coming?" Del called from the inside.

Will jumped at the sound of his voice. He stuffed the illumine into his own pack and dragged the rest of them into the Mausoleum.

Their packs were weighed down with magical books and items, and they had them cinched and ready to go when Isa asked: "What do we do about the dead monks and the Mausoleum door?"

The monks still laid where they had fallen and the door was smeared with Del's browning blood. It made them sick to look at it.

"Leave them," Elias offered. "We have what we need and we must be moving."

"But they're already hunting us," Isa replied. "Isn't it better they think we're running scared and stupid? Not educated and plotting?"

Del thought a moment. He looked at Will.

"What if we put the bodies in the Mausoleum?" Will suggested. "Then we'll clean the door and close it."

"Yes," Del said, stroking his chin. "They'll think the curious monks tried to get in. Maybe they'll even think they were mutinous. It would be something Kylan would try to cover rather than announce to his people. Plus, it will look like the monks killed each other."

"What about the things we've taken," Elias asked.

"I doubt they'll notice a few books and baubles," Del said. "We should try to offer ourselves the greatest benefit we can."

"It, at the very least, would afford us more time," Isa said.

Elias was unenthused (he wished to be away from this place more than any of the others), but the logic helped. He dropped his pack. "Fine, but I won't carry these bodies alone."

"I'll help," Del said. "You two gather more water and rub down the door."

They went their separate ways and completed the gruesome task of dragging the corpses into the Mausoleum and cleaning the door. After a short while the job was complete, and all felt rather unclean for having completed it, but it was done, and the Mausoleum of Magic sat as if nothing had ever molested it. Del managed to get the door closed, and it locked itself. He took the diamond shaped key from his pocket and place it in the keyhole.

"Why are you doing that?" Will asked.

"They'll think the monks tried to get in with their key, just as we did when the door slammed shut," Del explained, putting on his pack.

"We must get out of here," Elias said. "The day is waning and we have been here far too long." His traveling companions shared his eagerness to leave. They lifted their heavy loads and left the shadowy hollow of the Mausoleum of Magic, though all of them left something behind that would never be regained.

30

The long day turned into a long night with their yearning to put as much distance between them and the crypt as possible. They stopped sometime and somewhere near midnight to rest. Each dropped their packs from their strained backs and found the softest place they could to rest their heads.

From his sleeping position, Will watched Del dig through his pack and pull out his books. He rubbed the covers and glided through the pages as if caressing an old lover. Sleep crept further away from Will the longer he laid there and watched. After some time, awake and thinking, he grabbed the illumine from his pack and brought it to Del. The old wizard seemed to not notice his presence as he pored over the scribbled handwriting Will could not make out.

"What book is that?"

"A very old one," Del said privately. Dejection turned Will's face, and Del turned guilty with it. "It's Xenerac's Writings," Del said, his apology hidden in the quick retort.

"Was that a famous book?" Will asked.

"No, not at all, my boy," Del said, staring at it with fascination as it rested in tender hands. "In fact, I believe it's the only copy ever written."

Will leaned over and tried to read the words but couldn't. He blamed the failing light and the scratched handwriting, but he knew it was likely his education that prevented him from deciphering the words. He gave Del a few turned pages before he pulled out the illumine and presented it like a jewel. A gentle smile peeled across Del's lips.

"And where did you find that?" he asked, taking it as gently as Will held it.

"Elias found it … he said you invented it," Will replied.

Del looked over the illumine at Will. "I suppose I've always been a candlemaker of some sort." He smiled and Will smiled back.

"He said it can provide light for days or a bright burst of light in an instant," Will said.

"I'm sure it could have once," Del said. "But magic fades like the flavor in a wrinkled apple."

"How do you make it work?"

Del turned it so the moon reflected off the iridescent runes. "You must think of the light you need very deeply, then read the runes written on it." He handed it back to Will and returned to his book. Will looked down at the ball as if searching for something inside of it.

"What do the runes say?"

Del opened his mouth to answer, but stopped short. He closed his mouth and knitted his brow together. "For the life of me, I can't remember." He motioned toward the book. "Like most of our history, it's dead and gone. That's why we must read." He returned to his book without another thought. "It likely doesn't work anymore anyway."

Will looked at the illumine like some sort of dejected toy, his face screwed into a frown. "What would a person do with a burst of light?" he asked after a moment.

Del glanced at the boy. "A good magician would know what to do with it." Will looked deeply into the curious illumine. He guessed he had held many magical things in his time living with Del, but this was the only one he was sure about, and its strangeness captured him.

"Go get some sleep, Will. We have much traveling ahead."

Will scooted back to his makeshift bed and placed his head on his pack. He held the illumine in his hand and thought of light until his eyes closed and he fell asleep.

Del roused Will when morning began to lift the tint of night. He looked overhead. The sky was hazier than he remembered, and when he sat upright the ponderous smell of smoke drifted to him. Urgency rushed his traveling companions.

Del shook him. "Come on, Will. Up, UP!"

Will dropped the illumine his hand had gripped all night into his pack and hefted the thing over his shoulders as soon as the ball hit the bottom. He looked to Elias and Isa, both wearing mournful faces.

"What's wrong?" Will asked anyone who would answer. "Is the fire close?"

Elias answered: "It's on the other side of the King's Carve," he paused and looked at Isa. "But it's big." Isa looked away and wiped her face.

"We have to go," Del said.

They ventured swiftly from their camping place to the edge of the forest with Del and Elias leading them. Isa ran behind, unblinking and blank faced. Will trudged beside her, step by step.

They crossed a veil of smoke and the sun darkened overhead. The older travelers covered their mouths and noses with whatever cloth they could find. Will followed their suit and pulled a loose patch of cloak over his nose. His eyes burned the more they strayed into the smoke, and when he was about to ask why they were heading toward the fire, they emerged from the trees. The King's Carve stretched between them and the rolling blaze, a half-league of planed ground that gave way to a wall of flame. Judging by the size of the fire, if the King's Carve hadn't cleaved the forest they would have been consumed in their sleep.

They stared across at the thick, black, column rising to blanket the sun, now nothing more than a small candle in a dark room, a room as dark as the Mausoleum and much more destructive. They stared into the ring of light without its intensity forcing their gaze away.

Not a pair of their eyes were dry, and not because of the smoke. The forest was being burned down; its life and the life within it rose in the smog and dropped in floating ashes, indistinguishable from the tree or plant or animal that burned next to it.

Will looked at Isa. Her hand covered her open mouth, but she made no sound. Del stood in complete shock with his hands pulling at the hair on his head. Elias cried without shame.

Will ran to Del. "Do something! Can't you do something?!"

"It's too far gone," Del said.

"But Isa's home, the forest? Can't anything be done?"

Before Will could answer, men and women of the Guard emerged from the veil of smoke some distance ahead of them. Del grabbed Will and pulled him back into the tree line. Elias and Isa followed close behind.

"Guards!" Elias said. They peered through the waves of smoke and saw more emerge from the leaden cloud. Once clear of the smoke, the fleeing guards turned and watched the blaze—some bewildered while others ogled as if watching a grand show.

"This was intentional," Elias said. "We must attack them." His tears faded to throbbing anger.

Del stopped him. "No, we have to get out of here. Killing them won't change anything."

"Del's right," Isa said. Her blank and glassy eyes shined in the mottled light that dropped through the smoke. "We must leave. We're much too late."

Isa's words were quiet but final, and Elias acquiesced. They watched the fire a little longer as more guards materialized from the incessant flame and turned to gawk at its glory.

"Come," Elias said. "I know a place on this side of the forest, near the mountains, where we can hide." He turned first, then Del.

Will watched Isa stare, and for a moment he thought she was going to walk into the blaze, but she turned away and beckoned Will.

"We've already lost this fight, Will," Isa said, following Elias and Del.

Will came up beside her. He had seen his life taken from him at such a young age, and he extended his empathy to Isa with the touch of his hand. It was useless agony that *they* chose to inflict upon them for their own gain. Isa slogged on, and Will caught her whispering words.

"We've already lost this fight, but we will not lose the next." Her face turned and her teeth gritted, and she shed no more tears as they pushed toward the mountains on the edge of the forest.

◊

By dusk, they stopped in a clearing far north of the fire; their path ceaseless since they left the hungry conflagration. It lifted high above the trees to the south, its pillar to the sky lessening in width and intensity as the wind and sun dwindled for night.

They sat, drank, and ate what little they had without speaking. The smell of smoke lingered as if they had bathed in it, its memory not soon to leave them. After some time, Elias left them to patrol the forest and find water. Del, Isa, and Will said nothing, and all looked between their tired legs with no words to comfort the others. The dreary journey appeared to have no end, as all do in the moment.

Elias returned with swollen waterskins and an armful of watercress. He divvied it up between them and they resumed their silence, ruminating over their lonely thoughts and the leafy green food.

The water cooled Will, and he rubbed a palmful over his face to rid his skin of the smoky smell and the greasy soot. Dirt came off but the soot did not, and neither did the dense odor. His frustration grew at the tightness and stickiness of his clothes. He hated the dense miasma, but he wanted it to linger, he wanted the reminder to be there and to be angering, not to become a smell he tolerated or forgot about all together. The people of Umbrate, his home, had gotten used to the absolutist smell in their fearful surrender, but Will wanted its nagging memory as much as he wished to be rid of it.

"Why did they burn it down?" Will asked, unable to contain his frustrations any longer.

"Why is correct," Del said, looking around the group for an answer.

"Because the monks they sent to kill you never returned," Elias said.

"That's preposterous," Del retorted. "Why would they destroy all that wood and kill their game for an old man and a boy?"

"It's a small price to pay to erase a slight against their rule," Elias replied. "If their monks didn't return, that means they met something stronger than them, stronger than the crown. Kylan wouldn't suffer you getting away. He loves his power too much. He has nothing else."

"But to burn down the forest? It's ridiculous!" Del added.

"Not to them," Isa said. "Not to ones that only care about themselves, their power." She ran her hands over the grainy dirt. "A small price, indeed. They'll just pass it onto the cold and hungry, as they always have."

"At least now they'll think we're dead," Del said.

"We can only hope," Isa said, letting the soil fall between her fingers. "Or they'll continue to burn and burn and burn until there are no trees to shade the scorched earth, no animals to crop the grass, no birds to send songs and letters through the sky, and no homes for old witches to live in."

Del stared at the heavy pain sagging her face. He had willingly given up his home, but Isa had not. "I'm sorry, Isa. I shouldn't have said anything of the sort."

"It's not you, Del, it's the world we live in, the world we watched decay from a distance until it eroded our own doorstep. It's just as much my fault as anyone else's. I sat under my false shade, safe and fed, as others burned under a repressive flame. Today it came for me, as it already came for you. Now we're defeated and powerless, homeless and tired, just as they want us."

It pained them to look anywhere but down, and for a few moments all of the forest listened in, waiting for them to move.

"But at least we're homeless and tired together," Isa added. All breathed again and found the courage to look up from their navel-gazing.

"Where are we going?" Will asked after finishing his watercress.

"A cave where the forest meets the Glass Mountains," Elias said.

"The Glass Mountains?" Will said, his curiosity heightened. When the others gathered books of Magic in the Mausoleum, he took one of his own: *Tales of the Glass Mountains.* They fascinated him. His world was growing faster than he could map it. "But won't that take us by Mirror Pool and Sentinel's Village? Won't we get caught if we go that way?"

"No," Elias replied. "Mirror Pool and Sentinel's Village lie in a bowl shaped by the mountains and the border of the forest. We'll be much deeper in."

Will had only heard of the Glass Mountains, and it was rumored that they could be seen as a wavy blue line on the horizon from the top of Kylan's tower. Will doubted any person that ever told him that considering that none of the common people had ever been in Kylan's tower, but to the boy, like most things in his life, the mountains were once just a myth. Now, in the distance, he could see the wavy blue line of peaks, and they headed that way.

"But will we be safe there?" Del asked.

"Only traveling wizards know of it," Elias explained. "It's a protected place."

"So was Isa's home," Del said. He looked at Isa with apologetic eyes, she accepted the truth by turning to Elias for an answer.

"It's as good a place as I can offer," Elias said. Will watched him speak in his calm, taciturn way, but doubt resided there; Will couldn't blame him for that. "It will fit our needs."

"And what exactly are our needs now?" Del asked. It was a fair question that received no more blame than Elias's doubt.

"We need time, and we need rest," Elias said. "We have much to learn and much to remember. It's a two-day journey from here." Elias rolled to his side and placed his head on his pack.

They accepted the answer with confidence in Elias and with nothing better to offer. While Will's world expanded, the size of the world as a whole decreased with each move, and soon nothing would remain but scorched earth and darkened sunlight—a good wizard's nightmare.

Without saying goodnight, each rolled over on the gritty, hard earth and fell asleep, or at least pretended to with the smell of smoke lingering.

31

Rufus walked amongst the soot and floating ash and half-burned trees. His footprints left a white trail behind him where an impossible dark cloud hovered over each step. The fire had burned much hotter and hungrier than they could have imagined.

The black dust clung to the colors of his Royal Guard clothing, but he felt it was right considering the dirty task he had completed for reasons that still evaded him. Thirty members of the Royal Guard and thirty from the City Guard walked abreast from where the inexorable rage started to where it died of hunger at the edge of the King's Carve. The hot ground burning through his boots felt like easy penance for destroying so much—fifteen-thousand acres or more by Rufus's best guess; fifteen-thousand acres of fine wood and animals to eat, all for a boy and a geriatric candlemaker.

They had passed the ruins of some sort of cabin some ways back, but it was nothing more than a foundation and an old stove left over from a time gone by. There was no sign of life there. Not that it mattered, Rufus thought, because all signs of life had been burned away.

Looking to his left and to his right, he saw a line of guards kicking up a cloud of fine, throat-irritating dust like a traveling caravan a mile wide. Rufus wished to sigh, but the sticky air prevented him from doing so. He sucked in and coughed a dry, raspy note.

"I've found something," a guard yelled to his right.

Rufus ran over to the man digging through charred brush. The other soldiers started to follow him.

"Stay in formation!" Rufus yelled. The guards fell back in line reluctantly.

Rufus wanted to see for himself first. Alphonse had tasked him with burning down the forest and with saving the people the fire was meant to flush out. Completion of one and failure of the other was failure all around.

Rufus met the rummaging guard the same time as Yan. A cloud of soot lifted in the wake of each man's trail, promising to never come down as it caught the gentle breeze.

The man digging through the bits of burnt wood and ash revealed his find. Yan looked over it and smiled, his teeth white and alarming across his filthy face. Rufus looked closer and saw what appeared to be the remains of two carcasses stacked on top of each other.

Yan, without scruple, reached in and cleared the rest of the debris from the skeletons. His smile grew wider.

"I bet they were staying in that shack back there when we woke them with our little bonfire," Yan said. His steely smile turned into a fixed rictus as he rubbed his fingers over one of the smooth skulls. "Looks like you should have stayed in Umbrate," he said to it, his face holding its discomforting cheer. "Good, now we can return home and do the job we were trained to do."

"Sir," the guard said timidly. Yan dropped his smile and turned to the guard as if he had committed an insolent act by addressing him.

"What is it?"

"Well, sir," he began with a faint heart, "I thought we were looking for a man and a boy."

"Yes, and …"

"It's just that …"

"Go on," Yan prodded.

"It's just that these appear to be the skeletons of two men about the same size," the guard said, shrinking away. Rufus looked down and realized the guard's doubt.

Yan leaned down and dug through the bones and ash with more scrutiny. Rufus leaned down as well. They had been cremated in the intense heat, and besides the skulls they were just a pile of bones, indistinct from each other.

If Kylan had told Alphonse that two monks had gone missing in these woods then Yan would know as well. Yan had been eager to go back to Umbrate since their journey began, that much Rufus knew. He looked at Yan and seized his moment to allay the man's suspicion.

"I met the boy some days before they fled," Rufus lied. "He wasn't much smaller than the chandler, and the chandler was a stooped old man. These must be their bodies." He put his hands on the bones with an internal grimace and pushed them around. "Some of the bones appear smaller to me. Yan?"

Yan looked through them again, this time less willing to touch them. Rufus tensed at his prolonged thought.

"Yes," Yan said after a few moments. "I believe Rufus is correct." He stood and wiped his hands on his filthy cloak, leaving dark finger streaks fading down the side. "We will finish our scour to the road, and then we will return to Umbrate with the news that our escapees are dead and the job complete."

Yan moved out in front of the guards and yelled: "Continue on!"

The force, including the soldier that found the charred bones, commenced their march across the blackened remains of the forest. Yan waited until the guards were some distance away before he asked: "Do you really believe it's them?"

Rufus didn't, but he kneeled and looked them over again. It was a mess of bones, mostly broken from where a tree had fallen over them in the fire. Rufus couldn't distinguish which went to which skull.

"They are too broken and burned to tell for sure, but they have to be the boy and the chandler," Rufus said.

Yan nodded, but not convincingly. "How much did Alphonse tell you about this mission?"

Rufus shrugged. "Very little. He simply ordered that I take thirty members of the Royal Guard and join your force to burn down a portion of the Grim Forest to flush out some escapees."

"He told you no more?"

Rufus shook his head.

"Don't you think it's strange that Kylan had us go through all this trouble for a boy and an old man?"

"Alphonse said the old man was believed to be magical." Rufus laughed and kicked the remains with outside glee and internal strife. "It didn't help him much if he was."

Yan looked down at them and scoffed himself.

"Last I remember I'm a part of the Royal Guard and you're a part of the City Guard," Rufus said. "Let's get back home to where we belong. It was a fool's mission to begin with. There's no way those two could have survived long out here. If it hadn't been our fire, it would have been something else, magical or not." Rufus slapped Yan on the shoulder and a cloud of ash sprung up. Yan nodded and looked down at the remains.

"Yes, you are correct. They had no chance anyway. Let's get on with it."

Rufus didn't know if he had convinced Yan or not, but a man of such honor would not return to Kylan without completing his task, and the skeletons, while questionable, provided sufficient evidence. The leaders moved back into formation, following in the gray footsteps of the soldiers migrating across the desolation between them and the King's Carve. And the longer their journey went, the more time Rufus had to question whether Yan believed what he saw or not.

32

Two days after they left the sight of the devastating and defeating fire, Del, Will, Isa, and Elias climbed gentle rolling hills until the trees turned from gnarled and sturdy broadleaves to tall and hardy conifers. Will had never seen trees like that, or hills that rolled to peaks that extended beyond comprehension and stared down into valleys and draws that housed secrets undiscovered.

The Glass Mountains rose high and rocky and bare ahead of them, and their looming gave Will a sense of discomfort and awe. The rock walls towered like the walls of Umbrate, but much stronger and much older. He felt vulnerable below those wise, gazing peaks.

They rested on the top of a hill, and in the distance Will saw a rivulet of shimmering water flowing down the mountainside from a bank of snow. He followed its course until a distant glint blinked at him.

"What is that down there?" he asked Del.

Del, exhausted from the climb, looked up from his water and roughage Elias had gathered. A tired smile formed on his face.

"Ah, that's Mirror Pool," he said. "Always lit by the sun and moon, and always smooth as a piece of glass."

Will stared at it with new wonder. "Light always shines on it?"

Del nodded. "That's what keeps the Magic strong enough to hold the Evil Scourge below its placid surface," Del paused and absorbed the cost of its beauty. "And it is also why Umbrate is under constant shadow." His face turned to pain. He looked down and grimaced at the greens in his hand.

"Where's Sentinel's Village?" Will asked.

"Just beyond," Del said. "You can't hardly see it because of the light on the pool, but it's there."

Will squinted until his eyes burned but could not distinguish any part of it. He had always imagined a stout and proud city with great men and women, strong and selfless protectors, to match it. He pictured walls higher and thicker than Umbrate's, and armored sentinels keeping watch from great bastions of broad and ancient stone. His instructors had taught him that, and he still believed it to be true. He knew that the sentinels received the best food and living quarters as the guards of Umbrate did, and he had heard that they were allowed to have families to keep their community strong, because sentinels were only selected from their own village. Will had once wanted to be a sentinel, but he knew it wasn't possible because he didn't live there. Chewing on a leafy green, he wondered why sentinels could have spouses and children but the guards of Umbrate could not. Sentinel's Village must be a grand community, he thought, full of families and honor. He pictured clean streets and enough sunshine for things to grow and people to work under; a city that shined as bright as the pool before him. Will breathed in the piney air and felt satisfied for the first time ever.

"Are there magical people in Sentinel's Village that watch over Mirror Pool?" Will asked.

"No," Del replied. "Kylan is the overseer of the Pool, but it needs no overseeing. Powerful Magic resides over the pool, and every day the light of the sun and moon refresh it. Xenerac put the curse over the pool, and he was a very wise wizard."

Elias emerged from the trees. "We have to keep moving," he said, waking Isa from her nap against a pine trunk.

Each rose and returned their packs to their reluctant backs. Elias started off ahead of them at a pace that seemed cruel to all except Will. But Del managed to keep his grumbling to a minimum, and Isa grumbled not at all. No home waited back where they came from, and the only future they had remained ahead, even though it was shrouded in a mystery Elias kept to himself.

Will looked down at Mirror Pool one last time. The light reflected off it wherever he moved and whatever angle he looked down at it, until they crossed over another hill and it vanished from his sight. Someday he would see it again; someday when he was the great man Del said he would become.

By the evening of the same day Will looked down on Mirror Pool, the exhausted troop stood behind Elias and watched him run his glowing hands up and down, over and across, the front of a barrier of trees. Beyond the trees appeared to be nothing more than an impassable rock wall.

Will watched with fascination as Del and Isa leaned against trees with fatigue. They, at least at one point, had seen things like this many times before, but Will was witnessing it with virgin eyes, and an unconquerable part of him still searched to find the evil in Magic he had been eagerly taught by Umbrate's relentless instructors.

Elias dropped his scintillating hands and the trees seemed to step aside to admit them. Will rubbed his tired eyes at what appeared. An oasis stretched before them. The wall was not impassable vertical rock, but a large overhang that covered a shining pool. It went back some way, much farther than Will thought possible, and, when he squinted, he could see plants growing under there as if the pool emitted all the light the living things needed. Even the exhausted Isa and Del perked up at the sight of its promising refreshment.

Elias stepped aside to let them pass as if he were holding the tree-doors open for them. Will grabbed Isa's hand and pulled her in. She smiled and followed. Del came next and patted Elias on the shoulder.

"Thank you, Elias … again." Del entered the oasis of solace.

Elias gave a tired nod and turned to seal the passageway behind them.

The cool air wrapped them like a gentle breeze. They dropped their packs and cloaks, and the weary road with them. Isa ran her hands over the plants that grew out of the sandy bank so full of life and vigor for living under a rock. Will looked at the enticing water, its appearance too beautiful for him to dip his hands into; Del and Isa felt the same as they stared into its glowing presence.

Elias dropped his pack and approached the pool with an audience. He dropped his filthy cloak and removed his top. Squatting by the pool, he dipped his cupped hands in the glittering water. Will watched him with dry mouth and tempted eyes. Elias dipped his hands again and his whole body disappeared into the pool. They all stepped back, shocked. The man had vanished with hardly a splash. They watched, horrified, but he didn't rise back up.

"Get back from the edge, Will," Del said. The deft old man pulled Will away. Isa huddled close to them, and they watched with held breath, waiting for Elias to emerge.

"We have to help him," Will said. "He'll drown!"

Will worked free from Del's grip and ran to the edge of the pool. He looked into it and two large hands reached up and sucked him in. Elias's laugh echoed below the overhang as he wrestled a frantic, fighting Will into the water.

"No! I can't swim!" Will yelled.

"No need," Elias said, holding him above water. "You'll float if you believe you can." He launched the boy across the pool.

Will dipped below the surface and bobbed back up, struggling under the weight of his waterlogged clothes. His arms flailed and Isa yelled: "Help him!" But Elias ignored her plea. Will bobbed a few more times until his body evened out. He fluttered his hands because the water told him to, and he couldn't feel the weight of his body any more. He looked at Elias's dark eyes, the light of the pool shining through them.

"I'm floating!" Will yelled. "Whoo-hoo!" he launched himself backwards and dunked his body. The refreshing water charged through the pores of his skin and filled him with life he had never felt before. Will swam around the pool with not a wave or splash in his wake.

Elias turned to Del and Isa. "Come, it will restore those old bones!"

"I don't have old bones," Isa said with cocked hip. She smiled. "But it might be fun to have a swim again."

She stripped off her outercoat and dove into the infinitely deep pool. She rose for a breath with the dirt and grime erased from her face. Her wrinkles evened and Del remembered a time when he loved her, and wondered if it had ever passed.

"Come on, old man," Isa said, splashing water at him. Del scoffed. Maybe it had. He lifted off his cloak, then his shirt, and breathed deep, anticipating a cold entry. He hesitated.

"Come on, Del," Will yelled. "Stop being an Umbrate ninny and get in here."

Elias and Isa laughed; Del rolled his eyes. He prepared to dive with a cheering and jeering audience. He crouched and could feel the pain in his knees. Old bones? Definitely, he thought. Hesitating a moment longer he saw Elias grow suddenly serious.

"Look out behind you!" Elias yelled.

Del had a knife to his throat before he could turn.

"And who are thee that defiles the Radiant Pool with their filth?" the knife-wielder asked with the voice of a man. His hand shook at Del's throat as his other hand grabbed him over the shoulder and across his chest.

"Yes, who are thee but a group of scoundrels and thieves who stumbled upon a magical lair," said a second voice—the voice of a woman.

"We mean no harm," Del said, raising his hands above his shoulders.

"Yet here you are," the knife-wielder said.

"Yes, yet here you are," the woman echoed.

Will stopped his playing and Isa floated where the pool held her.

The knife seemed to shake at Del's throat, more from exhaustion than fear. He looked to Elias for help. A curious look grew on the large wizard's face. He tilted his head to the side as if to see the knife-wielder and the woman better. Del watched his face turn to relief, but the uncomfortable blade remained at his throat. Elias came to the edge of the pool and lifted himself out.

"You'll stop there if you know what's good for you," the blade-man said.

Elias lifted his hands and came closer.

"Doesn't appear to be stopping to me," the woman said. "Maybe we'll cut his friend's throat?"

"Yes, maybe we shall," the man agreed.

A small sound squeaked from Del, but Elias came closer with his hands still raised.

"This one doesn't know what's good for him," the man said. His voice shook like the blade at Del's throat.

"No, it appears he does not," the woman said.

"Stop, Elias," Del said. "Do as they say."

Elias smirked at him and passed beyond Del's peripherals. Del looked at Isa and Will, the pool shimmering in his wide eyes. They stared back at him, no more than helpless ducks paddling on a calm pond. The hand shook desperately at Del's throat. A shake no candlemaker could admire.

Del looked down and saw Elias's hand grab the quivering blade and move it away from his throat. The wielder seemed relieved that Elias did so, and his shaking calmed as he released his grip on Del's chest.

"That's no way to treat an old friend, Rolph," Elias said.

Del turned, quick with anger. "Rolph!" But he regretted the hostility he gave the word as he stared into the old, frail face. Del looked at the woman behind him. "And Gertrude." She was just as frail. Both were terrified and ashamed.

Rolph looked to the ground. "I have no old friends."

Elias grabbed the old man by the shoulders and pulled his head up. "It's me, Rolph, it's Elias, and Delier, and Isabella." The old man looked into Elias's eyes, trying to find something in them, or beyond them, that he could remember.

Isa came to the edge of the pool and lifted herself out. She turned and helped Will out.

"Who are these people?" Will whispered.

"Old friends," Isa explained. "Magical people we once knew."

She left Will to drip by the pool and went to Gertrude's side. The aged woman backed away and paused to stare dubiously into Isa's face.

"Gertrude, it's me, Isa," she said. The woman searched Isa with senile eyes in an odd attempt to remember.

Rolph looked from Elias to Gertrude. They shared a long knowing glance.

Gertrude looked back to Isa; her face more confident. "Yes, Isabella," she said. "Paulette's sister."

"That's right," Isa said. She pulled Gertrude in for a hug. "It's been so long. No wonder you didn't recognize us."

Rolph looked back at Elias towering over him. "I'm sorry," he said. "I … I guess we do have old friends. But faces change and memories don't linger forever."

Elias pulled him in for a hug, embracing the feeble man with his large arms. He let him go and Rolph looked at Del. "I'm sorry, Delier. I thought you were an intruder."

The offense faded from Del's face. "I understand, Rolph." He patted the old man on the shoulder and felt flabby flesh and hard bone. "It's good to see you again."

"I can't remember the last time I saw any of you," Rolph said, rubbing his forehead. "We've been hiding so long."

"As have we," Del said.

Will stood some distance away, dripping dry and watching the strange scene before him. They seemed to have forgotten he stood there until the awkward silence designated to old friends and former lovers set in.

Isa looked from Gertrude to Rolph, from Del to Elias. All were silent and searching for something to say. She turned and saw Will by the pool.

"Ah," Isa began, pulling Gertrude to her side. "Come meet Will, Paulette's great-grandson and my great-grandnephew."

Gertrude came forward and looked into Will's fresh eyes. "Yes, yes," Gertrude said, smiling wide. "I've seen those eyes before." She put her wrinkled hands on the supple skin of his cheeks. Without warning, she pulled him in for a hug, and there were tears in her eyes when she released him.

"Is he …?" she asked Isa.

Isa shook her head. Will felt suddenly weak and vulnerable surrounded by once powerful people, no matter how frail or old.

"And you and Del raised him?" Gertrude asked.

Isa and Del shared an uncomfortable glance.

"No," Isa replied. "Del raised him and brought him to me when they were forced to leave Umbrate."

"Unless my memory deceives me, I thought you two were—"

"Not anymore," Isa said, the frustration quick in her voice. Del looked away.

"What are you talking about?" Rolph asked Gertrude.

"They were married once, but now they're not," Gertrude replied. Her voice echoed in the chamber.

"Well, that's not right," Rolph replied. "Marriage is everlasting, eternal." They spoke as if no one else was there. Their new arrivals stared at anything to take them away from the conversation.

"Yes, but not for all people … apparently," Gertrude said.

"What! And why not. We've been married for three-hundred years and, sure, we've had our differences, but we've made it work. Why couldn't they manage to—"

Gertrude turned sharply. "Don't you know when to shut it?"

"You're the one that brought it up," Rolph scorned. He turned to a very vexed and embarrassed Del. "I'll tell you, if I had a gold coin for every time she told me to shut it over the past three centuries, I'd have—"

"Shut it!" Gertrude said.

Rolph smiled foolishly and lifted a cupped hand to his ear. "Did you hear that? The sound of a thousand gilded pieces clinking with greetings for a new friend."

"Give me that knife so I can gut you," Gertrude said.

"I've given her everything and now she wants more," Rolph said. He looked to Del. "You know, you might have something going with the axing of your marriage."

Gertrude planted her hands on her hips at the cold offense. "What did you say?"

Rolph slipped the knife behind his back and looked away like a dog that had eaten all of its owner's dinner. "I said how rude of you not to offer our guests some food. The boy looks hungry."

Gertrude turned her attention to Will. "Yes, how rude of me," she said, smiling motherly. "Would you like some food?"

All eyes turned to Will for relief from the marital bliss. He searched for the answer in the pleading faces and found a consensus.

Will said, "I would like that very much, thank you."

They sat around a stove of smooth rocks held together with caked and chipped mud. The pine wood fire dried them after their swim, and they became engrossed watching Rolph and Gertrude continue to bicker about a fight that started a few minutes before or a hundred years ago, it was too difficult for the newcomers to tell.

The pool glimmered by the opening of the cave Rolph and Gertrude called home. Beyond the stove they had a few trinkets that sat atop an uneven log they used as a shelf. Beyond that was a bed of dry grass over more uneven logs. But it had the appearance of a home in a strange way, or at least a place where people had been for a long time.

Will, Del, Isa, and Elias busied their hands by wringing their clothes, and once their clothes were dry and the stitches nearly torn, they went to fiddling through their packs or running their fingers over the smooth rocks of the cave. Their minds wandered, or at least tried to, to avoid listening to Rolph and Gertrude's arcane argument.

"And that's final!" Gertrude said. And it must have been because Rolph sat quiet on the edge of the bed, not defeated, but not willing to fight anymore. "Now," Gertrude said, finding time for her guests, "you said you'd like something to eat."

All eyes turned to Will again. He came awake and answered: "Yes, anything you have would be nice, Missus ..."

"Just Gertie or Gertrude, Will, anything else is too formal for a cave." She smiled jovially. "How about some turnip soup? It grows wild with the onions and watercress by the creeks."

"That sounds wonderful, Gertie," Will replied. It didn't, but Will knew his options were few.

The others shared Will's sentiment with smiles and nods to Gertrude. Each turned to Will with willful glances that not only held thanks but a bit of guilt for having a child act as their buffer. After living so long alone they seemed to have forgotten how to talk to others, or what people once talked about.

"I can't eat another bowl of that stuff," Rolph said, straightening from his crouched position.

"You don't have to, you old fool," Gertrude said. "That will leave more for our guests."

"I want fish," Rolph said, crossing his skinny arms over his chest like a toddler.

"Then go catch one!" her final note ended the conversation. She lifted a large kettle over the fire and sat beside Isa. She smiled at each in turn, waiting for any to open up and talk. She landed on Isa and the force of her constant smile and prodding gaze provoked her to speak.

"Uh, how long have you been staying here, Gertie?" Isa squeaked out.

"Quite some time, sad to say," she replied.

"Too long," Rolph clarified.

"Yes, too long," Gertie agreed. "We lived in Miner's Cove for so long. The people there kept us a secret because we helped them as we were able. The King had little presence there until some years ago, twenty I'd say, and then our work was exposed. It's all very strange. It seems so long ago, even in a life of four hundred years. We've been hiding here over a decade."

"Too long," Rolph said again. He came to her side and put his arm around her. She welcomed it.

"It's been a decade since I've seen you last," Elias said. "You must have been run out shortly after."

Gertie squinted her eyes and looked toward the roof of the cave. "Yes, I remember now." She shook her head. "I'm sorry I've forgotten so much. The memories drift when you spend all your time in a hole."

"How did they discover you?" Del asked. They all turned at his insensitive question. "It's just that Will and I were discovered in

Umbrate." He looked with guilt at the smooth rocks between his feet. "They tortured a friend and he said my name."

"It happened very similarly for us. All it took was for three guards to enter Miner's Cove. They were nothing more than table-turners looking for dropped coins to return to the king for a small bonus. We were fortunate to get away … others were not, and not one of them magical."

"You've been here for ten years?" Will asked, looking around the cave with surprise.

"Not quite. It's a long journey from Miner's Cove to the Glass Mountains, especially one made in the dark, but we had heard about this place many years ago and hoped we'd be able to find it. There's nowhere to go once you've been discovered."

"Evil world," Rolph interjected.

They all looked toward the ground and agreed in silence. The similarities of their situations were not coincidental and the truth of it pulled them closer.

Will looked at the old, haggard faces. All of them but Elias looked like they had lived a hard life, and even his age showed in the dancing firelight. He landed on Isa's face and she found something to smile about in his.

"Gertrude and Rolph helped us banish the Great Evil to Mirror Pool, Will," she said, attempting to lighten the situation. "They trained the great wizard Xenerac, who went on to become the most powerful wizard of all time."

"Long gone," Rolph said, swiping the attempt at cheer away.

"Yes, long gone indeed," Gertie echoed. "We can hardly start a fire nowadays, with no books to read and no memories to help us remember the Magic that saved all things. We're just cave dwelling common folk now. Soon we'll be blind like fish in a dark pool."

"We have books," Del said.

"What books are those, the foolish lie of *Mass and Umbrate History?* A dreadful piece," Gertie said.

"And poorly written," Rolph added.

Del reached for his pack. "No, we have books on Magic, written by Xenerac himself," he said. He dug through his pack and pulled out the three purloined books.

Gertrude and Rolph, nonplussed, stared at the books as if they were diseased.

"And where did you get those?" Gertie asked.

"Yes, where did you get those? I don't suppose you broke into the Mausoleum of Magic and selected them off the shelf yourself," Rolph said. He and Gertie snickered.

Del looked at Elias and Isa. "We did precisely that. And at a great price."

Rolph and Gertrude shared a glance and turned back to Del, their jaws resting in their laps.

"That's a bold lie, Delier," Gertrude said.

"Too bold," Rolph summed up.

"But it's true," Elias said.

The old couple looked to Isa. She nodded.

"How did you accomplish that?" Gertie asked with a sting of dubious arrogance.

"Yes, how?" Rolph asked. "There were a dozen monks around the place when we were there last."

"One-and-a-half dozen, I'd say," Gertie added.

Will watched the back and forth with growing anger as the aged magicians questioned their miserable day in choking darkness.

"There were only two guards. We," Del stopped and looked at Elias and Isa, embarrassed, "I mean, Elias and Isa killed the guards and we took the books."

"It couldn't have been that simple," Gertie said.

"I don't believe so either," Rolph said.

"They're numbers are not what they used to be," Del said, his frustration growing. "Oh, what does it matter. We almost died getting the books, but we have them now." Del passed the evidence to the doubters.

They thumbed through the pages, holding each with fascination and awe before they passed them to the other.

"These *are* Xenerac's books," Rolph said. "I remember discussing this idea with him. He is a great wizard."

"Yes, he certainly is," Gertie said.

"Was," Del clarified, catching a fierce glance from Isa.

Rolph looked up from his book and scoffed. "And what do you mean by that?"

Del shrugged and looked to his traveling companions. "It's common knowledge that Xenerac was imprisoned and killed."

"It's only common knowledge that he was imprisoned," Gertie said.

"Yes, that is the only knowledge that is common," Rolph replied. They went back to picking their way through the books. Isa directed her indignant eyes at Del, who shrugged. Xenerac had been like a child to Rolph and Gertrude, Del could remember that much, but it didn't change the fact that the wizard was dead. "And why would Kylan leave these books in a weakly guarded library in the forest? Surely even *he* is smart enough to understand their power," Rolph added, still retaining his reluctance to believe he was holding Xenerac's books.

"Kylan probably thought the books were useless, outdated. He had no respect for Xenerac," Del answered.

"Not unlike you apparently," Gertie said, still vexed by Del's comments about Xenerac's death.

Del scoffed. "Over a hundred years, people have forgotten about the books, about Xenerac, even." Rolph and Gertie shook their heads at his insolence. "And they're far too afraid to go into the *Grim* Forest. No one would ever go searching for books there."

Isa changed the subject. "We found other items as well," she added cheerily.

"Yes, yes, that's fine dear," Gertie said, ignoring Isa as she flipped through the pages of Xenerac's books. Isa sat back, deflated again.

This went on for a while. Gertie would pass a book to Rolph, Rolph to Gertie; she would show him a page, he would add commentary and remember suddenly that he had been there when it was written or that Xenerac had transcribed his own words in vivid detail. And after some time, they dropped the books in their laps and looked at each other, as if sharing their thoughts with blinks and face twitches.

"We must ask," Rolph began with his eyes on Gertie. He turned to Del and squinted in a skeptical shakedown. "What is it you intend to do with these books?"

Del reached for the books and Gertie and Rolph huddled them in close. Del rocked back on his rear.

"Well, we're, um …" Del began. He looked to Isa, but it was Elias that spoke first.

"We're gaining back what was taken from us." He reached his big arm over the stove and grabbed the books with no fight.

"Just the books, or do you mean …?" Rolph asked.

"He means a revolution," Isa said. "The books are just a start."

"And not a small start," Rolph said. "Foolish, but not small."

"It's not foolish, it's time," Isa retorted. "Or do you wish to live out your existence growing forgetful and blind in a cave?"

"If that's what we're doing then I can't help but wonder what brought *you* here," Gertie said.

Isa made no response.

"We came to buy ourselves time," Elias said. "They burned down Isa's home in the Verdant Forest, and we have no place left to relearn, to remember."

"And you've likely led the Guard here with your foolish games," Gertie said.

"Yes, and endangered us all," Rolph added.

"It'll be your fault if we get murdered in our own home," Gertie said.

"And we certainly will if they were willing to burn down the forest for your sake," Rolph said. "Foolish, foolish, I say."

"Fighting for truth and honor is not foolish!" Isa posited.

"It is if it means your life," Gertie said.

"And when did you lose your honor?" Isa asked. The question rocked Gertie and Rolph back. "You had it once, you know, and now it's gone."

"Gone!" Gertie said. "You believe my honor gone and you're off killing magical beings. How dare you …"

"No!" Del yelled. His voice echoed off the roof; Will watched the flames shake at the sound of it. "Those monks would have killed us in a heartbeat. One hit Elias because I had no strength to protect him, no honor."

"And two more tried to capture Will," Elias added. "They have no care for us except to see our light flushed out."

"They spent a whole day of darkness trapped inside the Mausoleum of Magic," Del said, pointing to his traveling companions. "Will, too. And they're doing much worse to the ones in the Reformatory. It's genocide!"

"Then what's the point in fighting?! Just so we can expose ourselves to that sort of hate? I won't do it!" Gertie said.

"There's no reason to!" Rolph asserted.

"No reason?!" Isa said.

Will stood with his shoulders slumped and his head down. They all stared at him. He looked into the old, wan faces. Each in turn.

"I would like to go fishing," he said. They stared at him with scrunched brows and hands scratching foreheads.

Will waited, searching each expression, then added: "You said if Rolph wanted fish then he should go catch them. Well, I want to go catch them."

"Oh," Gertie said, turning to Rolph. "Get the boy the switch pole." Rolph sat a moment in confusion.

"Rolph," Gertie said.

Rolph stared at Will. "Yes, of course, the pole." He got to his feet with some struggle and went further into the cave. He emerged with a willow switch taller than he with a length of line on the end of it. He passed it to Will.

"Thank you," Will said. "Now, I don't know how to fish. Would someone please show me?"

Elias grinned and stood. He had to stoop to keep from knocking his head on the roof. "I'll show you."

Del stood as well. "I'd like to come, too, if that's all right?"

"How about we all go?" Will offered to the crowd with a youthful, unwilted smile.

They stood as one and went fishing.

"I suppose that's reason enough," Gertie whispered to Isa as they walked to Radiant Pool.

And later they ate fresh trout with their soup.

33

Rufus stood before Alphonse with his hands behind his back and his chest popped out from his stiff stance. The colors of his robe were dulled by the tenacious soot and ash, and his face and body unwashed from returning so soon.

"Are you sure that's what you saw?" Alphonse asked after he mulled over Rufus's report.

"Yes, sir," Rufus responded. "We discovered two skeletons of similar size."

"And Yan seemed to agree that they were the chandler and the boy and not the monks that never returned?"

"He seemed … skeptical, sir," Rufus said, revealing his own skepticism. "I tried to convince him, and he in turn called the mission a success but, of course, I can't read the man's thoughts."

"A man like Yan won't report a failure to Kylan," Alphonse said. "Thank you, Rufus. I know it was not an easy mission. Princess Briella will hear of your sacrifice. You're dismissed of duty until tomorrow. Go clean yourself up."

"Thank you, sir," Rufus said.

He turned toward the door and left. He met Yan down the hallway, just as filthy and tired as he was.

"I've made my report to Alphonse," Rufus said.

"Good," Yan replied. "Then he will be briefed before we report to Kylan."

Yan walked past Rufus and stopped. He turned and asked: "Do you really believe those were the corpses of a man and boy?" This troubled Rufus. Men like Yan always knew the answers to their own questions.

Rufus turned on a slow heel, buying himself a sliver of a second. "Of course," he said with conviction. "It would be an awful coincidence that two other skeletons were found in the area the Guard lost them."

"Yes, an awful coincidence." Yan looked down at his ashy, dirty boots with the same doubtful gaze he gave the skeletons. He looked at Rufus with a small smile out of place on his face. "It would be foolish to report otherwise," he said.

Rufus gave him a curt nod and left the man in the stone hallway. Yan lingered a moment before he went to Alphonse's door.

◊

The two Guard leaders made the long climb to Kylan's tower. Yan, a usually dutiful and eager man, plodded up the stairs. Alphonse matched his gait as each grueling step seemed to challenge his equal more and more. Alphonse, sensing Yan's apprehension, grew uneasy.

"Are you tired from your journey?" Alphonse asked.

Yan emerged from his thoughts and looked at Alphonse. More than soot and weariness sullied his face.

"I can report to Kylan alone if you wish. Surely he will understand the fatiguing nature of your journey."

"No," Yan replied, unoffended. "I just need more time to think."

"About what?"

Yan looked at Alphonse as if he had read his mind and not simply asked a question.

"It was a curious journey," Yan said.

"Rufus said things went as expected."

"I fear Rufus doesn't know all the details."

Alphonse stopped Yan. He searched his bloodshot eyes before he asked: "What do you mean? He said you burned the forest and found two bodies. Wasn't that the mission?"

"Of course it was, but I can't help but wonder …" His voice trailed to an echo in the skinny stairwell.

"Can't help but wonder what?" The air warmed around Alphonse.

Yan searched Alphonse's eyes now. "Did Rufus know we were tasked with the mission because two monks went missing, or was that fact between us and Kylan?"

Alphonse cocked his head, but only to buy time. "No, he didn't know. I just delegated the mission and he accepted it. Did you tell your men?"

"No," Yan confessed. He stroked the stubble around his chin, smearing soot across his face.

"I'm struggling to understand the problem," Alphonse said. He wasn't, but it was not to his advantage to tell Yan so. "You burned the forest and you found two dead, correct?"

"Yes," Yan said. "But we should have found four bodies if the monks were killed."

"Rufus said the bodies appeared to be those of a man and boy," Alphonse reasoned.

"It was too difficult to tell. Everything was so burned and broken," Yan said. He stroked his chin even harder, nearly wiping the filth away. The unyielding man crumbled before Alphonse. That sort of doubt would not play well with Kylan. The old wizard would sniff it out quicker than rotting potatoes.

"I trust Rufus. He seemed very sure of what he saw," Alphonse said.

"But he didn't know all the facts," Yan retorted. The anguish spilled over in Yan's head; he tried to brush it away with a swift stroke through his greasy hair.

Alphonse put a hand on Yan's shoulder. "You can't go up there and be unsure, Yan. You either saw what you did or you'll be back on the hunt. The city is your domain to guard, not the forest. You know as well as I that a man and a boy raised in Umbrate couldn't survive out there, and they certainly couldn't outrun pursuing monks," Alphonse said. "And even if the monks did die there, it would have been nothing for you to have passed them."

Yan thought for a moment. "Do you trust Rufus?" He asked after a long pause.

"I wouldn't have appointed him leader if I didn't," Alphonse replied. He patted Yan's shoulder. "You're tired and just returning from a mission we both believed foolish. You need rest, and with rest comes clarity."

Alphonse turned and walked up the measured steps again. The long march up was having the desired effect on Yan's weary brain.

Yan sighed and turned to follow. He said without looking at Alphonse: "Do the talking, will you? I can hardly keep my eyes open or my head upright."

"Yes," Alphonse said. "I'll report to Kylan exactly as Rufus reported to me, if you agree with that?"

Yan breathed deep and nodded. "Yes, I trust Rufus as well, and I trust you."

The men said no more, and the guards at the door permitted them with quick and expected entry. Kylan finished his writing, making the men stand in aching anticipation, before Alphonse relayed the story as efficiently as he could. Kylan accepted with a nod and returned to his quill and parchment.

"Do you concur?" Kylan asked Yan, who hesitated. "You were there, weren't you?" he provoked.

"Yes, sir, sorry, sir. I'm quite worn from the journey," Yan said. "I do concur with Alphonse's report."

The tedious process made Alphonse sweat. Kylan wrote for some time, until the sweat beaded and fell down Alphonse's face in the high, hot tower. He attempted to look out the window to drum up the memory of a breeze when Kylan replaced his quill and looked at them with his enigmatic gaze.

"Good," Kylan said, and even the corners of his mouth curled into something of a smile, though the sight on the man's face was so rare that the two men weren't sure what emotion they witnessed, if emotion at all. "You're free to go about your business."

"Thank you, sir," each leader said with lighter shoulders. They turned and Kylan stopped them at the door.

"I would wish to remind you both of the upcoming festival. The lion's share of your guards will join the King and I on our pilgrimage to Bale's Victory, but I wish to leave a strong presence behind."

"Yes, sir," the leaders answered.

"Good," Kylan said, attempting to smile again. He went back to writing and Alphonse tapped on the door for the guards to let them out. He and Yan shared a relieved glance.

Yan stepped much quicker on the way down the steps. His livened pace gave Alphonse confidence, and he seemed to forget that Alphonse walked next to him.

They met a gray-cloaked figure walking up the steps as they went down. Alphonse moved aside and turned to inspect the being's desperate pace up the steps. Dirt from a long, fast journey caked the red trim on the bottom of his cape. He disappeared around the next curve, and Yan, pleased with his accomplished mission and the praise from Kylan, appeared to not even notice the passerby.

"How many guards are you sending to the festival?" Yan asked.

"Three-quarters, maybe more. All of the royalty is planning to attend. It would be useless to have any more in Umbrate protecting nothing," Alphonse answered, still considering the cloaked figure.

"Yes, I suppose I will send that many as well," Yan replied. "Should be quite an event."

"Quite an event indeed," Alphonse said hollowly. He turned and looked up the steps again, but the echo of busy feet was gone.

Yan continued to talk, and Alphonse considered that a good sign. The man's mind had dropped the haranguing questions and he returned to being the proud leader of the City Guard.

They separated at the bottom of the steps. Yan toward a bath, and Alphonse toward Princess Briella's quarters. He had news she needed to hear. And by the time he met with her, a monk sent to relieve the guards at the Mausoleum of Magic had relayed a very curious story to Kylan.

34

Will sat and watched Del read, and Isa read, and Elias read, and then Gertie and Rolph until his eyes began to burn. And when he'd had enough of them reading and nodding and discussing things in hushed tones, he would go fishing, but much to his surprise, even the taste of fresh trout started to dull, so he would catch them and toss them back, and then catch the same fish and toss it back.

He wasn't sure how much time had passed (he wished he had kept track) but he guessed they had been at least two weeks in the cave, and time continued to continue. After a while, when his curiosity glided to boredom, he began to wander through the cave, and when he wasn't wandering, he looked over shoulders to try and read what the adults were reading, because they wouldn't let him go out of the cave without a chaperone, and the chaperones were busy reading. Will could hardly make out the words, and they made very little sense to him if he managed to string them together. He wondered if there was a magical language or way of talking he couldn't comprehend. Maybe only magical beings understood it? He struggled to read his own book taken from the Mausoleum, *Tales of the Glass Mountains,* as well, but he attributed that to a feeling of futility.

He was beginning to feel quite useless with such a powerful, learned crowd around him. And he also, selfishly, wanted to see some Magic. It was the reason they were there: to rest and relearn Magic, but he didn't understand why he saw no flashes of light, or lightning bolts from fingertips, or dark curses that would cover their foes in boils. But he witnessed no such things, and he began to wonder if the old wizards and witches had fallen into procrastination once again and disguised it as learning.

Del put down his book and looked to the top of the cave, enlightened. He looked at Will fiddling with a pile of rocks and smiled. Will didn't smile back. His uselessness had turned into a millstone. Del could see it on his face.

"What's wrong, boy?" Del asked. Isa looked over the edge of her book at Will, and Elias paused on the page. Gertie and Rolph continued to read and bicker quietly some distance away.

Will flicked a rock and looked at Del. "How do you know I'm not magical?"

Del, Isa, and Elias shared an uneasy glance. "What do you mean?" Del asked.

"You know, why do you think I'm not able to do Magic? My aunt can do it. My mother apparently could do it. Why do you think I can't?"

"It really isn't that simple, Will. Magic isn't—"

"It's not hereditary. So you've said," Will interjected sadly, "but why was my mother magical?"

"We don't know if your mother was magical or not," Del said.

"But she saved me that day in the square. I remember this white light when Yan grabbed her, and he fell to the ground, knocked out."

"Wasn't he arresting a witch?" Del asked.

"Yes, but she was cuffed and ill on the ground."

Del went silent. It had been many years, and memories turned cloudy, especially for someone as old as him.

"You would know if you're magical." Isa said, picking up the conversation.

"How?"

"Well, for example, when I was a little girl of only four or five, I could heal plants that were dying just by touching them. They would perk right back up between my fingers, and then I would move on and do the same to the next one, giddy with the sight of brown leaves turning to green. And birds and animals always flocked to me. They found comfort in my presence, and I could heal the injured ones without a thought," Isa said. She smiled at the memory.

"And I stopped a stone mason from falling to the ground one day as I walked around the new walls of Umbrate," Elias said. "He fell right before my eyes and I caught him with my mind and lowered him to the ground. I was eight."

They all turned to Del, who looked into the distance, searching for a memory.

"How did you find out, Del?" Will asked.

"Yes, that's it, I must have been seven or so when I helped a girl that had fallen and broken her arm," Del said. "She took a tumble on the stones and wrenched her poor little elbow. She cried so horribly. I reached over and took ahold of it and she stopped crying. I can still see the shock in her brown eyes," he laughed a little. "She got up, kissed me on the cheek and ran down the cobbled road. Goodness, that must have been over two-hundred years ago."

With fond memories on their faces, Will turned glum; he would never have a memory like that. Isa saw his downcast eyes and came to sit beside him.

"Magic is something we're born with, Will, just like any other talent. And same as all talents, it needs to be cultivated, given lots of food and water and sunshine," Isa said. She hugged him close. "And our talents are nothing without conviction and hard work. We may have done Magic as small children, but it took us many years—decades even—to master it, and now we're sitting here trying to relearn what we foolishly gave up. It takes practice, and time, and, in many cases, love. Long ago, even the most magically talented got lazy and lost their ways. It made them slow, and often hateful of the world that continued on around them. That won't happen to you, Will." He looked up at her with sad eyes. "You may not know your talents yet, but I see one burning bright in you."

"You do?"

"I do, and it's something us magical people turned our backs on long ago. It's the reason we're hiding in a cave while our world crumbled for a century."

"What is it?" Will asked shyly.

"Bravery," Isa smiled, "courage to do what challenges us over what's easy. It's the same courage that made Xenerac stand up to Queen Sharon. It's what keeps Elias traveling to help others. And it's what you will offer the world when the time comes. Many have given up their fearlessness for what's safe in these strange times, but you never will, and that bravery is much more powerful than all the Magic inside of us."

"It's true," Del said. "If anything, you were born with the greatest talent of all."

Will gave a weak smile as he leaned into Isa.

"I hate to admit it, Will, but they're right." Gertie said. She and Rolph had moved closer during the conversation. "Rolph and I have lived over three centuries, with all the most magically powerful people ever created, and a frail old king, who started as nothing more than a sad boy, is the one that frightens us. He's the reason we're in a cave … but not much longer."

"Yes, not much longer," Rolph echoed.

"We just need a bit more time, more training to reawaken our own talents," Isa said.

"But you did Magic all the time at your home in the forest. And Elias does it out traveling. And Del does it with the candles," Will said. "What more do you need to learn?"

"Those things are simple for us, Will," Del said. "Trying to get in to a dark wizard's head so we can defeat him and his armies is not the same as growing plants or making candles that heal people, or even killing. We have to try and see Kylan's next move so we can cut it off. And since he was Xenerac's apprentice, the answer is likely in these books. We simply need more time to find the things we can't remember or never learned."

"I fear we don't have much left," Gertie said. The worried tone in her voice turned their attentive gazes.

"What do you mean?" Elias asked.

Gertie looked at Rolph and said: "We've been reading through Xenerac's writings and, it's not quite clear, but we think he's trying to warn us, only we can't get through to him."

"Warn us?" Del said. "Can't get through?" Isa asked.

Gertie and Rolph looked at the ground with guilty eyes.

"We didn't want to say anything until we were sure," Gertie said.

"Or maybe we chose to look away from it," Rolph admitted, rubbing his toe in the dirt.

"Yes, we were fools, the same way we were years ago when we let them take control of us," Gertie said.

"What on Mass are you talking about?" Del asked.

Gertie and Rolph shared a knowing glance, pausing as if conducting a conversation between each other's stares.

"Gertie? Rolph?" Isa interrupted their silent discussion.

Gertie turned to them first; Rolph dropped his head. "We've been noticing changes around here the past few years. The trees are sadder, the sun darker, the light shining off Mirror Pool less bright."

"We thought it was our own state of mind, our own situation plaguing our perception," Rolph added.

"Yes, but it seems more than that. It seems a more tangible thing now," Gertie said.

Gertie and Rolph shared another telepathic glance.

"Can you please get on with it?" Del asked desperately.

"We were fools," Gertie said.

"Yes, we've already agreed on that," Del said.

"And then you arrived," Rolph continued, ignoring Del.

"And we started to notice things," Gertie said. "And you brought these books, and it opened our eyes a little more."

"Things are changing," Rolph said, shaking his head.

Del put his head in his hands with frustration.

"Can you please tell us what you're talking about?" Isa asked, concealing her own annoyance.

"We've been through this book of Xenerac's writings," Gertie said. "And it appears that Xenerac could see very far into the future. It appears he saw a reckoning coming, but we can't get through to him."

"Yes, he's become very difficult to reach," Rolph said.

"You keep saying that. What do you mean he's become difficult to reach?" Isa prodded. She looked from Del to Elias to Will, their faces twisted in confused concern.

"As you know we have a very strong bond with Xenerac."

"Very strong."

"And one day, many years ago, he reached out to us," Gertie said.

"How?" Elias asked.

"With his mind," Rolph said.

"That's not possible, he's dead," Del said.

"He's not dead," Gertie retorted, offended.

"You think we just hear the voice of our former apprentice for no reason at all? Of course it's him!" Rolph said, mirroring Gertie's vexation.

"But even if he is alive, he'd be in the Reformatory of Magic. Magic only enters there, it never leaves," Del said with a shiver.

"You forget how powerful he is, Delier. And how powerful our bond is to him."

"Powerful indeed."

"Or maybe Kylan's power is cracking from lack of use?"

"As ours has." Their responses filled the space so quickly no others had the opportunity to speak.

"And when you arrived with these books, we thought we would try and reach him again."

"Very troubling things in here," Rolph said, holding up the book. "So, we tried to reach him." Gertie and Rolph went silent.

"And?" Del blurted when his patience ran out.

"He had very little to say," Gertie replied.

"That's it? That's all you have to offer?!" Del asked, his rising voice echoing off the cave roof.

Gertie and Rolph went back to their telepathic conversation. Del got to his feet and threw his hands in the air. He paced a few circles before they spoke again.

"It was mindless babbling," Gertie admitted.

"Jumbled nonsense," Rolph said.

"What exactly in the book made you want to try to contact him?" Elias asked, trying to find a point.

Opening to a page near the end of Xenerac's writings, Gertie passed it to Elias. "It's the last entry in the book," Gertie said sadly.

Elias read over it and looked back at Gertie and Rolph.

"What does it say?" Del asked.

All ears turned to Elias. "'A dream has presented itself to me. I watched from the top of the Glass Mountains as darkness covered the land. The trees wilted, the animals fled, the grass lost its sway, and the sun dulled over the pool. I watched years go by, chained to the peak of the mountains, and at the centurial null noon the discs clashed and broke, and eternal Darkness brought waves over the calm pool, and on those waves rode The End.'"

All eyes turned to Gertie and Rolph.

"What does it mean?" Isa asked. "Could Xenerac not tell you?"

"What's a centurial null noon?" Del pondered.

Gertie turned despondent and Rolph put his hand on her shoulder.

"He sounded like a mad man. 'Darkness … The end,' was all he muttered, over and over."

"What about the dream?" Del asked. "Do you understand it?"

"No," Gertie admitted. "But Xenerac was gifted with foresight; it's what made him so powerful. We need him here. We need his help."

"Of course," Del mocked, "let's just saunter into the Reformatory of Magic and see if they'll let us have a visit with him."

"Enough, Del!" Isa said.

Del took his seat and they all looked toward the gravelly ground, pondering the problem.

Will looked up first. "Why not?"

"Why not what?" Del asked curtly.

"Why not enter the Reformatory and free him?"

Del scoffed. "It's not the Mausoleum of Magic, Will. You've seen it. It's formidable, with no light, with no known entrance, and certainly no exit. Let alone the guards that monitor it always … and the monks."

"Don't forget we have friends," Will said.

Del avoided deriding the boy, but said: "And even if they could help us. How? And when?! We are but few."

Will slumped back, but not defeated. They scratched their heads and shared concerned glances for some minutes. Will's blank gaze landed on the Radiant Pool. The realization hit him like a fish landing on his hook.

"What about the festival?" Will said.

"What festival?" all but Del asked.

Del leaned back and considered the boy. His fear attempted to block him from admitting it, but Will was on to something … something bold, and brave … and very dangerous.

◊

"The centennial festival," Del explained, "to celebrate one-hundred years since King Bale banished the Great Evil of Magic into Bale's Victory … or at least that's what *they* are going to celebrate."

"And how will that help us?" Gertie asked.

"Yes, it sounds like it will bring many people *nearer* to us," Rolph added.

Del looked at Will. "I believe Will is suggesting we go to Umbrate to free Xenerac when all the guards and royals are at Sentinel's Village for the festival."

A small squeak escaped Isa and the rest of their mouth's dropped open at Del's momentous words. Will stared into each pair of bewildered eyes, one by one.

"It's our best opportunity to get Xenerac and any others out."

They turned their peeled, unblinking eyes back to Del.

"Do you really think we could do it?" Isa asked.

"Yes," Del answered.

The pithy word echoed between the walls of the cave, its wavelength striking them with realization. Elias went into thought; Isa's countenance turned to pure fear; Gertie and Rolph stared in telepathic conversation.

Del looked at Will, and Will at Del. They were on the same idea, but it didn't make it less terrifying or convincing.

"Yes, but at what cost," Rolph said as if the rest of the group had heard Gertie's preceding comment.

"No one can know that, Rolph. But Will is right, this is our opportunity if we were to ever have one," Del said. He couldn't believe the words were coming from his mouth. Feeling dizzy, he put his head in his hands to combat the nauseating pulse.

"How can we do it?" Elias asked.

"We have friends in Umbrate," Will said. His voice sounded small in the group of adults, but they looked to him for confidence. "Grace and Newt, and the Royal Guardsman, and Phin—"

"And Clyde," Del said rather meanly.

Will's shoulders slumped. He stared at the others, embarrassed. "Clyde's a donkey, but the rest are actual people."

"You're friends with a Royal Guard?" Elias asked.

"He helped us escape from Umbrate," Will confirmed.

"He'll be with the caravan going to Sentinel's Village," Del said.

"That doesn't mean he can't help us," Will countered.

Rolph, Gertie, and Isa watched the back and forth, feeling they had little to contribute to a conversation about a world they had excised themselves from long ago.

"Why would a Royal Guard help you escape from Umbrate?" Elias asked.

"He said it was what Princess Briella wanted," Del said, brushing the inquiry away.

The others turned to him with more confidence.

"So there are people who can and will aid us?" Isa asked.

"Does she wish to overthrow the king?" Elias asked.

"If so, she might be willing to help us free Xenerac," Gertie added.

"Certainly she would, if she helped you," Rolph said.

"But they will both be gone for the festival," Del reiterated, flustered. "And it's not like we can just walk right into the city and call on the Princess and the Royal Guard."

"Do you think Kylan and Father Renalt will also be gone?" Will asked.

"Yes," Del said it as a question. "Why?"

"What about Friar Emesh, then?" Will suggested. "He's part of the clergy. He could help get us into the Reformatory."

"But would he be willing?" Del asked.

"The real question is: would anybody be?" Gertie said.

"No," Rolph replied. They all stared at his abnormal disagreement with his wife. "The real question is: are *we* willing?"

They all thought a moment with much peering toward the ceiling and stroking of chins and flicking of pebbles. Will grew uncomfortable, then infuriated.

"What's the point in all of this reading and waiting if we aren't going to do something—anything?" Their faces muddied with the same countenance of shame only befitting an adult. "We can all stay here and wither, and never worry about the world or the people wasting away in it—but what if we can help? We've all seen people close to us killed, murdered, and we chose to do nothing. How long can it continue? What if you have the power to save the world from this evil? Would you rather die in this cave and never know if you could help, or would you rather die knowing you made a difference?"

They thought long and hard. Years of hiding can make one weak, frail, sleepy.

"Tell us about this Friar Emesh," Elias said after some internal thought.

"He's an old, chubby man of the clergy," Del answered. "He accepts our order of Altar candles each month before mass. He accepts all of the king's orders, in fact. Nothing with the king's stamp on it moves throughout the kingdom without him knowing."

"Altar candles?" Gertie asked.

"Mass?" Rolph added.

Del quickly explained the modern customs of Umbrate to the two outcasts and continued with his explanation of Emesh.

"He's a kind man, but the clergy seems to think little of him," Del said.

"And what makes you believe that?" Isa asked.

"Because he's been there for thirty years and they only let him accept boxes at the back door."

"I like him," Will said. "And I think he would be willing to help us."

"What makes you think that?" Del asked. "He's taken a vow just as the others of the clergy have."

"He's afraid of Renalt," Will said.

"Show me someone who isn't."

Will turned from squabbling with the incorrigible Del to the rest of the crowd.

"If Renalt and the others are gone, Emesh might be willing to help us. See, the Reformatory is attached to the back of the Cathedral where they conduct mass. I'm not sure, but I'd say that's how we get in, through the Cathedral. Emesh can help with that, especially if we can get word to Alphonse beforehand."

"And how would we do that?" Del asked.

Isa perked up. "What about Terron?"

"Who?" all but Elias inquired.

"The bird that found me wandering?" Elias said.

Isa nodded eagerly. "He could help us. He's a fast flier, and he has a good memory, unlike most birds."

"Even if we could get word to Alphonse, how would we get into Umbrate?" Del posited. "Guards watch all of the gates, and I'm sure Will and my likenesses are known by even the children of Umbrate now."

"What about Phin?" Will offered. "He could get us through."

"Maybe," Del said, not convincingly. "But how would we get all the way to the Cathedral and then into the Reformatory, and then all the way back out with the most powerful wizard in the world … and possibly others with him?"

"Could the guard that let you out let you in again?" Elias offered.

"It would be too much risk for him," Del said. "His duty is to protect the princess, and he would disown us if it came down to us or her. He was very displeased that Will came with when we escaped."

Will thought of their nighttime journey across those dull, flat plains. It had been difficult, but they had made it, and only with the help of some loyal and close friends …

"Grace and Newt could get us in," Will offered.

Del, stroking his chin hairs, examined him curiously. "How so?"

"If Alphonse gets the message from the bird and everything is in place, they could sneak us into Umbrate in bags of white earth."

"Bags of white earth?" Gertie said.

"Sounds uncomfortable," Rolph said.

"It would be," Will assured them. "But that was how they hid us from the hunting party. And Grace and Newt said that the king was taking all their white earth for the textile factory. They were taking so much that Del and I couldn't get any for candle making. They're ready for a revolution too." Will shook with excitement at the sprouting plan.

"It's true. And they said they would be willing to help," Del admitted, though the desire to stay in the cave at that moment tugged hard at him, and he guessed the others felt the same way, all except Will. Del felt it was much easier to live when he didn't have to do anything but hide; fear has its comforts.

"So, if we can get a bird to the guard, then get this Friar to agree, and then get word to your white earth friends, and *then* get all the way back to Umbrate in time to sneak in while the others are away, we can gain access to the Reformatory?" Gertie asked dubiously.

"Yes, there are many moving parts," Rolph agreed.

"When is the festival?" Gertie asked.

"On Mass Remembrance Day," Del said. He looked at Will. "Must be in a month or so."

"Or so?" Isa asked.

"I can't be sure. This cave doesn't have a calendar," Del mocked. Isa would have scoffed but he was correct in that regard.

"What if I dropped down to Sentinel's Village to find out while Isa finds her bird to send the message," Elias offered.

After some thought they all agreed that that was the best place to start, and also the most innocuous—their bravery needed building.

"I'll set out in the morning," Elias said.

"And I'll seek Terron tomorrow," Isa said.

"Can I come with, Elias?" Will asked.

Elias looked to Del, who turned to Will.

"I don't think that's a good idea," Del said. "I'm sure word of our escape from Umbrate has made its way to Sentinel's Village. They will be on high alert, even more so with the festival ahead. And we've already asked so much of you. It wouldn't be right to put you in any more danger."

"What about when we get into Umbrate? Will I be able to go then?" Will tested.

Del looked at the concerned eyes of his fellow adults.

"We'll discuss it when the time comes," Del said. "Let's worry about the bird for now."

Will shrank in the shadow of the cave, and all the others could offer were sad, weak smiles.

35

As Kylan was receiving news from a dusty, winded monk that no trace and no trail could be found of any possible intruders to the Mausoleum of Magic, and that the dogs could find no scent because of the ash and soot that fell from the fire in west Grim Forest, Isa was taking a seat on a bare hillside flooded with sun to find the roving mind of a small bird, and Elias was making his way down from the refuge of the cave toward Sentinel's Village.

But as Isa took her seat and closed her eyes, and Elias walked alone to Sentinel's Village, Will sat on the hillside with his knees hugged into his chest, a fire smoldering inside of him. He wanted to go with Elias, and he wanted to go into Umbrate to save Xenerac; and at the true heart of the matter, he wanted to do anything at all. He missed having a home, and he missed making candles, and a part of him even missed living in Umbrate and running through the dirty streets with his old friend Lyle. Beyond all of that, and even more so, he missed his mother. He closed his eyes as Isa did and searched, not to find the mind of a silly bird, but a memory of his mother. There were too many things there, too many apparitions coming and going. He closed them tighter to try and see her face, but a blur blotted where it should have been.

Will opened his eyes and the bright sun blinded him. He felt as if he had fallen asleep and returned once again to dawn after a night of hollow rest. Looking down the hill, Elias was nothing but a tall figure that blended in and out of the trees. Beyond him Mirror Pool glimmered in the morning light. Will shielded his eyes and looked at the sun; at his back, the edge of the moon dipped behind the Glass Mountains. They were always watching, always vigilant over the pool that imprisoned the Great Evil, the Great Scourge that boiled and wrestled below the calm surface. Will shuddered to think about all those dead, decaying beings climbing on top of one another, fighting to break the surface that Magic and the rotating watches of the sun and moon held fast.

He looked beyond the pool and beyond where Isa sat. The world looked so big to him, tilting over its edge before he could see the end of it. Until a few weeks ago, he had seen nothing further than Newt and Grace's cabin just a few miles from Umbrate, and now he had made it all the way to the Glass Mountains. Lyle would have more reason to be jealous of Will now than him simply being selected into the Guard. He pictured his old friend greeting him and asking of his journeys with wide, curious eyes and endless questions that Will knew all the answers to. It was a foolish thought, but Will allowed himself time to hold it.

Tales of the Glass Mountains rested in his lap. He had only glanced at it, and now it seemed foolish sitting in the shadow of the sharp peaks. He didn't need the tales any more, he was already there, and a part of him feared he would open it and find histories of great men and women that would make him feel even smaller and more useless.

He wondered if his mother would be proud of him for leaving Umbrate to avoid being part of the Guard that had ripped her from him. Or would she be disappointed that he put himself through such harm after she gave everything for him to live? His mother wouldn't consider the latter thought, Will knew it in his heart, but it still bounced around his mind like a court jester. She would have been proud of him; he would have no reason to go on if he believed otherwise. He would be just like the others in Umbrate and all across Mass, with nothing more to do than put his head down to not be seen by the Guard, as he and Del had done. Except he would be a part of that Guard, that fear machine that plucked people from the streets on empty claims and false charges.

Will shook his head to rid his mind of the filthy thought. He looked down the hill toward Mirror Pool and saw no sign of Elias, but when he turned to Isa, he saw something remarkable.

Birds and bees and butterflies and dragonflies orbited around her as if she were a transcendent flower. And not just a few, but hundreds of birds and thousands of flying insects. Their whirr made Will feel like he was sitting in a hard wind, but he felt nothing. Isa's hair floated here and there, and the hummingbirds dipped their needle-like beaks toward it and pulled away just before touching her, more out of respect than realized deception. Will could not believe what he witnessed, and he rubbed his eyes once or twice to make sure what he saw was actually there. Birds floated in and out and the hovering sphere of insects and bees expanded wider.

"Amazing, isn't it?" Del asked. His voice startled Will. He sat next to the boy and watched what seemed to be all the flying critters in the world gathering at Isa's calm presence. Del seemed less impressed than Will, but he continued to stare as though watching a fond, faraway memory. The old wizards and witches seemed to have many of those.

"How does she do it?" Will asked.

Del shrugged. "It's one of her gifts," he answered ambiguously. "Back in the old days it wasn't hard for a witch or wizard to practice their skills openly, to develop their born talents. The work keeps the skills strong, that's why we've lost so much of it over the last hundred years. But we're gaining it back, I assure you," he said, nodding to Isa. "Though I must tell you, her gift is as much a mystery to me as it is to you."

"What is your gift?" Will asked.

Del watched Isa with ease and said: "I was a great healer," he paused and corrected himself. "I *am* a great healer," he leaned toward Will, "and I've always had a way with light. Light is the ultimate healer—the great cleanser and guide."

"Well, what about Kylan? What's his gift?" Will asked. "Surely he wasn't always bad if he worked with Xenerac."

"I don't know what Kylan's talents are—I never knew him," Del said. "Likely the study of the sky and stars if he was Xenerac's apprentice. But unlike Xenerac, Kylan cultivated his gift with darkness and hate, not sunshine and care like Xenerac did." Del flicked his hand toward the sun and grabbed his wrist in pain.

"It still hurts?" Will asked.

"Yes," Del admitted. "Deep wounds take a long time to heal, though I'm guessing this one will take much longer."

"Why?"

"Because I inflicted it to tear away a bit of Dark Magic. Dark Magic takes sacrifice to implement, and sacrifice to brush away. Sadly, I don't think the pain of this sacrifice will ever go away."

Will took on a culpable countenance. "I never properly—"

"No need, my boy," Del said. "You would have done the same, and much quicker than I did."

"Thank you anyway, Del." Will looked into the distance and remembered the feeling of being afraid to blink to avoid being in the dark too long. He lifted his head toward the morning sun and the feeling faded like vapor. They watched the crowding birds and bees and flies buzz and flap and float around Isa.

"What's that you've got there?" Del asked, pointing to *Tales of the Glass Mountains*. Will grew shy for having taken it. He handed it to Del.

"Ah," he admired. "Have you had a chance to look at it?"

"Not much," Will said.

Del flipped through the pages and stopped on one, a picture. He showed it to Will. "Henry the Steadfast was the father of King Abiri, you know. He led the first expedition of the Glass Mountains and cleared the land around Mirror Pool to build Hornblower Valley, now known as Sentinel's Village, seeing it as fertile and warm land to grow crops for the Kingdom." Will looked at him, interested. "He was the father of Simon as well, Abiri's younger brother and father of Princess Briella."

"What happened to him, to Simon, I mean?" Will asked, very much intrigued.

"He tried to take his rightful throne as King of Mass and Bale killed him, or rather, Kylan did. Killed the whole family, in fact, except Briella, who was a baby at the time."

"Why keep Briella alive?"

Del shrugged. "Maybe he thought he could corrupt her because she was only a baby, as they corrupted the next generation." Del smiled at him sadly. "Seems it didn't work though. We owe Princess Briella much."

Will thought a bit longer and turned to Del and his fountaining knowledge. How did he know all this stuff? They had learned the history of Mass in school, but the part Del just told him was conveniently omitted. "Did they used to have schools for magical people?"

"Schools? No," Del said, almost laughing. "We were taught by masters of our crafts, just like you apprenticing under me at the candle shop. People were eager to pass their skills on then, not like now where they do as little as possible to remain hidden in the shadows of King Bale and Kylan. There were many great Magic teachers back then. Regrettably, it was through the teachers and their apprentices that Kylan was able to find and weed out witches and wizards. Our strength back then was in our numbers, but when we were off banishing the Great Scourge, Kylan and his goons hunted down the foremost men and women of our kind. They gave him names and locations to find apprentices they taught, whether through guile or force, and it was as easy as picking a bug off one's arm. They had the advantage when we came back. It was already finished." Del dropped his mournful head.

"Did you have a teacher?" Will asked after the storm passed from Del's face.

"Yes," Del said, smiling. His face quickly turned. "For the life of me, I can't seem to remember her name."

This plagued Del for a long time, before Will asked: "Was she hunted down?"

Del snickered. "No, they wouldn't have had a chance with her. She would have reminded them that she had saved their granny or birthed their child or fed that child when the mother couldn't, all with raised finger, mind you." Will laughed at Del's impression. Del's face turned down again. "She died many years before there were any raids. Fortunate woman."

Will looked at Isa, stuck in her galaxy with her wonderful stars revolving around her.

"How long do magical people live?" Will asked, rather shyly.

"Look ..." Del said. He pointed toward Isa.

All of the hovering, whirring, and buzzing creatures scattered as one small swallow swooped and perched on her shoulder. It appeared to have much to say, and Isa spent a significant amount of energy nodding her head and holding her hand up trying to get it to quiet down.

"Come, let us see how this goes," Del said, giving Will his book back.

Will made a point of hiding behind Del to not spook the bird, but Del made his way over without worry.

"Yes, yes, I know all about that, Terron. You told me all of this the last time I saw you," Isa said.

"Yes, of course I did," the bird said in a voice that sounded like a squealing mouse caught in a creaky door. Will couldn't believe he understood it.

"Can all birds talk?" he whispered to Del.

"Yes, but only once trained by a master like Isa. The trouble then is getting them to shut up."

"And who are these people?" Terron asked as Del and Will approached. The sound of his voice pained Will's sensitive ears.

"These are my friends Del and Will," Isa said. "Now, if—"

"Nice to meet you, Del and Will," Terron said, fluttering and alighting on each of their shoulders.

"Likewise," Del said. "Nice to meet you," Will said, staring into the bird's beady eyes. He couldn't even feel the swallow's weight on his shoulder, and with a flash and shimmer, the bird was back talking to Isa.

"Is this the same Del you were telling me about? The one you used to be married to and sometimes miss?" The words flitted out faster than the bird's wings fluttered. Isa looked out of the corner of her eye at a blushing Del.

"Yes, Terron. Now—"

"Well, it looks like you don't have to miss him anymore. Now that he's here, that is."

"Terron, will you please—"

"And a small boy as well, what a blessing. For humans, that is, our babies never stop barking at us. They're hungry all the time, and when they're not hungry they're fighting. Then comes the coarse, spindly feathers—they look like overused brooms! Not near as good looking as this little fellow. How wonderful to—"

"Terron!" Isa squawked as high as the bird's voice.

The bird fluttered to a stop. "No need to yell, Isabella. I am right here," Terron said.

"Yes, of course … sorry," Isa said, gathering herself again. "We have a task for you."

"I love tasks," Terron squeaked. "Go on."

"We need you to fly to Umbrate and—"

"No, I can't fly to Umbrate," Terron said.

"And why not?"

The bird turned his head and flapped acrobatically to catch a bug late to the winged-creature gathering. They all stared at him, and Will thought he could see the bird's blue and white cheeks blush.

"Sorry. Instinct," he said after gulping the fly down whole.

"No harm done … to us," Isa said, shuddering at the thought of the fly buzzing in the bird's gullet. "Why can't you fly to Umbrate?"

"That's Cliff Swallow country," Terron answered. "Nasty buggers, they are, building their nests of mud under eaves of stone around that cold castle—it's a terrible life for a bird, and their attitudes reflect it. I'm a Tree Swallow, and we have no desire to enter Cliff Swallow country."

"Not even if it's very important?" Isa said. Terron hopped closer at the conviction in her voice.

"How important?" he asked.

"Important enough to change the world."

If the bird had had a hand, he would have put it to his beak and thought a moment. Terron became so tense with silence that they wondered if he had spontaneously forgotten how to talk.

"That's good enough reason to enter Cliff Swallow country," Terron finally said. "Tell me more."

As Terron received his directions, his message, and a description of his target, Elias entered through the wooden gates of Sentinel's Village. The guards let him pass with little care for anything but his stature, because he carried nothing and hid nothing, and they seemed rather busy at the moment: the city was alive, and the gate was its funnel of commerce. Elias walked in with his hood down and his eyes up, for that is the best way to see things.

The village was old and constructed of wood once cut to keep the borders of the Grim Forest back, and of stone from the Glass Mountains. Its walls were warped and splintered, and its cobbled streets rattled the teeth loose of any cart rider or donkey that pulled the cart. It was a drab place, but the people were full of cheer and full of stomach. They seemed to get rosier-cheeked and fatter with each pass Elias made through. He couldn't believe the differences between Sentinel's Village and Umbrate. Umbrate was a brilliant city with dark streets and downtrodden people, and Sentinel's Village was a drab town with happy, smiling faces and laughter throughout.

Sentinel's Village was made up of guards and their families, and a few fortunate others that provided them with what they needed to keep all of Mass safe as they watched over Bale's Victory, or Mirror Pool as Elias knew it. Like the City Guard and the Royal Guard of Umbrate, the Sentinels and their closest people were provided for, and Sentinel's Village had the great advantage of eternal light, with enough water flowing off the mountains and cleared land to farm. Umbrate, on the other hand, was always shrouded in darkness, as if a great shadowy mountain rested at its back. Few things grew under such light, and the people starved at the great Altar of a wicked king. Yet in Sentinel's Village, home of the greatest protectors of Mass, the people were fat and slow, and had forgotten enough history to remember how great their city had been, or why the sentinels even watched over Bale's Victory.

It made Elias ill to think about it—how some starved while others had so much that they became fat from lack of discipline. Why not move all the people to Sentinel's Village, he had often wondered? The answer, however, was all too obvious to him: King Bale and his advisor Kylan loved their power. Give the people enough, but no more, and they won't complain; keep the light low and the Magic lower; keep those in power fed and strong, and no opposition will arise, and if it does it will be too weak to fight. Let them look at your tall, windowless towers of stone and fear the mysteries that take place inside so much that they never lift their eyes from their work for fear of seeing something they should not.

An opposite pattern took place in Sentinel's Village. Let the citizens and the Sentinels get soft and slow and fat; let them enjoy the spoils of life, the spoils gifted by their great king, and never let outsiders take position in their village without special grant. Elias knew it worked that way because eternal sunlight lifted the spirit too much, so why not make the people subservient and loyal in a way that makes sense to them?

But why would a king want his most prominent guards to get so fat and slow? The answer to that question was not so obvious to Elias. What he did know was that even if the Great Evil could rise from the depths of Mirror Pool (he couldn't bring himself to say Bale's Victory), the Sentinels would have little defense against it. Elias knew, he had faced it himself. The ancient scars still ached.

He had been to Sentinel's Village many times, but this time it looked different. People scurried through the streets, and banners and tapestries were being hung from the tops of buildings by men on creaky wooden ladders. The city buzzed like a hive.

"Well, you're a large one, aren't you," a woman with a round, ruddy face said. "Give us a hand with this flour, if you would, and I'll give you a loaf of bread."

An overfull cart sat before him piled high with large sacks of flour. Elias looked over the doorway and saw a wooden sign swinging from two lengths of chain that read 'Baker.'

"Of course," Elias said, attempting to mimic her smile but finding it a challenge to summon the cheer. He grabbed a sack in each arm and the woman stared at him with admiration.

"Oh my, you are strong," she said, giggling coquettishly. Elias nodded and she led the way into the shop where she opened the door of a pantry.

All the surfaces were covered in a fine flour dust and the room smelled of sweet bread and rising dough. Elias looked at the stack of endless wood piled by the stove and the flour that covered the floor. There were people across Mass who were not so fortunate to have either.

"Just there," the woman said, pointing into the pantry.

Elias stacked the sacks. "It's an awful lot of lifting for one woman," Elias said. "What do you do when I'm not around?"

"I wish you were always around—I'd have a lot of work for you." The woman giggled and touched his strong arm. "Normally, I'd ask a strong sentinel who might be about, but all are so busy getting ready for the centennial festival. It's so exciting," she shivered with uncontrolled giddy. She leaned in to whisper as if they weren't the only two there. "King Bale and Kylan Godea are coming."

"Then I've made it in time? Good!" Elias said. "How many days until the festival?"

The baker put one hand on her hip and counted by touching the tips of her fingers to her thumb with the other as she stared into the empty rafters trapping the heat of the stove.

"Three weeks exactly until the King and Kylan walk through the streets. Oh, goodness! And so much to do."

"How long does the festival last?" Elias asked.

She looked at him strangely. "Why a week, of course. Everyone except you seems to know that."

"You'll have to forgive me, ma'am. I've been traveling up from Bale's Bay and I was worried I had already missed it."

"No harm done," she said, waving his excuse away.

She gave him enough fodder for his ear to chew on as he made trip after trip with bags of flour. She described to him every event that would take place on every day of the King's visit, from the initial walk through the streets on the day of arrival, to the vigil and mass on the shore of Bale's Victory to remember the fateful day King Bale banished the Great Evil on the final day of the festival. She seemed particularly excited about that event and about honoring 'her sentinels', as she called them, at the greatest gathering that all of Mass had ever seen. And when Elias finished helping her, she gave him two loaves of still-warm bread and kissed him on his cheek.

"Thank you, Mister ..."

"Pierre," Elias said without a hitch—his usual alias. "Alfred Pierre."

"Well, thank you, Mr. Pierre. I'd like to see if those strong arms can lift other things someday." She giggled and blushed and skittered her way back into the bakery.

Elias walked the streets a bit longer, regretting not taking a corner of the bread as the warmth leached out of it. The people were so busy and excited. He wished he could feel the same way. After Gertie and Rolph confessed that things were changing, Elias couldn't help but notice himself. His travels had led him to the woods and mountains in this area many times and it was darker, and the trees looked lonelier, and few animals crossed his path on the way down, but the people seemed not to notice. They were too busy planning for a festival. He wished he knew someone there that he could talk to, but all had vanished years ago—the curse of being a wizard of long life.

He walked through the entire city without a glance in his direction. The people were busy with the work of their hands, and didn't have time to notice an illegal being traipsing through their streets. And when the sun began its downward descent, he made his way toward the gate and walked out without a look from the guards as people came and went through the inundated funnel.

Elias stopped by Mirror Pool and studied its calm waters. If it hadn't been so warm a person could have thought it was a sheet of ice. Its smooth surface reflected the jagged peaks of the Glass Mountains. He looked at the four sentinel towers built on the four cardinal points. They were careworn from a time when the Sentinel's actually cared and dilapidated from a lack of tending. And it appeared that no sentinels stood at the edges and watched the flat lake. If they only knew the power of what resided below.

Visions of that fateful day (or had it been night?) when he helped banish the true Great Evil to the depths of Mirror Pool flashed and burst through Elias's mind. He felt cold all over as if the memory itself had taken place in winter. Truly he couldn't remember if it had or not because all of the world felt cold and stormy back then. The Great Undead army had destroyed so many places, so many lands, and the sun and moon were so dark, as if great columns of smoke and shadow had blotted them out. Umbrate still lived under that shadow. Many towns across Mass had been destroyed before Xenerac and his army of witches and wizards chased and herded and imprisoned the Great Scourge into Mirror Pool. Few were rebuilt. And when it was all said and done, when the lives of many were left on the fields of battle, and those that fought and lived had no homes left, the great warriors returned to Umbrate to be greeted with incarceration and death, with they themselves being banished as the Great Evil.

That was the last time Elias had been in Umbrate, nearly a hundred years ago. He looked away from Mirror Pool and the lazy sentinel towers with a tear streaking down his face and hiding in his beard. He slipped into the trees, careful that none followed him, and made the forlorn trip back to the hiding place in the mountains.

At least he brought food with him, and the hope that the others would have better news to tell him than he had to tell them. Little time remained for their only opportunity to make a change in a changeless, lying world.

Sap expanded, popped, and sizzled in the handmade fireplace of the cave. Pleasant munching came from all as they dipped their bread in the weak vegetable broth. Its sweet flavor filled them with memories of days gone by as its density filled the voids in their stomachs for what seemed the first time in eternity.

For Will, it actually was eternity. Besides the biscuits at Isa's, he couldn't remember eating bread like this in his life, sure that if he had he would have remembered it.

"And she just gave it to you?" Will asked again.

Elias laughed. "I carried some flour for her, and then, yes, she just gave it to me."

"And they have bread like this down there all the time?" Will continued.

"Yes."

"Wow! We never had anything like this in Umbrate," Will exclaimed with a full mouth. The others smiled and laughed at him.

"I would imagine eating like this all the time has made the people of Sentinel's Village fat and content," Del said, content himself.

"It has," Elias admitted, not as contently. "It has also made the Sentinels fat and slow."

Del shook his head. "What did the king expect to happen after lying all these years? Of course they are going to get plump and sleepy when they don't even know what they're protecting Mass from." The others looked at the bread in their hands, considering this with some guilt.

"We don't have long," Elias said. "Only twenty-seven days, beginning tomorrow."

"It'll take us at least ten to get back to Umbrate, and at a trotting pace," Del said.

"But how do we get by them without being seen?" Gertie asked.

"Yes, there'll be a long line of them all the way up the King's Carve," Rolph added.

"We'll use the forest," Isa said. "It's our only option."

"We also have the option to not go," Del said. He caught the hurt gaze of the others and looked away. "Sorry." Old habits die hard.

"We must wait for Terron's return before we make any more plans," Elias said. "How long do you think it will take him?"

Isa shrugged. "I suppose it'll depend on how quickly he can get to Alphonse."

"Or if he can at all," Gertie said.

"Yes, another challenge," Isa acknowledged, looking downcast into her thin broth.

They hushed and thought of various things. One thought of a shiny lake watched by weak men; another thought of a place where everyone had enough and all were doughy and happy; and another still thought of a small bird flying somewhere in the wide world. They all sighed at the same time and went back to finishing their meal.

36

Being the Captain of the Royal Guard and personal attendant to Princess Briella, it was difficult for Alphonse to find time outside, simply because the doddering king and the imprisoned princess spent little time beyond the doors of the castle. It made his job rather dull on occasion. And to combat any dullness Alphonse spent time with the bright princess or walked through the halls of the royal chambers.

There were few windows in the halls of the royal chambers, but on his afternoon saunter, Alphonse enjoyed walking a corridor that overlooked Umbrate from high above. It gave him a full view of the city, and it helped remind him of the poverty and fear below. His walks also offered him time alone, time to think.

On a particularly dark and hazy day, Alphonse traipsed through the windowed corridor with his hands clasped behind his colorful robe. The humid air wrapped him and the mustiness of the enclosed Royal chambers behind him clung in his nostrils. The weather was always like this around the time of the Festival of Bale's Victory—always humid and hazy and musty—but Alphonse tolerated it, as did all of Umbrate.

He passed the first window, then the second, with the faint light clinging to the colors of his robes for just a moment before he returned to darkness. And when he came into the light of the third window, he looked into the small, beady eyes of a swallow with its head cocked to the side. It hopped closer to him and Alphonse cocked his own head at the curious animal. Two more skips forward and the bird never took his eyes off the royal guard.

"Well, you're an inquisitive little thing," Alphonse said, grinning. Most of the animals in the kingdom were like the people: they worked, and rested, and walked with their heads down, and even the swallows that built mud nests under the castle's eaves were silent hunters whose chatters never echoed between the stone walls as they might in a kinder, brighter city.

Alphonse reached out his hand to see if the bird would peck at his finger when the little creature hopped up on it. Alphonse's grin turned into a smile as he pulled the peculiar bird closer.

"And what are you doing so high on the castle walls? Looking for a treat?" Alphonse said.

"No, I'm looking for you," the bird replied in a series of high-pitched squeaks. Alphonse jumped back and flicked his hand, but the tiny talons remained latched.

"That's no way to treat a visitor, and one with so little time," Terron said.

Alphonse looked down the hallway and over his shoulder to verify he was alone.

"Did you say you were looking for me?" Alphonse asked; his voice squeaking a bit as well.

"Yes, if you're Alphonse of the Royal Guard. You look like the man they sent me to seek."

"I am," Alphonse said warily. "But who told you to seek me?"

Terron went right past that into his own troubles. "You're a very hard man to get alone, you walk too fast by these windows for me to get your attention. And those horrible Cliff Swallows have been badgering me day and night. I haven't had a chance to eat or sleep, and after all that flying from the Glass Mountains to catch up with a man who wouldn't dare be seen with me. I must say …"

The strength and speed at which the bird spoke astonished Alphonse, and gave him a bit of a headache. He attempted to speak a number of times but couldn't find a crack to sneak a word in, and it felt somehow disrespectful to interrupt such a small bird that had learned to talk.

"You said you were short on time?" Alphonse said, finding the courage to interject.

"Oh, yes, I've got a message for you from Isabella, aunt of William Chandler and ex-wife of Del Chandler. She wanted me to make sure I said that ex-wife bit, though I'm not sure why, Del seems like quite a nice man, maybe a little stodgy, but nice nonetheless, and young Will was so attentive, though in truth I don't think the boy had ever seen a talking bird." Alphonse could relate.

"You've word from Del and Will?" Alphonse exclaimed.

"Yes, and Isabella, of course," Terron continued. "They said the message might change all of Mass, and I hope they're right, having to fly so hard and put up with those incorrigible Cliff Swallows. Terrible beings they are, not like us Tree Swallows, much filthier, and much ruder, especially here in Umbrate. Though I can't possibly blame them for that. It's so dark here, and the air so heavy. I don't understand how a bird can catch a fly in such dense air. It really isn't fair, though I'm sure the fly would feel otherwise, if a fly could feel—"

Alphonse looked up and down the corridor, then back to the chattering bird.

"Please, I also have very little time, and many questions. It's not safe to talk openly here with a … you. Can I put you in my pocket and take you to my quarters where we can speak in private?"

"Pocket?" Terron asked. The bird seemed lost for words for the first time since it had learned any. He looked Alphonse up and down and nodded. "Fine, just as long as there aren't any nasty bits in there, and enough room to breathe. Us swallows can fit into many tight spaces but we're rather particular about our air."

"Of course," Alphonse said. He let Terron inspect the pocket over his breast and, after removing a piece of lint and loose string, the bird jumped into the pocket and quieted.

"Oh, it's you," Yan said, appearing at the end of the corridor. "I thought I heard someone talking … or squeaking, or something."

"I was whistling," Alphonse elucidated.

"Whistling?" Yan said, coming closer.

"Yes, it's a stupid habit I find myself doing when I'm alone. I don't even notice it's happening," Alphonse said, grinning.

"Well, it's not very professional," Yan critiqued.

"Yes, I suppose not." Alphonse turned to look out the window. He could feel the small bird fiddling in the folds of cloth like a mouse caught in a blanket.

"Are you and your guards prepared for the journey to Sentinel's Village?" Yan asked, coming up beside him and looking out the window on the dusty gray kingdom below. King Bale's fist pointed into the air as Xenerac stared up at them with terrified, bulging eyes from the statue below.

"Yes, of course. And you and your guards?" Alphonse replied. He stared into Xenerac's eyes and felt the fear in them like a sliver into the quick.

"Very much so, but I can't help but worry about the city while we're gone."

"It's difficult not to worry when it's your job," Alphonse said. Terron wiggled and a bead of sweat broke on his forehead.

Yan gazed out the window. "Yes, but at least the things you have to protect will be going with you."

"I'm sure the city will be safe as it is. The people are content with their lives; they have no desire to rebel because they wouldn't know what to do if they found victory in their hands; they are a defeated people, and in defeat is where they find comfort. Kylan and the monks would slice through them like a blade through water."

Yan looked at him from the corner of his eye. "Yes, but it's still enough to make a man consider."

"It proves you're in the position you are for a reason," Alphonse said. An abrupt squeak and movement popped from his chest. Yan turned and furrowed his brow, but the squeak vanished like an unimportant thought.

"Well, I'll let you get back to your ... whistling. Only five days until we depart and there is much to do," Yan said. He walked past Alphonse. "Hopefully I'll feel assured by then."

"You'll be ready for a festival, ready to celebrate a hundred years," Alphonse said.

Yan scoffed. "They'll do the celebrating. We'll be too busy guarding."

"Then your journey will not be in vain," Alphonse assured him.

"Yes, not like the journey to burn the forest," Yan said, his eyes reflecting on the past. He pivoted and left through the opposite doorway to the corridor. Alphonse put his hand over his heart and felt the bird's rapid vibration. He went the opposite direction of Yan and to his quarters where he released the swallow.

"That was quite unpleasant," he said. "Who were you talking to for so long?"

"Sorry, another guard," Alphonse explained. "And what is your name, Mr. bird?"

"Mr. Swallow to you—Mr. Tree Swallow, in fact. But Isabella calls me Terron, and you may as well." The strange sound of his voice pierced Alphonse's ear drums, but he was getting used to it.

"And what word do you have from Del and Will and Isabella, who I don't know, that has the potential to change all of Mass, Terron?" Alphonse asked.

"They would like to free a wizard from the Reformatory of Magic when the king and others are on their journey to Sentinel's Village for the centennial festival," came the nonchalant message. He searched the room with jerky head movements as Alphonse scraped his jaw off the floor.

"I don't believe I've heard you correctly," he said after a head shake to set things back in place.

"They wish to attack when the city is empty so that they can free a wizard from the Reformatory, or rather, as many magical people as they can. It seems a very simple plan, I'm not quite sure what you don't understand," Terron said quite haughtily for a one-ounce bird.

"Well, to start, I don't understand how they plan on breaking into the most guarded prison in all of Mass—it's impossible," Alphonse said.

"I suppose that's why they need you," Terron replied, growing distracted and hopping across the wooden table Alphonse set him on. "Oh, and they also need the help of a man named Emesh."

"Friar Emesh?"

"Yes, that sounds correct, and also some white earth miners named Newt and Grace." Terron fluttered from the desk to the small window sill. "Nice view," he said, staring out the window, "for Umbrate at least."

"Why do they need Friar Emesh?" Alphonse asked.

"Apparently he's a kind man of the clergy who can get things into the Reformatory," Terron said. A moth beat up from the corner of the sill and Terron fought the urge to snatch it.

Alphonse scratched his head. "They trust him that much?"

Terron didn't heed the question. "Can you help or not? I really must know before I leave for my long journey back."

"Where are they?"

"In a secret cave in the Glass Mountains—a magical place that's difficult to find, so don't try if you believe yourself a traitor."

"I'm not a traitor," Alphonse said, refusing to let a talking bird get him worked up more than he already had. "I wish to help, but it will not be easy."

"Good," Terron said, fluttering to the back of Alphonse's chair. "Let me tell you more."

Terron proceeded to divulge, with many tangential and erratic comments, all the details that Isa had passed on to him: the raiding of the Mausoleum of Magic, leaving the burned forest, finding the cave and two more magical people, and the plan to break into the Reformatory. They had left out the part about the wizard they wanted to save being Xenerac, because they didn't want Alphonse to deny the plan based on unsubstantiated claims, and because they weren't yet convinced that he was alive as Gertie and Rolph believed him to be. And when Alphonse asked who they wanted to save, the bird with the fantastic memory didn't know. They also kept the part about Xenerac's vision out—they themselves didn't know what to make of that yet.

"So, they wish to get into the city hidden in bags of white earth? And then they plan on using a doorman to get into a prison guarded by powerful dark wizards and witches?"

"Only with your help of course," Terron said. "They say the world is changing, that darkness is taking over again and, I must admit, I can feel it as well. I've had to move my home three times in the last year because of rot in the trees. It's very unpleasant—not healthy at all."

A light knock hit the door.

Terron and Alphonse looked at it, then back to each other.

"Just a moment," Alphonse said aloud.

"Will you commit your loyalty to their plan, yes or no? Time is short," Terron squeaked seriously.

Alphonse thought a moment, the sweat forming again on his usually cool brow.

"Yes," Alphonse said.

"Good. Thank you," and with that, Terron vanished through the open window.

Alphonse breathed deep and opened the door to find Rufus standing tall with patience.

"May I have a moment of your time, sir?" Rufus said.

Alphonse permitted him entry and closed the door.

"What is it?" Alphonse asked, his mind miles away with other issues.

"More monks than usual have been coming to visit Kylan on my watch, and if I'm not mistaken, I've heard the Mausoleum of Magic brought up more than once," Rufus said.

"I believe I can explain," Alphonse began. "But I must ask you: do you pledge your loyalty to me and Princess Briella?"

"Sir?" Rufus's face twisted. "I believe I have answered that with my actions."

"No, not yet, there is more to come—much more. But I ask again: do you pledge your loyalty?"

Rufus clicked his heels together and stood taller.

"In the name of my father and until my death, sir," Rufus said.

"Good. You will be staying in Umbrate for the festival," Alphonse began. "Now take a seat and let me explain further."

And when Alphonse finished explaining the plan to a bewildered Rufus, he went to Princess Briella's quarters to tell her of the day's strange events.

37

The last crumbs of bread sat on a board between the five grown wizards and the boy. They had eaten, and read, and fished, and walked, and swam, but the days seemed to only grow longer. Will found himself wondering how Gertie and Rolph had spent so many years in this cave before he realized that bickering was their own form of entertainment, as much as it annoyed everyone else.

It had been five days since Terron left with the message and, even dipped in the vegetable and fish stew, the stale bread became difficult to choke down. And worse than all of that, the once proud magical people were reverting back to the hopelessness they had so long made their homes.

Will looked at the bread on the board.

"You can have it, Will," Isa said.

"I don't want it," Will replied, wishing not to be discourteous but to tell the truth.

The rest of them stared at it and then back to their bowls. The dull sound of reluctant wooden spoons scraping up the lean fare filled the small cave. Elias tipped his bowl back and slurped the contents down.

"Well, I'll take it if no one else wants it," Del said. No protest came from the others, just pessimistic silence.

Will scooped his spoon under a turnip and it squeaked as if a metal spoon against a pottery bowl. He cocked his head, scraped the spoon again, and produced the same sound. He looked up and the adults stared at him. His spoon remained in place, but the squeaking continued. Isa put her bowl to the side and turned to the pool by the mouth of the cave.

"Terron," she said, struggling to her feet and running toward the entrance.

The others followed at a mad dash across the smooth pebbles. They broke through the magical barrier into the trees and looked around. The squeaking had stopped.

"Terron?" Isa yelled.

They looked to the sky with frantic eyes. Were they going mad?

"Terron!" Will called.

A chirruping cough came from behind them, and they turned to see Terron sitting atop a rock above the cave entrance.

"Sorry," he said, "I usually avoid eating moths, but I saw one in Umbrate and couldn't stop thinking about it the whole flight here, and then one of the little buggers fluttered out while I was searching for you. So dry, they are. Difficult to get down once you get started." He coughed-chirruped again.

Isa came to him with her hand over her heart, relieved.

"Oh, Terron, thank goodness you're back," she said.

"And I hope you brought good news," Del said.

Terron bobbed his head. "But a bit of water first would be nice," he said dryly.

In the cave, they gathered around the swallow perched on the edge of a wooden bowl. First he drank, then he bathed, and then he drank again. He asked for a bit of food, and with only lean broth and veggies to offer, Terron declined saying that the moth would be enough to hold him over.

After five days of waiting, the suspense felt like a hand tightening around their throats. They leaned in every time they thought the bird about to speak, and back out when they realized the chirrups were involuntary. And when it finally appeared that Terron was unaware they waited on him, Isa spoke up.

"Terron, do you have something you wish to tell us?"

"Oh, yes—he'll do it," Terron replied. He dipped his head into the water and shook the droplets down his smooth, waxy feathers.

"Who is he, and what will he do?" Del asked, exposing his lack of faith in the assurance of a bird.

"Alphonse of the Royal Guard said that he would pledge his loyalty to you and help you get into Umbrate the way you told me you wish to," Terron replied on the verge of strutting.

The group leaned back breathless and breathing deep.

"He seemed to believe it would be difficult, though. Difficult! *Cheep!*" Terron squeaked, annoyed. "Try living amongst filthy Cliff Swallows for three days waiting for a man in bright robes to walk by a certain window. The man knows nothing of difficulty." Terron dipped his head in the bowl and the water trickled down his pristine feathers once more.

The humans shared a glance, ignoring the swallow's diminutive annoyance. The realization of their situation clawed deeper every day they were there. If they stayed in the cave, they would always be in the cave, until Will was old and they were nothing more than a group of pensive stalagmites. Or, they could go to Umbrate, risk their lives to free the greatest wizard of all time, and probably die in a battle for all of Mass. It was proving to be a rather difficult decision. But Will, beginning to grasp the briefness of his life, said the thing the others were unwilling or unable to say.

"Then we must prepare for a journey back to Umbrate," he said. The others looked at him—some with hope, some with a hint of treason for the safety of the cave. "Five days are gone already, and we're no closer to freeing anyone or finding the truth of the dream."

Isa breathed deep. Gertie and Rolph stared at each other, engaged in telepathy. Del looked at the ground.

"We've waited long enough," Elias said, standing. "Our brave little friend has made a long and dangerous journey for us," Terron chirruped, "and now is the time to regain what, and who, we have lost."

Isa and Will stood with him, then Gertie and Rolph after silent deliberation. Del remained seated. Will put his hand on his slumped shoulder.

"We need you, Del. You've come too far to be left behind."

Del looked up and sighed. "You're a good boy, Will."

He stood and joined them: a scared bunch of geriatric wizards, a bird, and a boy with a heart that could not be defeated. The time to return to Umbrate had arrived.

38

A great procession lined the streets from the Cathedral to the gates of Umbrate. Guards stood shoulder to shoulder in taut lines that started with the City Guard and faded to the Royal Guard. In the center of the procession the Royal Guard surrounded a large force of gray-cloaked monks, who themselves surrounded the horse drawn carts of King Bale, Kylan Godea, Princess Briella, and Father Renalt. Behind the carts a second wave of guards waited at attention, and the distinguished members of the clergy stood in a tight circle behind them. All walked except for Yan and Alphonse, each the leader of their respected Guards, and each atop a chestnut horse.

The sight was a rare one, and the common people bordered the streets in full force, all remaining in Umbrate out of fear or poverty.

Alphonse looked at Rufus, standing before the remaining Royal Guard, and nodded; he returned it. He looked over at Friar Emesh and sighed. The old friar still had no clue of the part he was about to play. Alphonse thought it prudent to keep the man in the dark until they were gone because the gloom of Father Renalt hung always over him; but now the menacing father was leaving, and all the powerful clergy members with him. Some monks and guards remained, but Alphonse knew little Terron was right: it was their best opportunity for something big, something that could actually change the course of things. Waiting for the death of an old man wouldn't do any longer.

Alphonse, after a signal to Yan, gave the order, and the procession began. No cheers or claps or hoorahs came from the common people that lined the roads. No children tossed flowers into the streets or placed them in the hands of the king or princess.

All dropped their heads solemnly, too afraid to make eye contact with any in the procession, especially those in the carts.

Alphonse's eyes clouded with tears. What a dismal affair. Now was a time for celebration, a chance for an entire kingdom to rally around one event. Instead, the common people lowered their heads, not in reverence, but to avoid the sneering gazes from those above them. And to see the vibrant, clean banners and the shiny carts adorned with jewels and fine diaphanous curtains that separated the royalty from the dirty, malnourished, and unkempt working people, made Alphonse want to strip the clothes from his body and rouse them in revolution. It would come soon enough, and at the appropriate time, but in that moment Alphonse felt the truth in the rebellion of the small, stronger than he felt anything.

His part of the procession passed through the gate, and he closed his eyes to remember their faces: the young, the old, the bent too early for their age. He seared those pained gazes into his mind.

In twelve days, they would be walking through the streets of Sentinel's Village to the cheers of well-fed and happy people, and if there was any good in all of Mass, a group of wizards would be walking into the Reformatory of Magic and walking out with an army.

After the caravan was gone and the dust settled in its wake, Rufus ordered his remaining guards back to their posts. He lingered a moment and watched Friar Emesh enter his station on the side of the Cathedral. Once alone, Rufus approached the man's door and knocked.

Rufus's ears rang in the hush descending between the stone walls. The city was usually silent with downcast characters getting out of the way of guards, but the normal buzz of the place had left with the caravan.

Emesh cracked the door and peered out as if Rufus had roused him from his sleep. Seeing the colors of the Royal Guard, he threw the door open.

"Yes?" he said.

Rufus reached into his chest pocket and pulled out a sealed letter.

"The Captain of the Royal Guard requested I give this to you after the procession left the city."

Emesh looked at it curiously. He turned it over in his hands and saw the insignia of the Royal Guard and the insignia of Princess Briella stamped in wax, side by side.

"Fine, thank you," Emesh said, closing the door.

Rufus put his foot against the jamb. "He also requested that I watch you open it."

Emesh furrowed his brow, looking from Rufus to the letter.

"Fine, just come inside. It's too muggy out here for an old man."

Emesh admitted Rufus into the small receiving office. Rufus moved to the back, toward the Cathedral door. Emesh looked at him timidly, then down at the letter held cautiously in his fingers.

"What's this about?" Emesh asked, hesitant to break the seals. It was uncommon for a man like him to get noticed by anyone, let alone the princess, and he believed that to be a perk of the job.

"The letter should explain it all," Rufus said thoughtfully.

Emesh broke the seals with a shaky thumb. He read with a few glances at Rufus.

"I don't understand. I'm supposed to go pick up a load of white earth and deliver it to the Reformatory?" Emesh asked with scrunched brow.

"That is correct," Rufus said.

"But why can't the guards do it? They've always done it before," Emesh retorted.

"We're short on guards with everyone gone, but the King's loom will remain open. I will send one of my own with you to help load the white earth, and I will be here when the white earth is unloaded," Rufus replied.

"I don't mean to question the princess or your captain, but this is quite out of the ordinary," Emesh said. Doing anything but accepting and cataloguing commodities was far beyond Emesh's usual responsibilities.

Rufus stepped closer and the office became smaller. Emesh cowered, the fear heavy in his lachrymose eyes. "I don't mean to hurt you, Friar. I assure you that I am your friend in this matter, and I assure you that this is the best way for me to protect you."

"Protect me? From what?"

"Just do as you're told, and all will be well," Rufus explained. "I have the same orders from Alphonse and Princess Briella." He produced his own letter and presented it to Emesh, who scanned through it.

"But why do I have to take the load to the Reformatory? And why is the order coming from the Princess?"

Rufus grinned. "That is far above my head, Friar." He moved to the exterior door and turned. "Can you get the load to the Reformatory?"

"Of course," Emesh said, "but it will be a long, heavy haul."

Rufus nodded. "Good. I'll alert you when the order is ready."

Emesh stared, baffled, as Rufus left his quarters, praying that the old friar wouldn't take his questions elsewhere. He called on Asher, the man he would send with Emesh for the white earth. He slipped a letter into his hand and gave him a horse to send it with.

39

Gertie and Rolph stood at the opening of their cleared-out home. It appeared as if they had not been there the last ten years, and their hearts sank looking at what little impact they'd had on a place so important to them. The rest stood to the side and watched as the old pair said goodbye in their silent way. The cave had impressed on their lives as well. It had filled them with new breath and provided them with a quiet place to learn and remember, to rejuvenate and grow in strength again. Not even Del had anything cross to say … out loud, at least.

When Gertie and Rolph were finished they turned to the rest.

"Well, what are you waiting for?" Gertie said strongly.

"Yes, we have much road to travel," Rolph empathized.

And they turned away from the cave and started down the slope to a life they had circumvented long ago. The others followed, making their way into the Verdant Forest once again.

Will was relieved to be leaving the cave to get back to fighting in the real world, but he had made the journey already and knew of its difficulties, and he was not alone in wondering how a pair of very old magicians would handle it after spending so much idle time in a cave. But the pair sped ahead of them, appearing as eager to be on the move as Will.

Stepping out of the mountains and into the foothills above the forest, with one last glance down the hill, Will looked at Mirror Pool, the foundation of their modern civilization, and the greatest lie ever told. It gladdened him to look at it and see its truth—many had not and would not. How they had been deceived all these years, he didn't know—fear is a potent drug—but he would be deceived no longer, and he would try with what strength and experience he had to show others the truth. He would see Mirror Pool again.

Their journey would be long and difficult, but most worth making are, and soon they would change their world forever, or die in the process.

They made it out of the mountains and hills on the first hard day of their journey, and the next two were spent skirting and slinking through the Verdant Forest, though Will pondered the idea of it being named the Grim Forest once again. He didn't know if it was the fire, his last horrifying experience there, or if Gertie and Rolph's words about the world growing dark were coming true, but even in the few weeks since he had been through, the forest had grown grimmer. The greens were not as green, and the bark of the trees took on a sickly gray hue. Cloudy water ran out of the springs and the canopy refused to let the sun through. Walking through the forest was a gloomy affair, and not a pleasant omen for what they expected ahead.

Will walked with his head low, tired and defeated from carrying his pack through the melancholy woods. They traveled scattered, following Elias's flawless path. No one talked, because no one wanted to, and they only stopped for a break every few miles, if that. Will's head wobbled as he looked at the gray, sun-hungry ground, until he walked into Del's back.

The old man turned and put his index finger over his pursed lips. Will spun and saw the tense, pale gazes of his traveling companions as they crouched and stared toward the edge of the forest to their right. There were footfalls, many of them, and the sounds of wagons creaking and rocking in tune with the horses that pulled them. Will could just see the movement of a large force through a break in the trees. Arms and legs pumped in uniform motion as the caravan glided by the unmoving trees. It made his head hurt to look at the background moving so mechanically through the wild and knotted trees. Will recognized their uniforms as those of the City Guard.

Del grabbed his shoulder and forced him to squat. They watched for some time—longer than they should have—as the procession continued. A man on a horse flashed by the trained guards and the onlookers stooped lower. The uniforms changed from the City Guard to the Royal Guard. The Royal Guard expanded in its middle around a troop of monks surrounding four carts like a snake that had consumed a deer. Will could guess who rode in those carts. He looked at Elias, coiling as if to pounce. Was now their opportunity to attack? Del shook his head at him.

"There's too many. We could never get to them. If the guards didn't stop us, the monks would," Del whispered.

Elias gritted his teeth and backed away. The others followed. Will risked one last glance at the huge caravan before they faded into the trees. The man on the horse flashed by again, and Will thought he stopped and faced them, but he wasted no time to look with Isa, Gertie, and Rolph pushing him from behind.

They remained in their low retreat until they came to a flat opening where they could rest in hiding. The hoof and foot beats drummed in the distance, and the present company shared a knowing glance. Their enemy's motion led north while they headed south to an empty city.

They hunkered and waited for the footsteps to fade, and for the cover of nightfall.

◊

The sun lowered toward night before any of them felt safe enough to talk. The sound of the large snake had long slithered past, but its sinusoidal path, carved deep into the earth, still made them shiver to think about.

Del had pulled out Xenerac's writings some time ago and frantically flipped through it. Will scooted over to him and looked over his shoulder. "What are you doing?" he asked. They all turned to stare, acutely aware that he uttered the first words in many hours.

Del looked at Will, then around the group. "I'm trying to figure this out so I don't have to face that army of guards again."

Isa scoffed.

"Forgive me for trying to save my own skin, and yours," Del said.

"Luckily for you, they were heading in the opposite direction," Isa said. "They took all the guards with them."

"And monks," Elias added.

"And whether you figure it out or not, we still have to rescue those in the Reformatory," Isa said.

"And what if we get caught?" Del asked.

"Then we'll be in the Reformatory with them," Isa answered, "but at least we won't be hiding in a cave."

"Besides," Gertie began, "you won't be able to figure it out."

"Yes, if we can't, then you certainly won't be able to," Rolph said.

Del waved them off and went back to the book.

"We should continue moving," Elias said.

"But it's nearly dark," Isa disputed.

"And I feel no comfort talking openly when we don't know where they stopped," Elias said. "They could be walking in these woods now looking for water."

Each looked over a shoulder with newfound discomfort and rose as one to put on their packs.

Del looked at Will. "The answer is in here, boy." He said, holding up the book. "Even if we can't get Xenerac back, we still need to find it." Del stared at the trees overhead. "I may just be an old candlemaker who spent too many years in a dark shop, but things are changing, and they are changing rapidly." He adjusted his pack. "I've never thought much about the future, but I can't help but look at you and think about it now."

The other sets of eyes locked on Will, seeing the same future Del did. Will put his pack on and his head down, and they marched into night.

◊

They stopped and rested somewhere and sometime near midnight, and before Will knew it, the pale sky indicated dawn and Del was rousing him from his sleep. The journey had been long, and Will had no idea where they were or if they were getting closer, but there seemed to be a newfound comfort among his traveling companions that the bulk of the guards were far north of them now. Actually, the sheer size of their force seemed to cheer some of them, knowing that they wouldn't have to fight through a horde to get into Umbrate … not yet, anyway. Del did not share their cheer, and he loomed over Xenerac's books as if they were a fire providing him warmth on a cold, dreary night. His bloodshot eyes betrayed the fact that he had not slept, and when it was time to eat, Will brought him a bowl of whatever concoction Isa and Gertie had materialized. Del looked up at the bowl curiously, as if trying to read it as well, and accepted it.

"Ah, thank you, my boy." He slurped the broth and read the book rested on his knees.

"Why do you think the answer is in there?" Will asked.

Broth dribbled down Del's chin. He looked at Will and cautioned: "History has an extraordinary way of repeating itself, my dear boy, and if Xenerac believed these dreams and visions were a look into the future, they likely were."

"You really believe he can save all of Mass if we can free him? I mean, hasn't he been trapped in prison for a hundred years now, not doing any Magic?"

Everyone lowered their bowls and considered Will's question. Del looked at the others, hoping someone else would dare to answer first. They didn't. He stared at the boy.

"A fair question, Will, and I'm sure all of us have been wondering the same thing on this seemingly impossible journey, but you're forgetting something," Del said.

"What?"

"Well, hope, of course."

"Hope?"

Del smiled. "I know I'm not the greatest example of it, but that doesn't mean it doesn't exist, or that it doesn't have the power to change the world. Xenerac had hope."

"How do you know?" Will asked.

"Because he wrote this." Del lifted the prudent book of writings. "People without hope don't care about the future. The same way King Bale and Kylan don't care about the future. They just care about the reach of their power right now."

"But you've said it yourself—you've all said it: things are changing, and Xenerac's vision seems, well, hopeless."

"Hopeless only to those that don't care to change it," Del said. "That's how I used to be, and all those around me. But we have hope now."

The others agreed.

Elias stood and looked around. "We should be going."

Del reluctantly put his book away with a shaky hand. He put his pack on and felt its increasing weight, hoping dearly he wasn't lying about all that hope business. If not for his sake, then for Will's.

40

When Grace and Newt received the letter, they didn't think the order was possible. Could they not only hide Del and Will and their traveling companions, but also get them into Umbrate?

"You don't have to get them in," Asher informed them. "You just have to load the cart full enough to sneak them into the city."

"And how will we do that without killing them? It is heavy stuff," Newt said.

"I'm sure you'll find a way," Asher said.

"Do you really think they can do it? I mean, is it even possible to get people out of the Reformatory?" Grace asked.

Asher shrugged. "Only members from the clergy are allowed into the Reformatory. I know where the entrance is, but I know nothing else."

"And Friar Emesh is willing to help?" Newt asked. He had worked with the friar before, but only on a professional basis and only in passing.

"He's not fully informed of the plan," Asher admitted. "But if he refuses, I will be forced to kill him." Grace gasped. Asher continued, "I do not wish to do such a thing, but these are dire times, as you both know and understand." He looked from one worried face to the other. "Do I have your loyalty in this?"

Grace and Newt looked at each other. "Can you get us a bi-level cart?"

Asher thought a moment. "Yes, I believe I can."

"Then we're in," Newt said. Grace nodded.

"Good," Asher said. He went to the door, turned to them, and said, "Have a large load ready for when they arrive in the coming days," before he went out, got on his horse, and returned to Umbrate.

"So, now's the time?" Grace said after some silence.
"It's as good as any," Newt replied, taking her hand.

41

Isa stood before, or rather over, the ashes of her former home. They had crossed the King's Carve, its serpentine path carved deeper by footprints and cartwheels, and they were now standing in dusk light by an ashy mess. Tears rolled down her face; her hand muffled her sobbing mouth. It was a life she had lived, secret and alone, and it was a life destroyed. The others stood behind her and watched. Gertie and Rolph wrapped their arms around each other, thinking about their own lost home. Del looked at Will and pondered over his past home, and shop, and the time he had spent neglecting the boy. How quickly it could all be gone, with nothing left to show but a few charred boards and unidentifiable pieces that wouldn't even fit together.

Elias, with no home to speak of, was the only one that seemed concerned with standing exposed in the open. They could see for miles, and no one was around, but he knew the risk of being so public on the edge of the forest, or at least the new edge of the forest.

"We must get into the trees before dark," he said.

No one replied. Del looked at Elias and knew he was correct. He patted Will on the back and they both approached Isa. Del put his arm around her shoulder and Will hugged her waist. Her body shook under the weight of her grief, and she embraced them.

"It's so fragile," she said, the tears shaking down her face and dropping to crater the ash.

"There's a new life ahead for us, Isa," Del said. "It'll just take some rebuilding, is all." Del hugged her closer, and Will squeezed her tighter.

"Our time has come," Elias said. "Tomorrow we will be at the home of Del's friends, and we will enter Umbrate with the upper hand for the first time in a hundred years. There's no need to mourn over the fires of the past."

He was right. They left the site of ash and marched to the unburned portion of the woods to shelter under green leaves.

◊

"How far are we from this miner's home?" Gertie asked, peering through the trees.

"Yes, there is much open ground between us and Umbrate," Rolph said.

"It's some ways from here, but I'm not sure how far," Del said, standing behind them. He could see the hillside he and Will had popped out of from where they stood. The morning had been spent getting as far south as possible under cover of the forest, but their cover thinned.

"Didn't you come this way earlier? When you escaped?" Elias asked.

"Yes, but we didn't go over ground, we went under it," Del explained. Will tensed beside him.

"Then we should do the same," Gertie said.

"Yes, we've lived in a cave for a very long time. Underground is not an issue for us," Rolph added.

"No. Please, no," Will protested quietly. He grasped at the edge of Del's weathered cloak. None but Del had seen the boy in such pale fear, and he was the only one who could understand the sincerity of it.

"I agree with Will," Del said. "It's not safe, and Elias won't fit."

"What do you mean?" Elias asked, offended.

"I mean you're too big. Will and I could barely squeeze through. And not a pleasant squeeze, mind you."

"Then we'll have to wait for cover of darkness," Elias said.

"But we're running short of time," Isa said. "We're supposed to enter Umbrate tomorrow night."

"Then we have a long journey ahead, and now's the time to get some rest," Elias retorted.

"Why don't we just walk across the plains?" Will offered. Their eyes turned on him, stunned.

"We can't expose ourselves like that. It could destroy our whole mission," Elias warned.

"I don't think so," Will said, shrugging. He stepped forward and pointed. "We came out there in that hillside, and if we skirt along the edge, all the way around, we won't see anyone. No one veers from the King's Carve. And, besides, most of the guards are gone."

Del looked at him and rubbed his chin. "I think he's right."

"I don't," Elias said. "It's much too risky."

"I agree with Will." Isa picked her side. The four voters turned to Gertie and Rolph.

"Let's trust the boy," Rolph said as Gertie said, "No, we should wait." They looked at each other with furrowed brows.

"Four against two," Del said. "We'll rest here a while and continue this afternoon after a bit of watching."

Elias and Gertie shared a glance of betrayal, but they acquiesced and took a seat.

When the time came, Del was the first to step out of the trees. They had neither seen any movement nor heard any noise since their rest began an hour before, just the birds and insects chirruping at the humid day. And with little time to lose, the others followed the chandler. They made their way to the base of the hill and began to skirt around. They had waited till the sun dipped and now their shadows were long beside them. Will looked up at the hole in the hillside. His pulse quickened at the sight of it. Del sensed his apprehension and pulled the boy to his side.

By the time the hill faded to nothing more than a roll of earth, they had to squat to hide themselves. The sun was fading away and the moon had already risen behind it. There was not a person in sight, and as the light drained from the sky, they began to walk upright, holding tight to their vigilance until it all began to feel meaningless. Even this far out, the edge of the kingdom felt rather empty, quiet and content with the absence of life.

Dusk came and went, and they found themselves walking under the thin light of the moon. It was almost pleasant, as if they were out for an evening stroll in their old neighborhood.

"Stop!" Elias whispered. They stiffened and searched for a place to hide; there were few places on these dry, open plains. "Someone is approaching."

They couldn't see what Elias saw, but trusted his sight.

"Over there," Isa said, pointing to a small stand of stunted trees. They crouched low and duck-walked to the trees. There was not enough cover to hide them all, but they gathered around Will and watched through the skeletal branches.

A large figure appeared out of the dark like a moon-lit apparition. He, they guessed by his stature, walked casually along before stopping where they had turned. He headed toward the trees.

"Is somebody there?" the man called. "Hello, I mean you no harm."

Del stepped out of the trees, with Elias trying to stop him.

"Newt?" Del said.

The man turned at the sound of the voice. "Oh, Del, thank goodness! I've been so worried that you'd been captured. I've been walking out here every night since we received the message of your return." They hugged each other, unexpectedly but welcomed.

"Come out," Del said to the rest. "This is the man we've come to meet."

Will came first and the rest followed, still wary of meeting a wanderer in the dark.

"Will, my boy, how are you?" Newt said, the excitement palpable in his voice.

"Fine, Newt. It's good to see you again."

"And you, my boy. I'm glad to see you survived the cave.'"

"Only barely," Will said, downcast. Newt dropped the matter.

"And who are these folks?" Newt asked.

Del introduced them one by one and they each shook the stranger's hand without the opportunity to distinguish his face in the dark.

"Come, let's get back to the cabin. We have much to discuss, and I'm sure you're hungry and thirsty after your journey."

The quiet, dark walk to Newt's house seemed an eternity, but when they made it, Grace greeted them at the door with hugs and kisses to those she knew and hugs and handshakes to those she was just meeting. She let them in and fed them heartily. The affair was quite pleasant considering the long, hidden journey and what remained ahead.

Del told them of where they had been and what they had done, and Grace told them how surprised she had been to hear of their return and the mission they wished to accomplish. The new guests were not so eager to talk, whether from lack of trust or a deterioration of social skills from so much time alone, so Del and Will conducted the conversation, already having experienced Grace and Newt's loyalty and kindness for themselves.

"How did Alphonse get word to you?" Del asked as the usual pleasantries reached a quick end.

"Through a man named Asher, and another man named Rufus, both Royal Guards," Grace said. She gave him the letter and Del read it and passed it around.

"And Friar Emesh?"

Grace and Newt looked at each other. "Apparently he doesn't know what he's getting himself into," Newt said. "He thinks he's coming here for a delivery."

"And he agreed to that?"

"I'm not sure he had any choice. The order came from the Princess and the Captain of the Royal Guard," Grace said, adding soberly, "Asher said he would kill him if he resists."

"They can't do that!" Will exclaimed defensively.

Del put his arm around the boy. "They won't, Will. I'll make sure of it. Besides, Friar Emesh is a reasonable man, I'm sure he'll comply when we tell him of our plan. The clergy has not been kind to him all these years."

"But he *is* still a member of the clergy," Grace said, "and those loyalties are not easily broken."

"Then we will not easily break them," Del said. The room fell silent and he looked around at the tired, staring eyes. "I know him very well, and he will work with us, I'm sure of it. Right, Will?" If Del didn't believe in this wild plan, then the others wouldn't either, but it still took some effort to convince himself. They had come this far, now it was time to see it through, or die trying.

"I hope so," Will said. "He's always been very kind to me, unlike most in the clergy."

"Tell us about the plan to get into the city," Elias said, changing the subject to something he hoped had more foundation.

Newt began. "Tomorrow afternoon a multi-layered cart driven by Asher and Friar Emesh will arrive. We'll put you on the bottom level, and we'll fill the top level with white earth. Friar Emesh will present the order from Alphonse and the Princess, and the guards won't even consider stopping him. Getting in should be no problem. Getting out?" Newt shrugged. "I don't know what Rufus has planned."

"There are few guards to speak of in the city. We went there yesterday, and they didn't even stop us at the gate. The streets were empty," Grace said.

"It will be your best opportunity," Newt said. "Though I must say, I wasn't expecting five of you and the boy. I'm not sure how we'll fit all of you into the cart."

"Will's not going," Del said.

Will turned to him, shocked. "And why not? I'm smaller than all the rest of you. I can fit anywhere."

"We've already asked too much of you, and you've delivered even more. You'll stay here with Newt and Grace."

"But—"

"It's not negotiable," Del grumbled. No protest came from the others.

Will slouched in his seat and looked with disloyal eyes at his betrayers.

"Can you hide the rest of us?" Del asked.

Newt examined them. "It will be a tight, uncomfortable journey, but we can do it."

"The plan to get in seems feasible, but Newt brings up the question of getting out?" Elias cautioned.

"How many do you plan on saving?" Grace asked.

"One in particular, but as many as we can," Del said. "I know of a side gate—the same one Alphonse used to get us out—but it's far from the Reformatory."

Newt added, "You will have the cover of night."

"We must be careful to preserve life," Isa cautioned. "Too many have already died for this cause." They nodded but knew the impossibility of escaping without resistance.

Silence invaded the small cabin, and the weight of the job began to feel unbearably heavy. Gertie and Rolph stared into each other's eyes in a volley of silent conversation. Grace and Newt stared at them strangely, unsure of what they were witnessing. The rest waited for them to finish.

"We're not sure if we should go with you," Gertie said.

"Yes, we're very old and our Magic is spent," Rolph added.

Grace and Newt started at the word Magic—they guessed they always would being birthed in the middle of a Magic-hating world. But the world they lived in had failed them, and the alternative was clear.

"But we need you," Del said. "We need all the power we can get."

"If they don't go, then I will," Will said. Del glared at him.

"We've spent all of our lives hiding to avoid a cage," Gertie said.

"All our lives," Rolph echoed.

"And we don't plan on changing that now," Gertie added.

"Then why did you come?" Del asked. Gertie and Rolph fell silent again. "You have more to offer—I know it," he pleaded. "We know that you can contact Xenerac with your minds. He's the one we need."

"Xenerac … the wizard?" Grace asked, reminded of her history lesson. "He's dead."

"Apparently not," Del said. "They've been able to contact him."

Grace and Newt shared a confused glance. The boundaries of Magic were not well-defined to them.

"And what if he is dead?" Gertie's voice shook with fear. Rolph put his arm around her. "We haven't been able to reach him in years, and his mind seemed … lost the last time we tried." She put her head in her hands and cried. "We believed him to be our son. Nobody wants to see their son like that!"

Del swallowed hard and looked to Isa and Elias for help—they had none.

"Now is the only chance you'll have to save him," Del said. "You've come so far. Why stop now? We can't finish this without him."

"You saw what happened to him when he stood up to Kylan. We don't want to end up like him!" Gertie screeched. She cried harder and Rolph pulled her in to his chest.

Frustrated, Del stood and walked toward the door. "You're already like him: trapped in Kylan's restraints." He sighed. "You can stay, or you can go—it makes no difference to me—but I've hidden from that truth for too long, and I won't anymore." Del went out the door, into the night.

Will stood, looked around the table, and followed him.

Del looked up at the moon, and Will came up beside him.

"You have no right to not let me go with," the boy said.

Del breathed deep. "I know."

"Then why won't you let me?"

Del looked at him, the pale moonlight shining in his own mournful eyes. "Because if we lose you, we lose everything."

"That's not true. There's still a war to be fought!"

"Yes," Del agreed. "But you saw what I saw in there. They're giving up, just as I have for so long. You're their only motivation, and the motivation is waning. We need you alive, Will, and … I don't know what we're going to find tomorrow."

"But I don't want to be a symbol, I want to fight," Will said. The moon danced in his watery eyes.

"You have. And you will. Just not tomorrow," Del said. "I'm … I'm also scared of becoming like Xenerac and the others, just as Gertie and Rolph are, but if I'm meant to end up like that, I'd rather know you're not there with me."

The words sank into Will like the fangs of a snake, painfully true and destructive. But his bravery persevered. "I want to help … I *need* to help." The falling tears shook his words.

"No," Del said with finality, the sadness shaking his voice as well. "I can't see you trapped in the dark again." Will's head dropped. Del reached out to hug him, to touch him, but pulled away and walked into the night, leaving Will to cry alone.

◊

They scattered the floor of the large room in Newt and Grace's cabin. The only light came from the glow of embers that leaked through the seams of the stove door. None of them slept, and none of them would, but they rested in silence, most thinking about the years they had already lived to avoid thinking about the day to come. Will, however, could not get tomorrow out of his mind. He wanted to be there when they stormed into the Reformatory—he had to be. It wasn't fair, and he knew all of them believed that, but not a word was spoken in his defense.

He had as much stake in this fight as they did. It was his world too! While others thought of the past, he considered the future, and how he was going to be a part of it. If sleep would not come, then planning would suffice.

42

Morning dawned, low and hazy, as it often did under the perpetual shroud of Umbrate, and the mood inside Grace and Newt's house was just as gloomy. They had lasted the night, and now a long day stretched before them. Grace served them a breakfast of mealy porridge and dry bread, but no one complained. In fact, no one said anything at all, but deep consideration scattered the table as much as half-empty bowls and churning stomachs.

Will pouted, but the others remained oblivious, too deep in their own heads. And when the sun reached its noontime zenith, Rolph stood and presented himself.

"I've decided that I'm going with," he said.

Gertie gasped. The rest stared at him, taken aback.

"I'm sorry, dear," Rolph said to Gertie. "I know I've never kept anything from you, but I believe Del is right: this is our only chance to save Xenerac, and I've lived too long in a cave to not try."

Gertie stormed away from the table and out the door, teardrops marking the floor behind her. Del looked at the others and then to Rolph.

"Thank you, Rolph. Your presence will be a great help to us."

Rolph nodded and took his seat, but his eyes remained on the door, and the muffled cries drifting through it pierced his worn soul.

A few silent hours passed and the cart arrived. Their hearts pounded in their chests at the noise of axles squeaking without weight and shod hooves on packed dirt. The two men atop the cart stared down at them as they exited the house: one surprised, the other not.

"Del? Will? What on Mass are you doing here?" Friar Emesh said. "You're wanted by the king for defection!" The words settled in and the blood drained from his face. He turned to Asher, who remained firm. "You tricked me! You're going to let them into Umbrate under illegal orders. How dare you permit them after they shirked their duties!" He paused and turned back to Del and Will, his face a confused, betrayed mess. "Why *are* you coming back?"

"We've been friends a long time, Emesh," Del began, calmly, "and I've always trusted you, the same way I believe you've always trusted me."

"Yes, but that doesn't answer my question! And who are these people? More vagabonds and deserters?" Emesh said aggressively. The disgusted look on his normally jovial face was unfit for him.

Del looked to those standing by his side. "These are my friends … my *magical* friends, and we're here to free Xenerac and others from the Reformatory of Magic."

Emesh somehow leached to a paler shade of white. "You're … you're magical?"

"Yes," Del answered with calm confidence, though he shook below his weathered cloak.

Emesh's eyes rolled to the back of his head, and if Asher hadn't been so quick to grab him, he would have fallen out of the cart. He let him down gently.

"I'm Asher," he said as if he wasn't supporting a fainted man. "I've been appointed by Rufus, Alphonse, and Princess Briella to get you into Umbrate, and into the Reformatory of Magic."

Emesh's eyes burst open and he wavered upright.

"What happened?" he exclaimed, placing a hand on his clammy forehead. "I've had the strangest dream." He turned his head and saw Del and his motley crew; his rheumy eyes fluttered over his pallor. "I suppose it wasn't a dream." Emesh leaned forward and stroked his aching head. "Why me?" he asked himself.

"Because you've been kicked and beat just as much as we have," Del said with newfound and necessary gumption. "And it's time for a revolution."

"Revolution?" Emesh scoffed. "Mutiny, more like. It can't be done. And why should it be?"

"Because people like me and my friends have been oppressed and killed and silenced for far too long." Del came closer to the cart. Emesh recoiled. "You know me, Emesh, I'm the candlemaker, I wouldn't harm anyone, but you can't say the same for the king and his magical minion. They've had a stranglehold on everyone, not just magical people, for far too long. Don't you think it's hypocritical to use Magic to suppress Magic? Have you ever understood such a thing?"

"It's not my position to understand. I've taken an oath."

"Your position has been to stay out of Father Renalt's way," Del countered. Emesh shot him a foul glance. "Yes, I've seen the way they treat you, the way you cower from them. Does that strike you as kindness, Emesh?"

"It doesn't matter how it strikes me, it still can't be done," Emesh evaded. "And what is Will doing here? He's just a boy."

"Do you know how Will came to me?" Del asked.

"Of course not." Emesh wrapped his arms across his chest, petulant and resolute, and stared ahead into the distance. His world was changing far too quickly. It wasn't right!

"His mother was caught and killed by Yan Coaler of the City Guard. He ripped her from the streets for defending a magical woman caught in a kind act! And then they wanted him to serve that same man. Does that sound like a regime you want to follow?!"

Emesh softened, looked at the boy. "Is that true, Will?" Will nodded.

"And they were on their way to do the same to me. Alphonse warned me, and that's the only reason I'm still alive." Emesh refused to look at Del. "Now's the time, Emesh. I'm asking very little of you."

"Yes, all I have to do is sneak a bunch of criminals and their friends into the city they were banished from. Then I simply have to get them into the Reformatory of Magic," Emesh mocked. "That sounds like quite a lot to me, Delier."

Del grabbed Emesh's hand. Emesh avoided eye contact. "Will you do this for me, old friend? And if not for me, for Will?"

Emesh looked down at Del's hand and then into the distance. The battle waging in his head was apparent on his face. "Did they really kill Will's mother?"

"And many others like her," Del replied.

Emesh breathed deep. He put his head in his hands. "And if I refuse?"

"You won't be making the trip back to Umbrate," Asher answered.

Emesh moaned. "Why Xenerac?" he asked Del.

"He was unjustly accused, and he's the only one that can save us."

"Save us from what?"

"The end of all things."

"The end of all things?"

"He could see it long ago, and we need his help to avoid it."

Emesh didn't have a clue what Del saw ahead, and to be honest, Del didn't know either.

"We've done everything we can to protect you," Asher said.

"Yes, the letter worked well to get us out," Emesh reasoned. "But if you're caught, how will I be dealt with when they find out I aided you? Because they will!"

"We won't be caught," Del said. "We've traveled too many miles and put ourselves through too many terrible things to be caught, and so have Alphonse and his men."

Emesh scanned the expectant faces. He landed on Will's last.

"Fine," he said, and all shoulders relaxed. "I'll do what is expected of me—but no more!"

Wasting no time, Elias said: "Let us load the cart."

Will, feeling nudged out, refused to help load the cart. And while he watched the horse pull it to the mine as he stood alone on the porch, his plan fell into place. Once the cart was being loaded at the base of the hill, Will turned into the house and rummaged through his pack for the things he needed. He peeked through the door and, when he deemed it safe, went out and on to Umbrate.

The loading would take them some time to complete, and by then he would be far down the road with the hope of reaching Umbrate by nightfall. He turned toward the mine one last time and met the eyes of Elias. Will stopped. Elias stared right at him, he was sure of it, but the large wizard turned and went back to loading shovelfuls of white earth.

Will crossed the road and hid himself behind the stunted trees and shrubs. He would not be squeezed out of his own adventure. Now was his time as much as it was theirs. He tried everything to convince himself of that, but his erratic mind and his racing heart told him he was in for much more than he could fathom. But he had one comfort: nobody knew the streets of Umbrate as well as he did.

◊

It took them an hour to fill the cart as the sun shifted toward late afternoon. It was a few hours back to Umbrate with a full load, and it would be dark by then. The first shelf of the cart was stacked deep with white earth, making the second shelf look much more intolerable to the passengers.

"Get in," Asher said. "Time is short."

Del, Isa, Elias, and Rolph glanced at each other, then to the suffocating maw.

"Can't we walk down the road a ways?" Del asked.

"No," Asher said. "We can't take the risk."

Elias, standing to Del's left, began to sweat and shake thinking about the darkness of the Mausoleum when the door closed on them. Isa shared his sentiment. Del reached into the breast pocket of his cloak and pulled out a candle.

"For a bit of light," he said, and lit it. Emesh nearly fainted again watching him light the candle as quick as snapping a finger, and even stoic Asher, having never seen Magic before either, appeared stunned.

Elias nodded, filled his large chest with the fresh air, and climbed in first. The space shrunk with his large frame, and Isa followed after a quick hug with Gertie, Newt, and Grace. Del hugged them as well, and before he loaded himself in the cart, he looked over his shoulder at the house, hoping to see Will's face staring back at him; but no bright eyes or round child's face looked out. He sighed and got into the cart with the lit candle, leaving only enough room for Rolph.

Gertie looked at Rolph with hands on hips and her eyes locked on her husband, an angry love concomitant with fierce years of marriage.

"You want to be a hero, huh? Then go do it! But you better come back to me, you stubborn old kook," she said.

Rolph smiled at her as only a loving man can. "Gertrude, for once, I can't make you that promise." And she knew there was truth in his words. He kissed her and they melted into each other. "Goodbye, my dear."

"I'll be listening for you," Gertie said before she pulled away and wiped her eyes. Rolph slid into the cart and Asher covered it.

"Good luck," the four heard Newt say as the cart gate closed. Their world fell dark except for the nimbus of light around Del's brilliant candle, and the small space compressed even it.

The muffled sound of voices came through the slats of wood, but little could be distinguished. Then the cart began to roll away, and all they could hear was the sound of their own breaths and the turning of wheels taking them to their dreaded destination.

Purple dusk crept behind the setting sun as Will spied the walls of Umbrate in the distance. He could see the main gate, and he backed into the few trees around the city. There were fewer guards at the gate than he remembered, but he had no intention of going through it as the others did.

He scurried from tree to tree around the city wall. The door that Alphonse had let them out of was just ahead. Will approached it and, feeling no investigative eyes, put his hand on the door ring.

Holding his breath, he put his ear to the door—he heard nothing. Sucking in hopeful air, he tried to turn the ring and pushed at the same time. It didn't budge. Trying to avoid making too much noise, he leaned his shoulder into it and shoved. He might as well have been pushing the stone wall. Panic set in and he banged hard against the door with his shoulder. Nothing.

"Nonono," he repeated to himself. He had made a mistake, he knew it. Backing away from the door, Will looked down the length of the wall. He had to get in. The front gate was out, the side door was out, and darkness fastened around the city.

Will traced a path down the edge of the wall, looking for any entry. He saw no doors or drainages or cracks he could squeeze through. The wall was impenetrable. He stopped and thought a moment. As a boy who had grown up in Umbrate, he had spent much time with his eyes down—after all, there was not much worth looking up at, and looking up too often was seen as a sign of disrespect. But Will was not a citizen of Umbrate anymore, and he had learned over the past weeks that it was okay to look up. So, he did, and he found his point of entry.

A gnarled, spindly oak tree reached one branch over the wall as if peeking into the city. It was by far the largest tree near the wall, and he would climb it and get in—he had no other choice. Though another issue arose with being a boy raised in Umbrate: Will had never climbed a tree before. The time to rectify that had come.

The trunk of the tree was a good ten feet from the wall. It was bigger around than he could reach, but its knots and gnarls made it ideal for climbing. Will grabbed a low branch and put his tattered shoe on one of the twisted nodules. He lifted himself up and his foot slipped. Holding back his cry, he pulled with his skinny arms still gripping the branch and swung his legs up. With some difficulty he got his body on top of the branch and his legs straddled over it. His breath heaved with work and exhilaration. He found the branch that peeked over the wall and made his way to it with a series of awkward hand-over-foot exchanges.

It was dark now, but that was good for Will, because that meant nobody would be wandering the streets. He shimmied forward, low and slow, and as the branch began to thin, each movement rocked it up and down uncomfortably. If anyone had been watching on the other side of the wall, they might have thought the tree was coming alive. Will's legs and hands squeezed tighter the more it swayed. He scooted closer to the wall. In the distance he could see the moon taking its nighttime watch beyond Kylan's tower. Stars speckled the sky and he picked one to focus on. Moving an inch at a time, Will could almost reach out and touch the top of the wall. The branch creaked and moaned behind him, like a beast forcing him to scuttle faster. He was over the top of the wall now. He reached out to grab it and the swaying branch broke. Falling with a crash, the air was ripped from his lungs as his chest smashed against the wall. He heaved, legs dangling limply over the wall. Will pulled with all his might, but found nothing to grab onto. He sucked in a painful, choking breath and cold panic seized him. A rooftop looked up at him about six feet below the wall. Will tried to swing his legs up but something pressed hard into his chest. He stopped struggling and tried to catch his strained breath. He regained what he could with his body compressing his chest and the stone wall pressing up from below. He swung his leg around to get a hold and missed, and on the second try his toe caught a corner of stone. Slowly, he wiggled his entire body onto the edge of the wall.

He looked down at the rooftop below and swiveled his body over the other edge. The distance was too high for his legs to reach so he released his fingers, one at a time, until he slid down the wall onto the roof. He hit the roof and fell onto his rear but, luckily for him, the crash was light. He crouched there, waiting for someone to appear to see what caused the ruckus, but no one showed.

Will ran his fingers over his chest and scraped a tender spot. Wincing, he reached into the chest pocket of his tattered cloak and pulled out the illumine. It was intact and without a scratch. He wanted to throw it over the wall for hurting him. Why did I even bring this? he asked himself. It's useless—even Del couldn't remember how to use it. But its entrancing runes caught his gaze in the moonlight, reminding him of the power it once possessed. He felt that power, felt that it gave him something to contribute, even to a group of magical beings.

Replacing the illumine in his pocket, Will stepped to the edge of the roof. Another long drop.

In the distance, the moon clashed with the point of Kylan's tower. He breathed deep; he had made it into Umbrate. After a moment of relief, Will caught his breath and found a way off the roof.

◊

The hours in the cart seemed to triple the longer they jostled into each other. The light of the candle helped, but even the strongest among them faltered with the tight anxiety.

Del stared into the flame, with Rolph staring into it on the other side of the candle. Isa squeezed close behind Del, and Elias appeared to be asleep, but his heavy breath told them he was somewhere beyond dreams in a pleasant place his mind fought to keep alive.

Rolph's eyes widened, soaking up the light. Del looked at him curiously.

"Are you all right, Rolph?" he whispered.

The old wizard looked through the flame at Del. "It would appear we have a problem."

"What?" Del and Isa asked. Elias's breath shallowed, quickened.

"Gertie has reached out to me," Rolph said.

"Yes?"

Rolph wrestled with his thoughts, or with Gertie so far away—a strange sight for Del to witness so up close and personal with the candlelight on his face.

"Will was not at the cabin when they returned … and they can't find him."

"What?!" Del said, shouting in the small space.

"Quiet," Isa said.

Del tried again. "What do you mean they can't find him?"

"She said they've searched the hills and trees," Rolph explained. "He's nowhere in sight."

The anger flared on Del's face as the flame flickered with their conversation. "That little—"

"He'll meet us in the city," Elias said, his breath steadying.

"What?" Del said, louder than he should have.

"I saw him leave the cabin when we were loading the cart, and—"

"And you didn't stop him?!" Del tried to turn to face Elias but couldn't.

"It was not right for you to take him out of this fight," Elias replied, focused on controlling his creeping claustrophobia.

"But I'm his guardian, and I said—"

The touch of Isa's hand on his shoulder quelled Del's tirade. "What's done is done. If Elias thinks the boy will meet us in the city, then he will."

"And what if he gets caught?" Del countered.

"Then we'll save him too," Elias answered. "But he's too smart to get caught. You know that as well as I do, Delier."

Del relaxed as much as he could in the small space. He wanted to say more but it would have been a waste of precious air.

The cart rocked to a stop, and muffled voices were heard outside. All fell silent, pale. Del snuffed the flame, leaving them in complete darkness to listen. He could hear a laugh and some gentle banter. Good.

The cart began to roll again and the smooth dirt road turned to bumpy cobbled streets that clipped and clopped under the horse's hooves.

"We're in the city," Elias said. They all began to breathe heavily.

Will pulled his hood over his head and clung to the corners and shadows. He knew every part of Umbrate on this side of the Cathedral, and now he was slinking through the neighborhood of his old friend Lyle. His heart ached thinking about their last interaction together. The boy in him wanted to stop and apologize, but the budding man knew it would not help complete his dire mission.

The city was quiet, nearly dead, but Will remained watchful. The cart would be arriving soon, and he had to be at the Cathedral to meet it.

The curves and corners came to him like the city was a piece of his own body. Its familiarity comforted him, but Will knew that pleasant feeling housed a devious fraudulence that had stolen the lives of so many for so long. He stepped into a dark alley and the comfortable familiarity crashed into him.

Above his head a wooden sign hung limp from rusted chains. It read "Chandler." Will stopped and looked around. The only sound he heard was the sound of his own breath. He tried the door and it was locked. He reached above the door frame and felt the rounded bow. With shaky hands, Will slipped the key into the old lock and turned it. It sounded a dull pop that echoed in the quiet alley. He pushed the door open.

Once inside, Will closed the door and locked it before he dropped the key into his pocket. The entryway smelled dank and mildewy with disuse, staling the friendly scent of wax. Dust covered everything, as it always had, but now another layer settled over the top of the original Will had known so well.

The place had been turned over and, by Will's best guess, nothing had been found; Del was too intelligent for that. He ran his hands over the copper pot of the dipping station—the wax inside of it solid and dusty. His heart ached at the lack of use, the lack of work.

Turning about the workshop, he stopped at the door to Del's workspace. Without hesitation, he opened it and went in alone for the first time. It smelled of dry herbs, oils, and old wax. He looked at the different colors of wax lined in the depressed table in the dark. He ran his finger over one and the slick grit stuck to it. He smelled it and his mind told him it was lavender, though he knew not how the answer had so quickly fired into his consciousness when he had not remembered smelling lavender before. Lavender had been in the candle Del had given to Phin for his niece's cough. Will's mind slipped to the kind Mr. and Mrs. Grissom and how the candle Del created to help them had brought them to their end. What a strange world, he thought. He saw a pile of blue candles that looked like the ones Del had used in the cave. He grabbed a handful and put them in his pocket.

He closed the door on Del's room and glided across the shop to where he used to sleep what seemed like a thousand nights ago. The bed creaked when he sat on it, as it always had, and he felt that it had missed him as much as he had missed it. The room, like the rest of the shop, had filled with dust waiting for his return. Things had been moved, Will guessed in the sacking of the place, and his blanket and worn sheets had been ripped and tossed.

He reached into the side pocket of his cloak and pulled out the wax figurine Del had made for him. He marveled that it was still intact after the fall on the wall. It had been made by a wizard, he reminded himself, and a good one at that. The little figurine stood in triumphant victory. Will smiled, and a tear came to his eye. The pale statue glowed in the dark of the room and Will ran his dirty fingers and lucid eyes over it to remember every feature.

'I carved the man I believe you are going to someday be,' Del said. *'You're going to grow to be a strong man, darling,'* a tender voice echoed. Tears dropped from Will's eyes. He wiped them dry and took one last mental image of the figurine before he sat it atop the bedpost, valiant and victorious. Will stood, looked around the room, and exited the Chandler's shop to the dark, empty streets of Umbrate.

◊

The ride from the gate to the Cathedral left them with aches deep in their joints and bowels, partly because of the cobbled, bumpy streets and partly because they rode in complete darkness and complete silence, ruminating over the crucial task ahead. Del traced the turns in his mind, knowing the streets of Umbrate as well as Will did. Even more gut-wrenching, they rode on in the silent anticipation that Will would be there waiting for them. Or had he been captured? Or was he hurt along the way? The questions plagued Del worse than the pains of the drive.

He felt betrayed by Will, and Elias for that matter. The boy should not have been involved, but now the only option he had was to wait for him to arrive, or to be caught waiting for him to arrive—neither comforted him.

Del's judicious tracking guided him all the way to the Cathedral, where the cart came to a stop. Voices came to them from the outside as they tensed with breaths trapped in their lungs.

The board covering the back dropped and the heavy canvas sheet that covered the white earth was removed. Cool night suffused in and cleared the stale air. The four breathed deep again.

"It's safe. You can come out now," Emesh whispered in.

They wrestled themselves out, one at a time, and Del hobbled with stiffness over to Asher and Rufus waiting by the side door to the Cathedral.

"Have you seen him!" Del pleaded.

"Quiet!" Rufus hissed. "Have we seen who?"

"The boy? Have you seen Will?"

Asher and Rufus glanced at each other.

"The boy at the miner's cabin?" Asher asked.

"Yes, he ran away. Please tell me you've seen him." Del grabbed Asher's clean robes. He shook his head and Del looked to Rufus.

"I've been here for hours and seen no trace of anyone," Rufus said.

Del grabbed his throbbing temples.

Isa came up behind him. "He's not here?"

"No," Rufus said, "but we have no time to waste. We must go if you wish to get out tonight."

"We can't just leave him to wander the streets," Del said. "What if he's been caught by the Guard?"

"Then I will take care of them. I've been appointed by Yan and Alphonse to lead both guards while they are away."

"And why should we trust you?" Rolph challenged. To Isa, Elias and Rolph, Rufus might as well have been speaking a different language. They had been to Umbrate before, but not in a very long time, and not while any special Guards existed.

Rufus looked at the old wizard. "You can trust me, or you can leave," he suggested. "My name is Rufus, and I am second in command of the Royal Guard. I have pledged my allegiance to Princess Briella and to Alphonse, Captain of the Royal Guard."

"That means nothing to me," Rolph said, slouching away to stretch his tight body.

"We can trust him," Del said. "He wouldn't have gone through the trouble of getting us here if we couldn't."

"Don't mind me for asking," Rolph said, grabbing at a pinch in his back. "I've just spent what feels like half a day in a dark cell, and I don't wish to spend what's left of my life in one—the exact place they're leading us to."

Asher looked around for prying eyes. "We must be going. The boy will be fine, but our time is running short. Lead the way, Friar."

The city was silent—asleep or dead, they didn't know—but the air cooled the moisture into an eerie mist that shrouded the Cathedral looming over them.

Emesh, stuck between his duty and his friendship, searched Del's concerned face before he led them through the side door into the Cathedral, through the dark of the nave where they gathered for mass Del had once lit with his Altar candles. Del sparked the nub of the candle he had left from the cart ride and it provided enough light for him to see the step where Will had kneeled to pledge his allegiance to the King. The vileness of the moment punched his stomach.

Emesh rushed through a door at the side of the Altar and on down a long corridor. Del's candle provided the only light, but Emesh, Rufus, and Asher seemed to know their way in the dark. Isa put her hand on Del's shoulder to not lose him; anxiety flowed through her grasping fingers.

Asher stopped and Del nearly ran into him. Emesh stood before a door, listening at its slats like an inquisitive child.

"It sounds clear," he whispered.

Elias's deep breathing sucked the air out of the hallway.

Emesh looked into all of their faces as the light of the candle danced in the tight hallway with Elias's heavy breath and Del's shaky hand. The friar looked old and torn. He reached into his pocket and pulled out two keys.

"This one opens this door," he said, handing it to Rufus. "And this one," he held up a tarnished silver key, "this one will open the cell doors." He hesitated a moment before he dropped the key into Rufus's hand. "It's made of silver and cursed with the blood of dying wizards," he said, avoiding Del's gaze. "It will harm you Magic folk if you touch it." He wiped the sweat from his brow. "I accept deliveries for the Reformatory once a month." He swallowed hard. "I can't prepare you for the horrors you are about to see, but I can warn you that Magic will be very difficult in there. It's a place of Dark Magic, a place of death. The walls are lined with the same silver as the cuffs and cages that bind the magical beings. I don't know what you're looking for, and I don't wish to know, but it will not be easy for you in there. Four monks and four clergy members guard it at all times, and they are very skilled in the dark, but their job requires little activity. At night they congregate in a small room near the center of the prison." Friar Emesh's kind eyes filled with tears, and with a low head he began to walk away.

Del grabbed his arm as he passed. "If you see Will, take care of him and, I charge you, don't let him into the Reformatory!" The spittle flew from Del's lips.

Friar Emesh's whole body shook as he nodded. Del pulled him in close and hugged him. "Thank you, old friend. They will write good things about you when Mass is saved."

The culpable Friar Emesh left them with as much uncertainty as he'd had when he received the message from Princess Briella.

Even Rufus's brave countenance sagged with fear as he searched their eyes in the dark. "Do you have any more candles?" he asked. Del pulled two from his pocket and lit them. He gave one to Asher and one to Isa.

Rufus and Asher pulled their short swords and nodded to each other. Rufus inserted the first key and clicked the lock free. He opened the door, and they entered the Reformatory of Magic.

🔥

Will ran toward the faint light that leaked from Friar Emesh's office. He passed the horse-drawn cart and saw the back gate dropped and the second shelf empty. He was too late.

The tired horse didn't even bother to glance at him as he slipped by and into Emesh's office. He opened the door without knocking and ran into the friar.

"Will!" he exclaimed. "Oh, thank goodness, Del is worried sick about you."

"Where is he?" Will asked, wasting no breath. "Have they gone through already?"

"I'm afraid so, my boy, and Del told me to keep care of you until they return."

"But I have to get in there, I have to help them!"

"Quiet," Emesh whispered. "It's not safe for you in there. It's a terrible, terrible place where they do things a boy should not see."

"This is my fight too, Emesh! And you're going to let me in there!"

Emesh pulled himself sternly upright and crossed his arms over his hooded habit. "Del said to keep you out of the Reformatory. I *refuse* to show you the way."

Will pursed his lips. He didn't want it to go this way, but he reached into his breast pocket and pulled out the illumine that had taken his breath away at the start of the journey. The lamplight danced on its shiny, smooth surface.

"Do you know what this is?" he asked.

Emesh cocked his body and head to the side to get some distance from the peculiar item. "This is an illumine," Will explained matter-of-factly. "It's a magical bomb. Del gave it to me in case I ever needed to use it in a time of distress. He says it can destroy any target I wish it to."

Emesh backed away into his cluttered desk.

"You're not magical, you couldn't possibly use it," Emesh attempted.

Will held up the illumine with his lips tight in a devious smile. "You don't need to be magical to use it—Del invented it that way."

With one hand holding the illumine, Will reached into his pocket and pulled out a candle he took from the shop. He dipped it into the flame of the lamp.

"Now, how do I get to the Reformatory?" Will asked, somehow keeping his hand firm and his voice from quavering.

Emesh moaned weakly, and within a few minutes he was opening the door to the Reformatory of Magic.

◊

The painful, agonizing groans coming from the Reformatory had always served as the foundation of Del's nightmares, but as they tip-toed through the first corridor, he heard nothing but the swishing of blood in his ears and the sound of his heart beating in his chest.

It was so dark even his powerful candles failed to penetrate the atmosphere of anthracite black. The corridor was like any other; no cells lined the walls; no prisoners grasped for mercy, but the density of the everlasting night squeezed Del's throat, and he could feel himself weakening with each cautious step.

Rufus and Asher turned sharply in front of him and faced another door. Rufus stared back at them; the light of the flickering candles danced on his blade. He put his ear to the door and listened. He took the key from his pocket and inserted it.

"Wait," Del whispered, turning to Elias, Isa, and Rolph. "The candlelight will be our only source of light, and Emesh said that Magic would be very difficult. If you have to use it, make it necessary, and make it count." The three acknowledged him. Del turned back to Rufus and gave him a nod after a hard swallow.

"I'll leave the door open," Rufus said. "It will make for a quicker escape if I happen to fall."

The closeness of danger stopped their fluttering hearts. They were on a rescue mission, but that didn't mean Death wouldn't be attending.

With a moment's hesitation, Rufus breathed deep and turned the lock. The door opened smoothly, without a creak or catch, and the horrors of the Reformatory of Magic presented themselves.

A purple light, painful to the eyes, glowed from the floor, lighting the path at their feet that divided two walls of cells. Del's hand shook as he poked the candle into a cell at his right. A pair of dead eyes in a hanging head stared at him and he jerked back. They caught the light as if they were still alive, but the figure hung limp with its hands tied above its head in a Y-shape from manacles that dangled from the ceiling as its bony, bloody knees chaffed on the floor. He couldn't tell if it was a man or a woman, just a form that had the skin and bones of something that had once been one or the other. He stared into the blank and lifeless eyes that caught the light. Del moved the candle in closer, his partners watching behind him. The eyes blinked and the head lolled upright. Del jumped back and the others did the same. The skin-and-bones being was alive.

"Help," it said faintly, nothing more than a breath leaving a pair of dying lungs. "Help."

"Is that him? Is that Xenerac?!" Rufus asked.

"No," Rolph said.

"Then we must keep moving."

"We can't just leave him," Isa hissed.

"Help."

"He is not our mission," Rufus said. "Xenerac first, then the others." He continued down the hallway.

With another look into the cell, into the hollow eyes, Del and the others followed. They dipped their candles into each appalling chamber, looking for Xenerac but finding silent and haunting creatures much more terrifying than the fabricated screams of Del's nightmares. All the cells on their right were barred with the same silver material as the key Emesh gave Rufus, but all the cells on their left were made of rusted iron, and their occupants weren't tied but lying or sitting lifeless about the stall.

"The ones on the right are magical beings," Del realized.

"Yes," Elias said. He touched one of the bars with the tip of his finger and pulled it back as if it burned him. He shook the numbing pain out of his hand.

"Focus on the cells to the right," Isa said, feeling filthy for neglecting the others.

They dipped their candles into the cells and stared into defeated, dreadful, and dying troglodyte eyes. The blank orbs would look up, and see nothing, and the further they went into the Reformatory, the more pungent the smell became. It smelled of an injured and fouled limb in serious need of amputation. The miasma of stale sickness and blood curdled the food in their stomachs and made their own blood feel impossible to pump. Del swooned and wavered. The anti-magical silver weakened him. Isa put her hand on his shoulder and he could feel the weakness in her grip.

They knew nothing of the size of the Reformatory, or where the guards' station might be, but they continued down the repulsive hallway with the numbing purple radiance emanating from the path at their feet, sticking their weakening candles between the bars of the cells, one-by-one. The scaly scraping of prisoners moving in the dark like snakes slithering across the floor made them want to retreat back the way they came. The sound of bare kneecaps raking bone against stone would reside in their minds to forever wake them in the middle of the night. The cruelty of the place was repugnant and sadistic, and fitting for a class that desired to snuff all the light from the world.

Del had known Kylan was a calloused, hateful wizard, but even he was appalled by the extent of his viciousness as he sat in his tower over these decaying wizards, collecting their blood to bring down their fellows with evil devices. He could see now why some thought Magic was the Greatest Evil that ever lived. This was not Magic but a warped power created to put a dark blot over a lighter history. Del covered his mouth and nose to combat the smell but it didn't help.

"Stop," Rolph said. They all did.

"Darkness … The end," said a voice, faint and far away.

"That's him!" Rolph whispered excitedly.

They rushed ahead to where the voice became clearer.

"Darkness … The end," it said again, closer, but not close enough.

Before them, at the edge of the purple pathway, a thin line of light leaked under a closed door. Rufus's shaky hand lifted a finger to his lips, and then pointed to the light under the door.

"Darkness … The end," came the weak voice out of the cell across from the door.

They tip-toed to it, not a sound made between them. Rufus moved in front of the cage, and Asher stood in fighting position in front of the guards' door, his blade trembling in the dampened light.

Rufus pulled the silver key from his pocket, and with shaky hand in shaky light, attempted to insert it into the keyhole. He fumbled with the key and Del grabbed his wrist to steady it. They inserted the key together and Rufus turned it.

The lock clanged, cutting all breathing short.

"Darkness … The end," the prisoner whispered.

No sound came from the other side of the guards' door. Rufus, still quaking, opened the door to the cell. It squealed on sticky hinges.

"What on Mass was that," a faint voice said on the other side of the door.

"Darkness … The end."

Del's eyes glowed in the candlelight. "Hurry," he said to Rufus, before he turned toward the doorway to fight.

Rufus rushed into the cage with Isa providing him light and began to free the manacles. He unlocked the first one when the door burst open. A surprised guard stared into the faint eyes of Asher and Del, and with a calculated slash, Asher ended his staring. He dropped to the floor, and another man filled his space. Asher parried with him until a third man barreled into the second, knocking Asher into the bars of a cage. Del wrestled with the third man, and the sound of metal tearing through flesh forced a gasp out of the second man as Asher flung him away.

The room was lit by a lantern on a table, and as the fourth guard stepped into the doorway, Elias absorbed its radiance and sent a burst of light, as powerful as he could make it, into the station. The remaining guards toppled to their backs with the table in the center of the room splintering into a million pieces of shrapnel. The lights were snuffed as Asher slashed to kill the guard wrestling with Del. Moans came from within the guard office.

"I can't get the second lock!" Rufus said, exasperated in the dark of the cell.

Del stepped in and found the prisoner's hand, his own burning with a brush against the manacle. Despite the pain, he found the keyhole and brought Rufus's hand up to it. With a swift twist the prisoner flopped into Del's arms.

The moans turned to consciousness as the guards dug out of the destruction. Without hesitation, Elias grabbed the bony prisoner from Del's hands and put him over his shoulder.

"Run!" he yelled. They exited the cell and rushed toward the entrance.

Will's confidence diminished with each step down the long corridor of leaden light with only one exit far behind him. He arrived at the second door and saw it propped open. He peeked through the crack into the impregnable darkness. A whimper leaked from between his lips.

He opened the door and slipped in. The purple glow emanating from the floor hurt his eyes with only the candlelight providing any other semblance of light. Turning to his right he saw the first cage, barred with the tainted metal he had seen before. He dipped his shaking hand between the bars of the cell and the candle shuddered so furiously that hot wax dropped onto his wrist. The dead eyes of the chained thing stared back at him and blinked slowly.

"Help." The word escaped on a wisp of air.

Will jumped and dumped more wax onto his hand, nearly dropping the stick. He looked at the cage lock and realized he didn't have a key. He turned to the rusty iron bars at his back and looked in on the soulless beings that slunk through their caves, unchained and in silence as if searching for a crumb of food or a drop of water. He had never seen anything so terrible in all his life. The people in the cages had been reduced to *things*, dehumanized to something less than an eyeless pond animal that fed on movement and shadow.

Will stuck his candle into the first iron cage and the *thing* crumpled into the corner like a spider curling away from a flame, its face hidden in tangled hair and tattered clothing.

"Del," Will whispered.

He went silent, but the rush in his ears and the beating in his heart hindered him from hearing anything.

"Isa," he tried. "Elias."

He moved down the glowing path. This was the first time he had ever been truly alone, and the feeling grabbed at his chest like an iron rake across frozen earth. Had Emesh tricked him? Surely not. The cart outside was the one that arrived at Grace and Newt's, and the second door had been left unlocked for a reason. Will held the candle low and covered the light to peer into the distance. The dizzying purple glow twisted and contorted in front of him as the specter of the flame flickered in his eyes. Staring into the inky black made his head spin … and then the smell hit him, making him woozy and weak in the knees.

He leaned against the iron bars to his left and uncovered the candle. He held the flame in front of his face to see the light once again. Dropping to his knees, Will pulled the illumine from his pocket. The runes shined bright in the halo of the candle. Try as he might, he still couldn't use it, but the desperate need for light seized him like the desperate need for air underwater.

He heard talking and squinted his eyes to look into the distance. A flicker of light, real or contrived in the distorting madness of his mind, flashed for just a moment ahead of him. How far ahead? He couldn't tell in this deceiving darkness.

He lifted the illumine back into the candlelight and leaned in closer to the runes, grasping for some hope he might suddenly understand their meaning.

Arms reached through the iron bars and grabbed him. Will flashed the candle into the face, matted with hair and dirty from neglect. He fought to get away with the candle in one hand and the illumine in the other, but the caged beast was somehow too strong for him.

"Let go," Will hissed as the *thing* squeezed him against the iron bars.

Will lifted the candle to the face again in an attempt to scare it away, and he stared into calm, lucid eyes set deep in the malnourished face. He relaxed and the arms around him loosened.

"Will," the weak voice said.

"Mom," Will whispered back as weak as the voice came to him.

Down the hall a door opened, a light flashed, and a great crash sounded.

◊

Del bounded down the hall, his eyes filled with the burst from Elias's attack. Isa, he hoped, ran ahead of him, down the path that radiated up from the floor. A light shined ahead, he thought. He blinked the residual light from his eyes and squinted. It was a light, one of his own candles.

Isa's figure came into focus as she dashed down the hallway. The things in the cells were coming alive and reaching out to them. They dodged the arms and feeble moans, and a smoldering stream, purple like the glowing corridor, whizzed by them. One of the monks, maybe more, had risen and fired a curse at them in the dark.

Closer to the light, Del's surprise blinded him more than the burst of Elias's magic. Will held the flame, and a creature from within the cell wrapped him tight. Del hurried to Isa's side.

"It's Will!" he shouted. "Get that thing off him!"

Another purple streak blazed by and smashed the side of a silver barred cell. They reached Will and the boy was searching curiously in the eyes of the thing that held him. He appeared not to notice them approaching, and when they grabbed him, he fought back.

"No, stop!" he shouted. "It's my mother. We have to save her."

Completely taken aback, Del looked into the face of the caged person.

Elias ran by, carrying his precious cargo.

"Get a key! Unlock it!" Will shouted.

Del turned and saw Asher and Rufus approaching at a high rate of speed; Rolph lagged far behind, and behind him at least two figures pursued.

"Help!" Del said, grabbing hold of Rufus's robe. "This is the boy's mother."

"We have no time!" he shouted back, pulling Del.

"No!" the woman said in the cell, and Will echoed it.

Rufus pulled the key from his pocket and handed it to Del before dashing down the hall. Del pulled the candle from Will's hand as a flash of purple flared by and hit Asher in the back, toppling the guard.

"Will, get out! Go!" Del yelled. "I'll free her."

Isa pulled Will's arm, but the boy saw Rolph straggling behind. Del sank the key into the lock and turned it.

Somehow, despite the darkness, Will's eyes met Rolph's, and the old wizard spoke in his head. Will looked down at the illumine—he knew how to use it now, Rolph had told him.

Will stood, thought about light, and spoke: *Et lux in tenebris lucet.* And following Rolph's bidding, Will smashed the illumine into the floor of the Reformatory.

The world grew much darker for a moment, darker than even the depths of a cave that would shrivel and break at the sight of light. The illumine absorbed the light from the candle and the glow from the purple path. The world seemed to stop and all Will could hear was the ringing in his ears. In that split second, Rolph smiled at Will, and a burst of light rushed out of the ball in an explosion that threw them all back … into nothing. The bars of silver disintegrated and the heavy manacles fell, freeing the prisoners!

Rolph turned his back to Will and the light that expanded in his direction condensed into his core. Will could see the terrified faces of the monks. One of them struck at Rolph, but the power flowed through the old man, making him younger, taller, stronger, as he forced the concentrated light out from his hands, destroying all in its path.

Isa picked Will up, and Del took hold of Will's mother. They rushed down the hall and Rolph spoke to Will.

"Thank you, my boy. You've freed us all," and the roof of the Reformatory began to crumble down on him. And Will, whether Rolph intended it or not, heard the wizard's last words: *"Goodbye, my dear Gertrude. Take care of our boy, and remember I will always love you."*

In Isa's arms, Will was rushed out of the Reformatory of Magic with Del carrying his mother close behind. They made it through the second door as the Reformatory collapsed behind them. And Gertrude, a ball of agony and tears, collapsed on the floor of Grace and Newt's cabin.

◊

Emesh stepped into the nave of the Cathedral after a large boom shook his office. He ran to the door of the Reformatory and it slammed open and knocked him to the ground.

Elias stepped out with Xenerac on his back, and Rufus came out behind him. He helped the old friar to his feet as he held the door.

"He used it didn't he? Will used the bomb?" Emesh said.

Rufus, with dirty face and clouded eyes looked at him curiously. "How did you know about that? You let him in, didn't you?" Emesh looked away and Isa rushed by with Will in her arms; Del followed close behind with a tangle of tattered clothes and hair over his shoulder.

Rufus slammed the door shut.

"Weren't there two others?" Emesh asked.

Rufus looked at him sadly. "We must move before the Cathedral falls."

"What?" The blood rushed out of Emesh before the word was finished. Rufus grabbed his arm and dragged him through the Cathedral as another, closer crash rang out.

The floor of the building shook and the Altar of candleholders rocked and toppled over. They emerged from Emesh's office just in time to see the exterior walls of the windowless Reformatory lean inward and fall. The back of the Cathedral went with it, and

Kylan's tower wiggled from the bottom all the way through the spire, but remained sturdy.

Dust filled the cool, wet air, making it dry and sticky to breath. Elias placed Xenerac onto the tarp covering the cart of white earth.

"Darkness … The end," he said as he stared at the sky for the first time in a hundred years.

Isa put Will down and the boy rushed to where Del placed his mother beside Xenerac. He climbed up next to her, and she reached up with soiled, bony hands and caressed his face. "Will," it seemed to be all she could say, and it took all her energy just to cry, but life thrived in those tears, in those eyes, and Will cried with her as he hugged her.

Del fought the urge to castigate Emesh for letting the boy in, but he knew his mother would be dead if he hadn't, and they would have been as well if he hadn't used the illumine.

"We have to move before the people begin to gather," Rufus ordered. "There are horses saddled in the stable. I'll draw the guards away from the gate, and we'll drive the cart out after all is clear.

"Come with us, Emesh," Del said. "You have no life left here."

Emesh looked over his shoulder at the crumbling walls. He turned to Del and nodded. Rufus and Emesh climbed onto the seat of the cart, and Del led the rest to the stable. People already lined the streets to see the scene at the Cathedral. Rufus stopped at the stable and joined Del in gathering horses for riders. Within minutes everyone was on a horse and riding out. Del was last, and he heard a rather recognizable and defiant snort. He turned and saw Clyde the donkey. Begrudgingly, he dismounted and put a halter around the old donkey but, for once, the beast seemed eager to leave when Del pulled him along.

They stopped a few streets from the gate, at Rufus's instruction, and waited for him.

"The Cathedral is collapsing!" They heard him yelling to the guards. "Abandon your posts and take your assistance to it! Go! Now!"

The shadows of the guards rushed past. Rufus returned and led them through the unguarded entrance. The dust from the collapse rolled to the gate and provided cover as they rode into the night.

Will clung to his mother, and she continued to say his name as she stroked his hair. Xenerac stared at the moon and repeated over and over: "Darkness … The end," all the way to the Grace and Newt's cabin.

Behind them, the city startled awake and hurried to the Cathedral to see its glory crumble.

43

The morning sun crept over the hill to light the windows with the glow of dawn. The cabin was silent. Gertie had bathed and fed Xenerac and Will's mother, with Will never leaving her side. The rest had fed themselves and tried to wash away the death and defilement of the Reformatory with little success.

Gertie had said nothing upon their return, and they knew that nothing they could say or do would soothe her grieving heart. Will wondered if they had all heard Rolph's final words for not a one of them even told her what had happened. She tended to Xenerac and Will's mother in an attempt to not think about her dead husband. It was difficult to watch, but all who were witness felt fortunate to have survived, as much as they felt fortunate for Rolph's heroic and mystical stance of courage. He had saved them, and he put to rest so many that were living, if a person dared to call it that, in the most horrifying conditions they had ever seen, though some among them wondered what sort of assistance or knowledge those witches and wizards could have provided.

"I must make my way back to Umbrate," Rufus said as the purple light tipped over the horizon. It reminded him of the glowing floor in the Reformatory, and he wondered if he would ever look at those few seconds of dawn again without cringing.

"Why?" Del asked. "Stay with us."

He shook his dutiful head. "The guard will be in need of a commander. And I must return to settle things before word reaches the king and Kylan. This is only the beginning."

"Darkness … The end," Xenerac muttered.

"You have your man, and I have a city in chaos." Rufus leaned in and whispered to Del: "Your best chance of defeating Kylan and the king is while they are away from Umbrate. I will make sure they hear nothing of last night's events, but I have to be in Umbrate to be certain that no word reaches them."

Del, beaten, broken, and tired, knew that Rufus was right: it was just beginning.

He patted Del's shoulder and signaled to the others. "I will see you before the end." And Rufus left the cabin and galloped back to Umbrate.

Emesh looked as if he wanted to rise and join him, but the meek man sank in his seat and dropped his head.

All eyes fell on Del, but he had no encouragement to put forward.

"Darkness … The end," was the only advice offered. They looked toward the doddering Xenerac.

Gertie combed Will's mother's hair as the boy sat beside her, gazing into her eyes. There was life there, he was sure of it, but it rose slowly after being dormant so long.

"What's her name, dear," Gertie asked, gently smoothing the tangles of her matted hair.

"Isabella," Will answered.

Gertie looked at Isa. "After you, I imagine?"

Isa attempted a smile, "Yes, she's my niece."

Will's mother looked at Isa for the first time, and the look in her eyes realized her recognition to the likeness of her grandmother Paulette, Isa's twin. A tear trickled down her face. Will wiped it away.

"Call me Bella," she said. They were the first words she had muttered that wasn't her son's name. All in the room found confidence in the gentle glint of resurrected life.

"Darkness … The end." Until Xenerac voiced his ominous omen. The emaciated wizard laid on a small sofa and stared at the ceiling with cloudy, blind eyes. He had sucked down a thin broth and some water, but he lacked the life-glint that Bella had. After a hundred years in prison, they were surprised he lived at all.

When Gertie had undressed him the scars from deep wounds methodically carved were exposed all over his body, gashes inflicted to harvest the wizard's blood to make Kylan's terrible anti-magic silver. It wasn't the blood of dead Magic that was so lethal, but the threat of dying Magic. For that, at least, they praised Rolph for tearing the Reformatory down.

"Darkness … The end."

"What does he mean?" Emesh asked.

"He's talking about the cell he was in," Del answered, "… I think." He stood and looked out the window, eager for the sunshine of day.

"No, I don't think so," Grace said. They turned to look at her, like she was out of place in her own home. In fact, her and Newt had felt very out of place in their home with all of these people they didn't know, and people who had been imprisoned longer than they had been alive, and people of the Royal Guard.

"What do you mean?" Elias asked.

Grace looked to Newt for courage. "Well, why hasn't he died already? I mean, wouldn't you want to die if you were in a prison like that for so long?"

"Wizards are very difficult to kill," Del said.

"Yes, but I think he lived to deliver a message," Grace added.

"Darkness … The end."

"A message?" Isa asked.

"Things that want to die, do," Elias said, looking at Grace. "Bella lived because she wanted to see her son again. Maybe Xenerac also lived to deliver us a message."

"Darkness … The end." His voice lifted in a sympathetic tone.

Del bit his lip and paced the floor. He turned to Gertie. "Do you think you can … reach him?"

She combed through Bella's smoothed hair, comforting herself more than Bella at that point. Her hand stopped and she looked at Del. She sighed.

"I can try."

She kissed Bella on the cheek and left her side. Isa quickly took her place. The touch of her son and her grandaunt added another living sparkle to her eye.

Gertie kneeled next to Xenerac and put her hand on his. It pained her visibly to feel his bones through his thin and scarred skin. She brushed her thumb over the scars carved by the manacles and Xenerac relaxed further. Closing her eyes, Gertie transported somewhere else. Xenerac closed his unseeing eyes to lead her.

The onlookers waited a few tense minutes, and Del jumped at the sound of Gertie's voice as he gazed out the window.

"He keeps repeating the same thing," she explained; her eyes still closed. "Darkness … The end. His mind traverses a tenebrous sky. He's taking me with him."

"Darkness … The end," Xenerac whispered.

"But it's not dark like night … more like smoke from a fire dampening the sun's radiance." She went silent for a moment. "I see a crescent shape."

"The moon," Will said.

"Yes, but also no. It's round like the moon, but orange like the sun. The crescent is closing."

"Closing?" Del asked. He went to his pack and pulled out the book of Xenerac's writings.

"All grows darker. The world is falling asleep and something rises deep from within Mirror Pool." Gertie's voice became grim. "Waves are rocking its smooth surface. No, not waves, but … *things*—things emerging from the deep."

"Darkness … The end."

Del flipped to the dream that Elias had read in the cave. He read aloud: "'A dream has presented itself to me. I watched from the top of the Glass Mountains as darkness covered the land. The trees wilted, the animals fled, the grass lost its sway, and the sun dulled over the pool. I watched years go by, chained to the peak of the mountains, and at the centurial null noon the discs clashed and broke, and eternal Darkness brought waves over the calm pool, and on those waves rode The End.'"

Del looked up from the book, his face in pale shock. "It's an eclipse," he said, barely above a whisper.

"What's an eclipse?" Will asked.

"Darkness … The end." Xenerac's voice lifted.

"It's when the moon covers the sun, creating darkness in the middle of the day. The centurial null noon is when it's going to happen."

"Darkness … The end!" Xenerac said loudly. Gertie brushed his hand, soothing him.

"Centurial null noon?" Newt asked.

"It's been a hundred years since the Great Evil was banished to the depths of Mirror Pool." Del paced the room, his hand stroking his chin. "The magic is waning, and when the moon eclipses the sun at noon on the hundred-year anniversary of the banishment it will snuff the sun's light as the sun puts a shadow over the watching face of the moon."

"The true anniversary is on the last day of the festival," Elias said, "the day they will gather for the vigil around Mirror Pool."

Del stopped pacing and turned to them—realization clouding his face.

"When the moon blots out the sun and the sun quiets the moon, Kylan is going to raise the Great Evil from the pool and take control of Mass. This is what he's been waiting for."

Wide eyes and agape mouths swallowed the faces that stared at Del. They all instinctively looked at Xenerac. The old wizard smiled.

"Yes," he said with a whisper of a breath, his last breath. He relaxed further into the sofa and passed from Mass.

The silence in the room with the weight of the discovery was deafening. Gertie leaned over and put her hand on Xenerac's chest, though she cried no tears for the tortured wizard. He had lived a hundred years in pain and agony, with his blood forced out of his veins to imprison his own people so that the true Great Evil could reign again. Now, he was at peace for the first time in a century, with his heavy burden passed to another.

Will stood, holding his mother's hand, and said: "We have to go to Sentinel's Village."

44

With the morning sun on his face, Rufus rode to the walls of Umbrate atop a lathered horse. He approached the unguarded gate, and all was silent and empty. Looking up, he saw that Kylan's tower still stood, but a bit off kilter.

The dust had settled over the city, but the streets were empty. The closer Rufus got to the Cathedral, the more he realized the hard ride to Umbrate was going to be the easiest part of his morning. Shouting and quarreling came from the Cathedral square, and even Rufus, who had survived the rescue in the vile Reformatory, was not prepared for what he was about to enter.

He stopped his horse some distance away to decipher the scene for himself. The Cathedral had fallen, and in the square the common people of Umbrate were divided into two sides, shouting and haranguing each other as a man and a woman, each representing a side, stood in the middle attempting to calm them. Rufus came closer and found to his horror that the men and women of the City and Royal Guard were tied up and on their knees between the arguing crowds.

"It's time to make a decision!" the man shouted over the cacophony. "Do we kill them, or do we show them the mercy they never showed us?"

"Kill them!" "Save them!" "Murder!" "Mercy!" rang out. The two in the middle looked at each other, wondering what sort of mess they had gotten themselves into.

Cautiously, Rufus approached. The tied-up guards looked at him with relief; the crowds on each side looked at him with surprise.

"And who might you be? Atop your horse and not on your knees with your fellow guards?" the woman in the middle asked threateningly.

"I'm Rufus, appointed leader of the Guards in Yan and Alphonse's absence," he said.

"And where have you been all night?" the man asked.

"Freeing a wizard from the Reformatory." The crowd on the right gasped, and Rufus could guess their stance in the matter. "I was with the people that brought down the Cathedral." All gasped at that, including the kneeling guards. The crowd rose into a fury again until the man and woman in the middle settled them.

"What do you mean you were freeing a wizard?" the man blurted. The crowd, desiring to know the answer as much as he, quieted.

Rufus found no point in lying, and the truth would save more lives, so he told it: "A handful of wizards, a witch, a small boy, myself, and a fellow guard entered the Reformatory of Magic under the authority of Alphonse, Captain of the Royal Guard, and Princess Briella."

"Liar! Princess Briella would never allow that!" said someone on the right. The crowds jumped into a fury again.

"Enough!" the woman in the middle shrieked, piercing them into silence. "Why should we believe that nonsense? You're just trying to save your skin."

Rufus looked at the faces of anger, confusion, and fear.

"For too long, King Bale and Kylan have ruled over this city, this Kingdom. And if you had seen the horrors that I saw last night in the Reformatory, you would have witnessed the depth of their evils. But you do not have to see it, you just have to look at yourselves. You're underfed, overworked, all for a king and a dark wizard that care nothing for you."

"The Guard never cared, and neither do you. Kill them!" A woman shouted. Many shared her sentiment, but the bulk of the crowd grew quiet with internal thought.

"These men and women kneeling before you had no choice in their lives. Just as you had no choice. They were taught to be the way they are the same as the millers are taught to be the way they are, or the farmers, or the blacksmiths, or anyone of you." Guilty faces turned to avoid the glances of others.

"One of the brave wizards that entered the Reformatory with me last night is one of our own—Del Chandler. Many of you know him as the maker of the Altar candles for mass. Some know him for much more."

"He's a deserter—a criminal!" one shouted. No one openly agreed; Del was not the only citizen that had thought of fleeing the oppressive city.

"And how many of you really believe that?" No one replied. "Del has been helping people in this community with his Magic for a very long time, and at his own peril. I know for certain many of you have benefitted from his kindness."

The crowd went silent. Most looked to the ground, but a few looked around at the rest. A woman stepped forward.

"He gave me a candle that eased the pain of my last childbirth," she said demurely. "He knew I'd had trouble with the first two." She looked to the sky. "I always knew it was Magic."

A man stepped forward. "He gave me a candle that aided my mother to the other side. She even smiled at the end, after all those months of agony. Del did that; Del did what the clergy doctors wouldn't." Tears streaked his face as he stepped back.

"My niece had a terrible cough—she'd even cough up blood— and Del gave me a candle, right in front of the other guards, mind you, and she hasn't coughed since. And that wasn't the first time he helped my sister—and they need it, them being so poor," Phin said, kneeling among the other guards. "My sister and her kids are the only family I have left," he began to weep. "I owe Del everything."

"And I'm sure these are not the only three." The gatherers exchanged glances of guilt as shoulders slumped and eyes dropped. "And Del always had a boy with him," Rufus began.

"Will," Phin said, smiling at the image of the quiet, pensive child.

"That's right," Rufus said. "Will was orphaned as a child. His mother was forced to give him up after she attacked a guard, Yan Coaler, for assaulting an old woman. She gave herself up so that he could live. Will found her in the Reformatory last night, malnourished, soiled, and with hardly a memory of light or good days to grasp onto. Will saved her—he saved us all, in fact—and the boy helped topple the Cathedral, the source of your fears," Rufus pointed to the rubble behind them; the crowd turned and absorbed the sight of it, "the monolith we thought would never fall because of the iron shoulders that supported it. But it has fallen! And a boy with a little faith and a lot of love helped bring it down. We can do the same!"

The crowd cheered with Rufus, with a reluctant few glancing around, far outnumbered.

"If you believe in a new world, if you have even the smallest sliver of faith and love, then let these guards go and march with me to Sentinel's Village. Liberation is here! It's now!"

All of the crowd cheered, throwing their hands into the air. The man in the middle of the crowd bent to cut the ropes from Phin's hand. The woman stopped him, stared into his eyes, stooped, and cut them herself. The crowd cheered louder.

They were together, they were one, and they were going to march to victory or death, but never would they live another day in the world behind them.

45

As Xenerac rested in a hole beside the mine, the mourners began to wonder how they would find the courage and strength to march forward, away from their homes—again—toward an army of very powerful guards and wizards.

They took vigil by the side of the filled grave, hoping that Xenerac might have more to say, more to offer in their time of distress. A few against many did not comfort them, and more than a few of those many were monks loyal to a dark wizard. The king was not a problem. The doddering fool was on his deathbed every day of his life, and he had no more to offer than a paperweight without paper. Kylan was the man they needed to tear down. He had been trained by Xenerac, the greatest wizard that had ever lived, and now Xenerac reposed in the ground, and would have much sooner if he had not the determination to live to deliver the final truth of his prophecy. Kylan was the man running all of Mass, and soon he would release an Evil so great all light would be snuffed and Dark Magic would rule where Light Magic once reigned, open and free. He would be the most powerful wizard of all time, with the most powerful force behind him. He would be the master of Death, and Death would be his sword to swing.

And time was running short … very short.

The last day of the festival was in eleven days, and it was a ten-day journey to Sentinel's Village.

Gertie stood beside Del and stared hard at the fresh dirt turned over Xenerac's grave. Del put his arm around her and pulled her in close. Will hugged her as well, still holding onto his mother's hand. She had the strength to stand, but not for very long, and she stared at the grave of Xenerac with slight indifference; she had already died in many ways, and she remained numb in its presence. It wasn't long ago that she would have been jealous of Xenerac, but a healing warmth traveled through the hand that held hers, fading the jealousy and giving her the strength to stand again.

"I believe we should discuss our plan here, in front of Xenerac," Del offered. "He suffered much to pass the message onto us, and he deserves to know how it will end."

No one stepped through the door Del opened; even Elias looked lost. Will hovered by his mother's side, as Del looked from one face to the next.

"I don't have to remind you all that we have very little time to make a decision," Del said. "If we aren't on our way tomorrow, we won't make it in time."

Newt had his arm around Grace. They remained out of place in such a crowd, still unaware, and somewhat unsure of all this Magic stuff. They were young enough to grow up in a world where Magic was just a myth, a thing conquered by 'good,' and now they stood amongst it, a part of it. Newt looked into Grace's eyes and then at Del.

"I know we don't have much to offer," he said, "but we'll give you all we can, and go with if you need us."

Del smiled benevolently. "Thank you, Newt and Grace. You have more to offer than you think. We would have accomplished none of this without you." Newt and Grace smiled sadly, and Del pleaded with the remnants of the tired, defeated faces.

"What about the rest of you?" Del said.

"Of course we're going with," Isa answered. "But to what end? Most of our success has been while people weren't watching." She looked around the group cautiously. "Up there, all of Mass will be watching, and guarding. The people of Sentinel's Village live very well. They won't have the slightest understanding about the troubles of people in Umbrate and across Mass."

Before any could answer a horseman rolled passed them on the King's Carve. He pulled back on the reins and wheeled toward them at a gallop.

"Phin?" Del and Will said at the same time.

The guard jumped from his horse before it stopped and ran to hug Del and Will, with Gertie caught curiously in the middle. His breath seemed impossible to catch, though the horse had been doing all the running.

"What on Mass are you doing here?" Del asked.

"It's glorious, Del, outstanding, even!" Phin elated, oblivious to the mourners around the fresh grave.

"What's glorious?" Will asked, as eager as Del and as confused as everyone else.

"The Cathedral has fallen, and the people want to march to Sentinel's Village," Phin spit out between breaths.

"All of Umbrate?" Del asked.

"All that are able. And all that have resisted have been locked up, and there weren't many of those," Phin said, laughing.

Will and Del looked at each other in shock.

"Who has convinced them?" Newt asked, coming forward.

"Rufus. They had all the guards, me included, tied up in the Cathedral square. They were fighting about whether they should execute us or not, and he arrived and told us about Will saving you in the Reformatory, and how you rescued a wizard—and Will's mother! He talked about Del and all the good he's done in Umbrate, helping people in need and what not, and I spoke up for you then, and—"

"Thank you, Phin, that's quite enough," Del interrupted kindly. Will's mother seemed rather stunned by all the information, and they *were* still at a funeral, so Del seized his chance to silence the garrulous guard. "When are they coming this way?"

"Tomorrow, at dawn," Phin said. "I'm so excited. I've never been away from Umbrate before."

Del turned to the others. "Looks like we have a plan now," he said. The others agreed. Del turned back to Phin and thanked him.

"No, thank you, from all of us in Umbrate. The scourge of King Bale and Kylan has gone on far too long. I hate seeing people cower from me because I'm a guard. It's too much to handle really, and I can't stand to see my dear sister's family so thin while the king and his guards have so much, myself included in that, of course." Phin looked away guiltily. He turned to Del. "You're coming, right?"

"Yes," Del said. "All of us."

"Good." Phin smiled. "I'll pass the word to Rufus." He mounted his horse and turned to them. "No need to worry about food either. They've raided the king's store and now the whole city has more than it's ever seen. We'll meet you here in the morning." He turned his horse and kicked into a gallop.

Del turned and laughed to himself. "Well, we won't be traveling alone."

The others were delighted to hear it.

◊

Will spent the evening with his mother, close by and without any words, and she seemed to recover more and more with every kind touch and act. The others watched and marveled at the sight of a family reunited. Isa was never far away either, and Gertie clung to their reignited warmth, feeling herself all alone.

Del, Emesh, and Elias sat outside of the home and watched the sunset after dinner. They felt alone as well—in different ways, but in close proximity. Emesh had been distant over the past day, and Del could only imagine what a jostling he felt. One day he was a part of the clergy that lorded over a community of hungry and afraid people, a clergy that imprisoned those in opposition and bled them, and he had been a believer in it. The next day he was laying the most powerful wizard that ever lived to rest and planning a revolt against the cloth he had sworn to. Needless to say, it was all very confusing to the man.

Elias had always been alone, and he felt rather comfortable with it, but he had been weakened by the journey, and that was an experience altogether new to him. Del could see it in the broad traveling wizard. He had left something of himself in the Mausoleum on that horrendous day of darkness.

Del sat in the middle of them, also alone in a crowd. He had always felt alone, but Will had always been there. Now Will had his mother again, and Del pondered what *he* would have when all of this nasty business was finished. If it ever was.

"How are you faring, old friend?" Del asked Emesh.

Emesh feigned a smile and looked toward the ground. "I would say: imagine having your whole world turned upside down, but you can." He picked up a pebble and tossed it back and forth between his hands, following its arc like a fascinated child. "I always knew they were wrong: in how they treated people, in how they treated those in the Reformatory, in how they treated me, but it doesn't make it any easier to turn my back on it." He held the pebble in his fingers and looked into it like a crystal ball. "You know how children are Selected? Well, I was selected to be in the clergy. My father had been so proud. People weren't as hungry back then, and Umbrate wasn't so dark." He stopped and shook his head. "I'm glad I'm here now, though; I'm glad you returned. It seems a terrible lie that Kylan would release the true Evil back into Mass to enslave us all, but I suppose if a person had been watching, he would have seen it coming."

Del nodded. "We all looked the other way, and most, like you, were forced to. We have the opportunity to change things now, and we have the backing to do it."

"And tomorrow we journey back to Sentinel's Village," Elias said. There was no mistaking the exhaustion in his voice.

"Yes, and what a journey," Del said. "Yet it all seems to be starting again."

The night air cooled around them. In the morning, when the weak Mass sun would struggle to cut through the fog, they would be heading toward Sentinel's Village, toward the end.

Del wasn't sure how much longer he could go without sleep. He hadn't closed his eyes all night except to blink, resting on the same sofa where Xenerac had said his last words. The rest of the people tossing and turning about the room seemed to be facing the same challenge.

Will had stayed close to his mother all through the night as he had through the day, and Del watched the boy fall asleep for just the slightest moment when Bella sat upright, screaming and fighting some nightmarish thing none of them could possibly imagine. Will managed to calm her, and Del lit one of his special candles to give her a light brighter and closer than the cooling coals in the stove. She grabbed his arm as he turned back to bed and stared deep into his eyes.

"Thank you," she said, with silent, fearful tears streaming down her face. And she said it with such fervor that he knew she wasn't thanking him for the candle. She looked down at Will and began to stroke his hair as she closed her eyes again.

Del went back to bed and quivered in the dark as the whole journey, not of recent, but the ten-year journey he had been on with Will came to its culmination. He hated himself for how he treated the boy all that time, and he hated himself for even thinking of abandoning him when they fled Umbrate, and though joy had somehow bloomed in the decisions he had made, in the things that had been done, Del's heart ached of a slight crack, like glass spidering under too much pressure. He had to believe that what they were doing was right. People had died, close friends and distant rivals, but they had died nonetheless, and Del would not be able to sleep again until this journey met its end, or he met his.

Not long ago he had been only a simple chandler, diverting his eyes from the king and holding back his opinion about the meager pay for the Altar candles. How he had made so many candles to light the nave of an erroneous dark religion for so long, he would never know. He hated himself as much for that as he did for anything else and, compared to Emesh and all the others, he had no excuse when he could look back and remember a better time. But he had done it, and at their command. No longer. And in the next ten days, they would succeed or Mass would be covered in a darkness it would never recover from, but he would fight again and again ….

And herein lies the thoughts that kept Del and others up through the night, and a new dawn rose on those thoughts, clear and untainted by the dirty mist that long held the morning.

In the distance, a large caravan approached. They stood near the front porch with the horses they fled Umbrate with saddled and ready. The cart they had loaded down with the white earth was emptied and refilled with items for their journey, and a strong and eager horse danced ready in the harness.

Clyde stood next to Will with panniers draped over his back. They had considered leaving him behind, but the stubborn donkey refused, stepping in front of the horses each time they tried to saddle one before him. His life had been miserable in Umbrate as well. Wheat stubble had not been enough sustenance for him all these years. He wanted better as well, and he was willing to work for it. Will stroked his short, bristly mane.

His mother stood beside him. She was getting stronger, and she had as much right to be there in the end as any of the others, if not more. She refused to leave her son, as he refused to leave her.

Rufus rode ahead of the caravan, stalwart and dignified. He stopped and looked over the haggard crew before him.

"Where is the wizard you rescued?" he asked.

Del shook his head. Rufus slumped in his saddle. "But he revealed much to us in the end," Del said. "Things are much more dire than they appear."

Rufus repositioned in the saddle. "Is Sentinel's Village still our destination?"

"Yes," Del said, "and we have only ten days to get there, or it will all be over."

Rufus held his professionalism, but the blow shifted him in his saddle. The victory seemed won with the falling of the Cathedral, but the warning in Del's words told him the end was just beginning.

Rufus turned and saw the caravan approaching. "Then we have much to discuss. Ride up front with me," he said. "All of you."

They saddled their mounts, and Will helped his mother into the back of the cart with Gertie before he took the box seat by Friar Emesh. Del wasted no time in relaying to Rufus the history lost and the final realization with Xenerac, and the man who had maintained every stitch of his bravery in the Reformatory of Magic began to sweat.

"The end," he said. His mouth remained agape to let the portentous word echo out.

"Yes," Del said soberly. "The end of all things."

46

People jammed the streets of Sentinel's Village, leaving only enough room for the King's caravan to squeeze through. The citizens cheered with elation, and it seemed to shock not only Alphonse, but all the guards and monks that marched in formation around the carts of King Bale, Kylan, Renalt, and Princess Briella.

It had been nothing short of a funeral procession when they left the dreary streets of Umbrate, where few eyes dared to look up; now the people jumped and cheered and tossed flowers at their feet. Banners flapped in the wind, bright as birds floating through the air, and the streets were clean, despite the buildings being old and untended.

And the people were fat! All of them. Pudgy children ran ahead of the procession, and men and women lined the roads with their bellies poking into the streets. Alphonse and his guards had never seen such health. Being a part of the Royal Guard, he himself had never been wanting for a meal, but he had never seen a people so portly.

Cheers echoed between the old wooden buildings as they managed to get the carts up the mountain-stone streets that curved for what seemed an eternity all the way to the King's Manor. And never once did the cheers stop or the flowers cease to drop at their feet.

The people were happy, and Alphonse never thought in his life that he would be disgusted to see such a thing, but it made him sick to think of the skin and bones and defeated eyes sunken deep in emaciated sockets that had watched him leave a few days ago. He vowed to never forget those faces, and now the hot anger cauterized them on his heart. He looked up from atop his chestnut horse and the sun renewed him. It was warmer here, and brighter. The source of their food and happiness.

Looking from one round ruddy face to another, he wondered about the Sentinels. He had always believed they were hard men, willing to risk everything to save Mass if the Great Evil ever emerged, but he had yet to see a hard man, just squishy men with too many pies padding their guts. Alphonse thought his first journey to Sentinel's Village would be different. A place of stoic, carved faces and fierce women. It was not so, and he could imagine many of his guards felt the same way.

As far as he knew, the king had never been to Sentinel's Village in Alphonse's own lifetime. How could the people worship a king if they had never seen him? The bright sun and the loaves of bread and baskets of cookies that were passed from hand to hand answered his question. But why did the king want to visit now?

He looked across at Yan and saw the same confusion and near disgust in the man's face. Yan had been watching Alphonse for many days, and it was no wonder, because Alphonse could not help but think about what was happening in Umbrate: if the mission had been a success, or if a line of guards were galloping up the King's Carve to relieve his neck of his head.

Yan's eyes stayed on Alphonse as they reached the end of the street and the start of the King's Manor. It was an old wooden building, like the rest in Sentinel's Village, but not as dilapidated from years of use, and a large field surrounded it for a troops' cantonment. Bale's Victory lay in the distance to their right, serene and placid, with nothing to disturb its surface but the reflection of the Glass Mountains. Sentinel towers surrounded it, and the men and women on guard clapped and waved at them. Not one stared at the pool they were tasked with policing.

The guards, monks, and clergy members looped around the circular drive until the carts stopped at the front door. The members of the quadrumvirate emerged and the people cheered louder from the edge of the road where they had stopped. The old king raised his hand as he took Kylan's assisting arm with the other. Father Renalt came up the other side and assisted the king.

The stooped, old man looked like an ill child between the Priest and his Magical Advisor.

Alphonse dismounted and helped Princess Briella from her cart. She was far passed middle-aged, but strong and statuesque, and the people cheered at the sight of her beauty, and of the reign she would have when their beloved king passed.

Kylan walked by Alphonse and their eyes met. For people that never left their towers, they appeared uncomfortable in such brilliant light, but none more so than Kylan. He glared at Alphonse and the way he assisted the princess.

Briella took hold of his arm and Alphonse ordered members of the Royal Guard to enter the manor with them. The distinguished clergy followed at the back, and Yan was left to wait outside. A chubby manservant and maidservant greeted them at the door with strange sycophancy and led the royals to their rooms. The king, unable to walk far, was brought to the back of the house, and the maidservant guided Briella to her room upstairs. Her grip tightened on Alphonse's arm and he took it as an order to follow her. Once alone in the neat and tidy room, Briella turned to him.

"Is there any word from Umbrate?" she asked with quick and quiet trembling in her voice.

Alphonse shook his head. "No."

The princess tugged at her bottom lip as she paced the room. "Have we made the wrong decision?"

"No news is good news, Princess," Alphonse responded with a falter.

"Yes, I suppose you're right," Briella said. She took in the room with quick glances here and there. "I believe Kylan is planning something," she said as if thinking aloud.

Alphonse's brow furrowed. "What do you mean?"

"I don't know, but the man seems on edge, as if he's been waiting a hundred years for the coming days."

"Maybe he has," Alphonse said. The words did not comfort the princess. "With any luck, they will have freed the wizards and will be on their way here." That provided no comfort either. "I will protect you, my lady."

She turned to him and smiled. "You have been very loyal to me, Alphonse, and your debt will be repaid. Soon my family will be avenged and the throne returned to the rightful heir. I know these last few years have come at great risk to you. My cousin is old and sick. Only the Magic of Kylan is keeping him alive. But not for long, I fear. The wizard has other plans."

"And so do we," Alphonse reminded her. Silence filled the elegant room as the princess paced it. "I'll set guards at your door and take my leave, my lady."

"Yes, thank you, Alphonse … for everything."

Alphonse bowed and left the room. Normally a calm, calculating woman, Briella walked on the edge of fear, and that made Alphonse very nervous. She had planned for the death of the King and the transformation of Umbrate, but she had planned for it *in* Umbrate, not here at the edge of the world in a land unknown to them. Kylan held power everywhere, and even more so where the comfort of others was perforated, and he had brought most of his monks with them. Alphonse knew his guards would stand no chance against the trained wizards and witches.

He set a pair of guards at her door and left the manor. Outside, the guards unloaded the carts and began to erect tents in the open field. Many of them looked toward the city, where the streets remained lined with happy people and bustling business. They would have trouble keeping them in the cantonment, and sober. The more Alphonse thought about Briella's words, the more they made him uneasy. Kylan had crafted a web of lies that warped minds and convinced all of Mass that Magic was bad, though he himself wielded it over a fearful people.

The people in Sentinel's Village were soft, and soon Alphonse and Yan's guards would be soft with bread and ale. If Kylan were to make a move, now would be his opportune time.

Yan stood across the field and stared at Mirror Pool (Bale's Victory to him) in the distance. Alphonse approached.

"I've never been to Sentinel's Village," he said when Alphonse reached his side.

"Neither have I."

Yan's hands were behind his back; his eyes fixed on the pool.

"Bale's Victory is as brilliant as the members of the clergy have described."

"Yes," Alphonse said.

"The people are not."

Alphonse looked at the side of Yan's head. "No, they are not."

Yan dared to give Alphonse a side glance. They stood under the invigorating sun, absorbing its warmth through the fabric of their cloaks.

"I've been watching you, Alphonse. You seem … unsure."

"Unsure of what?"

"I haven't figured that out yet."

Alphonse grinned. "And what are you so sure about?"

Yan paused and looked out the side of his eye again. "I don't think Umbrate is safe." Alphonse tightened at the words. "And I don't understand why we are here."

"What makes you think Umbrate isn't safe?"

"Just a feeling, and I think you're having the same one. You've been uneasy since our departure."

"Yes," Alphonse said, though not in the same way Yan meant. "But what don't you understand about our pilgrimage here?"

"The king has never visited Sentinel's Village in my lifetime. We've celebrated many days of Bale's Victory in Umbrate, and now we travel here?"

"It's an important anniversary—a hundred years. That's worth more of a celebration, is it not?"

Yan turned to face Alphonse. "I did not know what life was like up here, Alphonse. The people are fat, happy, but they live in this shabby city with its rough streets and broken buildings. Umbrate is magnificent and proud, but the people are skinny, destitute. I cannot understand it. It's …" He stopped and rubbed the back of his head in question.

"Barbaric," Alphonse finished. Yan neither acknowledged nor accepted the word, but he didn't deny it either.

"I've never seen anything like it. We burned down half a forest for a man and a boy. And for what? So our own people could have less wood and food? Banners are made in Umbrate of all the finest cloths for a festival, and our own people, clothed in dirt and tatters, can't even attend?" Yan unraveled before Alphonse. "I thought I understood, but I don't have a clue anymore. And now we've traveled so far, and I can't figure out for the life of me why."

Yan took a deep breath and crossed his arms over his chest. "I was an orphaned child. No mother that I knew of, no father. The greatest joy in my life was the expectation that I would enter the Guard, that they would feed me, and clothe me, and that I would be a part of something bigger than myself."

"You are not unlike many others."

"Yes, but I've been much crueler. I believed the Guard would be my opportunity to destroy the evil I thought destroyed my family."

"What do you mean? Magic has been banished for a hundred years."

Yan paused, apprehensive, and continued. "When I went in for my confirmation to be Leader of the City Guard, Kylan told me how my parents died. They were part of the farming crew. He told me they had hired a witch in secret to help the crops grow. I was just a babe; I remember none of this. They were caught, and he told me they lived in the darkness of the Reformatory for twenty years before they died," Yan said. Alphonse, disturbed, made no response. "He made me hate my own parents more than I already had. I thought they had abandoned me, but somehow it was worse knowing they had fraternized with magical people. Kylan could see that anger in my eyes; it was why he promoted me. It took a journey here for me to see why my parents had done what they did. They did it to feed more people, and they were killed for it." Yan, a man so strong Alphonse wondered if he had been born without tear ducts, looked at him with misty eyes. "Why would they bring us so far? Why would they expose us to a world of decadence, just to send us back to the filth and mealy porridge of Umbrate. They live in fear there, and elate here. It's madness! I could see on your face when we arrived that you feel the same way."

"Yes," Alphonse said.

"But why?" Yan asked the sky, the earth, the grass, the pool.

"Power," Alphonse answered.

47

Del had plopped onto his rear some hours ago and there he remained, among the people of Umbrate, among his friends. Everyone gathered in their own groups, laughing and talking around small fires. He never knew the people of Umbrate could live with such cheer, even in the shadow of their grim journey. Word had been passed around that if they won, the world would improve, and if they lost, it would end. No one abandoned the caravan with the bleak news, and that put more confidence in Del than he'd ever had before. Though they grew up in a world that hated Magic, they were as oppressed as any magician that ever lived. They were one under the same banner, no matter their differences.

At Rufus's side, Del became somewhat of an advisor, a man that spoke for all his people as the wizard he was and the oppressed Umbratian he had been. The people had hope, a necessary hope, and even Lyle approached Will and apologized to him. The boys played when there was time to rest, but the playful ways of children didn't seem to fit them anymore, Will most of all. He had been through much, and now he had a mother to recuperate, and with his touch she was convalescing.

Bella began to walk more, leading Clyde by his halter as Will walked beside her. She spoke more, too, and the joy that Will brought her was a symbol for the life ahead, a life of recovery. Will sat next to her now, dipping bread in a simmering stew. He finished his meal, left with their dishes, and returned with a steaming bowl for Del.

"You should eat," he said. Del smiled at the boy's kindness and took the bowl, though he had no appetite and hadn't since their new journey began. Will sat next to him, and they watched Isa,

Gertie, and Bella talk in hushed tones. Bella smiled and Will smiled back.

They sat some distance away, under the shade of a cart, and the buzz around them was like that of a city market—a glorious sound! They marveled at it.

"You know, Umbrate used to always sound like this," Del said, shoveling a spoonful into his mouth. "Back when people were happy."

"It seems that things will return that way again," Will said. "Or end that way," he added darkly.

They fell silent. As much joy as they had, it was difficult to not consider the alternative to winning. Del finished his stew and bread and rested with his back against the cart.

"Do you think we'll make it on time?" Will asked. They had traveled hard for eight days, and by Del's best calculation, it would take more arduous traveling to make it by noon on the final day of the festival.

Del looked around. "I do," he said.

"The people are eager to get back to a life they once had," Will said.

"Back to a life they've never known," Del corrected. "I was around then, and even I can hardly remember what it was like."

"They believe in it—that's all that matters," Will said.

Del looked at the boy with pride and respect. They watched the people laugh and converse; the possible end had little effect on them, they had already been freed. Their lives had never been improved by the change of long ago. Fear had driven them this far, but the chains were broken.

"I don't suppose I can convince you to stay behind when we get to Sentinel's Village?" Del asked.

"Has it worked yet?" Will said.

Del chuckled. "No, it hasn't."

They had crossed the burned swath of forest, seen the destruction their rulers were capable of, and it had Will thinking: "If the Great Scourge was so bad for Mass, why would Kylan want to free it?"

Del considered him. "Power is like rich food, Will. Men like Kylan have tasted it always but will never have enough. To control the Great Scourge, to control Death, would make Kylan the most powerful man that ever lived, and we'd be no more than slaves, even more so than we already are, and his life would go on forever and ever while we wasted away. It would be the death of hope: the true end of all things."

They returned to silent staring. Will looked at the people and Del looked at Will's mother. He felt a deep jealousy he never thought possible.

"If we get home," Del said, "I would like to, well … I would very much like it if you became my apprentice again. In the candle shop."

Will looked at him and smiled. "*When* we get home, I would like that," he replied.

Will reached into his pocket and pulled out the key to the chandler's shop. He passed it to Del, who knew its edges and curves well. Del tried to hide the smile, but it crept up on him too secretly for him to stop it. He didn't ask how Will got it, he simply patted his back.

"You really think you're going to be a chandler after all this?" Will asked.

"That's all I want to do after this taxing adventure."

Will smiled. "Me too." He stood and returned to his mother. He spoke to her a moment and they all looked in Del's direction with satisfied smiles on their faces. Del smiled back.

Two more days and they would arrive in Sentinel's Village.

48

Ten minutes before midday, Father Renalt led a procession through the crowd. Behind him, Kylan aided the frail King Bale, and behind them Alphonse aided Princess Briella. Yan brought up the rear. The horde of people were divided from the King and the rest by a line of Guards that faded to monks where a platform had been built on the shore of Bale's Victory. The flat, inviting pool shimmered with the coming noon, and not a sound was heard as the gatherers held their breaths in anticipation for a great cheer. Now, however, the event was somber, official, and Father Renalt took his place on the platform to offer mass to the people.

The father, dressed in the finest robes, turned to the crowd as Kylan sat the king and Alphonse sat the princess. Alphonse took his position between Briella and Kylan. Yan took his position on the other side of Kylan. The gaunt and stern wizard showed no signs of distress or turmoil, just easy anticipation. Kylan turned his head on a tight swivel and stared at Alphonse. His eyes were cold and steely, and the only thing Alphonse saw in them was indifference.

Father Renalt breathed deeply, and the congregation seemed to exhale with him, their eyes never leaving their great king and his beautiful cousin, Princess Briella. They were myth brought to life for the people of Sentinel's Village, and the plump sentinels stood a little taller seeing the king that had banished the Great Evil they kept imprisoned at the bottom of the glassy pool.

"We gather here, at the edge of our world," Renalt began, "to remember the great sacrifice of the venerable King Bale Hornblower," the crowd struggled to maintain its cheers, "who banished the Great Evil of Magic into this pool after it stripped his mother from Mass. His name shall forever—"

"What's that?" someone shouted in the back.

All the bodies pivoted to a great wall of people coming around the edge of the forest less than a quarter-mile off. The people of Sentinel's Village thought it might be another treat gifted to them by the king to finish the celebration, but the royalty on the platform appeared confused.

Alphonse put his hand on Briella's shoulder and squeezed; she put her soft, confident hand on his. The guard looked to Kylan, his eyes aflame with anger. He turned them to the sky and stared right into the sun. Yan glanced at both of them, bewildered.

Alphonse looked up, shielding his eyes. The sun blazed bright, but not as bright as he remembered it being.

"Continue," Kylan hissed at Renalt.

"What's the matter?" King Bale muttered.

"Nothing, you old fool!" Kylan replied.

The people in the closest rows gasped at Kylan's insolence. Even Princess Briella and Alphonse turned in disgust. Yan perked upright. Renalt scoffed with impudence.

"How dare you, magical filth," Renalt said. Kneeling, he looked into the king's cloudy eyes. "Sire, it appears we have more guests approaching."

"More guests?" the king replied, squinting at the prospect.

"Yes, sire, for the final day of the festival."

"Guests from where?"

"I don't know, sire. Would you like me to wait for them?"

The king gave a terse nod.

Kylan made no point to hide his disdain. "You will continue, or you will get off this stage," he said.

"But the king said—"

"And the advisor to the king wants you to continue!" Kylan's voice hissed like water on hot iron.

Kylan looked at the sky, and then at the approaching people. They formed a line across the flat as if preparing for war. Father Renalt watched them approach, rather nervous himself. A group of mounted men and women led the charge, and they continued forward when they reached the edge of attendees around the pool, splitting them as Renalt had.

Alphonse saw Rufus, Del, and Will in the lead.

"Guards, surround us!" Kylan yelled. Monks filled the platform, forcing Renalt off. They gathered around Briella and Alphonse. He leaned down to her and said: "We must get you out of here." She tried to stand but Kylan commanded a guard to force her back into her seat. Behind him, Yan peeked over the lined shoulders of the monks. Alphonse stared at the foul wizard, and for the first time saw determination burning in his eyes.

The sky darkened overhead.

Del spoke. "Kylan Godea, you will surrender your position this moment! We know of your plan to raise the Great Scourge." He wished he had thought of something better to say, but the words seemed to strike Kylan, and the wizard rocked back, shocked.

"What do you know of my plan?" Kylan shouted. "You know nothing, fool!"

Del looked to the sky; time was running short. He advanced his forces forward, slicing through the crowd.

"Xenerac was freed from the Reformatory of Magic, and the Cathedral has fallen." Kylan tensed and shook with anger. "The people of Umbrate have come to take back what's theirs. They refuse to live under your rule any longer."

The people of Sentinel's Village watched with wonder, confusion, and silent dread on their faces, but the faces that weren't watching the back and forth looked toward the sky. A thin sliver covered the edge of the sun. They shielded their eyes and stared into its glory. Some pointed, some stared in awe, others gathered their children and fled.

"What on Mass is going on?" the king said.

Kylan turned his eyes to the sky. He looked back at Del with a glinting smile on his face. The monks crowded around him stood in unwavering formation. The time neared.

Kylan pulled a knife from his cloak and slipped the razors edge across the king's throat. And before the realization hit the king, or the first drops splashed on the platform, Alphonse pulled a dagger and began to hack at the monks that held Princess Briella down.

"No!" Del yelled, but it was too late.

Alphonse freed Briella, and the crowd fell into a frenzy as they watched their beloved king's execution. A purple slash of light burst from Kylan's hand and hit Briella in the back as Alphonse dropped his dagger and jumped from the deck with her. They fell into the crowd and Briella went limp. Alphonse lifted her and blended into the hysteria as the onlookers dispersed in any direction that allowed them to live.

Kylan slashed another ray of light at Del, forcing the wizard from his horse. Yan, stunned for only a moment, pulled his dagger and slashed at the monks before him. Kylan turned in the struggle and sent a purple beam into the man's chest, hitting some of his own protectors in the process. Yan fell dead from the platform, posthumously aware of the lie and fear he had spread for so long.

And then it happened. The moon shifted its weight in front of the midday sun and darkness covered the land. The people stopped their flight and stared up in terror. Flocks of birds lifted from the trees and scattered in dark clouds away from the pool as deer and squirrels and rabbits dashed from the forest. Kylan's face formed a disgusting grin and he turned to face the pool. The monks formed a tight circle around him.

He began to chant, and the calm waters of Mirror Pool began to rock back and forth with windless waves.

Mothers pulled their children close and fathers pulled in the mothers. Chaos set in motion.

Del looked up from the ground. Bravery faltered amongst his fellows as they stood motionless and watched the blotted sky and turgid pool. His horse danced in fear. He snapped awake and regained his mount.

"Charge!" he yelled, and spurred forward. The others followed his courage.

A stream of light ripped from a monk's fingertips and skipped over Del's head. They dispersed forces: Elias to his right, Isa to his left. Will had been directed to stay back, but he went ahead, and his mother rode next to him.

Elias flashed the first bright counterattack and a monk fell. His unexpected power stunned them and he was challenged with a magical barrage that unseated him from his horse. The people of

Umbrate, already having survived a death of their own, rushed in behind them and were met with a flurry of Magic. Many dropped dead, some fell in agony, but others continued forward—the only direction they wished to die moving in.

Del took his eyes off Kylan for a moment and stared at Mirror Pool. The waves, topped with white caps, swallowed the earth at its bank and receded to grow larger and larger until one wrapped around the base of a Sentinel's tower and brought it down. Del looked closer. The waves were not simply water, but the hands and bodies and legs of the dead.

Spray splashed Kylan's face as he stared into the eclipse and chanted. Del struck at him with a flash of light and a monk stepped in front to absorb the blow. Isa threw a bolt from her hands, missed, and her horse was struck with a volley. It rolled onto the ground and she flew from its back.

Rufus, in a feat of bravery, dashed ahead of Del and slashed with all his might, taking two monks before he was cut down by a third. Motionless, he fell to the earth. Gertie fired in from some distance away, diverting the returning blows.

The citizens of Umbrate rushed the platform, some getting close, but none close enough. Del turned and saw the desperate faces of Will and his mother as they ducked to avoid being hit. A wave rushed over the side of the pool and washed over his horse's hooves; it whinnied and screamed as if scalded. Del looked across the platform. Monks fell in committed servitude, but it was Kylan that needed to fall.

He spurred his horse and rushed forward, sending remembered and desperate Magic from his fingertips in a mad fury. He weakened under the lack of light, but pursued ahead. Two monks fell at his strikes and he wheeled his horse to the side of the platform. He pulled himself on top of it and a monk struck at him before Alphonse jumped on the stage and slashed his head from his neck. He pulled Del to his feet, and the two cleared the edge of the platform enough for the reinforcements to get up.

Alphonse slashed and parried, taking down man after man, while his own guards, or at least the ones that remained, watched in inert confusion. Del hit monk after monk, their screams and moans pounding through his chest.

A gap opened and he could see Kylan before him. He pulled in all the light he could and forced it through his fingers. Kylan turned his eyes from the sky and deflected Del's blow back at him, wiping everyone from the stage. From the ground, Del looked up at the platform. Kylan stood like a monolith.

Will watched Elias fall. He watched Isa fall, and Gertie fight with all her strength. And when Del tumbled from the platform, the hope sank in his chest. Alphonse got to his feet and began to swing at those that weren't stunned. Del remained on the ground.

Will spurred his horse forward.

"Will, no!" Bella shouted, but Will galloped over bodies toward the platform. His mother raced behind.

He jumped from his saddle onto the platform. On his hands and knees, he grabbed Alphonse's dropped dagger. He stood, pointed it into Kylan's side, and rushed forward—his target ahead for him alone to finish. With his head down, focused, he jabbed the dagger. Kylan stepped to the side and grabbed Will by the throat. The waves calmed on the lake.

"What a brave little boy you are," Kylan derided. He gritted his teeth and lifted Will by the neck. The boy dropped the dagger to grab the wizard's arm. "You'll make a great sacrifice to the dead."

Will could see the waves calm—just a few moments and it would all be over. He looked out and saw Elias fighting to get to his feet before he was struck down again. Isa lay on her back, staring up at the sky. The common people fought the monks and fell in droves. Del lay flat on his back, blood flowing from his left arm. Will turned his gaze to his desperate mother reaching for him as a monk ripped her from her horse.

Will looked down into Kylan's eyes and saw the end of the world in the face of the oppressor.

"What a fool you are to think you could defeat me," Kylan said.

The firm hand squeezed the breath from Will. A glint of light flashed behind his head and Will grabbed Kylan's forearm with his hand. He looked at Del and his struggling mother, and the thing deep within him, the thing he always knew to be there, flared between his grasped fingers.

Kylan looked at the light with horror, and the burst that flowed through the boy's fingers blew him back as he released Will from his grasp. He dropped to the deck and gasped for breath. He looked across the surface of it and saw his mother break free. Turning his dizzy eyes, he saw Kylan getting back up.

Will rocked to his side and tried to lift himself, but Kylan was on top of him. His face seethed with anger, and the man lifted his hand to strike the boy down when Will's mother launched herself into him. The wizard stumbled toward the edge of the platform, his face in complete shock. He tried to catch himself, tripped over a fallen body, and fell into the crashing waves of Mirror Pool.

Bella gathered Will to his feet and they watched as Kylan stood in the pool with water up to his waist. He struggled toward the edge and a wave battered over him. It sucked him under and his face emerged for just a moment when another washed over his bobbing head.

"We have to stop it!" Del shouted.

Elias stumbled to his side and Isa came to. Gertie rode up on her horse and sent the first burst of blinding light into the pool. The sun peeked around the darkening moon, showing its face again, and Elias found the strength to add his own stream of light. Del stood with his arm dangling at his side and forced a rivulet of light from his own fingers. Isa did the same.

The waves rocked with the hands and feet and faces of the dead reaching out to them. It wasn't enough power. Will stepped to the edge of the deck, soaked up the light of the sun, breathed deep, and the awoken thing inside him knew what to do, like when Rolph spoke in his head. A light stronger than all the rest flared from his fingers, too bright to look at, and the waves began to calm as the sun appeared from behind the moon, lighting the pool with its watchful gaze once again.

The pool turned into an expanse of ripples, and with one last effort, Will forced the Magic from within himself, and the pool went flat. The fire stopped burning from his fingers, and he fell to the deck, staring up into the bright sky, as the birds returned overhead and his mother leaned over him.

49

Will sat upright and looked around the room. He was in a grand bed in a place he had never been. He leaned over and tried to crawl out from under the sheets when a voice spoke up.

"Easy now, my boy."

"Del!" Will exclaimed. The wizard sat forward in his chair by the darkened side of the bed. His left arm was amputated just above the elbow. Will's gaze fixed upon it. "Your arm! What happened?"

Del looked at it. "Not even Isa could save it," he said. "But she made it as painless as possible." He gave a sad smile. In his other hand he rolled the key to the chandler's shop in his fingers.

Will tried to speak but Del stopped him.

"There's nothing to say, Will. An arm isn't so bad, considering …." He cleared his throat and shook his head. "If not for you, none of us would be here."

Will leaned back on his pillow. "Where are we? How long was I asleep?"

"We're in the King's Manor in Sentinel's Village, in the king's room, and you've been asleep for seven days."

"Seven days?!"

'Oh, yes," Del said. "You nearly exhausted yourself to death with that glorious burst of Magic you made."

"So, that did happen," Will realized, looking down at his hands. He wondered if it had all been a dream, but when he flexed his fingers he could feel the Magic, or something that made him wince.

"Yes, I remember feeling that tingle my first few times as well. You get used to it," Del said.

Will looked around the room, at the fine decor and soft sheets. It was the nicest place he had ever been in, and he felt greedy for being there. He turned to Del with an inquisitive tilt to his head.

"If I'm in the king's room," he said, thinking it all through, "and in the king's bed. Does that mean …?"

Del began to laugh. "No, you're not the king, my boy."

Will relaxed back. "Then Briella is the queen?"

"No, sadly, she died, but with her last words she appointed Alphonse to the throne."

"Alphonse is the king?!"

Del nodded and smiled. "And a good one too. He even let a boy recover in his bed."

Will smiled back.

"And there's another thing," Del said. Will's brow scrunched with curiosity. "He has appointed me to be his Magical Advisor."

"And you accepted?"

"I didn't have much choice in the matter. He thought I would be a fine fit, having lived in Umbrate so long."

Will looked dejected. "So, no going back to the candle shop, then?"

"No," Del said, looking down at the key, "but I would still like for you to be my apprentice."

Will's eyes lit up, but before he could answer the door burst open and his mother entered.

"Will!" She rushed to the bed with a deft speed that surprised him. He jumped from under the sheets and embraced her. She kissed the top of his head and hugged him so tight he could hardly breath. She let him loose and looked into his eyes. "How are you? Are you okay?"

"Yes," Will said. He couldn't keep the smile from his face or tears from his eyes as he stared at his rejuvenated mother. "You're better, too. You're … happy!" he said.

She hugged him in close. "Happier now that you're awake." She turned and looked at Del. "We're both happy. Del watched over you every hour he could," Bella said.

Will left his mother and walked over to Del. He hugged the wizard and said: "Thank you, Del. I love you."

Del embraced him with tears in his eyes. "You're a good boy, Will, and I love you," he said with a quivering lip. All eyes drained tears as if they had sprung a leak. Del wiped his away. "Look at me, the king's advisor and I'm blubbering like a baby."

Will laughed and wiped his own eyes. He turned back to his mother and said: "Del has offered to take me on as his apprentice, and I would like to accept … if you'll allow it," he finished, still not used to having a mother.

She came to his side and grinned. "I'll allow it."

Will turned to shake Del's hand and the wizard pulled him in for another hug.

"Come," Del said, standing, "the others wish to see you."

"The others? They all lived?"

"Yes, with some aches and pains, of course, but it will give them joy to see your face. Many were not so fortunate as us."

Will turned downcast at the thought of the lives that had fallen before the final victory: souls of good people who died for what they believed in, common or not.

"This is no time to be sad, Will," Del said. "This is a time to rebuild, and we'll need the strength of our young men and women to help."

Will smiled at him, and his mother and Del left the room so he could get dressed in the fine clothes they had laid out for him. He dressed slowly and methodically, feeling every stitch and seam of the soft cloth, but really, he was delaying. He stood in front of the closed door and it stared back at him. He had been here before, and he would be there again. Maturity waited on the other side.

Will breathed deep and pushed the door open.

50

A week after Will awoke, Alphonse stood on the edge of the serene pool with Del and Will to his right. In that time, he had appointed a new leader of Sentinel's Village, pardoned all that fought for Kylan, found a way to distribute food from Sentinel's Village to all the corners of Mass, and now spoke in front of the funeral pyre of the fallen.

"From this moment on, Bale's Victory will be known as Mirror Pool, as it once was," he said. "And it will be a symbol for all of Mass to look into to see the evil of our past. The ones that fell here did not die in vain, and a new Kingdom will bloom from the soil of their ashes below a sun that will never darken again." He lit the pyre, and the citizens of Sentinel's Village and Umbrate watched with somber faces and tears in their eyes.

The world was new to them, and the truth was rattling, but it would take much longer than a few weeks for them to understand the changes ahead. The pyre burned bright and hot, and the dead were lifted on ashes to their new homes as the glassy surface of Mirror Pool reflected the smoke that rose up.

The gatherers began to break up, and Alphonse watched until it burned down with the new warriors by his side. He turned to Del first.

"Tomorrow, we leave in the morning. We have much to do in Umbrate," he said. Del nodded, and their king stepped in front of Will. "I once wished to keep you in Umbrate to become a guard. What a fool I was. We all have much to thank you for, Will. Many more would have died if not for your bravery." Will blushed but held his eye contact.

Alphonse looked to the others. "Thank you. You are all welcome in Umbrate. Your help and power will be greatly appreciated." They bowed to their king as he stepped away to immediate questions from his attendants.

Del turned to the rest. Will stood beside him, and Bella put her arm around him. He looked to Gertie first. "We wish for you to come back to Umbrate."

She shook her head and looked toward the mountains. "I already have a home, and I miss it," she said.

Del nodded and turned to Elias. "And what about you, old friend?"

"I'm a traveling wizard—I don't do well in cages," he said. "Others will need me elsewhere."

Del bowed. Friar Emesh stepped up from beside Grace and Newt. "I'd like to come back to Umbrate and work for you," he said meekly. "I believe I can do some good."

"And so you shall," Del said. Emesh nodded and took a step back. Del looked to Grace and Newt. "I know you'll be coming back."

"Yes, and we have many suggestions for the king and his advisor," Grace said with hand on hip.

Del grinned. "And they will be given much attention."

Newt hugged her close and they smiled at him.

Del turned to Isa and she tried to look away from his gaze. He stared at her for a few moments until she acquiesced.

"Fine, I'll come back … but not for you," she said. "I'm doing it for them … my family." She looked at her lovely Will and Bella, then wagged a finger of warning at Del. "And don't think we're going to get married again—because we aren't! That's come and gone!"

Del rolled his eyes and the others laughed.

"I've been wondering," Will said. "You said it would be nearly impossible for me to have magical powers."

"I've been wrong before, Will," Isa said. Del glanced at her with surprise. "Oh, shut up, Del!" Del shrugged and the gathered few laughed.

"We all have some form of Magic in us, Will," Del said. "It's just a matter of finding the courage or the reason to drag it out. And you have many reasons." Del waved his hand over those before them, and the boy marveled at the family he never realized he had.

They took one last look at the pyre and turned back to Sentinel's Village.

It was a clear, sunny day, and with the new dawn, they would ride back to Umbrate.

THE END

9 798999 552600